Blueberry

Floyd Jones

Wooden Stake Press
Denver, Colorado

The characters and events portrayed in this book are fictitious. Any similarity to real persons, living or dead, is coincidental and not intended by the author.

Wooden Stake Press
Denver, CO

www.woodenstakepress.com

ISBN-10: 1-940936-17-9
ISBN-13: 978-1-940936-17-8

Cover design by Tatiana Jones, copyright © 2016

For Lulu, Magoo, Teej, and Bop. You are the beating of my heart.

And for Mom, who read to me.

We tried ruling the world; we tried acting as God's steward, then we tried ushering in the human revolution, the age of reason and isolation. We failed in all of it, and our failure destroyed more than we were even aware of.

~ Uncivilisation - The Dark Mountain Manifesto

I shall sing of Gaia, Mother of All, Strong-founded, Most Ancient, who feedeth all things that are in the world....

By thee, Revered Goddess, are men rich in children and harvests, and thine it is to give life to mortals, and take it away.

~ Homer, 8th century B.C.
Translated by John Edgar

400

parts per million
and climbing

Level of carbon dioxide in Earth's atmosphere
as of September 2016.

Junipero Bay, California
April 16, 2060

G aia Cadogan was kicking the skull of a seagull down the road when she heard the voice.

"Siafu! She comes!"

She'd given the skull a particularly good kick that sent it skipping and tumbling along the dirt shoulder, and the voice came just as the skull banked right, hopped, and disappeared over the edge of the bluff into the tangerine-pink Pacific a dozen yards below.

Gaia paused and looked up, but no one was there. It was the first time she'd lifted her head since leaving school, on a day she'd gotten hit with a hard dose of teasing. On the walk from school to her mom's office at the docks, she'd spent most of the time looking down, daydreaming, seething. With her natural blue hair, dirty-green skin, and ears so big she could barely cover them with her hands, getting worked over at school was as common to Gaia as breathing in and out.

And then there were her eyes. They changed color depending on how she felt moment to moment. First emerald, then azure, then gray—even light purple. And craziest of all, her eyes had no whites. Just colors. Gaia did love her eyes, especially how they scared people who saw them for the first time.

But her classmates had gotten used to her looks, which meant they teased her cruelly.

"Frog-enstein." That was today's nugget from a bully named Stacy Williams, the little bastard, the boy with the girl's name.

Deep down Gaia had to admit it was one of the more clever insults, and definitely new; but it stabbed her all the same, just like "booger" did, or "Syncro spawn," or "Halloween," or any of the others.

All through elementary school in little Junipero Bay, then through junior high, and now in her second year of high school, she'd had endless opportunities to employ countless strategies: ignore the idiots, plan and execute revenge schemes, rise above it and take the high road, fight back. She'd tried them all—rinse and repeat—but the teasing pounded on like relentless ocean waves. Whatever this unnamed disease was, she was saddled with it for life. Her parents were useless in telling her anything about it, and they refused to take her to a doctor. "You're perfectly healthy," her mom always said. "Whatever, Mom," Gaia would say. "You're perfectly helpful."

Gaia's running theory was that she wasn't the natural child of Maer and Jack Cadogan. Instead, she was a Croozer baby—the abandoned child of some hopeless drug addict who got pregnant and inadvertently poisoned her fetus with Croozer. Birth defects galore! Gaia imagined herself being found as a newborn between the legs of some comatose mother who was so strung out on Croozer that she wasn't aware she'd even given birth. Then the baby, Gaia, was turned over to some family—her family—that was kind enough to adopt such a freakish kid. The scenario wasn't hard to imagine. Croozer junkies were sprawled out everywhere in Junipero Bay. They were people who'd given up on life, on the world around them, and slid into the "happy death" the drug offered.

Giving up. That was a strategy Gaia hadn't really considered yet. But she waved it away, because she was enjoying her current strategy of "callous smartass" way too much. In fact, that morning after "Frog-enstein" came out, Gaia walked right up to Stacy Williams. He was a good six inches taller than she was, and he had pretty bad acne.

"What?" he said like some slow, dumb animal.

She locked eyes with him, got on her tiptoes so that she was only inches from his face, and whispered, "God help me, but I want you, Stacy Williams. I always have."

Stacy looked like he was about to lay an egg, or spew. Or both. That shut him up for a while. One down, 10 billion to go.

But she now had a new concern. This voice had snapped her awake. "Siafu! She comes!" It felt aimed at her.

A breeze floated in off the peach-colored waves, rustling her blueberry hair like curtains, and she drew a deep breath—something she did when she wanted to concentrate. The briny air was tinged with dust and piss. She turned and looked back up the straight mile of coastline road she'd just walked, eyeballing a few cars that hummed past on quiet electric motors but squawked artificial sounds from their NoisyBoys so that people could hear them coming: an old gasoline engine, a woman reciting *The Odyssey*, a cacophony of extinct tropical birds. NoisyBoys had gotten weirder over the past year. But being able to hear an electric car coming because of its NoisyBoy was better than not hearing it and getting run over, even if that noise was artificial fart sounds, which had just come out of the last car that passed her.

Gaia listened carefully. She found no escape from sound—ever—courtesy of her Dumbo ears. But she'd gotten good at filtering things out and tuning in to whatever caught her interest. Like this voice.

At first it seemed like it came from somewhere in front of her, but ahead lay only the dilapidated blue and white VW van she walked past every day, an old combie someone had abandoned months ago. She looked around. Gaia was certain the voice hadn't come from one of the passing cars, and aside from some old man droning on about his leg pains inside a lime green bungalow up the road, Gaia heard only normal things, like the roar of the sea, the NoisyBoys of the oncoming cars, and the bustling hum of tourists downtown a few hundred yards away. She scanned the brown stucco bungalows across the street, then trained her ears up into the neighborhood. She heard conversations about the drought, "The Worm" contaminating the sea, President Efrain and the coming election, food, and a man's hoarse, drunken complaint, "God damnit, God damnit, God DAMNIT, Ruth!"

For a moment, Gaia wondered if she'd imagined the voice or misheard something from one of the NoisyBoys. But no, it was distinct. The quality of the voice stood out, even spooked her—urgent, just above a whisper, and it seemed amputated—followed by a muffled slap, as if the speaker were being silenced.

Maybe it had come from a television. She felt foolishly paranoid.

Gaia made one last scan, shrugged, and started walking again.

Suddenly, a sharp pain burned in the back of her neck, in the spot where her new medical diagnostic implant had been inserted the day before. It was the fourth implant she'd gotten inside of a year, the previous three having vanished, disintegrated inexplicably, but none of them had ever hurt like this. She scratched desperately at the base of her skull, unable to reach the place between her skin and spine that burned like fire.

Then everything went black, and her body seized. Gaia felt herself falling in slow motion onto the hard dirt and heard the clatter of her metal bento lunchbox striking the ground and spilling open, and the only thought that entered her head was, *I hope a seagull doesn't steal the rest of my protein cake.* She lay there frozen, gritting her teeth against the searing pain, her body a heavy, suffering rock forcing it's weight into the earth. The urine smell was strong on the ground, and when she was finally able to suck in breath she coughed on dust.

Slowly, imperceptibly, the pain was subsiding, and she could move her fingers again, then her arms. *Did I just have a stroke?* she wondered. But as she began to push herself up from the ground, a vision—clearer than a videostream—started playing in her mind, becoming brighter and sharper as pain drained away. For the moment.

Fire. It was everywhere—crackling, spitting, towering over her against an empty black void. It washed her in angry heat, so real, so beyond a dream, that she was frightened she was actually in that place, about to be consumed. The fire was so unbelievably hot. *My skin is melting!* she thought, but in the vision she couldn't raise her arms to see if it were true. Gaia tried to move, tried to turn, but all she could do was lie in molten pain as the violent flames leapt into the void above.

"Help me!" she screamed. Then she caught movement beyond the flames. It was a shadow at first, but as the thing approached its edges were drawn by the fiery light into the shape of a person, a dark person—a man, young and black as charcoal—as dark black as she was dark green—running in slow motion toward her. "Here!" she cried. In the distance, his clenched white teeth were soon joined by a desperation on his sweaty face. He was getting closer, and Gaia now saw his colorful patterned shirt, opened clumsily at the top, bouncing in slow motion with his strides. Even in her terror, Gaia thought it odd that the flames were at full speed but he was in slow motion. The man dug in and began running harder. She wondered if there'd be nothing left of her but charred bones by the time he got there.

But the burning agony kept clawing at her. *Shouldn't I be dead by now?* she wondered through clenched teeth as her savior stopped at the edge of the flames. She was awed by his size—taller than the flames themselves. "Help me!" she called again. The man reached for her with one arm over the flames, but checked himself as the fire lapped at him, and he backed up. "Please!" she cried weakly, feeling her consciousness falter. Then Gaia saw resolve settle on his face, and he reached for her with both arms now, right through the fire.

She watched him. She listened to his slow-motion, exhausted breath. She heard his steady heartbeat. Bump-bump. Bump-bump. Bump-bump. She looked into his eyes. They seemed strangely old, milky white, with only the faint outline of iris and pupil. There was something else about those eyes, something unsettling, an opposite quality from the strain and effort he was making, different from his desperation or even his calm determination. *Death*, she thought. *His eyes are dead.* But she didn't care. He was going to save her.

"Cahm to me!" he called to her with an African accent. "I am thee only one who can help you! I am thee only one who undah-stands you!"

The man never reached Gaia, never saved her, never even touched her, because the vision faded, taking the heat and pain with it. Daylight grew slowly around her. When she opened her eyes, she saw the edge of the dusty Armor-Dillo blacktop road staring back at her and realized she was lying on her side, her skin crackling with a low, fading burn like the pain of her funny bone being struck. She grimaced and raised herself onto her elbows, then onto her knees. Her body was sweat-soaked, chilling in the breeze. Gaia heard the world around her again caterwauling with familiar sounds. She placed a palm over her chest, feeling her heart recovering from the roller coaster ride she'd just been on. Terror and agony. The otherworldly death in her savior's eyes. And now physical relief, coupled with the spooky man's promise to save her, which lingered strangely like a comforting blanket over her soul.

Then came the shock, the realization that what had just happened to her wasn't normal at all. As the puzzle pieces swirled in her brain, they slowly clicked into place. *No, this isn't happening!*

Gaia had heard about this sort of thing, but only as a theory. Nobody thought it was possible to tap into somebody's diagnostic chip and plant visions, thoughts, and feelings into them.

But there was no other explanation for what had just happened, and she shuddered. A surge of nausea forced her onto her hands and knees and she began to vomit.

Then a jarring noise caught her attention, a mechanical sputtering and coughing in front of her, followed by a deafening pop and a wheezy rumble. Gaia watched acrid black smoke erupt from the old VW van. It lurched into the road, labored to gain speed, turned left at the next street, and disappeared.

She threw up again, bile burning her throat as she tried to force something else out of her body along with the meager contents of her stomach: the feeling of just having been raped; though she wondered if physical rape would have been less terrifying than what had just happened to her.

Gaia Cadogan had just been hacked.

-2-
Music

G aia labored to her feet, brushed herself off, and looked around. Her blood was still sizzling. Had the hackers been in the VW van, or was that a coincidence? How close did you have to be to hack someone? She didn't want to stick around and find out, just sit there so they could do it again.

Then she heard another vehicle coming, blasting music. It was a lowrider pickup, dark purple and sparkly, slowly turning from a side street and coming toward her. The bass thundered and buzzed like a giant, sticky heartbeat, so loud and penetrating that she had to cover her ears. Even then, the sound penetrated her skin and pounded her organs. An electric guitar whined over the bass in a lazy, singsong melody as the singer rapscatted to the beat, repeating the same line over and over in a Brooklyn accent.

I think I'm losing my mind this time, this time, I'm losing my mind.

The truck approached, then slowed and stopped 20 feet shy of her. As Gaia started moving away, the back doors opened, spilling the music out even louder, and two Latino men got out. They were bald. One wore a long-sleeved, collared wool shirt that was buttoned only at the very top over a white t-shirt. He had a red bandana for a headband. The other wore a sleeveless collared shirt with ratty edges that showed thick muscles covered in tattoo ink that rose up onto his neck. He looked at Gaia, then gave her a quick chin raise and pointed at her. Then they both started coming toward her.

So what'cha what'cha what'choo waaaaaant, the singer shouted.

"Hold up!" one of them shouted, but Gaia was already running for town as hard as she could. She reached the old cypress tree that marked where the bluffs swung out to the right, leaving the road and bending into a block of row houses. She ducked right and picked up speed, not bothering to look at the houses she passed. Her lungs were burning. A quick glance behind her showed she wasn't being followed—yet. She still heard the rap song, but it didn't seem to be getting any closer. Were the men on foot? She imagined them jumping out at her from one of the yards. They were much stronger and probably faster than she was.

The street ended at a guardrail at the bluffs' edge. Gaia hopped it and tore her hands up sliding down the steep slope of dirt she normally climbed down to reach the luggage-size boulders on the beach. It wasn't until she hit the bottom that she realized how stupid it was to take this route today. She growled at herself. The fastest way would have been to stay on the road and head straight into town. But muscle memory had brought her here. For the past year she'd taken this secret way along the coastline to avoid the pointing and stares of tourists who constantly crammed the little downtown.

But it was too late. She was already committed. The good news was that the tide was out, so she didn't have to navigate surging ocean whitewater. Gaia stood on a boulder and looked up at the guardrail high above her, then scanned the bluffs on either side. Nobody was there.

Then, the old scary rhyme popped into her head, the one Selene sometimes taunted her with.

Run, run, run, you little goat. Last Coyote gonna slit your throat!

When she was younger, Gaia didn't know what it meant. It was just a scary thing to say. But soon after in class, Godpappy Lane talked about Chief Last Coyote after a Chinese bullet train exploded near Bakersfield. Apparently Chief Last Coyote had done it. Then Jeremy Mendez had piped up and said, "Yeah, and the dude's a cannibal. He eats little kids for breakfast." The rhyme and rumors about Chief Last Coyote never truly spooked her until now. She knew it was crazy to think the terrorist was after her, but maybe this is how he operated: scare a kid into doing something stupid, like running down to some hidden part of the coast, then snatching her.

Last Coyote is not after you, she told herself. *And I'm almost 15. I'm not some little kid.* Then, to make it true, she said aloud. "Last Coyote is not after you!" But it didn't help.

Gaia bent over to catch her breath. She had to keep moving. She needed to get to her mom.

"Get it together. Think!" she scolded herself.

Her scientist mom was always telling Selene and her to think. Gaia scanned the boulder field ahead. With the tide out, she had a few yards of dry coastline to navigate. Her mom also scolded her about going this way. "You won't be so cavalier about The Worm when your belly's the size of a basketball," she'd say. But Gaia also knew you got The Worm mostly from drinking poorly treated sea water, and it was usually low tide when she went this way. But The Worm was the least of her worries right now. She looked back up to the bluff half expecting to see the men hopping over the guardrail after her, followed by Last Coyote, who looked like a blood-soaked savage in her imagination, then grabbing her and slitting her throat.

Gaia began boulder hopping toward the next section of bluff, which jutted further out toward the tide. She couldn't hear the rapscat music anymore, and as she neared the ocean, the cluttered street noise above gave way to the roar of the surf against the boulders a few yards away, a sound that usually calmed her. But now it sounded like a hiss.

She stepped recklessly from rock to rock, stumbling, occasionally glancing back. Gaia hiked up the legs of her baggy hemp pants as she neared the water. Today she didn't wait for the tide to recede before making a move around the point, and the oncoming wash of surf soaked her sneakers and calves. Gaia imagined microscopic nanobots—The Worm—crawling up her legs, trying to eat her like they were supposed to eat the Great Pacific Garbage Patch of plastic out at sea.

Around the point, she moved up away from the tide, then looked back again, then at the top of the bluffs. Nobody. So she sat down on an old piece of concrete protruding from the ground to catch her breath.

"Why am I even running?" her voice faltered. "Calm down, Cadogan! Calm down. Calm. Calm."

Cahm to me! The memory of the hacking man's voice called. *I am thee only one who can help you! I am thee only one who undah-stands you!*

She leaned back into a boulder, trying to slow her breathing to match the rhythm of the pounding surf. Her mind started to settle as the briny air washed up through her nose and into her brain. The man in the vision came back. He was so alien, yet so intimate, like he knew her. *I am thee only one who undah-stands you!* He was both frightening and reassuring, like a demon who turns out to be your friend, or the other way around. She'd made a dumb move coming this way, but at the very least she'd probably gotten herself out of hacking range. *Why would somebody do that? Why me?* Gaia shook her head and clenched her teeth, trying to clear her head of craziness.

Then something made the craziness worse. Another kind of music drifted into her mind. She'd started hearing it a week ago, a slow, faint, harmonized melody of voices and instruments mingling and blending so that she could discern neither instrument nor voice. At first she thought the music was coming from an open window in the distance, but it seemed to follow her wherever she went, until she realized she wasn't really hearing it with her ears. It was coming from inside her head. The music came to her at random times for only a few minutes before fading away. It was annoying, but it was also comforting; primal and nourishing, lulling, almost like the comfort she felt from the vision of the dark man. But the music felt more a part of her than the hacking, more real. Maybe she really was losing her mind. Maybe the rap music was imaginary, too, and it was speaking truth to her: *I think I'm losing my mind this time, this time, I'm losing my mind.* Maybe the whispered voice, "Siafu! She comes!" came from the same place as the music. Maybe the vision of the dark man trying to save her from the fire was part of the same insanity creeping into her. *How many 14-year-olds get schizophrenia?* she wondered.

The music gently wove along, and she felt less and less like running. Calming down and getting her mind right might be the thing to do.

To her left, seemingly right on top of her, giant Chumash rock towered over the end of the bay like a stone Titan rising from the sea. Behind Chumash Rock on the gray horizon, barren clouds brushed themselves into the sky like a painting—a promise of rain that never comes.

A lone seagull glided past, cocking its head as if to ask, "Well? *Do you have schizophrenia?*" Its scrawny body and disheveled feathers looked more regal with the grace of flight as it hugged the coastline, then landed on a distant boulder. Gaia got up and started moving again. Regardless of what was happening to her, she just wanted to be in the safety of her mom's office.

As she picked her way along the boulders in her wet, squishy sneakers, the eerie-but-comforting music in her head was like a soundtrack to her movements.

She noticed something in the boulders ahead, crouching beyond where the seagull had landed. It was a small, dark-haired person. The seagull that had flown past her and landed seemed very interested in something, tilting its head and hopping from rock to rock to follow whatever it was.

Suddenly, many things happened at once. The gull dove into the rocks to grab the thing it was chasing, but it came up flailing, struggling to take flight while the person—a shirtless, one-armed boy, Gaia could now see—jumped up from his hiding place. The gull thrashed and squawked, desperate to free itself from the fishing line in the boy's hand. As the gull struggled to stay in the air like a struggling kite, the boy deftly pulled the line through his legs to reel the bird in, feeding the slack end into his teeth to hold the line in place for the next pull. Gaia watched in shock. She'd heard of "gull kiting," but this was the first time she'd ever seen it. Her stomach flipped as she watched the boy grab the bird's head, wedge its flailing body between his legs, and wring its neck.

Realizing she was standing still, Gaia started to move again, looking ahead for any path she could take around the boy. But he noticed her, and instead of running away, he waited—and to Gaia's discomfort began angling toward her as she approached. In only bare feet and ragged shorts, he was much more nimble over the rocks than she was, so graceful and practiced that he may as well have been walking on flat ground.

Before she knew it he was at her side, and she could take in the gruesome picture of him. The boy, who was clearly Hawaiian, was horribly disfigured. His missing arm wasn't missing at all, but was a short stub with a tiny, useless hand at the end of it. The whole left side of his face seemed to be melted, bone and all, with his mouth gaping hopelessly open. Gaia noticed what may have been an eye slit, but she wasn't sure.

Then she noticed the seagulls. The one he'd just killed hung limply from his hand, but a rope of four or five more dead gulls was looped around his neck and hung down to his knees like a giant, feathery boa. When the boy saw Gaia eyeballing the gull in his hand, he quickly shoved it between his legs. Then he knelt and made a quick, one-handed slipknot at the bottom of the rope, slipped the gull's head into it, yanked the end of the rope tight, and stood up proudly.

Suddenly, one of the gulls in the middle of the rope began to flail and jerk, scaring Gaia into a careless step backwards, and she fell awkwardly onto the boulders. She got to her feet gracelessly, as quickly as she could, and saw the boy calmly grab the flailing bird by the head and snap its body like a whip to send it into eternal slumber.

The music in her mind wafted on.

"You thish lady daughter?" he slurred with surprising clarity given his ruined mouth, speaking without the use of his lips like a ventriloquist.

"Fish lady?" she repeated to make sure she'd heard the right thing. The boy nodded. Gaia wasn't sure if he meant her mom.

"Doat that say telican?"

"Boat that says Pelican? The Pelican boat?" Her mom's boat was called The Pelican. The boy nodded vigorously and seemed to smile on the good side of his mouth.

"Yeah..." she hesitated. "That's my mom's boat." She wondered where this was going, but more important, how the boy even knew.

"Wha ha'n da you?" he cocked his head, concerned.

"What happened to me?" She wondered if all his conversations with people went like this, with the other person repeating everything. He nodded. She looked down at her right hand. She'd come down hard on it when she fell, and her middle finger was cut and bleeding. "Oh, I just cut my finger on the rock. I'm fine," she said, looking ahead for an escape route.

"No," he shook his head, unfazed. "Earsh. Hair. Shkin." Then his eye grew big as he studied her face. "Eyes!" His rising voice drew the word out with awe.

Gaia dropped her head, embarrassed and frustrated. She looked at her bare arms, green like string beans, then reached up to cover her ears with her blueberry hair as best she could, though she could never fully cover them. She wished for sunglasses to cover her eyes, though for some reason it was nearly impossible for her to see through sunglasses.

"You Island? Like Lohi?" He seemed more curious than judgmental, looking for common ground. *Maybe he's relieved to see another freak,* she thought. Gaia realized she'd never escape from being a freak show, that even somebody as freakish as this boy would gawk at her, the whole damaged package.

"Your name's Lohi?" she asked, feeling obligated to keep the conversation going, but occasionally casting a glance behind her. He nodded vigorously again.

"I'm not Hawaiian," she said. "I don't know what's wrong with me. I was born like this."

"Ut's er nane?" he asked, matter-of-factly switching from the uncomfortable topic of her physical appearance as if it were some insignificant detail. Gaia was grateful for this. It was even a little endearing, and she relaxed a bit.

"Gaia," she answered as a surge of tide swept in and drenched their lower legs. "Ah, shipwreck!" she spat, pulling the bottoms of her soaked pants up over her knees and peeling off two small jellyfish that had washed onto them. Lohi stood there calmly, oblivious to the ocean. She wiped her hands on the tops of her pants.

"Worm water!" she said.

Gaia saw blood on her pants from her finger and quickly raised her hand, fearing the water had touched her open wound.

"This is GREAT!" she spat, picturing the microscopic worms swimming into her bloodstream, then making her belly swell over the next few months until she burst like a tick.

"'Sokay," Lohi smiled. "Don't touch your nouth." He was grinning at her. He seemed amused by her discomfort—at both talking to him and with worm water—quizzically watching this strange girl who had no idea about the true difficulties of life. But then his smile faded, and he became all business.

"You trade thor thish?"

Gaia looked back up the coast, then scanned the tops of the bluffs. No one. But she still felt uneasy and wanted to keep moving. She needed to ditch Lohi. The question he'd asked finally hit her.

"What? You want to trade for fish?" This was quickly turning into a barter situation she wanted no part of. Lohi nodded. "Trade for *seagulls*?" she asked incredulously.

The boy's face lit up, and he lifted the rope of dead birds. "Gull? Yesh? You trade thor gull?"

Gaia felt bile rise in her throat. Eating seagull was supposed to be worse than eating out of the trash. She shook her head. "We don't get any fish. My mom just tries to grow them. They usually die after she releases them into the ocean, because they get infected with The Worm."

Lohi stared at her a few long seconds, weighing whether or not to believe her. "Dethore they go in the ocean, good to eat? I trade thor work! Ina good worker!"

Gaia noticed that the music was fading, leaving her. She looked back over the boulders. "It doesn't work that way. I'm sorry, I have to go. I'm in a hurry."

A few moments later, when Gaia checked to see if she was being followed by Lohi or anyone else, she saw him standing where she'd left him, watching her go, looking like a small, brown, disfigured ghost with a rope of dead seagulls hanging from his neck.

Gaia didn't look back again.

-3-
Crazy

ire danced in the blackness ahead of her, a blackness so deep that the fire appeared to float in midair. Within the crackle of flames a baby cried out. Gaia panicked and tried to run to it, but her legs felt like they were pushing through thick batter. After what seemed like an eternity, she reached the fire and found it to be waist high, lashing out at her, but without heat, blazing in a circle around something. Gaia feared what she might see in the middle, because the baby had stopped crying. As she peered over the flames, she saw a seagull with a broken neck lying on a patch of perfectly green grass. "I'm too late!" Gaia cried out. But the seagull opened one eye, and Gaia felt a rush of hope that she wasn't too late after all. "Nice try," the bird croaked, then closed its eye, and exploded in a puff of dust.

Gaia woke to the sound of the Saturday morning People's News Service blaring across the house from the kitchen. The eerie choir of phantom music was back in her head. It sounded like both a choir and an orchestra were trapped inside a didjeridoo being blown on by a Siberian throat singer, weaving a heartbreakingly sweet melody over the jangle of news.

"Nice try! Nice try!" a male voice on the news kept saying over and over. A female voice responded, "So there's no way I can convince you that President Efrain is a murderous, blood-sucking robot?"

For a second, Gaia thought her sister had said that. It was just the kind of thing she'd spout. But this early, on a Saturday morning, there's no way Selene would be awake, much less talking.

Mean Selene. That's what Gaia called her. Mean Selene, with her normal red hair, white skin, and green eyes that never changed color, and her grating, 16-year-old attitude. *Selene's the best sister in the world—when she's asleep*, Gaia thought. She trained her ears on the room next door and heard Selene's heavy breathing. Out cold.

Gaia rolled onto her stomach and pulled the pillow over her head. "Why do they have to play it so loud!" she grumbled, vowing once and for all to tell her family about her sensitive hearing. But she planned to never tell them. Gaia's hearing was her one real gift, an advantage, and she wanted to keep it secret.

Starting to suffocate, realizing she'd never get back to sleep, Gaia tossed her pillow and tore the sheets off of herself. She sat up and gazed morosely around her cluttered room at the misshapen family of potted cacti, the bonsai cypress tree inside her frog tank, her dad's old surfboard that hung suspended from the ceiling inside an ancient fishing net, which made it look like some strange, ancient fish captured by mistake. She wondered if there had been fish that looked like that.

Just like me yesterday, she realized, picturing herself lying in the dirt, trapped in an invisible net while somebody hacked her like a helpless jellyfish. The dark man's milky eyes swam into her head, and she shuddered and rubbed the back of her neck as the nutty smell of mush wafted from the kitchen.

Cahm to me! the African voice echoed.

"The hell I will," she mumbled, imagining a pair of pimply kids peeking out from the curtains of a house, laughing at the effect their prank was having on her as she twitched in the dirt. "Idiot kids," she said. But then Gaia remembered the VW van sputtering away, and she felt a sick darkness descending into her stomach that it wasn't just idiot kids.

For two seconds she considered telling her parents about the hacking, but then decided not to. Big ears. Weird eyes. All the wrong color everywhere. Phantom music in her head. A hacking that was probably only schizophrenia. More trouble from an already troubled kid. *There's nothing wrong with you, baby, you're fine!* Whatever.

"Girls!" her dad's voice boomed from the kitchen. "It's about to come on! Selene! Gaia!"

As Gaia hobbled out to see what her dad was talking about, she heard Selene grumble and pull at her covers behind her bedroom door. Gaia stepped over a scattered wad of clothes that Selene had left in the hallway, too lazy to carry all the way into her room from the laundry five steps down the hall. The dark bamboo floor was cold on Gaia's feet despite all the calluses she'd built up from constantly going barefoot. She ran a knuckle along the smooth, uneven adobe wall until it ended and opened up into their small living room decorated with her dad's "classic" old wood-framed, plaid-covered furniture. Through the living room's French doors, Gaia saw their ancient hound dog, Prop, rolling in the graveled back yard and lifting a light dust cloud. He spotted her and raced to the door, pleading for entry with a paw that scraped the pane of glass he favored, adding to its brutally scratched surface. Long ago they'd quit yelling at him to stop, realizing it was hopeless. Gaia decided not to let him in yet, because he never left her alone. If she were a light, Prop would have been a giant moth, and she needed a little space this morning.

The kitchen-slash-dining-room was just an extension of the living room, separated by a counter that was covered in randomly piled books, the bookshelf in the living room having long ago reached capacity.

"Morning, baby," Gaia's mom said from the pot of mush she was stirring at their ancient electric stove. Gaia's dad pulled out a chair for her at the round, battered dining room table. When she sat, the chair rocked backwards slightly on its loose joints. The aroma of mush was smoky sweet, and her stomach growled.

"Here," said her dad, grinning as he handing her the silver-dollar-sized hologram projector disk. "It's about to start!"

Gaia yawned and set the disk on the table and poked it. A videostream appeared in midair above the disk. She was still too young for a Telepath, so she had to watch things this way instead of in her head, like her mom, dad, and Selene could do.

"What is it?"

"Come on, you know. Hasn't your godfather been telling you about this in school? The Huo Shui Ban ji?"

"Oh yeah," she said. "The Chinese fire water jet. Runs on sea water." She thought about being at the ocean yesterday talking to the boy Lohi.

"Just think of it!" he said. "A jet engine that runs on water!"

"Oh, we're suddenly all excited about the Chinese?" her mom said, still stirring the mush. "Like they need any more power.

They're even doing this from their Nebraska air base. Just rubbing our noses in it."

"Easy, Maer. They're sharing the technology with us."

"Yeah, at what cost? More farmland? It's eventually going to get shot down just like everything else."

"Shhh! It's starting. Selene!" he shouted so loudly it made Gaia jump, but she tried to disguise it by dropping her spoon on the floor. "Turn it on! Watch on the Alliance feed!"

The hologram above the disk was a sleek-looking black jet that slowly taxied on a white runway. Heat waves blurred the jet's body behind the engines, which sounded like screams to Gaia, and she ran her hand through the hologram to turn the volume down. The announcers spoke in quick Chinese that Gaia had a hard time keeping up with, but she could catch enough to know that they were mostly being self congratulatory about the wonders of all things China and Chinese. The camera zoomed in on the tinted, unmanned cockpit. A minute later the jet shot forward, launching itself into the sky like a bullet. There was applause, and the announcers became more animated and arrogant. The camera stayed with the jet as it streaked across the gray sky.

Suddenly, a flash of white from below, like a straight lightning bolt, struck the jet, which started cartwheeling through the air and breaking into pieces of wing and body before exploding. Gaia sat there, shocked, listening to yells from the announcers as the flaming pieces tumbled to earth, landing in a cornfield, and setting the cornfield ablaze. The hologram disappeared, but it was replaced a few seconds later by the hologram of an American news anchor.

> ANCHOR: "We interrupt this broadcast with breaking news. A group has just claimed responsibility for the downing of the Chinese aircraft Huo Shui Ban ji, the fire water jet, on what was to be its maiden flight. The group claiming responsibility, Native Americans Against America, led by the terrorist known as Chief Last Coyote, released the following statement. Quote, 'That was for Crazy Horse.' Unquote."

"Wow," Maer said. "What was I just saying?"

"Wow is right," her dad said, shaking his head sadly. "Damn."

"Run, run, run, you little goat! Last Coyote gonna slit your throat!" Selene said. She'd sauntered into the dining room, all grins, and sat in the chair opposite Gaia. Gaia was still in shock. Her family seemed so callous about what had just happened. Gaia had never seen anything like this before, and combined with what had happened to her the day before, she suddenly felt ill.

But Maer was chuckling.

"What the hell, Maer!" said their dad. "This isn't funny."

"From whose perspective is it not funny, Jack?"

"From—anyone's."

"Ma, I'm hungry," Selene whined, apathetic to anything and everything that didn't have to do with Selene and her needs. Gaia wondered if her sister's narcissism ever took a break.

"Turn it off," Maer said, "before your father has kittens."

Selene reached over and flicked Gaia's disk, but Gaia had already gotten up and was heading back down the hallway. The music had come back into her head, swirling in graceful, melodic plumes like a distant sandstorm rolling and curling back on itself. Seconds later, the music vanished.

Gaia felt drained. More than that she had to pee, so she grabbed her soccer uniform and long-sleeved shirt from bedroom floor before heading into the bathroom, where she immediately saw her reflection in the mirror. Her straight hair was balled up on one side from sleep, looking like tangled blue seaweed, letting a giant green ear stick out like a dirty teacup saucer. Gaia scowled at herself, then ran her green fingers—darker than green beans—over a dark blue eyebrow and down her cheek.

Her green skin reminded her of the big day today, one that she'd been excited about for weeks, ever since her soccer coach told the team they'd been invited to play a game on The Green. Rumored to be the most amazing field of green grass, *real* green grass like in the dream she'd woken up from that morning, the Green lay inside a mysterious white dome she'd driven past a dozen times on the canyon road. And today was the day she'd finally get to run around on it, touch it, smell it, feel it. The Green. Godpappy Lane said was going to be there, too. But her Uncle Cloudy couldn't come. He had to work.

But she'd lost some excitement between the hacking and the shock of the water jet. Her mom and dad were still arguing in the kitchen, and Selene had gone into her own room and slammed the door. Gaia's mind went back to brownness, to dirt, dusty and choking. Just yesterday she'd been lying on the side of the road, crippled, unable to do anything but cough and sweat as she was assaulted by the fiery vision. She knew it was an illusion, but it seemed so real, so full of pain and meaning, so intentional. *His eyes were dead.*

Gaia leaned closer to the mirror to watch her own eyes, which were anything but dead. They were currently purplish-black, with sulphur-yellow edges, like storm clouds swirling around a dark alien planet. The yellow, she'd been told, came out when she got worked up. And when the strange music was playing in her head, she'd noticed that her eyes seemed to change in time with it.

But nobody would ever ask her what the music sounded like, because nobody would ever find out about it. *To hell with everybody*, she thought. She turned from the mirror and sat on the closed toilet with her head in her hands, giving in to the news her parents had turned back on in the kitchen.

> REPORTER: "President Efrain, still no comment on the latest attack by Chief Last Coyote?
>
> PRESIDENT: "Still no comment, Kim."
>
> REPORTER: "Very well, let's turn to the ocean."
>
> PRESIDENT: "Which one, Kim?"

The news blathered on. Gaia pictured the ocean, pink in the morning and orange in the afternoon. All the grown-ups said it used to be gray and blue—so blue that from space it looked like a blue marble instead of Mars's twin. Blue like her hair, like a blueberry.

> REPORTER: [Chuckles]. "Your opponent says this is an election year stunt, saying, quote, 'This is black magic smoke with no real basis in science or reality.'"
>
> PRESIDENT: "Tell me exactly what that scatterbrain Israel Martinez is desperately whining

about this time, and I'll tell you whether or not it's a stunt. How's that?"

"Don't you say it!" Maer growled from the kitchen. "Don't you dare talk about *my* fish project just to get re-elected!"

"They're gonna say it," Jack droned.

It was only April, and Gaia was already sick of hearing about the presidential election, which was still seven months away. There was still a few more months of Efrain and Martinez trashing each other in the primary, then another few more months of one of them trashing the other party's candidate in the general election, dragging each other through the mud. Excavating each other's demons.

> REPORTER: "Fish, of course. Madam President, your Department of Ecological Recovery claims that it's now possible to grow a worm-resistant species of fish."

"Idiot! God damn idiot!" Maer said. "Are you *trying* to get me kidnapped by the Chinese?"

Gaia froze. She knew that her mom did something for the government having to do with growing fish, but up until now she never realized it might be something that could put her mom in any kind of danger. *Is she serious?*

"Easy," Jack reassured. "Don't get overdramatic. It's not as bad—"

"OVERDRAMATIC?!" Maer shouted, then shushed herself to a whisper, which Gaia could still hear. "Overdramatic, Jack?"

Her mom was serious as cancer, and her urgency spooked Gaia.

> PRESIDENT: "Oh, I assure you this is very real indeed, based on very real science. The fact that we're about to make the greatest breakthrough in food security in the past fifty years is not lost on my opponent. America is going to start feeding the world again—under my Administration."
>
> REPORTER: "So you're confirming that this is true?"

PRESIDENT: "Yes I am, Kim. Truer than true."

REPORTER: "And what about the Chinese?"

Gaia remembered she needed to study for her upcoming Chinese language test on Monday.

PRESIDENT: "What *about* the Chinese?"

REPORTER: "They've said that as part of our debt repayment terms they can claim co-ownership of any new food-related technologies."

PRESIDENT: "Let me worry about the Chinese, Kim."

REPORTER: "And the terrorist organization Native Americans Against America. Chief Last Coyote. Any concerns there about possible sabotage? We've just gotten a fresh reminder of how dangerous Naaa is. The N-triple-A."

PRESIDENT: "I'm confident in our ability to protect our interests."

REPORTER: "You mean like our satellites?"

PRESIDENT: "You know as well as I do that the satellite program was abandoned due to atmospheric conditions. And as for fish growing, Chief Last Coyote and his organization stand to benefit just as much as the rest of the world. He's gotta eat just like everyone else."

"Off!" Maer snapped, and the news vanished. Gaia heard a series of jarring slams from her mom angrily putting bowls on the table.

"Whoa," Jack said. "Take it easy."

"Oh, *now* you wanna take it easy? You get all worked up about the poor Chinese and their plane, but you're willing to take it easy when they hang your wife out to dry on the Alliance news? The *Alliance* news, Jack? The whole world just heard that."

Gaia tensed. She'd never heard her battle-tested mom sound this worried before.

"A lot of people are working on this project, Maer," Jack said.

Gaia pictured her mom pointing a bamboo spoon at her dad, which she often did.

"Sure, but how many lead scientists are there. Two, Jack. Me and Lane Ripple. Oh, don't you shake your head at me like I'm crazy."

Wouldn't making a worm-resistant fish be a good thing? Gaia wondered. She, and the rest of the country, were tired of eating fonio and synthetic food—and seagull, if you were Hawaiian or desperate enough. Gaia thought of the melted boy from yesterday. Dangling, contaminated bird meat. The desperate flailing at the end of the fishing line, the broken necks. Being hacked, being on fire, gagging on dust. Getting teased every day of her life, mercilessly. Bizarre music that only she could hear, coming and going. *And Mom's worried about being crazy? I'm a blue-haired, green-skinned, big-eared, schizophrenic freak!* She pictured Stacy Williams sneering at her, saying, "Guy-uh is gay-uh!"

She suddenly felt like screaming and curling up into a tight little ball.

"And it's not Last Coyote I'm worried about, it's the Chinese. I cannot believe she just told the world about my classified project!" Gaia heard a piece of bamboo-ware rattle in the sink where her mom had tossed it. "Fuck it. I'm gonna go help Gaia get ready."

Desperate to avoid her mom seeing her upset, Gaia quickly stripped off her jammies, donned her long-sleeved shirt, and swam into her oversized soccer jersey, which fell to her knees like a dress. Her socks would cover the rest of her green legs. As she opened the bathroom door to make a quick exit, Gaia saw that she was too late.

"What is it, baby?" Her mom was blocking the path to her room. "Are you crying?"

All Gaia wanted to do was fall onto her bed, but she covered her face with her hands and buried herself in her mom's neck.

"What is it?"

Gaia wanted to tell her mom about the hacking, but she hesitated. She'd been hearing weird music, which means the hacking could have just been in her head, too, like some neurological disorder. Maybe her disease really was starting to invade her brain. She was ashamed, scared, and didn't want to talk about it right now. So she went with anger instead.

"You know what it is!" Gaia snarled.

"Somebody tease you?"

"No!" she pulled away. "Why won't you take me to the doctor?"

Her mom closed her eyes and drew a deep breath.

"Because, baby—we've already been through this—there's nothing wrong with you. You're perfectly healthy."

"Oh! Right! I forgot!" She pushed past her mom and stormed into her room, throwing herself face down on the bed. Her dad's boot steps echoed in the hall, along with the tick-tick-tick of Prop's claws on the hard clay floor. She felt him jump onto the bed and roll over against her with a groan, and she draped her arm over him. Prop's graying fur was warm and soft across his bumpy ribs.

"Stupid dog," she whispered, as he let out a labored sigh.

"Are you forgetting what today is?" Her mom sat down on the foot of the bed.

"Yes."

"Oh, really."

Gaia smiled wearily into her pillow. *How can I be depressed one minute and happy the next? I HATE this!* Her mood swings lately made as much sense as rain falling when the sun is shining. But Gaia couldn't help but smile. In an hour she'd be playing soccer on The Green, and her heart bounced a little as she tried to picture the field.

"I probably won't play anyway," she mumbled into her pillow. "I suck."

"Who cares? It's real grass, Gaia. Beautiful, lush, real grass. Roll around on it while you're on the sidelines!"

Gaia couldn't imagine. She'd seen pictures and videostreams of real grass, rolling hills of it. Parks and golf courses used to be nothing but unbelievably green grass. *Today I'll get to see it. I'm going to do cartwheels on it.* She wondered how it would feel. Would her feet sink into it? Would it make her itch? She loved anything that grew from the ground no matter what it was, from patches of invasive crab grass to broad-leafed rhubarb plants that snakes loved to sleep under (until Gaia showed up, when they would inexplicably slither over and try to curl around her feet). Gardening, growing things, soothed her when nothing else would; and she had a particular soft spot for the growing things that struggled, stubbornly clinging to life—the underdogs. "Playing with your only friends?" Selene mocked her whenever she caught Gaia spending time in their sad, front yard garden. And Gaia would always say, "What choice do I have with a retarded sister?"

But today there would be a sea of rich, green grass! The phantom music rose in her mind again, accompanying the visions of grass.

Gaia rolled onto her back and tried her best to scowl. Prop slid his head backwards to stay pinned against her, sticking to her like a shadow, and she stroked his velvety ears.

"Why are they letting us play on The Green, anyway?" she asked. "We're just going to tear it up. It doesn't make any sense."

"That's the whole point!" her dad said from the doorway. He was dressed in his desert-camouflaged fatigues, which meant he was leaving again soon.

"*What's* the whole point?"

"It's a new strain of grass. It supposedly draws moisture from the air, so you never have to water it. Or, not very often, anyway. That's in theory. They want to see how it reacts to stress."

"They should try to figure out how freakish kids react to stress instead," Gaia deadpanned.

"Hey! That's enough of that." Her mom slapped her butt. "We'll talk about this later."

"There's nothing to talk about."

"Later! We need to feed you and go."

Gaia rose laboriously and squeezed past her dad to go to the kitchen.

"Baby," her mom asked behind her as they walked down the hall. "I got another message from the Health Department yesterday. Something about not being able to read your heart rate or blood pressure remotely through your diagnostic implant. Did you feel anything that might have, um, made your D.I. malfunction?"

"No," Gaia lied, plopping into her chair at the kitchen table behind a bowl of steaming fonio mush, wondering if the "oatmeal" her parents talked about eating in the old days tasted any better. She was convinced that if her freakish body hadn't dissolved her fourth D.I., the hacking definitely had.

"Okay. Just asking," Maer said, joining her at the table. "You'd tell me, right?"

Gaia shrugged. Her dad sat down and flipped through the colorful images floating in a loose sphere above his palm while he sipped chicory coffee. Gaia could never see exactly what he was seeing, because the security settings built into his Telepath blurred and scrambled the images and videostreams for everyone but him.

"Where's your lunch box?" Maer asked suddenly. The spoon in Gaia's hand stopped what it was doing: sculpting a face in her mush that was vomiting mush. She remembered the hollow clang and clatter of her bento box spilling all over the ground yesterday. She hadn't picked it up before she started running.

"I—" Gaia started, rolling through lies in her head, but she was saved by her mom mom's yell, so sudden and loud that it made her jump.

"Selene! We're leaving in five minutes with or without you!"

Gaia heard her big sister mumble "Shut up," too softly for their mom to hear, and Gaia hoped she'd just stay in bed. But she knew Selene was dying to see the grass, too.

"Gaia, stop playing with your food and eat," Maer said, and Gaia was relieved she'd forgotten about the lunch box. "If they catch us throwing out food they'll fine us."

"They never check," Gaia said.

"Oh, you'd be surprised."

"You eat it, then."

"No. It's yours. EAT!"

Gaia shoveled a heaping spoonful of sticky mush into her mouth and choked it down.

"Up! Up! Up!" Mar tried steering her to the front door, but Gaia spun and made for the side kitchen door instead.

"Gah," Maer sighed. "We're late. Go to the truck. You can spend time in the garden when we get home."

But Gaia ignored her. She needed a few minutes of solace, and she knew she'd be sitting in the truck, waiting, because Selene was just sitting down to eat and wasn't even dressed yet.

The morning was chilly and dewless, and relatively quiet despite the music in hear head, though she could still hear a thousand things anyway: dogs barking in the distance, people talking and cooking in their homes around the neighborhood, news and videostreams colliding with each other, NoisyBoys, a baby crying, Maer hassling Selene about always waking up at the last minute.

Their garden, not unlike most other house gardens, was fenced in with rusted tin sheets to help keep critters out, and topped with high voltage wire to help keep people out. Gaia meandered through the rows of motley tomatoes, zucchini, and carrots, running her fingers over brown-edged, leafy plants that were thirsty but trying their best. Some of the vegetables, though shriveled and small, were nearly ready to eat. The quinoa plants were getting white fly again, and the bugs wafted like smoke when she bumped the thick stems.

Her underdogs. Her only friends.

Gaia wondered more about the music, trying to figure out what might have triggered it. The music began at school a week ago, right after she overheard D-Day Perez get frustrated with Maggie Ancheta and tell her, "Why don'choo leave me alone and go bug The Thing instead." The Thing was another nickname for Gaia, but the kids had stopped saying it to her face when Gaia started hissing at them like a cat. Right after Maggie said, "Shut up, D-Day," the music began to play, floating through the classroom. When she looked up and nobody else seemed to hear it, she thought it was coming from another room. But when she went outside for recess and still heard it, Gaia realized it was coming from somewhere inside her head, so naturally she started to think that she really *was* going crazy. Maybe the simplest explanation really was the right one. Godpappy Lane, who was also her teacher, had called that "Occam's Razor" in class, and Stupid Stacy Williams had asked him what shaving had to do with it.

The front door opened, then closed, and Gaia heard her mom and dad walking to the truck. "Gaia, move it," her dad's voice came from the other side of the fence.

"Okay," she said dully, but continued to wander the garden.

"What in the world is she doing?" Gaia heard her dad ask her mom as they climbed into the truck, clueless about Gaia's eavesdropping.

"She's stalling, Jack."

"I can see that, Maer. I thought she was excited about this."

"She is."

"Then why is she taking her sweet time?"

"I think something happened. Somebody must have teased her or said something."

Yeah, like you guys talking about me is any better, Gaia thought.

"I figured we were past all that," her dad said. "All those kids know her by now."

"Apparently that doesn't matter. Kids are little assholes."

Duh.

"So what do we do now?"

"We? We, Jack? If you were ever home for longer than an hour you could say 'we.'"

Gaia hated it when they argued, especially on the day he was going to leave. Why did they always do that?

"Dammit, Maer. That's not—"

"Not now, Jack."

"But you—"

"Not. Now. Jack."

In the few moments of silence that followed, Gaia heard the soft roar and hiss of the Pacific a mile down the hill. She scanned the sad, wilting garden, taking in each sorrowful-looking plant, each resembling a weary refugee bent and bowed by its own thoughts of a troubled past in a different land. In a way, they reminded Gaia of herself. *These* were her people.

She was startled by the front door slamming and Selene stomping to the truck.

"I guess it's a good sign, as strange as it sounds," Jack said. "These moods. Looks like she's going to suffer through puberty like every other kid. I have to admit, I had my doubts."

"Jack!" Maer cut him off.

Gaia froze. Was he joking? She'd never heard anything like that before, and he sounded serious. *I'm not going to go through puberty?*

"What? You think she can hear us?"

They stopped talking for a few moments, and then Maer spoke, a little louder than before.

"She's the most incredible person I know. The only thing wrong with her is that she's better than everyone else. Someday she'll see that. Someday, everyone will see it."

The truck horn blared, but Gaia didn't look up. She was kneeling behind a tomato plant, nervously digging at the base of a thistle weed to pull it out without getting poked. She needed a little more time to process what she'd just heard. *These moods.* Her blueberry hair hung like ragged curtains, and it framed her hands working at the weed. For a moment, her hands looked like somebody else's—like they belonged to a creature, a "thing" other than her. Her hands had a tinge of brown against the dirt that Gaia hadn't noticed before. But maybe that was her wishful thinking painting an optical illusion. There was no mistaking the greenness of her hands, of her skin. It covered her body like moss bathing in the last rays of afternoon sun.

With her dangling hair, Gaia suddenly felt like a skinny frog that somebody had jokingly costumed with a blue mop. She felt beaten down by teasing, by hacking, felt the burning fire of the vision tingling on her skin; the burning of her classmates's mockery and the jarring pity the deformed Hawaiian kid had given her.

"Move it, you little krill!" Selene yelled from the truck window.

"Selene!" Maer snapped. "Shove a rag in it."

"I had to wake up just to wait around for Little Miss Sadness?"

"You know, you're absolutely right, Sweetie. Why don't you go in the house and go back to sleep. Oh! Or better yet, go back into the house and empty the toilet compost like I asked you to yesterday. The 1-2 truck is coming to pick up our bin on Monday."

"No way! I'm not doing that. It's gross. I just woke up."

"Then just keep your mouth clamped. Give your sister a minute."

"Jesus," Selene huffed.

"You called?" their dad joked. Nobody laughed.

A minute later the truck horn blared again, but Gaia stayed put. Her vision had gone blurry as tears tried to escape from her eyes and plunge into the parched ground—but she caught herself and quickly wiped her face on the arm of her shirt. "No!" she scolded herself. "No crying."

Maybe it's the world that's going crazy, and I'm in the eye of the storm, she thought, but then, *Yeah, sure, blame it on the world, you green-skinned freak. It's you. You're finally losing it.*

The thistle she was pulling at came free, but it gave her a sharp little poke as it left the soil, its one final act of defiance. Gaia held it up to examine it, small and limp and dirty green. It looked like she felt—like a bizarre little weed that everybody wanted to yank.

She stood and lifted her shirt to wipe her face, then tossed the thistle into the dirt. She was about to step on it and grind it into the ground, but she remembered she was barefoot. Stepping on it barefoot would hurt. The weed lay there, pathetic and prone, it's poky leaves spread wide like little praying mantis arms daring the world to "Bring it on!" With respect, she stepped over it as she went to the truck—to drive to The Green.

"See you later, weed," she called back to it.

But the weed didn't respond.

-4-

Communion

S unlight filtered through eucalyptus leaves as they wound their way through the canyon, and Gaia watched stubbly patches of wild grasses already shaded brown with death whiz past the window. Jack poked a button on the NoisyBoy, and the rusty jingle of an old-fashioned ice cream truck tinkled into the air.

"Jesus H, Dad. Every time. It's embarrassing," Selene whined.

"What's embarrassing, Princess, is when somebody slams into you because they don't hear you coming."

"Dad, this truck already sounds like it's gonna fall apart. I can hear you coming a mile away whenever you pick me up!"

"That's because I play the ice cream truck."

"Can't you put something else on?" Selene scrunched down in the seat and rested her head on the dusty window, dramatically folding her arms across her chest.

Gaia tried to tune them out as she watched skeletons of California oak and sycamore pass. She wondered how they could grow in the brick-hard earth. Some of the trees, the ones that weren't burned, clung to a few green leaves that were oddly tinged with life. They reminded her of the human corpses she had heard about whose fingernails and toenails continue to grow in the grave. She always felt an odd sensation that she should do something about the dying world around her. But what?

As they emerged from the canyon into the flatlands, they reached a towering wall that blurred as they drove alongside to it. The Chinese government built it to protect their crops from theft and vandalism, which reminded Gaia of the rusted tin and high voltage wire protecting her sad little garden at home; though her crops would be easier to steal than those behind this giant wall. She craned her neck to read the large Chinese characters: "New People's Paper." She'd asked Godpappy Lane in class one day what New People's Paper was, and he'd said that the Chinese were growing hemp on the other side, presumably, as advertised, to make paper. But after he said it some of the kids in class had laughed and pinched their thumbs and forefingers together pretending to smoke.

At the end of the wall, somebody had spray-painted what was becoming a common tag, one she didn't understand: "ZAZ - Prepare the Way." After the wall, acres of drought-ignorant fonio draped the ground like a brittle yellow carpet as far as the horizon. It was everywhere, this "poor man's wheat" as everyone called it, the ubiquitous food staple of the Central Coast protected by an invisible electric fence.

Selene was quiet for a few minutes, but it didn't last long.

"I'm hungry," Selene muttered.

Shut up, Gaia thought.

"Well, did you eat breakfast like I asked you to?" Maer asked.

No, Gaia answered in her head.

"No."

"Well maybe that's why."

"Can I have something out of the lunch basket?"

"No, that's for lunch. That's why it's in the *lunch* basket."

"Fine. Just *let* me die."

"Just let her die, Mom," Gaia said and was rewarded by a slap in the head from her sister. She tried to do it back, but Selene blocked it.

"Knock it off, both of you," Jack said. "Selene, you're not going to die. Not today, anyway."

"Wanna bet? It's a spook year. I bet we all die this year."

"What?" Jack chuckled. "What on earth is a spook year?"

"Wow Dad. You don't know what a spook year is? Ma, do you even know?"

Maer shook her head and sighed. "Enlighten us."

"It's a year with two zeroes in it. Baaaaaaaad things happen in spook years."

"Okay, like what?" Maer said.

"When did the last whale die?"

"Christ, do you *have* to bring that up?" Maer sighed. "Fine. 2050."

"See?!" Selene said triumphantly. "The last spook year!"

"Sure, but the last satellite was shot out of the sky two years later," Jack said.

"Oh, like that's as bad as the whales, Dad. Tell that to Mom."

Selene argued back and forth with her parents about her spook year theory, and Gaia tried to tune them out. She also had other troubles to marinate in. Gaia was a mess inside. Her dad had called her impending puberty a good sign because he doubted it would happen, like there a chance she *wouldn't* go through puberty. She wanted to ask her dad what he'd meant, but that just made her innards churn. In asking, she knew she was about to betray her own secret—the secret of how well she could hear. Her heart pounded in her throat, stopping the words from coming out. Instead, she asked something else.

"Mom, what's Zaz?"

"Zaz?" Maer turned in her seat to face Gaia. "Zaz is cult bullshit."

"Please don't cuss, Mom," Gaia said.

"Look, baby, this is me. You're going to have to deal with all kinds in this life, starting with your mother."

"Good luck with that," Jack said, turning his head to wink at Gaia as the truck went over a bump.

Maer punched him in the arm and scowled. "Watch the road, smartass. Anyway," she addressed Gaia again, "I don't know a lot about it, but it sounds like an alternative Bible, or gospel that was discovered a few years ago. The Christians and Muslims hate it, which does make it more endearing to me, I'll admit. The irony of religious bull poop—is that better?—calling bull poop on religious bull poop is a gorgeous little circle, like a donut with extra sprinkles. Anyway, it's new. The darker the times, the thicker the bull poop, I guess."

"A bull crap donut. Yum," Selene said. "Nothing like rambling on with authority about a topic you know absolutely nothing about. Great parenting, Ma."

Jack chuckled. Gaia wondered if her parents had ever seen a live bull when they were younger, but she didn't want to derail the conversation about Zaz. She wanted to know more, but she wasn't sure why.

"And you're suddenly some Zaz expert, my dear, sweet princess?" Maer said.

"We actually talked about it in class."

"Oh?"

"Some female savior, but not like Jesus or Mohammed. Something greater, like nature itself, or the Earth Mother. Like—" here she smirked at Gaia. "Like Gaia in the old Greek myths, creator of the earth and all the big, nasty monsters on it. By the way, have you been holding out on me, you little snot? Are you really the Earth Mother but haven't told me? That would be just like you."

Gaia saw something pass between her mom and dad, so subtly that it might have been her imagination. But Maer became quiet and turned to look out her side window.

"Oh, wait!" She dug into the back pocket of her pants. "I've still got this!" She unfolded the paper. "We all had to read part of the gospel out loud. This was mine." She reached her arm out for dramatic effect and read in a low, thespian voice, rolling her Rs.

> "And the grrrreat hound laughed aloud and began
> to devour the living and the dead on the land and
> in the barren sea, and the host cried and wailed
> and ate stones for bread, and laughed with the
> hound saying, 'Consume us not, Father!'
> "But a small voice arose and shook the World, and
> commanded the hound, 'Lie down.' And the great
> hound obeyed."

"Oh, boy," said Maer, and Jack laughed, which only encouraged Selene. She raised her hand and wiggled her fingers like a preacher. "This is where you come in," she paused, backhanding Gaia on the arm.

> "And a child sprrrrung from the poisoned ground
> and stood before the hound. And the hound
> bowed its head saying, 'Who art thou, mistress?'
> 'Thine is not to ask, but to obey,' saith the child.
> 'Go thy way, and laugh no more.'"

Here Selene let loose with a deep, boisterous, theatrical laugh.

"And the great hound went his way, the great
beast, and the children rejoiced and cried, 'Mother,
thou hast not forsaken us!'
"And the child said, 'Nay, call me not Mother,
whom thou hast forsaken. I am AIA, and I am ZAZ,
the first and the last. I am thee. Rise up.'"

"Pretty impressive, eh Ma?" Selene said, leaning back in her seat
and folding her arms in victory.

"Anybody can say the word 'and' over and over," Gaia said.

"AND anyway," Selene raised her voice, "my take is that Zaz
AND is going to save us from the AND evils of the genetic food
AND conglomerates."

Now Jack joined in. "Either that or Prop is the hound, and he's
going to go rabid and turn on us when we get back home. Careful,
Red, he'll latch onto you first because you're so *spicy*."

Red and Blue, the pet names for the Cadogan girls. Gaia played
with the idea that their parents had brought colors into the world
rather than children.

"Veritas to the mothership, Pop," Selene said.

"It's official," Maer said. "I live with the insane."

"Don't forget the deformed," Gaia said, but Maer didn't laugh.
She turned in her seat with a scowl and slapped Gaia's leg. "Knock
it off. You're not deformed."

"Speaking of donuts," Selene pointed out, turning to Gaia, "I
hear Last Coyote loves to eat deformed children the most, because
he knows their parents won't miss them. Run, run, run you little
goat. Last Coyote—OWWW! Shit, Ma!" Selene moved back to
her side of the truck holding her head. "Are you trying to make me
retarded?"

"Too late," Jack said. "I hear he likes to eat special needs
gingers, too."

"Pa, you're an ass."

Selene shut up, but what she'd said had gotten Gaia worked up
again. She thought back to the hacking, of being chased from the
road and along the coast by a phantom named Siafu, her fear
being fueled by the myth of Last Coyote slitting her throat. She
suddenly wondered if Siafu was some secret code name for Last
Coyote.

"Dad?" Gaia said. "Is that really true, about Last Coyote eating kids?"

"Who knows about somebody like him. I doubt it, but who knows."

Selene touched Gaia's leg and slowly nodded with very wide eyes.

"I do know he's truly an evil genius," Jack continued, becoming serious. "We think he's responsible for the fact that we no longer have satellites, and why nobody dares put an airplane into the sky. Just like what happened this morning with the water jet."

"The Pulse," Gaia said.

"The Pulse, that's right. The most dangerous weapon we've ever seen, short of a nuclear bomb. And we've barely seen it. Before today, it was never caught on video. That's all I can say without being hung for treason. Whether he created it or stole it, we don't know. But we do know—we think—he's the only one with it. New Persia doesn't have it, neither does China. We sure as hell don't."

"Mom, Dad?" She was making another attempt to tell them about the hacking. But when her mom turned to face her and her dad looked in the rear-view, she got cold feet. So she lied. "Nothing. Just nervous about the game, that's all."

"You're gonna kick some grass," her dad said.

"Who cares about the game," her mom said. "Enjoy yourself. Especially the grass. I don't think you know what a big deal it is. Actual, living grass."

But Gaia did know what a big deal it was. She felt as if she were about to be reconnected to a lost part of her soul.

They hit the section of road where the Armor-Dillo blacktop undulated up and down like a black sea monster, turning the trip into a roller coaster ride, courtesy of San Andreas fault, Maer always said. Gaia quietly looked out the window as her father sped up over the swells in the road. The landscape and her guts lurched up and down. Maer groaned and gripped the dashboard. Normally Gaia loved this section of road, but now she was distracted by Last Coyote, by the hacking, and now by this Zaz myth.

Then Gaia heard a whisper. It was Selene. So soft were the words that nobody else would have been able to hear them. Gaia almost looked over at Selene, but caught herself just in time. It was another of her sister's tricks, testing how well Gaia could hear. So far, Gaia had always been able to pretend she couldn't hear it.

"I hope you move faster on the soccer field than you do getting into the truck."

Gaia looked at the window and ignored her.

"I know you can hear me, you little shit."

She glued her eyes to the scenery as she tried to slow her breathing. Even if Selene only suspected, Gaia obviously wasn't doing a good enough job of hiding it. *What? You think she can hear us?* Her dad's voice from inside the truck earlier that morning echoed in her brain. She'd have to be more careful.

But Selene didn't whisper another word. She turned her whining back to her parents.

"Can I drive home after the game?"

"We're going to get IceKream at Salty's after the game," Jack said.

"Then can I drive to Salty's?"

"Gee, I don't know. Do you have your permit yet?" Maer said.

"Almost!"

"Well, then, I almost said yes."

"Shhhhhhhhhhhhhhhhhhhit," Selene softly exhaled. Clearly, it was one of her favorite words.

"What was that?"

"What was what?"

"That's what I thought."

"What, Ma, you can say it but I can't? You say it all the time!"

"That's correct."

"Hypocrite."

"Listen. As soon as you show me you can express yourself competently, you know, say what you feel with meaningful words rather than lazy swearing, *then* you can start saying it."

"Mom, I'm frustrated by what I perceive to be your belittlement of me and my capabilities. How's that? Better?"

"Much."

"Then SHIT!"

Their dad nearly drove off the road, he was laughing so hard. Even Gaia had to admit it was funny, but she kept her head pressed to the window.

As the truck slowed and turned into the parking lot, Gaia sat up and swallowed hard against her excitement. She heard the bustle and chatter of the growing crowd, and the scraping of what seemed like a million feet. She heard bits of conversation, too, but nothing was worth listening to.

"I wonder if Lane's bringing his niece," Maer said to Jack.

"What?" Gaia said. "Godpappy has a niece?"

"Never mind," Maer said. "Shouldn't have said anything."

"You mean his Croozer baby niece?" Selene said.

Gaia perked up. Godpappy with a Croozer baby niece? She couldn't believe it. If this were true, Gaia was dying to see what she looked like, to see if she looked anything like Gaia herself.

"Hey!" Maer snapped. "Not cool. And how did you know about that?"

"I was in your office when Lane was telling you about it. Remember? Selene? Your invisible daughter?"

"That's enough," Maer said. "That's enough, all of it."

"How old is she?" Gaia asked.

"Your age. Never mind. I shouldn't have said anything. I'll let Lane tell you, if he even wants to."

They drove through a tall, solid green gate onto a new Armor-Dillo parking lot that was as black as space. Its smooth surface was thick with cars and people hurrying toward the giant white bubble that looked like a celestial circus tent. The Cadogans waited in line while some cars were let in and others were turned away. Finally, when it was their turn, a green-suited guard stepped to the window.

"Help you?"

"We have a player!" Jack announced with embarrassing enthusiasm as he gestured to the back seat.

The guard peered into the truck, and his gaze lingered on Gaia for a few uncomfortable moments.

"Name?"

"Cadogan."

"Is that a K or a C?"

"C."

"First name?"

"Gaia."

"Kya?"

"No, Gaia. G-A-I-A."

The guard's eyes glazed over to check the list of names in his Telepath. "Got it. They'll tell you where to park inside. Not a lot of space, so park closely. Enjoy The Green. No smoking."

A claustrophobic itch jumped into Gaia, and she had to get out of the car. She had to get to The Green. Her body thirsted for it.

Her mom turned to her, holding up a hair tie.

"No!" Gaia said, and instead of reaching for the hair tie, she grabbed her soccer bag and hopped out of the car. "You know I hate those. They make my ears stick out." She slammed the door and was on the move, weaving and darting in and out of people in her stocking feet, moving ever closer to the giant white bubble.

"Guess *somebody's* excited," she heard her dad say.

"Guess *somebody's* gonna get her period any minute," Selene commented.

Gaia slowed to let Selene's words sink in. Selene was being a jerk, but Gaia found hope in what she'd just said, and it couldn't have come at a better time. She needed reassurance that she was normal in some way, even if it did come from Selene.

The acrid smell of the heating Armor-Dillo surface reminded Gaia of the rotting fruit some farmers tried to sell at the market every week. But as she neared the bubble, her nose picked up on a fresh, rich, and earthy scent. She bulled her way through the crowd. Normally she wouldn't have been so pushy, but she couldn't control herself. Her body, her being, craved the living grass.

But something was wrong—something she was hearing. She realized she'd been hearing it since she'd escaped from the truck but had tuned it out in her excitement. It was a small child crying. As she paused to listen, to pick up where it was coming from, she felt the crowd forcing her along. The crying was up ahead in the direction she was walking.

Gaia wasn't even sure why she was doing this, trying to locate this child, when every fiber of her longed to get into the bubble. But something about the cry haunted her, as if a part of herself were out there, frightened and hopeless, and nobody was listening. What she found a few moments later was a pathetic-looking little boy with wild brown hair and a face that was red and melting with tears. He stood there completely still, bawling away, facing the flow of the crowd with his arms limp at his sides like a hopeless doll with one of his overall straps undone and dangling. It was one of the saddest things Gaia had ever seen. Grown-ups, people with children of their own, moved right past him like he was invisible.

When Gaia stepped in front of him and he saw her face, he stopped crying for a second and looked as if he might turn and run away.

"Don't worry!" Gaia said. "This is just a costume! I'm just dressing up funny today."

This seemed to help, because the boy's face softened.

"Let's go find your momma," she said, holding out her hand. He hesitated but took it and let Gaia lead him back toward the bubble. His hand felt so little in hers. She concentrated, listening for any conversation about a lost child. A few moments later she easily had it, coming from inside the bubble. "He was right next to me!" she heard an anguished woman saying. "My hand was on his head! He just disappeared!"

"I think I found your momma," Gaia leaned down and told him. She felt his hand grip hers tightly as bodies pressed in on them. At one point when she thought the crowd would pull them apart, Gaia picked the boy up and he wrapped his arms and legs around her like a monkey. He wasn't much bigger than the soccer bag draped over her shoulder.

As they neared the mouth of the bubble, the humidity and moisture struck her like an epiphany, saturating her face and seeping into her roots. A few moments later they stumbled from the crush of people into the open, cavernous bubble. And there it was. Grass. Slowing in disbelief, her knees wobbled and she felt faint. She was certain she'd passed through the portal of Heaven, because nothing like this existed on Earth. The brilliant green—greener than the sky was blue—lit from within by some God of Pure Life.

Then she remembered she was holding the boy. "What's your name?" she asked him.

"Taz," he said softly. For a second, she thought he'd said 'Zaz'.

"What's your momma's name?"

"Mommy."

"Do you know her *real* name?"

"Mommy."

Gaia started shouting. "Taz's mom! Taz's mom! Taz—"

The boy's arm shot out and pointed at a frantic-looking woman running toward them. She reached out and scooped the boy from Gaia and rocked him back and forth in a tight squeeze.

"Thank you!" the woman said. When she looked up at Gaia her face changed—just like everybody's face changed when they first looked at her.

"No problem," Gaia said and quickly walked away. She didn't want *that* tedious old awkwardness again. But more than that, she had to get to the grass.

When she reached it she slowed, marveling at it, taking it in. Then as if she were taking her first step into a strange new parallel universe she'd just discovered, she gingerly stepped onto it, and she felt it give under her stocking feet. It was like a sponge.

Gaia ripped off her socks and took a few slow steps. The blades were rougher than they looked, and they poked between her toes. It tickled. She caught a whiff of a pungent mustiness, and she was filled with a buzzing vibrancy. She walked to a more open area where nobody was standing. Slowly, one limb at a time, she lay facedown on the grass. It poked her face and tickled the inside of her big ears when she turned her head.

"I'm here," she murmured.

Gaia's first communion with the grass lasted only a few seconds. A sharp slap on her butt jolted Gaia from her reverie. It was Selene.

"You *are* alive!" Selene grinned. "Bummer!"

Grabbing her bag and socks, Gaia just shook her head. "Can't leave me alone for five seconds, can you." She got up, grabbed her bag, and started walking toward the group of white jerseys where her team was warming up.

"Pretty cool grass, huh?" Selene called out, but Gaia kept going. "Hey, Blue! I know you heard me in the truck. Faker."

Gaia froze. She turned slowly. She tried to think of something to say that would throw Selene off the scent.

"I'll bet the whole parking lot heard you—Red," she snapped. "You and that mouth. You're starting to sound Street. You in a gang pack now? Trying to cuss to impress your pack dogs?"

Selene's grin widened.

"You know that's not what I meant. Nice try. How much do you hear, anyway? Don't worry. I won't tell hardly anyone."

Gaia rolled her eyes and jogged over to her team.

"Don't get your ass kicked by those mean girls out there," Selene said softly, well out of normal earshot.

What Gaia did next was driven by a flash of pure anger. She extended her arm and flipped Selene the bird. It was a huge mistake, but Gaia didn't care.

"Ha!" Selene burst out triumphantly. "I knew it! I friggin' knew it!"

-5-
Snap

Most of her teammates were already paired up and making halfhearted attempts to kick a ball back and forth, but mostly they were kneeling down to touch the unbelievable turf. Still in awe, Gaia felt like keeping to herself and savoring the coolness of the prickly grass. She loved the feeling of the moist ground on her hands and bare feet as she turned slow, deliberate cartwheels. She could feel the humid air in the bubble heating up, and giant ceiling fans droned in deep baritone ohms. A mockingbird chattered in the dead sycamore trees outside of the bubble, and Gaia wished she could fly—without leaving the grass.

"That has to be the most revolutionary way of playing soccer I've ever seen!" a deep voice said to her. "You need to teach your goalie that move." A bear of a man in sloppy clothes stood scowling at her with his arms folded across his broad chest.

Gaia did another cartwheel. "I'm completely revolutionary, Godpappy. See me revolving?"

"I see you *rotating*, if that's what you mean."

"Oh, come on. We're not in school right now."

"You don't think so? The world is a classroom, my dear. Don't go getting squishy lazy brain on me." Lane stepped up and gently poked her in the forehead.

Despite her godfather's gruffness—or maybe because of it—he was always able to make Gaia forget her troubles and feel lighter.

"What're you doing here?" she asked, seeing if he'd volunteer any information about this mystery niece.

"You think for a second I'd miss seeing this place?"

"And watching me play has nothing to do with it, I guess."

"Oh! Are you playing here today? My, my! Actually, I have other reasons for being here. Oddly enough, my life does *not* rotate around you, Miss Wonderful."

"You mean revolve."

"Good girl. You're not as dumb as I look!" He crossed his eyes and let his tongue hang out the side of his mouth.

"Sure it does."

"Sure it does, what?"

"Your life. Revolve around me." She grinned back, hoping that would make him volunteer more information.

"Sheesh! The arrogance is *thick* around here! Why is it, do you suppose, that it's the beautiful people who are the most arrogant? I've never understood that. You'll have to explain it to me sometime."

"Good one, Godpappy. You're a great liar."

"'Scuse me? Liar? I do not lie, ma'am—not unless I really have to, and now is not one of those times." His eyes grew wide as he looked at her. "Oh, my!"

"What? What is it?"

"Your eyes!"

"What! What's wrong?" She looked down.

"No, no. Don't you dare look away! Nothing's wrong. I've just never seen them turn that color before. They're like bright emeralds. What are you feeling right now?"

Gaia blushed but didn't say anything.

"I take it you're enjoying the grass?"

She nodded, feeling peaceful and overwhelmed at the same time, unable to put it in words. "I've never seen anything like it."

"Well, there you have it. I had a feeling that you, of all people, would take to it."

"Why? Why me of all people?"

In answer, he gave her a rough kiss on the top of her head. It was another odd reference to something that was being kept from her, like puberty or her period. Or even Zaz. It was frustrating.

"That's from your mom and dad. They sent me over. They didn't want to smother you."

He turned her by the shoulders and pointed her to where her team was gathering, and he gave her a playful kick on the butt.

"And that's from me! Give 'em hell out there." He winked at her as he turned to walk back to the sidelines.

"Why did you say me of all people?" she called out, trying to pry an answer out of him, but he just waved and kept walking. "Is Uncle Cloudy coming?"

"Can't," he called back without turning. "He's on patrol."

"What about your niece?"

He stopped, then turned slowly. She couldn't read his face, but it slowly grew a smirk. "All in good time, my dear. All in good time."

He walked to her parents on the sidelines and brought them into a little huddle. Gaia tried to eavesdrop on their whispered conversation, but she was distracted by Coach Luke who was calling the team over for their pre-game talk. He read out the starting lineup—Gaia was playing at center midfield, which was the position usually reserved for the best player on the team. Worse, she was to be a captain, too. Was this a joke? Not only would she have to play a position that saw most of the action, she'd have to walk out to the middle of the field and shake hands with the other team's captains before the game—with everyone watching.

Gaia pulled Coach Luke aside. "Coach, are you joking around with me?"

"No," he smiled. "Captain and center mid, just like I said."

"You know how terrible I am."

Coach just kept smiling.

"Are you *trying* to lose today?" Gaia said.

He laughed. "I'm *trying* to help all of you learn how to play the beautiful game, which means you have to actually play it. Come on. Look around you. Look where we are. Do you really care whether we win or lose today?"

Gaia scanned the brilliant green field, which seemed to infuse everyone with energy and life, even happiness. The world here, thick with lung-saturating humidity, felt heavenly, and it must have shown on Gaia's face.

"That's what I thought," Coach said. "Get out there, and don't worry. You'll be fine."

The ref blew the whistle for captains, and Gaia made the eternal stroll to midfield with Meg Branch, who was her co-captain and goalie. Gaia was glad it was Meg, because even though Meg kept to herself, she played her position with the fury of a hurricane despite—or maybe because of—her short stature. And unlike most everyone else around them, Meg's skin was natural. Like Maer, Selene, Godpappy, and Uncle Cloudy, Meg also wasn't vain enough to take Derma pills to make herself tan. Everyone who took Derma parroted the notion that it was for natural skin protection even though it had been scientifically proven to *cause* skin cancer over time. And Gaia, of course, didn't take Derma pills, even though her skin looked like Derma gone wrong.

Three players in purple jerseys from the other team joined them in the midfield circle, and they all shook hands. Two of the other team's players, perfectly tanned, stared a few seconds longer at Gaia, then looked down at their feet or looked away. The third, a shorter girl about Meg's height with badly cropped black hair and pale white skin, quietly studied Gaia without looking away. Her eyes were black marbles. The girl leaked a tense energy like a stray dog—like one that would try to bite you if you held eye contact too long.

The ref flipped the coin, the purple girls chose the side of the field they wanted, and the ref told the girls to have a good game. He was the English ref Gaia loved, but as she turned to walk back to her team, the ref said to her, "Planning on wearing your boots today, Luv?"

The tanned girls sniggered at Gaia's bare feet. On the way to their huddle she heard one of them say, "Wow, nice ears! She's gonna take off and fly if she runs too fast."

"I had to bite down to keep from laughing! Are you *kidding* me? Where do you even start? That's some serious Derma trauma right there!" the other cackled.

Gaia felt the familiar wall rising inside of her. The good feeling from Coach Luke's pep was evaporating. She didn't want to play anymore.

"And don't forget to tuck in that jersey!" the ref called to her.

Gaia pulled her socks on over her wet feet and laced up her cleats while Coach Luke told them how lucky they were to be playing at The Green, and that they needed to be on their best behavior. Water was slowly soaking into Gaia's shorts where she sat, and she marveled at how water could come up from the ground so freely.

She wanted to melt into the grass, to let her skin, guts, and bones merge with its soil and roots. So many girls wanted to be famous singers or actors. But, not Gaia. Right now, she wanted to *be* The Earth. That's all. It made perfect sense. Her ears would be the mountains, her blue hair the sea, her skin the patchwork quilt of land from season to season, and her eyes deep lakes that gently shift hues as the days wax and wane.

"Gaia! Get up! Kickoff!" Coach said. She reluctantly got to her feet, tucked in her shirt, and shambled onto the field as if she were walking to her own execution.

"Remember, pass to open space and keep moving," he called out, clapping his hands. "Let's go, hustle out!"

Gaia broke into a slow trot, trying to stay as inconspicuous as possible. She wanted to turn and sprint back to the sidelines, or to go anywhere else on the expanse of grass other than the playing field. Her one bright thought was that she'd play so badly that Coach would have to pull her.

Finally, the starting whistle blew and the match got underway. The ball traded sides often, staying mostly in the middle of the field, and for Gaia's first few touches, she felt like she was kicking a cabbage, which made her regret doing cartwheels instead of warming up.

From the whistle, it was clear the little black-headed, stray-dog girl was mean, and a bully. She threw elbows and pushed and smack-talked. "You ain't nothin'," she kept saying to girls on Gaia's team. "I own you." And pretty soon it was Gaia's turn. The black-headed girl made a run directly at Gaia. The girl juked to one side, and when Gaia bit on the fake and tried to block her, the girl cut the other direction, leaving Gaia flat-footed and off balance. "Nothin'!" the girl called out. Gaia heard a collective groan from the sidelines.

Then an odd thing happened.

Something snapped inside Gaia's head, like a bone had splintered in her brain, and she dropped to her knees.

It wasn't painful, but she went dizzy, and the world was blurry. The strange music suddenly filled her mind. This time, though, the music had a faster pace and greater energy, like a choir building to its climax in a symphony. She closed her eyes, and images flashed through her brain, landscapes of deserts and forests and plains she'd never seen, along with intense feelings of sadness and exultation, of biting cold and humid, sweltering heat. She heard laughing, and crying, and screaming in the music. The whole experience felt as if someone were trying to upload memories into her. But the effect was both pleasant and comforting, friendly even. At first it reminded her of the hacking, but the two were completely unlike. The hacking had felt like an attack. This felt like a relief, like an answer of some kind. Images flashed and feelings flowed for what seemed like a week.

And then it all stopped, fading to silence with a gentle, trailing hum.

Gaia reeled and steadied herself against the ground, but she kept her eyes closed. Her breathing was easy, and deep, and her heartbeat felt slow and strong. The grass smelled earthy and sweet.

This was no hacking. Nothing had been asked of her, or even taken. Quite the opposite. She felt as if she'd been given something. Something very important.

Gaia felt different. More grounded. More confident. It felt as if a new person had entered her body, but it was much more subtle than that. It was still her, but her nature was somehow different. She felt stronger inside, above pettiness where little things didn't matter; and she felt resolve, a fire to make right what was wrong. The sensations were confusing, and she didn't know what to do with them.

Gaia shook her head. The snap felt both violent and invigorating, like the sudden release of being hugged and feeling your back suddenly crack.

She opened her eyes and saw a blur of green grass. As her vision cleared, she looked at her hands to make sure all her fingers could move and all of her limbs were still connected to her body.

She wondered if she was getting her period, if this is what it felt like. She'd been told her whole life what a gift it was, what an incredible right of passage it was to become a woman. But this thing? What had just happened to her? It was more than some right of female passage. Much more.

Someone shouted her name again, and she felt the referee's hand on her back. He was asking if she was okay. She turned around and saw the game. Then she remembered what had happened. The black-headed girl had made her look foolish and, worse than that, she was a bully. It wasn't right, and it needed to be fixed. Determination filled her.

Pulling away from the referee, nodding that she was fine, she saw the ball bouncing around as both teams tried to get control of it. They hadn't stopped the game. She was amazed to realize that no time at all had gone by.

Then Gaia saw the black-headed girl push one of her *own* teammates out of the way to take control of the ball.

Gaia launched forward, her eyes fixed on the #1 on the back of stray-dog girl's jersey. She was weaving in and out of Gaia's teammates until nobody stood between her and Meg in the goal.

Gaia was gaining ground, a feeling of justice pouring energy into every stride. Her legs spun faster, faster than she ever imagined they could go without tripping herself. She heard her name shouted, and at first she thought it was because she was out of position. But when she'd kept charging and catching up to the girl, she realized they were cheering her on.

But none of that mattered. Stopping #1 was Gaia's world, and she was almost on top of her.

A second before the girl shot, she stutter-stepped to get the timing right on her kick. Gaia slid and felt the sweet contact of the ball rocketing off her foot, flying safely away from the goal and out of bounds. The black-headed girl tripped over Gaia's legs and face-planted in front of a crouching Meg who let out a surprised laugh.

Gaia sprang to her feet and came up limping, feeling a sharp pain on the inside of her knee. A mad asylum of cheers, angry yells, and whoops rumbled the sidelines, and the opposing coach was screaming at the ref, "That's a red card! That was in the box! That's a penalty kick!" But the ref, who had run up to the action blowing his whistle, was shaking his head and sweeping his arms from side to side saying, "That was a clean play! Clean play! No foul! Are we all right, Ladies?"

#1 was slow to get up, nodding that she was okay when the ref checked on her, but she gave Gaia a murderous look. One of the girls' teammates ran up and shoved Gaia, and the ref had to separate bodies that were itching to fight.

Furious, Gaia dove back into the growing scrum of fighting girls to go after the one who'd pushed her. But someone was grabbing her jersey from behind and pulling her away from the melee. She struggled free, turned, and took a blind swing at the person. Meg easily ducked the blow.

"Whoa, whoa, whoa, Killer!" Meg shouted, holding her hands up. "Friend! Friend!" She was laughing. "Holy Zaz, where did *that* come from?"

-6-
Death

F uming and nursing a knee-throbbing limp, Gaia tried to catch her breath as Meg went back to pull more girls out of the dwindling fight. The shouting on the sidelines had died down to chatter and laughing, and there were a few calls of, "Way to go, Gaia!" and "Great defense, Gaia!" Her vision was floating, and the black-headed girl, purple and white jerseys, the grass and goals, the lines on the field, and the inside of the bubble seemed a surreal dream. It took her a few seconds to register that Coach Luke had his arm around her, and he was helping her off the field.

"Gaia Cadogan, I don't know what you ate for breakfast, but you need to keep eating it from now on." She smiled but noticed that her knee was swelling and getting stiffer by the second. She wondered if she'd broken it. Gaia was still on fire inside, and for the first time in her life she didn't want to leave the game.

"I wanna go back in, Coach."

He just laughed. "Go easy. Let's get you checked out. That knee looks bad."

On the sidelines Coach examined her leg, and Gaia was barely aware that another older man, the white-haired league medic, was looking her over as well. The game had started up again, and Gaia was sucked into the action. She kept her eyes on #1. It was obvious the black-headed girl was a gifted player, but something was off about her. Her brutal shoulder slams knocked Gaia's team off the ball, and she passed to her teammates only when she knew she'd get the ball back. Gaia's anger festered, and she lusted for action.

This new feeling frightened her almost as much as it excited her, and she wondered if other girls often felt the same way.

Maybe #1 has a brother. Girls with brothers tended to be rough—not just physically, but socially as well, like Everly Demond. Everly was in Gaia's work group at school, and she had four brothers who ran in different packs. Not long ago, the youngest—Junior—was shot in the arm through the back window of his friend's car. The story went that he had his arm around his girlfriend in the back seat, and if it weren't for his arm, his girlfriend would have taken a bullet to the head. Gaia wondered if that's why Everly was always cussing, smoking, and getting into fights. She wondered if the constant feeling of battle embeds itself under a person's skin and penetrates the muscles. Compared to Everly, Gaia led a pretty tame life. When she and Selene fought, they rarely hit each other even though Gaia wanted to.

Most people went around angry and cantankerous. Gaia thought back to an incident at Junipero Bay in front of the Speedy Füd snack bar. Two men duked it out in a bloody fistfight that ended with one man drawing a knife and the other taking off, all because the man with the knife was protecting his daughter's food. If she hadn't seen it with her own eyes, Gaia never would have believed it. And what shocked Gaia most was how the little girl reacted—or didn't react. When the man sat back down, she didn't cry or ask if he was okay. She didn't even look up. They just went back to eating their lunch.

The halftime whistle blew, and Gaia watched her exhausted teammates walk slowly to the sidelines and collapse. She noticed that a cold pack was strapped to her knee, and without thinking she tore the tape off and dropped it on the ground.

Gaia's knee was looking and feeling normal again, and she tested it by jogging limp-free across the field. When she turned to jog back, she saw that her mom was talking to Coach.

"If she feels fine, let her play. You have our permission. She's a quick healer."

The old medic had joined Coach and Maer in watching Gaia run back, and the two men looked stunned. The medic knelt and examined her knee again, squeezing it here and there, asking if it hurt anywhere, shaking his head with disbelief when Gaia told him no.

The medic shrugged at Coach, and Coach shrugged back. "Okay," Coach said. "I guess you're in the second half."

"Damndest thing I've ever seen," she heard the old medic say as he walked away with his bag.

"GC!" Heather Frye shouted, motioning Gaia over to join the girls as they chugged water and caught their breath. Heather held up her hand for a high five, and Gaia awkwardly slapped it and sat down. They'd never acknowledged her like this.

"I wanna hurt that girl," Heather said, and everyone laughed. "Cadogan, I want you to slide tackle that 'itch again. That kited her, most utterly, jes like a Raftie catchin' a gull." More whoops of laughter. Gaia smiled, but cringed at the memory of the boy Lohi catching the seagull yesterday.

"Let's get that girl a red card," Caitlyn Roberts said, always ready for a fight.

"I'll give her something red. Blood gushing out of her nose!" Heather said, handing Gaia a water bottle. It flickered in Gaia's mind that Heather had two older brothers.

"Gaia, don't drink that worm water!" Caitlyn shouted with fake urgency.

"Ain't no worm water, 'itch!" Heather shouted back, slugging Caitlyn in the arm. "I look like a Raftie to you? Belly all swelled up? If this wuz seawater, I'd go give that girl a drink—see how number 1 she is when she gets The Worm."

"That guhl even looks lak a Raftie, sho'," Savannah Lee drawled. Gaia didn't know Savannah very well. All she knew was that she was from New Texas, formerly a state before The Great Secession of '47. She and her family were granted U.S. citizenship because her dad was a scientist.

"Oh, shut it, Doing Doing," Heather said. "Raftie ain't much worse'n a damn Reb Southie!"

Savannah stared at the ground, embarrassed and hurt. Meg tossed a soccer ball that ricocheted off Heather's head.

"Goddamn Southie lover!" Heather yelled at Meg as they both leapt to their feet and went after each other. Once wrestling turned to punching, Coach had to separate them. Blood trickled down Meg's cheek from a scratch, and Heather's lower lip was bleeding a little. Then they grinned at each other and sat back down.

"Hey Moco," a girl called, and it wasn't until Meg slapped Gaia on the shoulder and pointed that Gaia realized Lupe Antunez was trying to get her attention. Moco was Spanish for booger, but she wasn't used to hearing one of her nicknames in Spanish.

"Nice going," Lupe said. "Hey, I forgot to tell you. My cousin Chooie said he saw you lying in the road yesterday, and you ran away from him when he tried to help you. What the fuck you doin' lyin' in the road?"

The hacking. The smell of dirt and piss came back to Gaia, and the feeling of angry bees coursing through her. She remembered the lowrider truck blasting rapscat and the men getting out of it and walking toward her.

"Chooie said that white girls run from him all the time, but this is the first time he had a green girl run," Lupe said, laughing. "Orale pues, I got your lunch box. I'll give it to you at school."

"Thanks," Gaia managed, and was grateful when Lupe got up to go pee and didn't seem to care why Gaia had been lying in the road. She was now relieved the men hadn't been chasing her. But that didn't explain the hacking. Someone else had done it. The man in the vision had said, "Cahm to me." Maybe somebody *was* after her. But why? It made no sense. She did her best to shrug it off, but she found that trying to forget about it was like having a banana slug crawl on your arm: You could pull it off, but the sticky slime stayed there for days.

When Coach called Gaia's name to start the second half, that was the welcome distraction she needed. And as the second half got underway, Gaia still felt strong and confident. She also learned the name of her nemesis.

Quinn.

Something had changed in Gaia after the brain snap. On the field she didn't hear anything outside of the game. Her body seemed to flow on its own, and her mind was clear. As she dribbled, passed, and defended, she saw the field and its players like a chessboard—paths of attack, opportunities, and potential checkmates. Nothing got past her, and a couple of pinpoint passes she made resulted in two goals that put her team in the lead. She instinctively knew where the other team would pass or which direction a player was going to dribble, including a visibly frustrated Quinn. Seizing a quick opportunity, Gaia stole the ball from Quinn and shouldered her to the ground on purpose, which got her a yellow card from the ref. Quinn's teammates had to hold Quinn back as she tried to claw through them to reach Gaia, and

Gaia realized that her teammates were pulling her back to stop her from going after Quinn. If it weren't for Heather's strong grip, Gaia wasn't sure what she would have done if she made it to Quinn. She only knew that she had never felt such rage and ferocity.

It was Heather's laugh that brought Gaia back to earth. "What's your *name*, you total wicked *'itch*, and what have you done with Gaia? Blue-headed demon, you are officially my new hero!"

After the ref calmed the girls down and restarted the game, Gaia got back into her groove, feeling like she'd stumbled into a hidden passageway and discovered the secret to life. Everything was effortless, even her newfound intensity. But, as she positioned herself to trap a ball that was lobbed in her direction, something heavy and sharp slammed onto the top of her right foot. She cried out in pain as she saw the opposing jersey next to her, and then on top of her. She recognized Quinn, and without warning there was a flash of elbow and Gaia's nose exploded as she fell backwards through space onto the turf.

She gasped for breath through her mouth, through a lightning blast of pain, and in the back of her broken, flattened nose she recognized the scent of her own blood. She struggled to open her eyes, but the light disappeared as a body fell on her and started yanking her hair.

Then a fist smashed into Gaia's temple.

This fight was for keeps.

With a rush of adrenaline, Gaia thrust her arms forward and shoved Quinn off of her. She scrambled to her feet and through a blur of involuntary tears she saw Quinn holding her own face. Then she rushed Gaia, and they hit the ground again, grappling and rolling over each other. She felt the meat of her hand pressing against Quinn's face, then a bolt of pain as Quinn bit down.

A deeper anger erupted inside of Gaia, and she forced herself on top of Quinn, pinning her against the turf, and punched wildly at the girl's face. Her only thought was of wanting to bash this other human being into oblivion.

And that was her undoing. The moment she thought of Quinn as another living being, she hesitated, and Quinn rolled Gaia onto her back again, her hand clutching Gaia's throat, clawing in and clamping off her air.

Gaia heard feet surrounding them, and Quinn leaned in and hissed, "Go back to MARS, mutant BITCH!"

Then Quinn was off her, pulled away by many hands. Gaia covered her face and rolled onto her stomach, shaking with pain and rage. She felt warm blood pooling in her hands, and she sobbed when she heard her parents' voices. She also heard Godpappy's angry voice yelling Quinn's name. Was that his niece? It couldn't be.

Her dad's strong hands were moving her into a sitting position, and she heard her mother gasp. Gaia tasted the blood running over her mouth as her dad stripped off his camo shirt, then took off his t-shirt and held is up to Gaia's bloody nose. When Gaia was able to see clearer, she saw Godpappy pulling Quinn away by the arm, scolding her. The sight filled Gaia with hatred.

Then Gaia was aware of something else—something eerie. Everyone except her parents were slowly backing away as if Gaia had a disease. She saw Selene backing away, too, looking more frightened than Gaia had ever seen her. She heard whispers as they pointed at the ground.

Cowards, Gaia thought. *Haven't they ever seen a freak bleed before?*

Jack lifted her up, cradling her as he carried her away.

"No, Daddy," she said through clenched teeth. "Put me down. I want to walk."

He stopped, and without saying a word he gently set her down, but he held his arm tightly around her shoulder as she limped along with her mom on the other side of her. The pain throbbed rhythmically in her face, and for a few moments the only sound was their footsteps and the droning fans in the bubble.

"Look! It's spreading!"

"It started right there, where she was on the ground!"

"Look! Look where she's walking!"

Gaia didn't recognize any of the voices. Then someone called her name, and she stopped and slowly turned. Gaia looked down where she'd been walking. The once lush, green grass was now a trail of brown death that led back to where she'd been lying. And it was spreading. She watched it slowly broaden—a withering shadow of death on every spot of grass she'd touched.

She looked at her feet through teary eyes. The grass beneath her was spreading into a larger circle of death, stopping only when it reached the dirt track at the field's edge.

Somewhere in the core of her soul, she knew. She understood that this was her doing, and that the change she'd felt earlier was somehow deeply connected to this. Gaia didn't know why, but she knew this was her fault. She was killing the grass.

But she didn't care. She knew nothing good ever lasted, and she hated herself more than ever. She hated the grass. She hated everything.

Unable to see beyond the flashes of light and shadow, she sobbed as she hobbled off the field, vaguely aware of her parents' arms around her. And she prayed. She prayed that whoever had made her—God or the spaceship that abandoned her on Earth nearly 15 years ago—would fly by and vaporize her for good.

Then, as if in response to her prayer, the long, ominous whine of emergency sirens broke out across town.

"Sandstorm," her dad said. "Let's get moving."

-7-

Confession

Dregs from the last gasp of the sandstorm rapped against the windows of the medical clinic as Gaia quietly sobbed into her dad's blood-soaked t-shirt. The waiting room was clogged with people taking refuge from the storm. A few chairs over, a man held the hand of a woman whose entire body, especially her belly, was swollen with the telltale signs of worm infection.

The storm hadn't been terribly heavy, but it still managed to blanket everything outside with a layer of grit. Questions and answers flitted in and out of her mind, only to be devoured by bursts of hopelessness and hate. *What happened? Something freakish, just like me. Who am I? Nobody. What are my parents keeping from me? What is Selene not telling me? Or Godpappy Lane? Or Uncle Cloudy? Probably that they found me in a dumpster when I was a baby, tossed in there by a Croozer addict. Or maybe I'm an abandoned Syncro baby. That would make sense.*

Gaia's stomach curdled at the thought of being a Syncro baby, a deformed creature born of somebody who was surgically fitted with both sets of sex organs—male and female—and shot up with DNA scramblers so that he-she could self reproduce. She thought of the ads against synchronous hermaphroditism, which always showed the puke-inducing videostream of Siamese twin babies joined at the face, accompanied by large text and a deep, ominous voice: "Syncro: Against the Law. Against Nature."

Syncro baby, Croozer baby, or whatever, Gaia felt something rot inside of her whenever she considered that she might not be the natural child of Maer and Jack Cadogan. She'd heard stories about Selene's difficult delivery, but whenever she asked about her own, her mom always said she'd rather not talk about it. Some other time.

Who leaves a wake of death wherever she walks, killing what she loves so much? Gaia longed for an answer to her questions, or at least for a logical explanation for the dead grass. It didn't need to be a complicated explanation. Something simple would do just fine, like a chemical in her clothing or the new strain of grass reacts horribly to stress. She'd be able to understand those. But in her soul, Gaia was certain she'd killed the grass in some other way, and the shocked faces of everyone on the field confirmed it. Instead of awe, she felt a scolding deep shame. She was glad the ivy plant next to her in the waiting room was fake. No danger of her killing *that*.

She rocked back and forth and fingered the base of her skull where she'd felt it snap on the soccer field. There was something significant about the snap, like a misaligned bone had popped and settled into its right place. Except that there wasn't anything right about the dead grass. She felt both right and wrong at the same time, both centered and bent.

A blonde bulldozer of a nurse named Bernice plowed into the lobby and began shoveling people out the door. "Storm's over, folks!" she hollered. "Out you go! Got real patients to help here! Out! Out!"

As the lobby drained, Selene wandered off to the next room, and Gaia heard her complain that the only thing in the vending machine was stupid jellyfish leather. *I wish I had your problems,* Gaia thought, slumping in her seat.

Maer and Jack resembled parental bookends as they sat on either side of her. Maer stroked her hair and rubbed her back but kept quiet, seemingly deep in thought. Gaia was barefoot now, and a light bruise was spread across the top of her right foot where Quinn had stomped on it. The pain was almost gone, and Quinn's bite marks that had broken the skin on her hand were barely visible. The throbbing in her nose was subsiding, too, and she could even breathe through it a little.

"Mommy?" She was going to ask the question she wanted to ask on the way to the game.

"I'm here, Baby. What is it?"

"What does it feel like to get your period?"

Gaia held her breath. She hoped her mom would say something like this: *Of course it feels like something snapping in your brain. Of course you're absolutely normal in every way. The fact that we hinted otherwise was just our usual sarcasm. Pay no attention to us. We're just horrible, insensitive parents. And oh, by the way, don't worry about killing the grass. That wasn't you. That's just how that kind of grass is.*

"Oh, God! Are you—" Her mom cocked her head and started to stand, looking ready to whisk Gaia off to the bathroom.

"No," Gaia said, shaking her head and looking at the blood on the t-shirt she'd set in her lap. "At least I don't think so."

"You sure?"

Gaia shook her head.

"No, you're not sure, or just no?"

I never should have asked, Gaia thought as she tried to find a graceful exit from the conversation.

"I think Selene needs me in the other room," her dad said, standing up to give them some privacy.

"No, Daddy, it's okay. Sit."

He raised his eyebrows.

"Yes, I'm sure. Sit down." She looked at her mom. "Please stop making such a big scene."

They both sat, watching her, waiting. Now was Gaia's opportunity to say, *Never mind, I was just curious*, and leave it at that. But the words just kept coming. They were too big to stop.

"Does it feel like something snaps in your brain? Like a violent pop or something?"

They stared blankly at her.

"Uhhh..." Her mom was clearly confused.

"Never mind. I guess that's a no."

"Did that happen to you? Your neck popped?" her dad asked a little too enthusiastically. Gaia suspected he was happy changing the subject.

Gaia shrugged. "More inside my head."

"When?"

"Right before I started playing well."

"Not at the end, with—" he started.

"The grass dying?" Gaia finished for him. There. It was out in the open. She'd named the real whale in the room.

Her dad paused for a second, his eyebrows furrowing in thought. "Was it painful? Are you, you know, okay?" His voice trailed as he looked at Gaia.

"I'm okay."

"Yeah?"

"Yeah."

"Let's be sure to tell the doc about it," Maer said.

"About the grass? The dead grass?" Gaia was getting agitated, and she was determined to keep her parents pinned to the real issue. If she couldn't get out of it, then neither could they.

"Okay, tell me about that," her mom cut in. "Tell me about the grass."

"What's there to tell?"

"What were you feeling? What was happening?"

Gaia shrugged. "I've never been that mad before, ever. I wanted to kill somebody. I wanted to kill that girl."

Her parents looked at each other, like they did back in the truck on the way to the game. Gaia could see something pass between them. Their eyes shifted almost imperceptibly with a silent communication that lasted a bit too long. Her mom was the first to break the communion when she looked at Gaia, and her next words nearly gave Gaia whiplash.

"Baby, I—we—have something to tell you."

Gaia looked down at the bloody shirt, waiting, her body rigid and still, her breath chopped into small bits. Now a giant wave was about to crash back onto her, and she braced herself.

"You sure about this, Maer?" Jack asked. "Here? Now?"

"Jesus, Jack. I mean—don't you think so? What else is it going to take?"

Gaia's stomach pitched.

Jack looked down at the floor, nodding. He looked more vulnerable than Gaia had ever seen him, with his camo shirt untucked and unbuttoned halfway down, showing his bare chest.

"What's going on?" Gaia asked.

"It's time," Maer said. "It's just time. Enough!"

"Time for what? Enough what?"

But Maer's confidence broke. She cradled her face in her hands and shook her head.

"Why?" Maer cried. "Why, why, WHY? Why, Jack? Why are we squeezing this secret so tightly? I swear this is going to give me cancer."

"Easy, Maer," her husband said, reaching over to touch her back. "We talked about this. We talked about it over and over. You *wanted* to keep it a secret."

"Talked about what?" Gaia asked.

"No. Not anymore. It was a mistake," Maer said. She sat up and closed her eyes, inhaled deeply, and wiped her face with her hands. Then she looked at Gaia.

"Honey, we've been lying to you. All of us. Everyone. Not direct lies, but lies of omission. We did it because we thought it was best for you. But that was wrong."

Godpappy's voice suddenly echoed in Gaia's head from the soccer field: "*I do not lie, ma'am. Not unless I really have to.*" At the time, she assumed he was joking. Maybe he wasn't. Maybe he knew something, too. He'd said, *You of all people* to her about liking the grass.

"What, Mom?" Gaia asked just as Selene shuffled back into the room chewing her jellyfish leather. "What have you been lying about?"

"Oh, God, what happened?" Selene's eyes flicked from Gaia to her mom and dad and back to Gaia. "What did you say?"

Maer studied her oldest daughter. "The truth, Selene. That's what's happening."

"Oh, praise the King of Miracles! Really? You're finally telling her about being adopted?"

"Selene Isabella Cadogan!"

Gaia caught her breath. So there it was. *Gaia Cadogan, Croozer baby.* Selene sighed as she plopped into the chair next to her dad and kept yapping.

"Wow, what a relief, not having to swallow that firecracker anymore. Guess you don't have to worry about getting cancer now, huh, Ma?" She bit off another hunk of jellyfish and made a face.

"Jesus, Selene!" Maer said. "We hadn't gotten quite that far in our conversation. But as always, *thank you* for your valuable and timely input."

"You're welcome."

"Selene!" Jack stood suddenly. "Come with me, please. A word."

"Oh, so we're *not* being truthful? I'm confused."

"Now." The word slithered out of Jack so softly that it seemed to be generated by pure menace.

"That's enough, Selene," Maer said, shaking her head.

"Oh!" Selene jumped to her feet. "*Is* it, Mom? *Is* it enough? Yeah, yeah, I *know* it's enough—Mother!" She threw what was left of her jellyfish leather against the window with a thud. The second it hit the floor, a rat appeared from nowhere, snatched it, and scurried off.

Selene's face was turning nearly as red as her hair. "Shut up, Selene! Leave her alone, Selene! Don't say anything, Selene! Don't tell anybody, Selene! I have to walk across broken glass, and you want to carry the little princess across so her feelings don't get cut?"

Selene looked at Gaia. "Nothing against you, Gaia. Your whole life they've treated you like a fragile little mouse, and I catch hell every day because I think it's stupid. Time to wake up! We're living with hypocrites!"

Fragile little mouse? The words blindsided Gaia, who had *never* felt treated like a fragile little mouse! Ever! How dare she say that! Selene never heard the whispers, the teasing, the hurtfully empathetic comments that strangers made. *Poor thing, I wonder what's wrong with her?* Selene never had to wear the "freak" label wherever she went. Selene never got called "Dumbo" or "Booger" or "Frog-enstein!" Gaia was about to tell her to shut up, that she was the one talking to her like she was a baby, but she didn't have a chance, because Selene had already turned and stomped out of the clinic.

"Oh boy," Jack said as he followed his daughter outside.

In the opposite corner of the waiting area, a gangly old man with wild white hair and a ratty coat was giggling, drooling, and staring at them occasionally, shaking his head, as if they were the ones who were weird.

"Oh, go change your pants, Bum!" Maer said with disgust, which made him giggle even harder.

"Ca-*dog*-an?" the receptionist called from the front desk.

"*Ca*dogan, yes," Maer said. She sighed and turned to Gaia. "Well, that all went down in pure Ca-*dog*-an fashion. Nothing graceful about *this* family—*your* family. Just a few more minutes more, Baby. We'll continue this fiasco after we get you checked out." She kissed Gaia on the head. "You look good. I reckon you're just about healed up. Another ten minutes or so and there probably won't be a thing wrong with you. But let's be sure."

Gaia's mind was spinning. Adopted! Completely healed if she waited ten more minutes! She wanted to race from the clinic all the way to the ocean and start swimming until she either drowned or reached Hawaii. She wanted to cry and scream. She wanted to sink into the ground and become brainless soil. But instead, she got up and followed her mom into the examination room feeling confused and numb, and for the next stretch of time she had only a vague awareness of being poked, prodded, and blinded by light, until her mom patted her leg and told her it was time.

Gaia felt something firm stuffed into each nostril. She'd been so elsewhere in her head that she hadn't even noticed the doctor put anything in her nose.

"Go back to the waiting room and sit with Dad. The doctor wants to talk to me for a minute."

"About what?" Gaia asked.

"About your diagnostic implant. Your D.I. Go on. It'll just take a minute."

Gaia did as she was told, and by the time she reached the waiting room her dad was leaning forward in his chair again. Without a word, she slipped in beside him and gently leaned against his shoulder as he put his arm around her. The old man was gone and Selene was in his spot, her chair flipped around so her back was to them with only the top of her head showing. They sat quietly as a light breeze tapped the clinic windows with dust.

"So how do you like your first trip to the Emergency Clinic? Bet you'll want to do this every weekend from now on." Her dad's feeble attempt at humor didn't make her feel any better.

But she heard something interesting and tuned out her dad. Gaia straightened and she was suddenly alert again. She heard agitation in her mom's voice.

"You okay, Blueberry?" her dad asked.

"Shh! Quiet, Daddy!" She held up a hand and closed her eyes, concentrating. She was hearing multiple conversations and trying to tune into her mom's voice.

"Do you have a headache?" her dad asked.

"Shhhhhhh!"

"And you're certain about the D.I. chip—the diagnostic implant?" the doctor was saying. "It says here she had a new one put in two days ago—actually, let's see. Wow, her fourth one since last July? The records show it was implanted in the normal spot, here, in the neck."

"That's correct, yes," Maer said.

"But I don't see any scar tissue at the normal point of insertion."

"Are you saying I'm lying to you?"

"No, of course not. Could it have been implanted somewhere else, maybe?"

"No. You're looking at your records. What do they say?"

"Our records show she had it done. Four times."

"Well, there you go."

"But there's no scar tissue."

"She doesn't tend to scar."

"Everybody scars, even if you can't see it with your eyes. I'm telling you, there's no scar tissue. At all. And when I scanned for vitals there was nothing there—no D.I. chip, not a single one of the four! That's why we had to check her blood pressure and take her temperature manually. I've never seen a D.I. dislodge before."

"Doctor..."

"Medina."

"Doctor Medina. It's pretty clear you neither trust me nor your own records, and you're implying that this is somehow my fault."

Gaia felt nervous at her mom's rising anger and wondered why she was being so snippy with the doctor.

"Don't you want her to have a D.I. chip?"

"Honestly? No. No, I don't."

"Mrs. Cadogan, I'm sure you realize I'm trying to be nice about this. But now I must insist. Everyone needs a D.I. chip. The government requires it. This facility can get into serious trouble—*I* can get into serious trouble—if the Health Department finds out we let your daughter walk out of here without a D.I. chip."

"Ah, so it's a health concern, is it, Doctor? You're being artificially nice to me because the government is concerned about my daughter's health? Or, are you smokescreening the fact that the government requires the chip in order to keep track of our constant whereabouts?"

Gaia was getting more nervouse. Was she in trouble with the government? She put her hand on her dad's leg to make sure he was still next to her.

"Mrs. Cadogan, that's a myth."

"Oh, is it? Really. A myth. Doctor, let's just say I run in mythical circles within mythical agencies every day. Bottom line is I'm within my rights to state an exemption for a D.I. chip for her."

"That's highly frowned upon, Mrs. Cadogan."

"Then highly frown all you like."

"Very well." There were shuffling noises. "Let's get back to the real point of interest here. Take a look at the scan of her nose. And you're positive she's never broken it before?"

"Doctor Medina, do I have the word 'Liar' scrawled across my forehead? Yes, I'm positive. One-thousand percent. She's never broken her nose."

"So look right here. This is incredible!"

Gaia's heartbeat quickened and she tensed, hoping her dad wouldn't take that moment to talk to her again, because she didn't want to miss what was coming next.

"See this line, curving around and back down? That's the break, that piece curved like a thumb tip."

"I see it. So?"

"It's nearly fused, Mrs. Cadogan! Here, let me zoom in. Watch." Neither of them spoke for several seconds. "You can see it actually reconnecting! This is bone! It's happening faster than a tongue injury!"

Gaia's heart jumped, and she felt its pulse throb in her nose. She knew she was a quick healer, but this surprised even her.

"You say she's your daughter?"

"What? Of course she's my daughter."

"By blood? You delivered her?"

Gaia's heart dropped. It was getting quite a workout. A few minutes ago she would have expected her mom to say, *Yes, of course by blood!* But like everything else lately, Gaia thought, that would have been a lie.

"This was a mistake," Maer said. "I'm sorry. We should go."

The doctor laughed. "Are you serious? This is the most miraculous thing I've ever seen. A mistake? Mrs. Cadogan, something very special is happening here, something we need to learn more about. You of all people—a marine biologist—yes, I know who you are—the importance of this can't be lost on you."

"Doctor Medina, thank you for your help. We're leaving."

"I wish you wouldn't."

"Or else?"

"I'm sorry, but I don't understand your dismissiveness about this."

"Doctor, with respect and a calmness I can't promise a few seconds from now, we're not here to put you on the map and turn you into a research celebrity."

"So you admit there really is something special about your daughter."

"Doctor Medina, I don't know what's going on any more than you do."

She's lying, Gaia thought, and felt suddenly innocent and clueless. She wondered how she could ever understand the subtleties of the adult world. How could she ever fend for herself if she needed to? Maybe she *was* a fragile little mouse in a complicated, chaotic world.

"You know very well I can get a government order based on New Biological Discovery," the doctor was saying.

"Have fun with *that* paperwork."

"Mrs. Cadogan—" The doctor followed her into the waiting room and paused as Jack stood up.

Maer reached out and locked her fingers with Gaia. "Come on, Baby, let's go," she said, pulling Gaia out of the building while her dad shook hands with the doctor, obviously unaware of what had just transpired.

"I knew this was a mistake," her mom said as they got outside, pulling Gaia toward the truck as they turned their backs to the dusty breeze. "They never do anything you couldn't do yourself, and they always find something to harass you about." She stopped and turned her body to block Gaia from the stinging grains of sand.

"How are you?"

"You tell me!"

"He seems to think you'll be fine. I have to admit, so do I."

"That's not what *I* heard!"

Maer just looked at Gaia, her expression changing between searching for an answer and choosing between inadequate things to say. For the first time, Gaia realized she was tall enough to look her mom in the eyes—which were tearing up again as her dad stepped in and folded them both into his arms. Selene shuffled sideways toward the truck with her back to the breeze, keeping her distance.

"What happened in there?" Jack asked.

"Might have trouble with that doctor. I'll tell you about it later."

"Did you talk about the snap that Gaia felt in her head?"

"With *that* doctor?"

"Why are we going to have trouble with him?"

"He noticed how quickly she heals."

"Ah," he nodded slowly, looking carefully at Gaia, saying nothing.

"Say it," Gaia said. "Stop holding back. Whatever you have to say, just say it!"

But Maer spoke to her husband instead. "Right now, I need you to get Lane Ripple. You can't call him with your Telepath, because the stubborn man doesn't have one of his own. And Cloudy. Bring him, too. Meet us at Pelican Bluffs in an hour. Take Selene with you."

"What should I tell them?"

"What do you mean, what should you tell them? Tell them it's time! This is the day we've been waiting for all these years." She kept her arm tightly around Gaia and maneuvered her toward the truck.

"Oh!" Maer called over her shoulder. "And bring the Sequoia. And the vine."

-8-

Orange Smoothies and Dead Hawaiians

Gaia fidgeted in the passenger seat of the rattling, rickety old truck as she and her mom left the clinic for Pelican Bluffs. The truth about her was finally going to come out, and she couldn't sit still. But instead of pressing her mom with questions, she squirmed and held the suspense like a wrapped gift, forcing herself to wait before opening it.

Somewhere up ahead Gaia heard a gaggle of voices in Chinese mixed with the low rumble of a big engine. As they turned the corner that put them on the main stretch of downtown, a giant bus loomed in the middle of the street up ahead in front of Salty's IceKream and Hashish Bar, its tail end jutting so far out that the cars in the other lane had to swing around it.

"Oh, no," Maer growled.

A group of well-dressed Chinese spilled out of Salty's and onto the road, pointing up and down the street, and toward the brown hillside as if measuring for renovation. Maer slowed and stopped at the red light, which gave Gaia time to read the Chinese writing on the side of the bus: Beautiful Land Touring.

"Shit. Over my dead body," Maer said, shaking her head.

"Don't cuss, Momma. You sound like Selene."

"You mean Selene sounds like me."

"I hate cussing."

"Baby, like I told you a hundred times, there are no bad words—just misused words. If a swear word says exactly what you mean, it's the right word. I said exactly what I mean." Maer frowned. "That bus means a mess of shit for us. Looks like the

Chinese want to buy up more of Junipero Bay and close it off for themselves."

"Why do they do that? Why do we let them?"

Maer sighed. "You remember Maya?"

"Of course I do! She was the best friend ever. She didn't care about how I looked. She liked it. I miss her."

"The Gaia and Maya show. Well, do you remember her parents getting a divorce before they moved away?"

Gaia looked down at her hands.

"No. I didn't know they got a divorce."

Maya and her family, the Alistairs, had lived three-and-a-half houses down from the Cadogans. Gaia and Maya counted the fire-gutted Lancaster house as half, and Gaia remembered hearing the nightly fights between Maya's parents. Gaia was only eight at the time, and the fights scared her.

And then, there was nothing. The fights were gone, and so were Maya and her family. Just like that. And Maya never even said goodbye.

Maer paused, watching Gaia.

"Anyway, you know the big wall we drove past on the way to the game, the Chinese hemp farm?"

"Yeah. The paper farm."

"That's it. Well, that land used to belong to Maya's daddy. He raised cattle."

"We used to go there!" Gaia remembered sitting in the field with Maya, watching, waiting for a cow to lift its tail and gush pee like a waterfall. How they'd laugh and laugh.

Maer smiled. "Yes we did used to go there. Anyway, that's when our government in its infinite wisdom banned livestock, and Maya's dad lost everything. And, because he wasn't a farmer, he had no way of making money from his land. They were desperate, so he had to sell."

"Why did the Chinese get it? Why didn't our government take it?"

"It's a little complicated, but I guess it boils down to the fact that our government owes China a lot of money, so they can do a lot of things we wouldn't otherwise let them do—like build an air base in Nebraska. That's where the Chinese water jet took off today, before it got shot down."

Gaia thought back to the videostream that morning, watching the jet tumble through the sky in flames like it was rolling across flat ground. She looked over at the bus. More Chinese were spilling out of it, clogging the sidewalk, and she wondered how they felt about the water jet getting blown up. Chief Last Coyote. He was the one who'd done it. She felt herself running along the coast after the hacking, running from an imaginary Chief Last Coyote. She hoped it was imaginary, anyway.

"Enough of that!" Maer said, which made Gaia jump. "It's a battle for another day. Right now, the most important thing in the world is you, Gaia Grace Cadogan."

Maybe it was all in her head. Maybe what her family was about to tell her would explain everything, explain why she was hearing music and seizing up while videostreams played in her head.

The stoplight turned green, and Maer watched the bus as they drove past it. "Beautiful Land, my Irish arse."

"Stop!" Gaia shrieked. Her mom wasn't looking where she was going. The truck screeched to a halt just shy of a group of older kids who'd swaggered into the street in front of them. Their only reaction to nearly being leveled by the truck was to glare into the windshield as they continued across the street.

There were seven of them. A few whites, the rest Mexicans and Native Americans. Gaia recognized a shorter white kid from her neighborhood who looked at her and smiled—not a friendly smile, but the smirk of a devil. The flannel shirts that were draped over their gaunt frames looked like they were washed by shotgun blasts. Their skin was stretched to their skulls, and they looked starving, but not hungry. One of the Mexicans, a girl who was probably 16 but looked 40, slammed her fist on the hood of the truck, yelled "Puta!" A lanky Native American boy behind her glanced in at Gaia, but he did a double-take and slowed down, almost as if he wanted to stop and talk. There was something wrong with the side of his face, and his t-shirt sported a familiar, grinning cartoon of Chief Last Coyote riding a missile. The terrorist was a cult hero for some, and the cartoon was a meme for Native Americans Against America. The boy reluctantly kept going, a look of wide-eyed wonder never leaving his face.

Somebody else staring at the freak, Gaia thought.

He paused for a moment to look down at the front of the car. He seemed to be reading the license plate. Then he trotted to catch up with his pack, glancing back at Gaia one more time.

"Oh, don't you mark me, you little bastard," Maer said.

Gaia hated when people gawked at her. But the look on this boy's face was different. It wasn't gawking. He seemed to recognize her, though she'd never seen him before. There was an awe, like a fan suddenly realizing he's in the presence of a film star. She'd never gotten that look before. It was refreshing but spooky, even spookier after he read their license plate.

Gaia and Maer watched the pack angle toward the Chinese, and when the Chinese land grabbers finally noticed them, they swirled like a school of clogged, panicking fish pushing and shoving to get back onto the bus. Some ran up the street and nervously looked back. Breaking into a trot, the pack reached inside their shirts and pulled out dark, round balls and began hurling them at the Chinese. As the balls hit, they splattered in burnt yellows and deep orange-reds, and then a massive brawl erupted.

Maer let out a frightened curse and hit the accelerator, which scared Gaia even more as she looked back through the rear window. A huge Chinese man flailed at the pack with a fat stick as he pushed through the crowd. A couple of the pack fell to the ground, but the rest were able to jump him. The brawl quickly turned into a twisted, writhing pile of bodies.

"Don't watch, Gaia!"

Gaia was all adrenaline, and when they were finally at a safe distance Maer pulled the truck over and tapped the view screen on the truck's dashboard. "Cloudy," she said. A few moments later, Uncle Cloudy's blond, crew cut head appeared onscreen.

"Chang's Dolphin Pizza!" he said brightly, looking away to fiddle with something.

"Not funny, Cloudy," Maer said. "Is that how they're training deputy sheriff's to answer calls these days?"

Cloudy laughed. "I was on my way to meet you, but I just got an urgent call from the dispatcher—something about a riot at Salty's. They must have run out of Chunky Seaweed IceKream again. What's up?"

Gaia wondered how he could joke when he knew he was heading into the middle of a riot.

"That's what I was afraid of, you getting called to handle this. We just drove past it."

"How bad?"

"Six or seven bay kids going after a land grabber bus. The kids were throwing orange smoothies."

"Oh, Christ," Cloudy said wearily. "Are you okay? You clear?"

"We're clear."

Gaia was confused. They sounded more worried about the orange smoothies than they did about the fighting.

"Good. Get out of there. Don't hang around, and don't worry about me. I'll be fine. Wait—did you say 'we'? Who's with you?"

"Hi, Uncle Cloudy," Gaia said.

"That you, Blueberry?" Maer reached forward to twist the ancient little dashboard camera toward Gaia. Uncle Cloudy's gaunt, yellow-bearded face and sad eyes smiled onscreen.

"I'm sorry you had to see that, Blueberry. You hang on to that big love of yours, but be wise like a serpent. Lemme see that serpent tongue."

Gaia flicked her tongue at Uncle Cloudy.

"That's my mean little snake!" he laughed, but his face settled and his eyes softened. "I hear you had quite a morning."

Gaia nodded. She felt her nose throb at the memory of Quinn's elbow slamming into it.

"I'll be there as soon as I can. We have a lot to tell you."

"Just be careful, Cloudy," Maer called out. "Those kids looked serious, and they didn't run. They stayed and fought."

"We're seeing a lot of that lately. Worry not, Maer. I got my booster shots last week, and my kung fu is unstoppable these days."

A flash of color glinted on the truck's side mirror, and Gaia looked back to see the lights of Cloudy's patrol car arriving at the scene.

"Wow, this looks like fun!" Cloudy said. Then Gaia heard a sudden thud on his patrol car, and she saw him jerk back in his seat. "Okay! Gotta go! I'll bring some IceKream later!" The screen went blank.

As Maer pulled the truck back onto the road, Gaia pictured one of the balloons splatting on their own windshield.

"Mom, what's an orange smoothie?"

Maer looked straight ahead, not answering, as if she didn't hear.

"Fine," Gaia said as she began poking at the dashboard screen again to look up the answer.

"Okay, pushy girl!" Maer said, poking the screen off again. "No way to explain around it, I guess. They're balloons filled with piss and blood, and they look orange when they splatter." She glanced at Gaia and saw the disgusted look on her face. "Hey, you asked."

"How do they get that stuff into the balloons?" Gaia wasn't even sure she wanted to know, but morbid curiosity made her wonder whether the people filling them were in as much danger as the people being hit by them.

"Wait, I tell you what's in them, and your only concern is how they're filled?"

"It's just nasty, that's all."

"It *is* nasty, Baby. And the kicker is that the blood is usually diseased. That's why I called Uncle Cloudy to tell him to watch it. Glad you asked?"

Gaia didn't answer.

As the rest of the little downtown rolled past the window, she wondered about how bad things must be in bigger towns and cities with all those people crammed together. The stories she heard about the cities were always bad, and if things were this bad in little Junipero Bay, she couldn't fathom city troubles.

Gaia rolled down her window and drew a long, deep breath. The breeze whipped familiar scents through the truck; burnt cigar from her dad, mixed with an odor wafting from the plugged-in air "freshener"—a Mother's Day present from Selene. The label on it said "Maple Syrup," but it smelled like farts, and Gaia decided that if that's what maple syrup had really smelled like she wouldn't have touched the stuff.

Mother's Day. Her mother. The woman who adopted her. The sudden remembrance of where they were going and what they were about to do rekindled her excitement and angst with such intensity that she teetered on the brink of fainting. *It's time,* her mom had said. *It's just time. Enough!* Gaia knew her world was about to change.

As they pulled up to the entrance of Pelican Bluffs—or Mommy Bluffs, as Gaia called it, a familiar feeling of impatience began to grip her. She called it Mommy Bluffs because it was her mom's government-funded project to restore fish populations and coastal ecosystems, which meant she knew everyone there, which also meant there would be a long-winded conversation with the guard before they finally drove in, which meant it would take longer for Gaia to finally hear this "truth" her mom was promising. This time, however, Maer cursed as the camouflaged guard stepped out of the booth. Gaia hadn't seen him before.

"Well, look what the tide washed in!" the guard drawled, as he stepped to the driver's side window. The rifle strapped across his back looked colder, blacker, and more intimidating than any of her dad's rifles. "It's been a while, ma'am."

"Not long enough if you ask me, Corporal. Or is it back to Private now?"

"Shoot, Mrs. C. Ain't we had a few months of water under that bridge? And at this happy reunion, you wanna try to court-martial me—wait, no," the man paused, looking up and counting on his fingers. "Let's see, Corporal, PFC, P2, Private. I do believe that was a *quadrupal* court martial you got goin' on there. HooWEE! Back to my enlistment pay! And after all the troublesome nonsense and legal mumbo jumbo you already put me through to get me fired? Why in fact, as you *very* well know, you may address me as *Sergeant* Renneck now—that is, if it pleases yer ladyship," he said reverently, switching from his southern drawl to a butchered Cockney accent.

"You belong in prison, Carl," said Maer, looking straight ahead.

Gaia wondered for a second if her mom was kidding, but when she realized she wasn't, Gaia tensed and looked away out her own window to get as far from the argument as possible. Caution signs on the tall, black fence surrounding the preserve warned against high voltage.

"Apparently, I do not," he continued with mock woe, removing his cap and clutching it to his chest, "in that my person is, let's see, how did they call it? Ah! 'A model of exemplary stewardship and bravery in these volatile and dangerous times.' Why, that sounds like some mighty fancy praise if you ask me. Downright congratulatory, if I read that correctly, especially with the pay raise."

"*Sergeant*, you killed people!"

Gaia's heart jumped. She'd never heard about this, and she definitely had never been in the presence of a killer. She pressed her back against the seat and wished that her mom would drive away.

Then Maer's voice took a dark turn.

"You gunned down families—*families*—whose raft smashed into these very bluffs. Families who survived across thousands of miles of angry sea, and who clawed their way up to shore. Good God! They were barely alive, unarmed, and you *shot* them. *All* of them! They were *people*! There were *children*!"

Gaia wanted to scream, *Mom, drive away! Go!* as her own right foot pressed hard on an imaginary accelerator.

"Ma'am, ain't we spinnin' like a windmill with this old conversation? With all due respect, this spinnin' is beginning to give me the dizzies." The soldier's tone softened and blackened. "But I will say this: They wasn't people. No, ma'am. They was Hawaiians. Worm-infested kite niggers. They know they ain't supposed to come across, though a couple did look a little lighter skinned. Hard to tell so early in the mornin'. But that raft? It was one'a them newer ones. Had a neat little water purifier that I still use from time to time."

"Jesus, man, my daughter's here!" The soldier bent down and looked at Gaia with a stony, lingering appraisal. Gaia froze. She could feel cold goosebumps on her skin as he tipped the brim of his cap.

"Young ma'am."

He stepped back. "Grow up fast, don't they? Good lookin' kid. Could almost pass for one'a them purdy island girls."

Gaia took a quick glance at his rifle again. Her mind transported her to a made-up scene where she was on the raft with the Hawaiians as they reached the shore just before dawn. She was frozen and starving, weakly climbing off a raft through the cold, surging tide, and using her last ounce of strength to pull herself up the bluff. Hunks of dirt disintegrated under her feet, making her slip backwards and lose her footing, but she kept at it until she finally crested the bluff to find pure, solid bliss. It was the first land she'd felt under her feet in weeks. The images swirled in her mind's eye, and Gaia watched as a large, dark figure approached. A friend? Somebody to welcome them? As the figure got closer, Gaia saw it raise something to its side, waist high.

Then—nothing. A blinding flash catapulted her into darkness.

A pure, empty, and final darkness.

Gaia heard her mom speaking, a spring-loaded warning to the soldier. "Listen to me you sick, damaged Neanderthal. Enjoy your smugness. Enjoy the fresh air, because I'll do everything I can to make sure you spend the rest of your days lugging *shit* buckets in a refugee colony."

The soldier stiffened. "Are we havin' an altercation, ma'am? Because I'm supposed to deal with those. It's in my job description."

"Mom! Go!" Gaia's voice shook with fear.

Maer punched the accelerator and held up her middle finger as the the truck lurched forward, snapping and splintering the striped wooden plank of the guard gate.

Gaia glanced back through a cloud of dust expecting to see the soldier leveling his gun at them, aiming, and ready to fire just like in her daydream. But he wasn't. He stood calmly in the dirt road, hands on his hips, sporting a confident, predatory smile, looking right at her.

Truth

B etween her fight with Quinn, the dead grass, and now this menace of a guard, Gaia felt the confidence that blossomed earlier on the soccer field being ripped from her like roots yanked from the ground—popping, tearing. And she was about to learn things. Secrets. Things that had been hidden presumably to protect her, but which only made her feel paranoid and hormonal.

Waves of anxiety and excitement crashed inside her as if she were in a tiny rowboat among fifty-foot swells.

"Oh, Sweet Girl, don't cry," Maer said. "I'm so sorry. I shouldn't have stopped to give that Neanderthal the time of day."

"You're right, you shouldn't have stopped." Gaia said, wiping her eyes.

"Damn this world! We need to get out of this truck."

"Damn this *world*?" Gaia flared. "What does the world have to do with your picking a fight—another fight—with a man like that?"

Maer looked proud of her daughter's sass. "When did you get so ornery?" she said.

Gaia was about to say she'd always been that way, but when she thought about it, she couldn't remember a single time she'd been ornery. She recalled getting scolded for things, like when she was little and put some of Prop's poop in the shiny new grain incubating machine because she wanted to grow another puppy. But that wasn't because she was ornery. She just didn't know any better. *Have I always been so spineless?* she wondered. *No wonder I'm always getting picked on.* Gaia savored the feeling of this new strength and confidence, this purification of speaking her mind, and she wanted more of it.

"Well?" Maer said. "I'm serious. When did you get so ornery? I've been trying to drive some spunk into you for years."

"Maybe I've always had it. Maybe I had it all along but there was never any room for it because of you and Selene."

There. It was finally out in the open, something she'd always felt but never said. She braced for the impact of her mom's hurt feelings. But Maer's laugh surprised her.

"You're blaming Selene and me for you keeping your mouth shut?" She leaned over and pulled Gaia into an uncomfortably strong hug. "Oh, Sweetie. You think there's only room in this world for two strong women? My goal is to start an army of 'em."

Maer released Gaia and got out of the truck. "Bring the food," she said as she grabbed a folded blanket from the gear box behind the cab. Gaia hopped out and lifted the bamboo food basket from the back seat. *What just happened?* She glanced at her mom who was shaking her head and smiling.

"Gaia Grace, we should call this the Day of Truth. It's like somebody flung open a cage door and little birds of truth are flying out everywhere."

Maer was smiling when she said it, which meant the "truth" might not be as bad as she'd pictured. Maybe she wasn't a Croozer baby after all, or a Syncro baby. But what? Gaia picked up the food basket and slammed the truck door. Her stomach grumbled, then she imagined lifting the basket lid and watching doves fly out.

She was starving. She couldn't remember what her mom had packed that morning, but it was probably fonio cakes and spiced jellyfish salad. And if she were really lucky, there might be tomatoes from their tiny, struggling vegetable garden.

Gaia heard a rhythmic whoosh overhead and watched the blades of the giant windmill slicing the air in the corner of the preserve. Her eyes traced the thick white pole down to the ground where she noticed the remnants of a seagull that had flown into the blades—the very reason her mom was trying to get the windmill relocated.

"Hungry?" Maer smiled, and Gaia nodded. "I brought a little surprise, originally to celebrate your big day on the grass. Now I realize I should have brought something more. Shall we eat in the gazebo?"

Gaia nodded again, but food, doves, and dead seagulls twisted and coiled in her head, and she wondered whether the kids who caught birds with fishing line, the kiters, would eat a gull that was already dead.

Gaia's feet scuffed the dirt as she walked, as she tried to decide what questions to ask her mom first on this Day of Truth. She sidestepped what looked like a small, wrinkled, dead jellyfish, and she would have thought nothing more of it, but her mom made a disgusted noise and kicked dirt over it with her foot.

"What, Momma?"

"Bleh. Nothing. I wonder how they got in here. Probably climbed the bluffs. I guess security is only strict when the raft people show up."

"What is it? A jellyfish?"

"No. Keep walking. I'm just grateful that whoever was here isn't procreating."

"Oh," was all Gaia said, though her mind reeled a little that it wasn't a dead jellyfish at all, but the remnants of sex. The world seemed so much larger to Gaia right then, as if it were a globe-sized cabinet of hidden drawers. Hidden drawers filled with hidden things.

The white gazebo was perched precipitously at the bluffs' edge like a spaceship ready to blast off. Its open pentagonal structure offered a commanding view of the ragged, hazy, salty-pink coast. To the south, Chumash Rock dominated the middle of Junipero Bay's calm breakwater like a giant's big toe, and if she squinted she could see Point Conception melting into the horizon. Looking north, she saw Sunset Hills and a corner of the "wave eater" power generator in the distance. The vast, dead Pacific loomed straight ahead, orange-pink and pouring out to the edge of the world, sending back swells to the kelp-draped rocks that looked like a giant's mouthful of jagged, crooked, awful teeth.

Maer parachuted a blanket onto the gazebo floor and pulled Gaia into a long, rocking embrace. The breeze fluttered in their hair, and Gaia thought the tide's rhythm sounded like her mom's heartbeat. She floated in the warmth of her mother's chest as a gull called out somewhere down the coast, and she felt like a small child again, swaddled, surrounded by a lullaby of tide, breeze, and bird calls. Her mom let go and gently fussed with Gaia's hair.

"I think you can take the plugs out of your nose now."

Her nose! She'd stopped thinking about it because it didn't hurt anymore, but now the plugs shoved up her nostrils suddenly felt thick and alien. She hesitated and cocked her head.

"Go ahead. I think you'll be fine."

"Are you sure?"

Maer nodded.

One at a time, Gaia slowly extracted the plugs, wincing as stuck parts peeled away. Her mom handed her a few tissues and, after a minute of blowing, Gaia breathed freely. She reached up to touch the side of her nose, stunned that there wasn't any pain at all.

"Holy mother..." She pushed a bit harder on her right nostril.

Maer grinned. "Well, I don't think I can take credit for it, as much as I'd love to. And that spot you're touching, that's the spot."

"What spot?"

Her mom's expression said, *Oh, come now. We're way past pretending.*

"Where my nose was broken?"

"So you *did* hear," Maer smiled and handed Gaia a mystery package from the lunch basket. "I figured you did."

The package revealed a piece of thin, brown, and wrinkly food, but Gaia was focused on the fact that her mom really did know about her extraordinary hearing. How long had she known?

"It's beef leather. Try it. It's cow meat. The old timers called it "jerky." I've been holding onto a stash of it for about five years now."

Gaia sniffed it and set it in her lap. It didn't smell like much, though she was still distracted by the thought that she'd broken a bone earlier that day and it was already healed. Between her hearing and her self-healing, she wondered—this time seriously—what kind of a mutant she was.

"How did you know?" Gaia asked, suddenly feeling like she'd been the one lying by omission.

"You mean about your hearing? Oh, Cutie, when you were little you'd tell me all about the things you heard."

Gaia thought back and realized she *had* actually done that, but at the time, it felt so normal to her that she didn't consider how incredible her hearing would seem to someone else. *How could I have overlooked that?* She felt stupid for holding onto this big secret that was absolutely no secret at all.

"I think the last time was when you were about five. It was bedtime, and you'd been waiting for me to read to you. It got later and later, and when I finally came in, you were almost asleep. I said I was sorry and you said in a sleepy voice that it was okay, because you'd already gotten your story—the one Mr. Alistair read to Maya. In her room. Four houses away."

As foolish as Gaia was now feeling, she smiled at that. "I remember that story. It was about how an elephant got his trunk."

"Yes!" Maer said. "And the next morning, when we went to pick Maya up for school, you asked Mr. Alistair if he would read that story again. He asked, 'What story?' And you said, 'The one about the elephant!' And I remember the look on his face!" Maer burst out laughing. "Like somebody cracked an egg over his head. I remember frantically thinking for a few seconds as I tried to figure out how to explain that one away, but there was nothing I could say. So I just grabbed you and Maya by the hand and whisked you to the truck as fast as I could, trying my best not to laugh out loud."

Gaia didn't remember that part, and now she was dreading the notion that her hearing ability was even more public than she'd ever dreamed.

"And did Mr. Alistair ever know? Did he ever find out? About my hearing, I mean."

"Oh, I don't know. I don't think so. He never mentioned it."

"So you've known..."

"Yes, your father and I know. And probably a babysitter or two."

"And Selene," Gaia said. "She knows. She finally figured it out today."

Maer nodded. "I think she always suspected."

"What about Godpappy Lane? Does he know?"

Her mom hesitated as she picked a sand burr out of the blanket, her smile wilting as she seemed to go to a deeper place. "I think it's safe to say he does, yes."

Gaia was quiet for a moment. Godpappy Lane had been her teacher three years in a row, since the fourth grade, and it was rare for a teacher to keep the same class for that long. She tried to recall moments when she'd eavesdropped in class, and the hurtful things kids said were smack dab at the front of her line of memories. But she couldn't remember anything involving Godpappy, except that he was always quick to step in, especially during the first year when he caught the whispers about Gaia and seized the opportunity for a "teaching moment" to give a lesson on the value and wonder of difference, about how everyone has strange characteristics. And he'd been unusually kind to her when she cried in class the first few times. So he probably did know.

"I can hear really well, Mom. I mean, really well. Sometimes I think I'll go crazy with it, because nobody ever shuts up. I think that's why I don't talk very much. Everybody else is doing too much of it."

The look on Maer's face made her regret that last part. "I didn't mean you, Mom."

"What? Oh, no! I wasn't thinking that at all. It's—" Her mom hesitated. "Can I ask you something? I've always wanted to know."

Gaia nodded.

"When we're talking right now, just the two of us, is my voice so loud that it's uncomfortable?"

Gaia scrunched her nose. "No. Not really. I'm used to it. Sometimes people talk extra loud, or have a pitch to their voice. Then it hurts a little."

"I wondered about that. I've seen you wince sometimes."

"I try to hide it, Momma."

"I know, Baby. I know." Maer sighed. "I'm so sorry."

"So I really am a mutant, then."

"Don't ever say that!" her mom snapped. "Never, ever say things like that about yourself. I'm not sorry about your hearing at all. That's not what I mean. I mean, I'm sorry that we kept things from you. I'm sorry that you felt you had to keep things from us. Maybe I should have talked to you soon—"

"Yes, you should have, Mom!" Gaia interrupted.

"I guess I didn't because I didn't want to confuse or frighten you. We want you to live a completely normal life, and for the most part I think you have. The worst of it, so far, has been the need to cope with your differences, mostly the differences in your looks."

"The *differences* in my *looks*? Mom, I'm a freak show!" The core pain triggered again. Her looks, her hearing—and now even her self-healing—were the undeniable daily reminders that something was wrong with her. Or at least different about her. And nobody was leveling with her.

"Nobody looks like me! Even people who have allergic reactions to Derma look sort of normal, even when their skin turns orange. Look at my eyes, Mom! Look at my ears! Look at my hair!" Gaia's tears returned.

"Lots of people color their hair, Gaia."

"Mom! I don't have any whites in my eyes! I look like an alien! I *do* look like a booger!"

"Who said that?"

"Nobody."

"Who?"

"Some jerk boy named Stacy."

"Is that why you were sad this morning?"

Gaia shrugged.

"Stacy. You mean a mean boy with a girl's name called *you* a name? Kind of cancels itself out, don't you think?"

"Mom, it's not funny!"

"Oh, come on. You have to admit it's a *little* funny." Maer bumped Gaia's shoulder playfully.

"It's all easy for you to say, because you're beautiful! You said it was time for honesty, so just say that I'm freakish and ugly. I won't trust you if you don't!"

"Listen to me." Her mom's eyes and voice bored into her. "You're growing up so fast. Before we know it, you're going to be out on your own. You're going to have to be very strong." She paused. "You, in particular."

"Why me in particular?"

"Just listen. It's time to start learning this now. You need to do two things. They're going to sound contradictory, but they're not. And, they're the most important things you will ever do for yourself."

Blah blah blah. The last thing Gaia wanted right now was advice. Advice would never change the way she looked, so she tuned out her mom and just sat, staring at the expansive horizon. Storm clouds formed in the distance, and Gaia wondered if a hurricane was heading in their direction.

"The first thing is you need to stop feeling sorry for yourself. No self pity, no wallowing in your perceived misfortune. Be tough like you have been these past few minutes. If you need to grieve about your looks, then grieve. I mean really grieve. But then let it go. Drop it." She shook Gaia a little by the shoulders for emphasis, and Gaia slowly looked at her mom.

"Are you hearing me?"

"Yes. Tough. Grieve. Drop it. Got it." She stared out to sea again, catching the flare of a tiny flash of lighting in the distant clouds.

"And here's how you drop it," Maer said, as Gaia felt her mom's hand gently moving her face so that Gaia was looking into her dark brown eyes. "You drop it with the second thing I'm going to tell you. And that is, you have to go back into yourself. And, by that, I mean love yourself, cherish yourself. *Revel* in your gifts and embrace your faults and mistakes. Laugh at them, and forgive yourself. Cherish those things that make *you* a human being—just like *every other* human being—because in the end, no matter what, your humanity is the only thing that'll make a difference in this world."

Gaia tried to understand. The human being part was reassuring. But the rest of it? She heard only her mom's words flowing like water across bone-dry ground.

"I know," Maer said. "It's hard for you to understand right now. But you will."

"Like this great truth you keep promising me?" Gaia feared that this wonderful, unwrapped gift of truth would turn out to be something completely ordinary. *Maybe I just fell into a vat of acid when I was a baby.*

Maer moved in and cradled Gaia again, squeezing her. Her voice cracked.

"I think—I know—that you are the most beautiful creature on this earth. Sometimes I think my soul will burn up with the love I have for you."

Gaia closed her eyes and felt sadness creep into her own soul, a tormenting sadness telling her that she'd never find a satisfying answer about anything.

"I hate that it hurts you so much, and being your age doesn't help. I guess you have the same hormones that every other girl your age has."

"And the same mirrors," Gaia grumbled, taking out her frustration on the beef jerky by trying to tear it in half, which she wasn't able to do.

"Wait!" Gaia stopped. "What do you mean you guess I have the same hormones? I heard Dad say it in the truck this morning, too. Why wouldn't I have the same hormones as everyone else?"

Her mom squeezed her harder in reply, as if she were trying to protect Gaia from something, and that frightened her.

"I *am* a human being, right?"

No answer.

"Mom!" Gaia's panic rose and she sat straight up, trembling. "What is it? What's *wrong* with me? Seriously. I think I killed grass without doing anything, by just being furious. Do I come from another planet? Is that what's going on? Am I an alien? *Tell* me!"

"No, Baby. I don't believe you're an alien."

"You don't *believe*? But *maybe*?" More fear tore through her. Gaia couldn't believe what she was hearing, and she wanted to reach into her mom's skull and yank every thread of knowledge out of her brain.

"*Truth*, Mom!" Gaia yelled. "You said it's the Day of Truth!"

Maer nodded. "Yes, I did," she said calmly. A lone seagull soared past the gazebo and shrieked, eyeballing the food basket.

"So?" Gaia hollered. "Spit it out! Now!" Her mom's shoulders caved, and she suddenly changed from a confident woman into a small, helpless child.

"I'll let your godpappy and Uncle Cloudy tell you the story of how you came to us. So yes, Baby, you're adopted. Well, not exactly adopted. Found. They found you and gave you to me."

Gaia's mouth hung open. She didn't know whether to scream or cry or laugh. Adopted. No, worse. Found. By Godpappy and Uncle Cloudy. Suddenly, her heart sank.

"So it's really true," said Gaia. "I really am a Croozer baby."

"No. Not a Croozer baby. Or a Syncro baby, like you've spouted before."

"What then?"

"I hate myself for holding out on you. It was irresponsible, and I'm sorry. I hope someday—"

"Mom!" Gaia shouted.

Maer flicked a thought away with her hand. She seemed suddenly small to Gaia and very, very un-Maer-like.

"I'll tell you exactly what I know, Baby. There's your nose, for one, and now your foot. Look at it."

Gaia, who had taken off her shoes as soon as they sat down, looked at her once-injured foot. It was completely normal, dirty, gross green and all. The swelling and the yellow bruise had completely vanished.

"So?" she said. "What am I, the first Croozer baby who's not retarded and has amazing self-healing powers?"

"What?" Maer looked like she'd been slapped. "I said you're not a Croozer baby."

Gaia lifted her arms to signal, *What else am I supposed to think*?

"Gaia! You're the furthest thing from a Croozer baby!"

"WHAT THEN?" she hollered. "WHY AM I LIKE THIS?! WHAT *AM* I?"

Her mom drew a deep breath, then closed her eyes.

"You're Gaia."

"Oh, please! Please just tell me! Please! Don't play these games with me! Why are you dragging this out? I don't care what the truth is! I just want to know!" Sobs wracked her body. "Please, Momma!"

Maer didn't say anything for what seemed an eternity. She just stared past Gaia out to sea.

"Momma! Wake up! Tell me!"

"I just told you, Baby. You're *Gaia*."

"What?! What does that mean?" Gaia had no idea what her mom was talking about.

Maer sat up, bracing herself. "Okay, here goes. Shit. Get it together, Maer," she whispered to herself.

"What, Momma?"

Thunder bellowed in the deep distance.

"There's a myth, an old myth. It's as old as humans. Well, modern humans, anyway. Actually, that's not quite accurate, is it. The Lower Palaeo period—"

"Mom!" Gaia said, sensing the build-up of a technical diatribe, a comfort zone her scientist mom fell back into when she was nervous, which made Gaia even angrier.

"Hear me out, Baby. It's not what you think."

"Speak English, then!"

Maer sighed, regrouping. "I've had a long time to research this, and discoveries in Kenya the past few years put this myth at a couple million years old. Most people think Hesiod and Homer and the old Greeks came up with it, but they didn't."

"*What* myth?" Gaia knew she was being testy and impatient, but she felt it was her right after being lied to for so many years, and she had no idea what some stupid myth had to do with her. Was this another stalling tactic?

"You've heard of Mother Earth."

"Yes," Gaia said cautiously, wiping her eyes. "I've heard of Mother Earth. So what?"

"Some vague concept we use as a cute way to describe the planet we live on and the things that grow out of it, right?"

Gaia wiped her face and swallowed.

"Well," Maer continued, "wrong. The ancients—hundreds of thousands of years back—believed Mother Earth to be an actual person who walked among them."

"And did what?" Gaia asked, her mind beginning to make a connection that she was simultaneously trying to suppress because the thought was too impossible. Her right leg had started to go numb from sitting on it for so long, so she shifted to sitting on her left leg hoping the movement would make the thought go away. Another rumble of thunder rolled across the horizon.

"Grew things. Plants. Wild things, especially plants they could eat. Mother Earth—the Earth Mother—was as real to them as I am to you. She was their goddess, a very practical and real goddess. And apparently she'd vanish for long periods of time only to reappear again."

"What do you mean, 'long periods of time?'" Gaia asked as an ominous chill surged through her.

"Millennia. Thousands of years. But she keeps showing up again and again in different parts of the world, though less frequently. It's been tens of thousands of years since her last appearance, according to archaeology, anyway."

"So..." Gaia started as a lump swelled in her throat, which took some effort to swallow. "What does this have to do with me?"

"It had been so long since her last appearance that even the Greeks of three-thousand years ago spoke of her as only a myth, a story." Maer rested a hand on Gaia's leg. "And do you know what the Greeks called her?"

Gaia stared at her mom, paralyzed.

"Gaia. They called her Gaia. And I believe, with all my heart, that the goddess has returned again."

-10-
Stories

The first thing that came into Gaia's mind was, *what bullshit.* Then it came out of her mouth. Her entire being had just burst like a balloon inflated with too much air and too much excitement, and now nothing remained inside of her. As the sun tried to make up its mind about late afternoon, she felt peaceful in her emptiness, her deflation. She gazed at the sea, listlessly pondering whether or not the storm was inching closer.

Maer said nothing. The Earth Mother? Of course her mom was joking. Her mom didn't believe in God, much less goddesses or the Earth Mother. How odd. *What a strange joke,* Gaia thought.

In a feeble attempt to re-inflate herself with *something, anything,* Gaia tried to decipher the hidden meaning behind her mom's strange confession. But no matter how hard she tried, she wound up with the same thing: nothing. So there she sat, marveling at how her mom could be so direct one moment and so abstruse the next. *Oh well, the Day of Truth was interesting while it lasted.*

Abstruse. Gaia rolled the word around in her mind, floating in her new vacant buoyancy that was completely free from rational thought. She liked using the word "abstruse" because Selene didn't know what it meant, which was doubly funny because Selene's ignorance was the only reason Gaia remembered the word. She'd come home from school one day having just learned it, and Selene asked what it meant. "Hard to understand," Gaia told her. But Selene thought Gaia was teasing her, and she threw a pen at Gaia. "Fine! Don't tell me, you stupid twat!" Selene blurted. The incident had become a family joke.

Abstruse. Take that, Selene.

Clearly, her mom was using some sort of psychological ploy to smooth the edges of Gaia's raw emotions. Gaia arrived at the bluffs with anticipation in her heart and a deep thirst for the truth, and this is what her mom handed her? Cold Psychology? In her flippant mental state, Gaia found it amusing, so she laughed.

"What's so funny?" Maer asked so gravely that it made Gaia giggle even more.

"Nice, Mom." Gaia caught the hum of a vehicle and noticed Uncle Cloudy's squad car arriving and parking next to the old truck. Her dad, Godpappy Lane, and Selene were with him. Gaia thought the four of them looked like dolls in a toy car.

"Nice Mom, what?"

"Whatever," Gaia said, shaking her head. "It's okay. I'll stop asking."

"Stop asking what?"

Car doors opened, then slammed. Footsteps.

"About me." Gaia felt like a small mouse in a world of giant tiger lies, and she wanted to crawl into her little mouse hole under the gazebo and sleep. Just sleep. Forever.

Maer tried stroking Gaia's hair, but Gaia pulled away.

"Did you hear what I just said to you?"

"Yeah, I heard, Mom."

"And?"

"And what? It's okay. You don't have to tell me the truth. I mean, why start now? You probably don't even know the truth, anyway."

"Didn't start without us, did you?" Godpappy's voice boomed just as Maer opened her mouth to speak. The gazebo bloated as Godpappy, her dad, and Selene squeezed in, claiming their spots on the blanket. Uncle Cloudy remained outside and leaned on the railing, and when Jack waved him in, he shook his head and said he was fine where he was.

Selene immediately dove into the food basket. Normally, Maer would scold her daughter's greediness, but this time she didn't seem to notice.

"Whoa!" Selene gasped, pulling out a small roll. "Where'd you get this? Is this—wheat bread?" She tore off a big bite and closed her eyes as she chewed, her cheeks puffed like an oversized, satisfied rodent. "What's *that*, Grumpy Mug?" she mumbled over the bread in her mouth, now pointing to the beef leather in Gaia's lap. Her finger was so close to it that Gaia, out of reflex, snatched it up and held it away from her sister. But Gaia really didn't care if Selene stole her food. In fact, nothing Selene did tweaked her in the least at the moment. And the upshot of her lack of caring was the feeling of a strange, new inner armor.

"Selene!" Jack snapped. "Stop acting like an animal. We all eat together. Nobody eats ahead of anyone else."

"I'm huuuuuungry, Pa!"

"Knock it off or you don't get any more. Fathom?"

Selene shoved another bite into her mouth and frowned while she chewed, raising her eyes to check out her dad's reaction.

"So!" Cloudy said. "That guard at the gate is a real piece of work, eh?"

"Speaking of animals," Lane said. "Seemed to tighten his jib a bit when he saw Jack in the car, that's for damn sure. At least he still respects military rank even if he doesn't respect anything else. Like human life."

The soldier at the guard gate. And for some reason, Gaia's mind started to go other places, too. She thought back to that fight she'd seen at the Speedy Füd snack bar with the apathetic little girl whose dad had pulled a knife on a man trying to steal their food. Then to the pack fight at the Chinese land grabber bus. Her own fight with Quinn. The hacking, the flames, the pain, more vivid than a memory. The black man who'd reached out to her with his ghostly stare. Dead grass. The violent world was seeping into her like an infection, growing with the claustrophobia of family around her chit chatting in the gazebo while her entire world was falling apart.

"Stop!" Gaia exploded. One by one, the chatter ceased and there was silence—except for Selene's chewing.

"I told her my theory," Maer confessed.

"You mean," Jack started, and Maer nodded. He blew an incredulous whistle, and then rested his hand on Gaia's knee.

"I had to, Jack. I'm done. I'm finished creeping around and worrying about knocking things over."

"Hell, why not?" Cloudy said. "It is what it is."

Gaia glanced up at him. His smile was peaceful and empathetic, and he leaned on the gazebo railing as casually as if he were watching a baseball game on a lazy Saturday afternoon.

"What is what it is?" Gaia asked. And that's when it hit her. Her mom *wasn't* joking.

"Mom. You mean...you were being serious? You weren't just being abstruse?"

"Oddly, yes, I was being serious, not abstruse. Is that what you've been thinking this whole time?"

"I know what that word means," Selene grumbled, nearly choking on the last of her bread roll.

Gaia scrutinized the group. Not one sarcastic smirk in a gazebo full of smart alecks. Every face was solemn, almost reverent, and when Gaia's eyes met Selene's, Selene looked down.

"So you think I'm what?"

"How about this instead," Maer said, reaching into the food basket and handing Gaia a bottle of tomato juice. "See how this feels to you. Why don't we just tell you stories about yourself, tell you all the things we know, and we'll let you make up your own mind about who you are."

It was a heavy thing for her mom to say. Who she was? As in, they didn't really know themselves? Gaia stared back at her mom as if she'd bounced a ball off her head. Did they all really, truly, honestly believe she was the Earth Mother? It was too much—too much, too big, and too strange to sink in, so Gaia just nodded. The cool April breeze gave her goosebumps, and more splinters of lightning blipped on the horizon.

"You've never been sick. Not a day in your life," Maer began. "And you obviously heal quickly."

Gaia knew she'd always been a quick healer, but she assumed that was normal. *I've never been sick? Not even a cold? Never stuck in bed, moaning for soup or medicine?* Maybe that was just Selene. Gaia remembered lying in bed with her mom once when her mom was sick. *Maybe it's true. Maybe I haven't been sick.*

"By the way," Lane said sheepishly. "Gaia, I'm so sorry about my niece. I know this isn't the time to talk about it, but I had no idea she was that—well, as bad as *that*. Her mom, my little sister, is back on Croozer, and I need to figure out what to do with Quinn." He smiled weakly. Godpappy looked haggard. "But it looks like you're all healed up. No surprise there. But I'm sorry you had to go through that. I—"

"Yeah, that's weird and completely messed up that that kid is related to you," Gaia said. "And I want to talk to you more about that sometime. But what's really weird and completely messed up is the fact that you and Uncle Cloudy apparently found me as a baby, and nobody, oh, ever bothered to tell me about it!"

Lane glanced over at Maer, then looked down and picked at the gazebo floor.

"He left it up to me to tell you," Maer said. "Please don't blame him, or Cloudy. It's my fault."

"Fine," Gaia said, starting to feel angry again. Angry about being left in the dark. Angry that she was allowed to think she might be a Croozer baby. Angry that her mom had just pulled some ridiculous mythological theory out of her scientific hat. Angry about being hacked and not feeling safe enough to talk about it with her family, because she felt she was going crazy enough about the cause of her looks, and the weird music she was hearing, which added even more fuel to her anger about being left in the dark.

"It's your fault, fine" Gaia told her mom. "Whatever. Now will you please tell me what the hell is going on? Really?"

"I've been trying to," Maer said. "Just keep listening, okay? You make up your mind."

Gaia sighed and nodded, feeling impatient, but after nearly 15 years this was better than nothing.

"You cried a lot as a baby," Maer said, "when Lane and Cloudy brought you to us."

"Stop there," Gaia interrupted. "Where did you find me? You found me and brought me here, right?"

"We found you," Godpappy said, "on the side of Mt. Kenya. April 22, 2045. A newborn."

Gaia just stared at him, then gulped, then asked a question she never imagined having to ask.

"Who was—is—my mother?"

Godpappy Lane looked over at Cloudy.

"You don't, we think, have a human mother," Cloudy said. "We think you were born from the earth itself."

Gaia froze. If this was a hoax, or a joke, she'd have sniffed it out. Her mother, Godpappy, and Cloudy just didn't act this way when they were joking, especially all at the same time. She had no idea what to do with this information.

"How—" she started, "why do you think that? Was there some magic vagina in the ground that you saw me come out of? Stop laughing, I'm serious! You already know this and I don't!"

It had been a bit of comic relief, but Maer stopped smiling and Godpappy and Cloudy stopped chuckling, probably realizing she was right. It wasn't fair to laugh.

"Well, not that we saw," Godpappy said. "But, well…"

"Well what?"

"You had an umbilical cord. Attached to you. You were just lying there on a patch of grass."

"On the side of Mt. Kenya," Gaia said. "That *is* in Africa, right? Kenya in Africa."

Godpappy nodded. "Kenya in Africa." But he didn't elaborate.

"Fine," Gaia said. "Keep talking, Mom. Tell me all this amazing stuff." Her tone was cutting, but inside she felt herself going from frustration to wonder.

Maer smiled. "You wouldn't take milk. The only food that made you happy was a mixture of tomato juice and corn syrup. We had to get the ratio just right."

"Seriously? Are you making all of this up?"

"No, we're not. Nothing we say here today will be made up. Tomato juice and corn syrup. Found on the side of a mountain. I'll save the rest of that story for Godpappy and Uncle Cloudy. But think about it. What's your favorite drink now?"

Gaia examined the tomato juice bottle. *I could drink myself to death on this stuff,* she thought.

"Yep, tomato juice. Don't you think that's a little strange, for a kid to love tomato juice?"

"No, because I love tomato juice."

"Touché. That's my girl." Her mom was fully present and engaged again, and she was just getting warmed up, which comforted Gaia. "We thought you might be jaundiced, before we realized your fantastic skin wasn't going to change. So in the first days I put you in the sunshine next to the terrarium in your little bouncy lounge. Prop was just a puppy then. He'd lie down like a log with his nose near your toes, not moving a muscle even when you kicked him in the head. He never left your side. And he'd let out this low, hound dog growl if anyone came near you, even us.

"The terrarium," Maer continued. "I've mentioned it to you before, but not the whole of it. I told you about how you loved things that grew and how they seemed to grow better when you were near," she trailed off, chasing a memory.

"One morning, I cleaned out the terrarium. Things were wilting, so I pulled everything out, rotated the soil, and added some 1-2 toilet compost. You know, the normal routine. I wasn't going to plant anything that day, so I moved you and your bouncy seat back to the front of the terrarium. Prop even nipped at me when I moved you. Anyway..."

She paused, then launched a sob.

"It's okay," Jack said, rubbing his wife's back. "Take your time."

Gaia sensed a big moment coming, so she sat up to make sure she heard all of it, which struck her as silly, because she could have heard this from down the road.

"I walked back into the kitchen to make tea," Maer continued, wiping her eyes. "A minute later, I heard little Selene say, 'Mama, look!'" She paused and glanced at her oldest daughter. "Do you remember this at all, Selene? You were only two."

Selene studied her lap before she answered, and when she did answer there was a challenge to her voice. "I remember a lot more than you think from those days. I remember you yelling at Dad, and Dad leaving. It was like clockwork. I remember being invisible to you."

Maer hesitated, studying Selene, looking as if she wanted to reach out to her, but she didn't. Selene kept her eyes down on the stick she was trying to poke through the blanket.

"Okay if we talk about this later?" Maer asked.

"Whatever," Selene shrugged. "If you don't want me to talk then don't ask me questions."

Maer opened her mouth to speak but apparently thought better of what she was about to say, then looked back at Gaia.

"Anyway, I panicked and ran in to where you were because I was expecting to see something awful, and I saw Selene pointing at the terrarium with a big grin on her face."

"Invisible," Gaia heard Selene mumble, but nobody else seemed to hear it. Gaia couldn't tell if Selene was sad, or scared, or angry—or just bored.

"My God. I nearly passed out," Maer said. "The first flowers I noticed were the sunflowers. Dozens of them! Maybe a hundred! Tiny ones!"

"In the terrarium?" Gaia asked, wondering if her mom was implying that she had somehow created them.

"In the terrarium! The one I had just cleaned out. The one that was nothing but soil a few minutes earlier."

Goosebumps.

"Then I saw something else at the back, and I had to get on my hands and knees to see it. It was a tree. A tiny tree, like a bonsai tree, that looked like a small replica of a giant Sequoia. It was fully formed, but tiny, and less than a foot tall."

Gaia's mouth fell open. An image of the scene flashed through her mind, but whether it were remembered or invented, she couldn't tell.

"Wait. Are you saying I had something to do with that? Are you saying *I* grew those things?"

Gaia looked from amused face to amused face.

"Yes, Baby," Maer laughed, wiping her eyes again. "That's exactly what I'm saying."

Gaia realized her dad was holding something in front of her. It was an old shoebox. She took it, placed it in her lap, and opened the lid.

Inside lay a small withered tree, almost as long as the box, resting on a pad of green cloth. The tree was so dry that Gaia spent a few moments deciding which were the roots and which were the branches. She traced her finger along its rough, grooved trunk, and she thought it looked very much like the beef leather. Jerky, her mom called it.

"Woopdie-doopdie," Selene deadpanned. "Happy birthday. It's a dead tree."

"Hey!" Jack scolded. "Knock it off. Don't ruin this."

Selene started to get up and leave, but Jack grabbed her arm and forced her to sit back down. Selene yanked her arm away and turned her back on them.

Cloudy and Lane stayed quiet, letting the family play with their own demons.

"That's the tree," Maer said. "The very same tree. We saved it. I found out what kind of tree it is, too."

Gaia looked up. "What kind?"

"It's a Sequoia."

"Like..."

"Like the tallest trees in the world. Like the one you can drive a car through at Sequoia National Farm. And this one? It's fully grown."

Gaia lifted it by the trunk and examined it as her excitement mounted and tingled in her arms.

"We tried replanting it in a bigger pot, but it didn't take."

"I don't understand," Gaia said, still struggling to believe any of it. "You're saying I did this?"

"Yes, Sweetie. You did that and more. You did it over and over. When the plants in the terrarium died, I'd clean it out, add some more 1-2, and you'd do it again. I'd watch it happen—watch the little sprouts pop up and grow right in front of my eyes in a matter of minutes. And speaking of eyes, your eyes! They'd go from green to blue to purple, changing so quickly it frightened me, like they were making the plants grow!"

Gaia closed her eyes and zoned out, trying to imagine it all.

"The tree only happened once," Maer said, "but you'd grow all kinds of other things, things I'd never seen. I have all of them pressed in that little book at home."

Then it clicked. Gaia knew that book better than any of her other books! When she was little, she always asked for it at bedtime—page after page of the most beautiful, whimsical pressed flowers she'd ever seen.

Maer lit up. "Yep! The flower book! *You* made those. Of course, we never told you."

"Why? Why didn't you tell me?"

Maer's face dropped. "Well, after a couple of months it stopped happening, and by the time you could talk you didn't remember any of it."

"You still could have told me."

"Would *you* have told you?"

Then Selene spoke. "I would have told you if they hadn't been telling me to shut up all the time."

Something was definitely boiling in Selene, who usually dropped a verbal bomb and walked away. But today she was persistent, like she'd been holding something in a long time and was about to blow. Why today? Why now? Why at the most important conversation in Gaia's life? It was just like Selene to spoil something big, like the year she told Gaia everything Gaia was getting for Christmas—including the flower book—before Gaia had a chance to open her presents.

But oh, the flower book! So *she* had grown those? Gaia pretended her mom *had* told her she'd grown those flowers. She pictured herself as a little squirt strutting around telling people, *Hey, look what I did! I grew these with my magical powers!* Then she heard the laughter, and she saw creepy little Stacy Williams' face again, taunting her, saying that if she could really do it then why doesn't she just do it again? Then she imagined blaming her parents for making up stories and for lying to her, and for making her believe she really had grown the flowers. Gaia sighed uneasily, deciding her mom and dad were probably right for holding out. At least when she was a little kid.

"So today, with the grass..." Gaia started.

"...was the first time since you were a baby that anything like that has happened," Maer finished.

"But I killed it!"

"I know."

"Why?"

Maer shook her head and shrugged.

Now Godpappy spoke. "You said you were furious."

Gaia nodded, and Godpappy nodded back.

"I think it works both ways," he said.

"But that's what I mean. What is *it*? *What* works both ways?"

"Life," Godpappy said. "And death."

-11-
Cheese, Scotch, & Croozer

When Godpappy said "death," the dark, ghostly eyed man in the fire materialized in her head again, reaching out to her—or reaching forward to grab her, it now seemed. The vision wasn't as vivid or alive as when she'd been hacked, but the memory was more permanent than normal memories. It was terrifying. If she really had been hacked, if this is how it felt, she never wanted anything inserted into her again, which meant she'd never have a Telepath. But it was worth the tradeoff if it meant not being hacked. Those nutball Luddites who sabotaged tech companies probably had it right.

But then the chilling question came back to her: If she had been hacked, who could it possibly be? Was there someone else who knew about her, somebody her parents and Godpappy and Cloudy weren't telling her about? Or maybe somebody they didn't even know about?

Gaia rubbed her face with both hands and shook her head fiercely to dislodge the insanity that was starting to whirl through her mind again.

"What the hell was *that*?" Selene guffawed.

"Leave me alone," Gaia growled. She'd been seriously considering telling them about the hacking, but they'd probably think she was nuts. The Day of Truth didn't need to go that far, and she didn't owe them *any* truth. They owed it to her.

"Selene, that's enough!" Maer said. "Put this in your mouth. We'll all be happier, especially you." Maer was passing beef leather and bread rolls to everyone, then produced a jar of strawberry preserves, something normally reserved for Christmas. The men were giddy about the beef, but it wasn't until everyone slathered their rolls and began munching that Maer pulled something from the basket that Gaia didn't recognize. She thought it looked like an orange brick, and when the men saw it, they immediately stopped chewing. Whatever it was, Gaia didn't like that it was distracting from the storytelling. She was desperate to hear more, to try to make sense of what was happening to her, but nobody else seemed to care. Why would they? They already knew!

"No! It can't be!" Godpappy said with awe.

"Mom, Godpappy, please don't stop the story!" Gaia pleaded.

But Maer only smiled. She seemed annoyingly pleased with herself, like there was no hurry in the world. She carved a slice off the end of the orange thing and handed it to Gaia.

"Patience, my love. The past isn't going anywhere and moments like this, well, they don't happen too often. Enjoying the moment is a very special power in itself."

Gaia sighed and examined the strange food, wondering if the comment about power was a reference to *her* confusing powers. Everyone stared at her except for Selene, who'd turned her back to them again only after she'd gotten her food.

The slice of orange thing was firm and smooth between Gaia's fingers, and it flexed as she took a quick, mindless bite. But when the flavor crept through her mouth, she paused. It was like nothing she'd ever tasted. There was a savory tang that nipped and played with her tastebuds, though Gaia wasn't sure she liked it.

"Maer, is that cheese?" Cloudy asked, looking covetously at the orange brick. Maer sliced off a piece and tossed it to him. He caught it carefully with two hands and examined it from different angles, then sniffed it. He took a bite and chewed, slowly, closing his eyes. "How in the world..."

"Do I even want to know how you got ahold of this?" Jack said, but he didn't refuse when she handed him a piece.

"No, you most definitely do not want to know," Maer said. "For all you know it fell from the sky."

Gaia had heard of cheese, but she had no idea it was *this* big of a deal. The way the adults went on about it, it seemed just as important as the news that she was the Earth Mother—like they were grieving something from their past, something they'd lost and figured they'd never see again. Gaia wondered if they'd be more surprised to see an extinct dolphin pop its head from the waves and start squawking at them.

Then an odd thought struck her. She'd killed that day. She'd killed the beautiful grass, and she felt that some of her own innocence had somehow died along with it. Would she ever get that back? *Could* she? Were the adults feeling that kind of loss? Was this what growing up was all about, suffering loss after loss? *It works both ways, life and death*, Godpappy had said. As Gaia nibbled another bite of the cheese, it seemed to her that death was winning.

"Thanks for the food, Maer," Godpappy Lane said. "All we need now is a little Scotch!" He chuckled and shook his head. "Ah, dare to dream."

"Lord, wouldn't that be nice! Those were the days," Jack's voice trailed off, lost in memory.

Maer grinned at them as she reached into the basket and slowly withdrew an old glass bottle that was curvaceous and green.

Eyes popped, jaws dropped.

"You're kidding me, right?" Lane said. "You found Scotch?"

Maer ceremoniously twisted the top out, which made a light pop as the corked lid came free, and she placed six small glasses on the ground, pouring a little amber liquid into each one. No one spoke as the glasses were passed around. Apparently, this must have been good stuff because Cloudy entered the gazebo and knelt down, rubbing his hands together.

Selene spun around, suddenly interested. "Indian water?" she asked.

Maer scowled and reached for the glass she'd handed Selene. "You can give that right back if you're going to talk that racist crap." But Selene launched into a rapid apology as she held the glass just out of her mother's reach.

Gaia held up her glass and sniffed. The sweet pungency of the liquid stabbed her brain. The vapor coming off it made her eyes water.

"We're all going to need this where we're going next," Maer said. "Lane? Cloudy? You boys ready to tell the story about how this amazing girl came to us?"

Lane and Cloudy locked eyes for a moment, and something passed between them.

"Sweetie," Maer said, "I said something very big to you when we first sat down, about whom I think you are. If what we've told you so far doesn't convince you, then what you're about to hear most certainly will."

What's the big deal if I can't do any of that stuff anymore? Gaia wondered. *What can they possibly tell me that will make me believe I'm the Earth Mother?* But then she thought about the dead grass.

"To truth," Maer toasted, holding up her glass.

"Finally," said Jack as he, Lane, and Cloudy hoisted their glasses. Selene and Gaia kept theirs down. After the adults sipped, they all grimaced.

"Hello!" Lane said. "I remember that. Whooo!"

Maer's smile widened as she looked at Gaia. "There's something else in the box. Did you notice?"

Gaia lifted the little Sequoia out of the box again and saw a piece she'd assumed had just broken off the tree. But on closer examination, the branch or whatever it was was different than the tree. It was also withered, but it was smoother than the tree and had a round ball at the end. She picked it up and held it to the light, scrunching her eyebrows.

"That fell off about a week after they brought you to us," Maer said.

"Fell off what? What is it?"

"That's the cord. That's what made your belly button."

Gaia turned the thing over in her hands, examining it. She lifted her shirt and put the ball end of the thing into her belly button. It was a nice fit.

"Your mom had it analyzed," said Jack. "It's some kind of vine, but they were never able to get an exact match against anything that exists today—or has ever existed."

Gaia's heart stopped. "What do you mean, it's a *vine*? That doesn't make any sense!"

"Well," Jack said, rubbing the side of his face, "I'm afraid that what Lane and Cloudy are about to tell you may confuse the issue even more."

"I'm afraid it will, too," Godpappy said.

"Hell, *I'm* still confused by it," Cloudy put in. "To this very day it baffles me—baffles *all* of us."

Everyone slowly nodded. Even the short little trees behind them in the preserve seemed to nod in the breeze, as if all of nature were kept out of the secret as well.

"What do you mean? What are you talking about?" Selene demanded. "I've never heard about this!"

Overwhelmed, Gaia set the vine back in the box and downed the alcohol in her glass.

Wham! As she swallowed, her throat convulsed with fire, and the back of her eyes sizzled and filled with tears. Then she started coughing uncontrollably.

"Here, let me help you with that!" Godpappy chuckled, and she felt him gently slip the glass from her hand. She was certain her esophagus was melted and that the poison liquid attacking her gut and making it do flips would burn a hole right through it.

When the wretched coughing stopped, she realized that Selene also completely finished her Scotch, but without a fuss. She wasn't even making a face. The grown-ups were so focused on Gaia's agony that none of them noticed Selene stealthily refill her own glass to the top and quickly down it with only the slightest little cough, and then filled her glass again to the level which Maer had originally poured it.

"Not tomato juice, is it?" Cloudy grinned at Gaia.

"I had a vine for an umbilical cord?!" Gaia sputtered, trying to regain her composure as the Scotch kept up the assault on her throat. "Gah, that's the worst stuff ever!" She wondered how Selene could stand it. Gaia unscrewed the cap on her tomato juice and drained the soothing liquid in giant gulps to drown the Scotch.

"Well, I guess it's an acquired taste. And definitely not the worst stuff ever!" Lane took another slug, then he and Cloudy exchanged glances.

"The worst thing ever, Blueberry," said Cloudy, "would be Croozer."

Lane stared at the ground, nodding.

"How do *you* know?" Selene piped up, demurely sipping her third glass of Scotch. "I bet you guys have never even smoked herb. Obviously you've never been on Croozer."

"Why do you say 'obviously?'" Cloudy's eyes narrowed.

"Because you're not on Croozer now. Nobody kicks Croozer. Once you're hooked, you're hooked."

"And you know this how?" Jack asked.

"Dad, come on. What, am I? Five? Are you still going to tell me that the people I see lying around on the side of the road are just taking naps? I see the garbage trucks all the time stopping to 'pick up the trashed.' Like I'm the only one of us who sees it? Name one person you know who's kicked Croozer."

Gaia was getting impatient. "What does this have to do with the story?"

"Actually, it has quite a lot to do with the story," Lane said. "In fact, it's a perfect place to start the story. You want to know the name of one person who's kicked Croozer, Selene? Cliff Barr. Cloudy. The man sitting right across from you."

"Uncle Cloudy?" Selene gawked, then laughed. "No way. There's no *way*!"

Cloudy's eyes glistened. Whether from the Scotch or emotion, Gaia couldn't tell.

"If he hadn't have been on Croozer, I wouldn't have found him, and you wouldn't be calling him Uncle Cloudy. And, most important, Gaia probably wouldn't be here with us. Funny how things work out."

"I wouldn't exactly call it funny," Cloudy said.

"Wait. What? I wouldn't be here?" Gaia was intrigued by the notion that her very existence could hinge on something unstable and unpredictable, on random events—and worse, random events tied to a dangerous drug. What if Godpappy had slept in the day he found Cloudy? What if he were out of town, or what if he had simply walked down the wrong street? Would any of that have changed her own fate, her own existence?

"Damn!" Selene said, awestruck. "Respeck, Uncle Cloudy."

Gaia noticed that her own presence, her own story, seemed less interesting to Selene than Croozer—or Scotch—which ignited a fresh heat of resentment toward her sister. And didn't they notice that she was getting drunk?

Maer reached for Selene's Scotch, but Selene quickly downed the rest. She grinned and held the empty glass out to her mom. "Morepleas!"

"Oh, you're way done," Maer said, who needed both of her hands to pry the glass from Selene.

"Well—why? Why'djou get on Croozer, Uncle Cloudy-oudy?" Selene slurred a little, releasing her grip on the glass with a flourish.

"Escape," Cloudy said quietly. He seemed lost in his own thoughts, oblivious to Selene's obnoxious state, which made Gaia even angrier. "Total and complete escape. Cowardice, if we're calling a rock a rock. Just like anyone who's too chicken to commit suicide. Drinking something that sends you into a state of living death seems, I don't know, easier, I guess. It was after Sally and Grace. After I went through with—" His voice glitched and he tightened his lips, holding something back. Everybody left a respectful silence for him, and Jack rested a hand on his shoulder.

Gaia softened at Cloudy's confession, and she wondered how taking Croozer was cowardly if it was the most dangerous thing you could drink short of poison. She wanted to ask him why anybody would want to kill himself, but the sorrow in his eyes convinced her that it was possible, even if she didn't understand it. Cloudy never talked about the tragedy, but Gaia knew it was his wife and infant daughter. Baby Grace. They'd been killed during a fight in a water distribution line. Gaia suspected it was the reason her own middle name was Grace.

"Anyway," Cloudy continued, looking out to sea, his blond stubble and drooping blue eyes evoking a lost sailor, "Lane saved my life, even though I didn't want him to." The focus suddenly came back into his eyes, and he looked worried, like he understood something. "Selene, you seem awfully curious about Croozer. Why is that?"

Selene paused and took two deep breaths as if preparing to slip under water, then launched something that jolted everyone. "Becuzzai almos tookit tha other day! I. Almos. Took. Croozer. Anyou wanna know why?" She stuck her chin out.

Maer covered her mouth with her hands.

Gaia snapped. It was too much. Her selfish, over-dramatic sister was trying to steal her day. Before she had time to think about it, Gaia found herself shouting, desperate for the page to flip back to her story.

"I was hacked! Somebody hacked my D.I. chip and gave me a vision!"

Stunned looks bounced between Gaia and Selene. She'd gotten their attention. Maer looked ready to faint, and Jack's mouth hung open limply in lobotomized shock.

"There was a black man, reaching out to me! He was trying to grab me, and he was on fire. His eyes were white and dead!"

She looked from face to face and caught something that scared her. Both Godpappy and Cloudy looked frightened, like they'd seen a ghost.

-12-
Life

S ilence lingered as the orange-pink Pacific pushed at the bluffs, its rhythmic slapping on the shore punctuating the tension in the air. This wasn't going at all as Gaia had hoped. Her head was spinning with questions. Her mom considered her to be the Earth Mother. The Sequoia, the flowers, the vine umbilical cord. Lane and Cloudy's untold story about how they'd found her. Seeing death spread across beautiful, green grass, knowing that she was causing it. Her broken nose—and probably broken foot—healing in a matter of hours. The fright of being hacked, with a vision that felt more and more threatening as she replayed it in her memory. She needed answers more desperately than she needed to breathe. She wanted to know what the hell was going on, and after all these years of secrecy she knew she deserved it. How was it possible that Selene could now steal this from her?

"Gaia," Maer cautioned, keeping her eyes on Selene. Gaia knew what was coming next. "Hold that thought. Please."

"Selene, tell me you're joking," Jack ordered as Selene glared defiantly back at him. "I know you're probably a little tipsy right now."

"I can't believe you're falling for this," Gaia said. She'd bet her life that Selene would sooner swallow ground glass than take Croozer.

"Are you kidding, Selene?" Uncle Cloudy asked calmly. "This isn't something to joke about."

But Godpappy stayed focused on Gaia. "Wait a minute. You said you saw a black man on fire? In a vision?"

"What if I'm *not* kidding?" Selene bulldozed through, spitting a little as she fired her question back at Cloudy.

"Oh, shenanagins!" Gaia growled with disgust, ignoring even Godpappy Lane as she got up to leave. This phony Croozer drama made her want to puke.

"Sh'nan'gins?!" Selene yelled after her. "The perfect li'l princess with the perfect little life calls sh'nan'gans? The one who's gotten all the attention from the day her cute li'l green ass landed on our door-shtep?"

Gaia lost it. She whirled around and stormed back to Selene, bending down so their noses almost touched, her teeth clenched with fury. "Perfect? Little green ass?" She wanted to bite Selene's face. But instead she screamed—an almost inhuman screech. Selene's swift slap stung her face, and the next thing Gaia knew, Selene was on top of her, pinning her shoulders to the ground like Quinn had done on the soccer field.

"You wanna know why I'm gonna take Croozer?" Selene shrieked. "Because of YOU, that's why!"

Jack stepped in and pulled Selene off, and in a flash Gaia rolled over and sprinted from the gazebo, crying and kicking at a few seagulls that were moving her direction, drawn to her like all animals were. In the middle of the dirt field, she slowed and crumpled to the ground, lurching with violent sobs.

"Leave me alone!" Gaia screamed at Godpappy, who had started walking to her but stopped in his tracks and sat on the ground watching her.

Gaia rolled over, face down on the hardpack ground, and bawled into her folded arms—a deep, cleansing bawl, draining her of thought and feeling. Time passed. Her breathing slowed as the sobs died, and the pulsing comfort of her own heartbeat gently resonated once again. She reached forward, placed her palms on the ground above her head, arcing her back upward in a gentle curve. The stretch felt good. She pretended to be touching skin, placing her hand on the pregnant belly of her mother—not Maer, but the earth. She wondered what it must feel like to be a baby growing inside of the ground. She knew the thought was ridiculous, but she didn't care.

Without warning, Gaia felt a snap deep at the base of her skull similar to what she experienced on the soccer field, but this one was stronger, like a giant thumb flicked her head loose. He mind was floating, her thoughts and feelings drifting to the ground like fall leaves. The snap had thrown her into a cocooned in peace, almost the opposite of how the hacking felt.

The unyielding ground dissolved into fertile softness, and she felt one with it, melting into it like a root slowly snaking down. Drinking. Being. As she descended, she felt a warm current, and in the flowing was the music! The same music she'd been hearing the past week, only louder—not melody, but an unending note—thousands of indecipherable voices and instruments all blending together, deep and rolling, carrying her along, feeding her. She lingered, hoping the moment would never end.

But something was tickling her. Gaia quickly sat up and swiped at her nose, thinking a bug had flown into it. But it wasn't bug. It brushed her arms, too. Her eyelids fluttered open, heavy from her deep meditation, and she saw what it was.

Flowers.

Poppies. Deep reddish purple, nearly the color of blood.

They blanketed the floor of the park, the once-desolate ground now a thick carpet of swaying crimson and green. Gaia looked around. The poppies were everywhere, extending in all directions, all the way up to the parked cars and all the way down to the bluff's edge. She just sat there, staring in disbelief, wondering if she was hallucinating.

"Oh, my sweet Jesus!" Gaia heard her mom say. Gaia glanced at the gazebo and saw Maer stifle a laugh with her hands, crying openly.

Living polka dots of shadow and light began dancing on satin leaves, and Gaia looked up and saw the cause of it: more birds. Clouds of them came, descending in silhouetted vortexes of orchestrated chaos like upside down tornadoes—seagulls, sparrows, sandpipers, and and a few big, massive-beaked birds that Gaia had never seen in real life, alighting among the poppies.

"Pelicans!" Maer said, her voice barely a whisper, her index finger pointing into the flowers. "Honest-to-God, real pelicans!"

Gaia stood and strolled dreamily back to the gazebo, swishing through the flowers and scattering birds, trying not to step on any of them. Godpappy got up from where he was sitting as she approached, and he walked the rest of the way with her. Everyone in the gazebo stood and stared, even Selene.

Next to the gazebo, one of the pelicans caught Gaia's attention. She'd only seen pelicans in videostreams because they were thought to be extinct. It was much bigger than she'd imagined. Its feathers were dark charcoal, and its beak pouch was full and fat. The pelican turned and waddled toward her, approaching in a cautious zigzag, cocking its head sideways to examine her.

Gaia watched, transfixed. The pelican stopped, tossed its beak up and down in a frenetic convulsion, and produced a fish in its mouth. The pelican lowered its head and flipped the fish toward Gaia where it thudded and vanished in the crimson flowers.

Maer crawled to where the fish landed, and she carefully picked it up, awestruck. Its spiny dorsal fin looked like a mohawk, steep and sharp, and it wriggled half-heartedly in Maer's hands. Everyone gathered to look. Gaia had to cover her ears because of all the bird screeching as more and more landed.

"It's one of my rock fish!" Maer gasped, laughing. "Gaia, look! It's an actual rock fish! One that we grew with the fish grower! He got it! Crikey, he got it! A *pelican*—caught one of my *fish*!" She offered it to Gaia, her face open with wonder. "And he brought it for you! For *you*! Even the birds know who you are!"

Gaia stared wide-eyed at the fish without taking it, then looked at the pelican. She felt as if she were inside a Salvador Dali painting, where everything looked real but nothing belonged together and things were melting at the edges.

"I'm having a dream," she whispered.

"We're having the same dream," Jack said.

Then Selene spoke, vacantly, without a hint of edge to her voice. "It's you."

As Gaia took in her sister's bewildered eyes, Selene suddenly seemed like a tiny girl just learning to speak.

"It's...it's *really* you."

The pelican suddenly raised its wings and flapped itself airborne. As if it were a cue, dozens, then hundreds of birds took to the sky, the muffled beats of their wings drumming the air as they rose and flew off in all directions, melting into the coastline. Only a few straggler seagulls remained to raid the picnic basket while everyone's back was turned.

And then, Gaia knew. The sticky fog in her mind lifted, and she realized something with simple, matter-of-fact clarity.

She was the Earth Mother.

But she was also feeling an odd sensation in her pants.

Maer dropped the fish and drew Gaia into a strong embrace. But an odd feeling nagged her, and Gaia pulled away.

"What? What is it, Baby?"

Gaia turned her back to the group and untied the drawstring on her pants. Maer came over and Gaia pulled open the top of her pants.

"Oh my," Maer said.

"What is it?" Gaia asked. "What's happening?"

Maer smiled, still crying. "Looks like somebody just got her period."

-13-
Godpappy's Journal

S elene sat down in the poppies and was staring at Gaia as if Gaia were a ghost. She seemed frightened and lost. Lane, Cloudy, and Jack seemed equally stunned, watching a sky suddenly full of seagulls, and even a few more pelicans, swirling and landing among the poppies.

"Selene," said Maer, who seemed to be the only person who'd retained her senses. "Selene!" she snapped her fingers. Selene looked at her slowly. "I'm sorry, baby. We'll continue our conversation about Croozer. But right now you're needed. Please go to the truck and get the lady pads out of the gear box."

Selene stood and walked to the truck with her arms pinned to her sides.

"You have pads?" asked Gaia. "You and Selene don't use pads."

"I've been carrying those pads around for a year," said Maer. "To be ready for this."

After Selene returned, she sat back down in the poppies and quietly watched Maer help Gaia with the pad.

"So what do you think now, about what I said earlier?" Maer wiped new tears from her eyes. "About who I think you are?"

"I—" Gaia started, taking in all the flowers and birds. The poppies. All over the bluff. It was such a contrast to the grass she'd killed on the soccer pitch. Godpappy's earlier words came back: *It works both ways, life and death.* But what did that mean? Could she both kill and give life without much control over it? The thought made her dizzy.

"Ready to hear more of your story?" Maer asked as she went over to help Selene up. The three of them walked back to the gazebo to join the men.

"Lane, Cloudy, you're on," Maer said. "Don't hold anything back."

Gaia liked the sound of that. *Don't hold anything back.* Lane and Cloudy sat across from her on the picnic blanket.

"Well," Lane said, reaching to his back pocket and retrieving an old, black, weathered journal. Slowly, almost reluctantly, he handed it to her. "Here you go. I think it's best if you just start reading."

Gaia turned it over, examining it, running her green fingers over faded spots, stains, frayed corners. She flipped through the old paper which was warped and discolored on the long edge like an ancient accordion. Scribbled writing filled the pages. As she caught a few of the words while skimming through it, she realized it was about Godpappy and Cloudy's journey to find her. Gaia's hands trembled at a surge of excitement that collided with disbelief, and she squeezed the cover to steady herself.

"What is it?" she asked, even though she already knew. She just wanted to hear them say it in their own words.

"That's your story," Godpappy said. "Your birth story."

It was titled, *Mt. Kenya - April 2045*. Fifteen years ago.

Her skin buzzed. She quickly opened to the first page and began to read like a parched desert traveler drinking from a hose. Everything around her disappeared as she dove into this universe of words and story, unfolding in her mind like a videostream that paused momentarily each time she stumbled over one of Lane's indecipherable scribbles. She was only vaguely aware of gulls landing, screeching, and squabbling, and of her father kicking and swatting the birds away if they got too close.

In the narrative, Godpappy was sitting at a bar, slowly getting drunk on broo, hunched over a bowl of jellyfish chowder, talking into it like a madman. He was arguing with a voice in his head—a voice that had materialized a few days before, ordering him to go to Africa.

When Lane first heard the voice, he was frightened. The demand was so random and idiotic that he feared somebody had laced his food or drink with Croozer, and he was beginning his slow decline into oblivion. When he went to the clinic for a blood test, they didn't find any Croozer in his system. Yet the voice kept after him. His doctor was no help. She ruled out schizophrenia and other mental disorders, because Lane was lucid and high-functioning in every other way. He'd go out on his boat every morning, check the fish eggs he'd planted, move to another section of the artificial reef, pull on his wetsuit and diving gear, spend the next hour attaching more egg sacs to the reef, then head back to the office to meet with his boss, Maer Cadogan, and work on his report. He'd shop for food, have normal conversations with people, walk home, cook himself dinner, and perform every other function normally. But it was "that damned voice." It was relentless. He described it as sounding like "a man who'd gone Syncro, where the hormone treatments put a soft edge on a deep voice," but he also described the voice as "more thought than sound." Whatever it was, it was driving him to drink, talk into bowls of chowder, and on this particular afternoon at the bar, spray vomit all over bartender and owner Eddie McGee.

After Eddie threw Lane out onto the street, Lane wandered, drunk and aimless, in whatever direction his body was currently pointed. He swam through clumps of tourists who quickly moved clear of the giant man threatening to mow them down. He kept plodding along, following the road as it climbed and wove into the hills.

Turn left, the voice told him.

"No!" bellowed Lane. "Fuck you!"

Then the voice did something it hadn't done before. Rather than a simple demand, it began a conversation.

Look, it said. *You're pretty dense. So if you won't listen to me, maybe you'll listen to somebody else. You're running out of time.*

Lane stopped. This was new.

Turn left.

He looked left, but there was nowhere to go. Just a gentle hill of weeds and scrub oak.

"Running out of time for what?" he said out loud.

Turn left.

Lane sighed, then turned left.

He climbed the hill, which flattened out on top, and after a few more steps something caught his eye. It was a faded blue tarp tucked under a bush. Then he noticed a large cardboard box lying under a tree, and then saw other trash scattered about as if somebody had camped there and not cleaned up after themselves.

After a few more steps he started seeing bodies.

There was a body in the blue tarp, and there was a body under the cardboard box. Bodies lay under trees and bushes and more taps and makeshift lean-tos constructed sloppily out of weeds and tree branches.

In the journal, Lane never said the words "Croozer camp," but he didn't need to. Gaia knew exactly what this was: a place where people without hope went to trip out and slowly starve to death. The drug apparently gave one a feeling of bliss, which is why it was called the "Happy Death." The "HD."

Another pelican—or the same pelican—waddled over to her, dropped another rock fish in front of her, cocked its head, then pumped its wide wings and flew away. Gaia felt the wind from it and smelled its dusty feathers. Maer let out a happy shriek and reached in to grab the spiny-backed fish as its gills fanned open and its big mouth gulped at the useless air. In a house somewhere nearby, as an odd coincidence to what was happening in front of her, Gaia heard a woman with a southern accent saying, "Dejalo! Git that thing outta yer mouth!"

The afternoon sun striking the poppies, and the rustling of gulls, and the breeze drifting in off the unseen waves at the bluff's base, produced the smell of sweet, earthy plant stalks edged with brine.

Gaia turned her attention back to the journal.

The story took an interesting turn when Lane discovered Cloudy in the bodies—Cloudy, Lane's old college roommate. On Croozer! She couldn't believe it. Gaia looked up at Cloudy and was about to ask him something, but he was looking down and picking at the blanket, so she kept reading. She'd never get to the good parts if she kept stopping.

After Lane carried Cloudy home, he tied him to a bed and watched him writhe and scream for seven days as the Croozer left his system. When the Croozer hold finally broke and Cloudy was able to keep food down, Lane was getting worse. The voice was nagging him harder than ever, and it was making him physically sick. Unable to hide it from Cloudy any longer, he explained what was happening to him. That's when Cloudy finally convinced Lane to go to Africa. Just stop fighting it and go. As soon as Lane agreed, he felt better immediately, and the voice stopped nagging him. Mostly.

Next in the journal came more boring bits about getting ready for the trip, and a few more incidents regarding the voice, and Gaia found herself skimming.

"Blue," Lane said, and she looked up. "How's it going?"

"You guys just got on the water tanker in Louisiana, bound for Cameroon."

"Skip ahead a few pages. I forgot about that part. It's probably pretty boring. Cloudy just got sick a lot."

She looked over at Cloudy.

"You were really on Croozer?" she asked.

Cloudy smiled sadly. "Crazy, no? Don't worry about that now. I'll tell you more later. Keep going."

Gaia heard a hummingbird whir past, then heard a thud over at the windmill as another gull was caught by the spinning blades. She watched its odd, broken shape fall to the ground.

Lane had reached over and was leafing through pages in the journal.

"Here," he pointed. "Start reading here."

The section was titled simply "Day 7." They were in Nairobi, and they'd just hired a local man to guide them up Mt. Kenya. His name was Matthew, and Lane described him as "tall, taller than me, and taller than any African we'd seen so far. He was bone thin, all angles. At first, Cloudy and I thought Matthew was blind, because his eyes were milky with only a shadow of iris. But it turns out he could see perfectly well."

Then the eyes of the man in the hacking popped into Gaia's mind, and she felt cold all of a sudden. The eyes were milky like that, haunting, like a dead person walking the earth. Like a zombie. She wondered, hoped, that eyes like that were more common than she'd thought. Maybe it was a sign of malnutrition. But then she realized many people were malnourished in Junipero Bay, and she'd never seen eyes like that. Maybe it was common in Africa. She shuddered and brought her focus back to the journal.

Halfway up Mt. Kenya, Lane had to stop every five minutes to dry heave. He said it was due to "an excitement I couldn't contain, but not my own excitement. I could tell it was coming from somewhere else, someone else. From whoever the voice was. I was getting closer. But to what, I didn't know."

It was me, Gaia realized as goosebumps sizzled on her arms. *You were getting closer to me.*

Matthew, their guide, was getting angry. He kept telling Cloudy to take Lane back down the mountain, thinking Lane had altitude sickness. But when Lane dug in his heels and stubbornly insisted they keep going, Matthew said they were on their own and stormed off to hunt hyraxes among the boulders.

Strangely, Lane noted, his stomach calmed the moment Matthew was out of sight. Lane got to his feet, wiping his mouth with his shirtsleeve. (Gaia didn't understand why he'd bother to put details like that in the journal.)

Suddenly, something large swooped past their heads, and Lane and Cloudy nearly toppled over. A giant bird. "The wind from its wings was like a sonic boom," wrote Lane. "Its wingspan was massive, and it cocked its vulture head at us as it barreled past, then rose into the sky like an old B-52 bomber and joined four more vultures."

The birds soared up the mountain, and when they reached a higher ridge, they turned and began circling like a wheel turning in the sky, then slowly descended. Before they were out of sight the voice said to him, *Go. Now.*

Lane started running. He ran like a wild man, stumbling and falling and scrambling "until I thought my lungs would rip and my legs would seize."

When he crested the ridge, Lane stopped to catch his breath. Then froze. The ground sloped downward into a bowl that was shielded by rock walls. A light fog had formed, and the bright sun behind the walls caused the tops of them to glow, "sending diffused shards of light into the mist like the entrance to some heavenly portal."

Cloudy caught up to him. "What the hell *is* that?" he said.

Gaia shifted from sitting on her butt to her knees.

The vultures, which were half the height of a man, were standing on something. As Lane and Cloudy stepped closer, a breeze swirled the mist away and they could see more clearly.

"It's a glacier!" Lane said.

Sure enough, it was an oval-shaped glacier, maybe 20 yards long.

"Whoa," said Cloudy. "There haven't been any glaciers—anywhere—since we were kids. But what's that in the middle of it? What are those birds looking at?"

Gaia held her breath. Was this real? Was it really about her?

Lane and Cloudy stepped onto the glacier with a crunch, now only feet from the giant birds. But the birds didn't scatter. Then the one closest to them shuffled and clumsily stepped aside as if inviting the men to enter.

Cloudy gasped.

What the vultures surrounded was a large patch of the greenest grass. And on the grass, tiny pink and blue and white flowers sprouted everywhere. Wild little bushes grew heavy with berries of red, blue, and yellow. At the far end of the little garden, a tiny tree bore small orange fruit, and another was heavy with something that looked like small pomegranates. In the middle, a tomato plant sprouted fat, oblong fruit.

Next to the tomato plant, a thick, gnarled vine curled upwards, looping, then twisting back down, connecting with what at first looked like a long, oddly shaped, dark green melon. It had a dense, blue tuft of fuzz on one end of it, like a plop of hair.

Is that me? Gaia wondered with a shiver.

They knelt on the grass, crawling on their hands and knees, and the vultures croaked and ambled away to give them room. "The grass felt unusually warm," wrote Lane.

Then something moved. Slithered. Cloudy jumped back as two snakes, yellow and black striped, twisted and moved over the melon, which Lane realized was also moving. It had legs. And arms, and he realized the blue tuft really *was* hair!

Gaia unconsciously felt her blue hair. Her heart was hammering.

Lane crawled closer. As he did, one of the snakes hissed, but the two of them relented and slithered away.

"Oh my!" Cloudy said.

"It's a baby!" Lane said. "Holy shit, it's a baby!"

Language, said the voice.

Gaia's skin was burning with goosebumps.

The twisted, curled vine was attached to the baby's belly.

"It's a girl," said Cloudy. "It's a baby girl."

Both men stared at her. She gurgled and kicked like she was riding an invisible bicycle, and "when she opened her eyes," Lane wrote, "I thought I was looking into the eyes of God. Or some demon. There were no whites, but the colors changed from blue to black to green to purple as she grunted and kicked. She was the most beautiful, otherworldly thing I'd ever seen."

Gaia had to steady herself because she was spinning. It couldn't be real. And Godpappy's first thought of her was that she was beautiful. Her eyes still did that.

"Pick her up," said Cloudy, who had come to his senses first. Then the two argued back and forth about how to deal with the vine, finally agreeing that it was probably okay to cut it off like a normal umbilical cord. Cloudy moved to the other side of the baby girl to help steady the vine while Lane cut it with his big knife, which Lane described as "the most nerve-racking thing I've ever had to do." But he did it without cutting the baby.

Lane realized how tiny she was the moment he picked her up. She fit in his hand from her head to her butt. He was afraid he'd break her, and for a second he thought he did, because she started crying. But Cloudy told him she was probably hungry.

Gaia caught herself smiling. No, grinning widely. When she looked up at the two men who were in the story, they were watching her intently.

"Uncle Cloudy seemed a lot more paternal, than you did, Godpappy," she said.

Lane smiled. "That's because he was. I was in complete shock. The only time in my life I've been in greater shock, well, that was just a few minutes ago, when you grew all these poppies." He kicked at a gull who was trying to go after a piece of cheese on the blanket.

"You should have seen us trying to feed you," Cloudy said. "I know it's probably in the journal, but boy, what a comedy that was."

"How *did* you feed me?" asked Gaia. "I'm sure you didn't have a bottle since you didn't know you were going to find a baby. And what was at the other end of that vine? My umbilical cord?"

Lane froze. "Damn!" he said. "I just realized we never checked."

"What do you mean you never checked?"

"You'd started howling up a real squall, something awful. So we were a little distracted. And by the time we had you settled in my backpack, all the grass, the flowers, the bushes, the vine, shriveled and blew away before our eyes like they were never there."

"Really?" She couldn't believe it. "But what about the piece of vine Mom showed me earlier today?"

"That fell off you later," Cloudy said, "after we got you home."

"So," Gaia started, then paused. "I didn't have a mother. Or a father." But when she saw her mom look down, a pang of guilt made her correct herself. "I mean, birth parents."

It seemed to help. Maer glanced back up at her and winked, but she looked sad, or uneasy. Jack looked off out to sea pensively. Selene was sitting cross-legged back behind their parents seeming wilted with her chin resting in her hands. Gaia felt the urge to go comfort her sister, but the urge wasn't strong enough for her to leave the story she'd been needing to hear her whole life.

Godpappy twisted his mouth up. "I wouldn't say you didn't have birth parents. Something put you there, or grew you. That voice I was hearing was somebody. And they left that food for you."

Gaia considered all this, still not able to wrap her mind to it. Where did she come from? It was a mystery she realized might never be solved, and she wasn't sure how to feel about that.

"Wait, what food?" she asked. "You said *they* left me food. What did you feed me?"

"I had some powdered milk," Cloudy said. "We mixed it with tea, because that's all the liquid we had, and we tried to feed it to you through a bandana. Tried to make you suck on it." He laughed. "But you just got madder and madder, so mad you were turning purple, and no sound came out when you cried. You were so distraught you passed right out and didn't wake up until we were halfway down the mountain. Then you woke up and started bawling again. You were really hungry."

Gaia was still confused. "But you said they'd left me food. What food?"

"Oh yeah," said Cloudy. "I was getting to that. Pretty much the tomatoes, the bullet-shaped tomatoes growing next to you. On a lark I gathered a bunch of them up and brought them along, just in case. Smartest decision I ever made."

"Why?" she asked.

Now Godpappy jumped in. "Well, when you started crying again, we were at a total loss. We'd stopped and set the packs down to try feeding you powdered milk tea again. That's when the monkey came."

"The monkey?"

"A damned monkey came out of the trees and dove right into Cloudy's pack. I tried to shoo it, but it didn't budge. It just grabbed one of the tomatoes."

"What happened?" Gaia leaned forward to hear, even though she could have heard Godpappy from literally a mile away.

"That monkey jumped over to me and dropped that tomato right on top of you, then scampered to the edge of the trail to watch. You'd really started coming unglued again, and I started putting two and two together. 'Why were those tomatoes growing next to you?' I wondered. So I bit off the tip of it. And when I did, I nearly dropped you, because what came out of it was sweet, sweet beyond anything I'd ever tasted. Like some new kind of fruit. So I gave it to you. The fruit was gooey and poured right out of the skin. Ten minutes later you'd gone through four more. Then you farted and fell asleep for a very long time."

Gaia tried to picture the scene. The monkey. She tried digging far back into her mind for some spark of memory, but nothing came.

Maer spoke up. "Now you know why you love tomato juice so much."

It was true. She loved tomato juice more than anything in the world.

But something had come over Lane.

"What's wrong, Godpappy? You look like somebody just died."

Lane drew a deep breath. "That thing you said earlier, about being hacked through your D.I. chip."

The memory of it flew back into like a dark poison. "What about it? What does that have to do with this story?"

Lane and Cloudy exchanged a look, then Lane turned back to Gaia. "You said the man in the vision had eyes that were white and dead looking."

"Yes," she said slowly, trying to connect the dots. Then a thought, one that had remained in her subconscious, bubbled up. In the journal, Godpappy had described their mountain guide's eyes the same way. "They sound like the eyes of your guide. That Matthew."

Lane nodded. "They do. There's another part of the story I didn't put in the journal, a part that Cloudy and I have never told anyone." He glanced at Cloudy.

"What?" Jack jumped in, suddenly in the all-business military mode Gaia knew so well. "What is it?"

"Matthew tried to take you from us, and he almost succeeded. Right up there on the mountain."

"What?" Maer and Jack said in unison. Maer looked angry.

"Apparently," Cloudy said, rubbing his neck, "he got me with one of his darts. I don't remember any of it because I was unconscious."

"He tried it on me, too," Lane said. "It turned into a struggle, and in the end I left him for dead. I hit him in the head pretty hard."

"Lane, why didn't you tell us this before?" Maer said.

"Admit to you that I'd killed a man? What would you have done with that information?"

"I—" Maer began, then stopped, thinking about it.

"It just would have been good to know," Jack said, "to have all the details when we took her in, is all."

That stabbed Gaia. Was her adoption conditional? Would they not have taken her had they known? But Maer quickly jumped in.

"It wouldn't have made one single difference to us, Baby."

"No," Jack stammered, addressing Gaia. "That's not what I meant, Sweetie. Not at all."

"You need to know we chose you," Maer said, "because we fell in love with you."

Gaia had to smile. Seeing her parents tripping over themselves to reassure her was all she needed.

"But this new intel sure seems relevant," Jack said. He turned to Gaia. "You really think you got hacked?"

Gaia nodded. She didn't want to be reminded, and now she was worried that their mountain guide and the hacking might somehow be related.

Jacked turned to Lane. "And that this Matthew guy, you think he might have something to do with it, or is it all just coincidence?"

"He's dead as far as I know," Lane said. "And if Gaia says she was hacked, I believe her. What's got me uneasy, though, is that I stopped believing in coincidence a long time back. Fifteen years ago."

-14-

The Gate of the World

"Gaia," said her dad, setting a hand on her leg. "Can you tell us more about what happened to you yesterday?"

Gaia sighed and gazed around the bluff at the surreal sea of crimson. She didn't want to think about the hacking, but she was the one who'd blurted it out, and the talk of Matthew the mountain guide had unnerved her, especially the description of his eyes. So she recounted what had happened, from first hearing, "Siafu, she comes," to the old VW van sputtering away, to the Latino men in the lowrider trying to talk to her, even the part about meeting Lohi with his necklace of seagulls. Anything could be relevant.

"I'll go talk to some folks in the neighborhood," Cloudy said after she'd finished. "Maybe they can tell us more about who was in that van. Sounds like those may be our guys."

"I'll run the name 'Siafu,'" Jack said. "I'll also have one of my guys look at the Net traffic in that area."

All Maer could do was shake her head and say, "This is too much. It's all too much."

Gaia noticed Selene again. She was still sitting among the poppies outside the gazebo, so Gaia went and sat next to her.

"I'm sorry," said Gaia.

Selene looked up at her. Gaia couldn't read her expression. "For what?"

"For being an 'itch and stomping on your story. You weren't really thinking about taking Croozer, were you?"

Selene was quiet for a moment. She looked down and brushed her hand over one of the poppies.

"It doesn't matter," she said. "Everything's different now."

"Is it?" Gaia asked, meaning whether Selene felt differently inside.

Then Selene did the most wonderful thing. She looked at Gaia and crossed her eyes and stuck her tongue out the side of her mouth and said, "You're questioning whether or not everything's different now? Good. At least you're still stupid. My special needs little sister."

Sister. That was all Gaia needed to hear. She'd just heard the most incredible stories about herself, which included the fact that she had no real mother or father. But she did have a family, she realized, and Selene still called her 'sister." Gaia wrapped Selene into a hug, and they both cried a little until Selene playfully pushed Gaia away, saying, "Now get the fuck away from me. People will talk."

A few minutes later, Maer came over to Gaia.

"Listen, Sweetie. You've had, well, quite a day, to put a euphemistic spin on it. What do you want to do now?"

Gaia thought about that. It was an excellent question. What now?

"Do you want to go home?"

"No," Gaia said.

"Then what?"

She ran her fingers through the poppies. The sun was warming them, and the aroma of earth and petals and green stems floated up into her brain and settled behind her eyes, then drifted down into the rest of her.

"I want to try growing again," she said.

"Do you?"

"Wouldn't you? I just don't know where to go and do it."

"If you're serious, I know a place."

"Where?" Gaia was now starting to second-guess herself. What if the poppies were a one-time thing? What if she couldn't do it again? Or if she could, what was the point of growing poppies everywhere?

"Remember Liesl?" Maer asked.

"Crazy Liesl? From the farmers market? The one who cusses all the time?"

"Crazy Liesl, yes. Her community farm is just a few miles away, and it's got the blight. Everything's dead."

Gaia didn't voice her doubts.

"Okay."

"You sure? You don't sound so sure."

Gaia stood up. "Let's go. I want to."

In a few minutes they had everything packed up. The Cadogans piled into their old truck with Gaia in the front seat, and Cloudy and Lane followed them in Cloudy's squad car.

When they were close to the guard booth, Maer gunned the motor and plowed the truck through the exit gate, snapping it like she'd done on the entrance side. Maer let out a whoop and held her middle finger high out the window. The scary guard hollered after them from the booth. Cloudy flipped on his siren and lights, pretending to chase Maer as they made a hard left onto the old coastal road.

"Maer," Jack said, still shaking his head at his scofflaw wife, "are you sure about this?"

Gaia's mind went to the farm, and the responsibility of it suddenly washed over her. It felt heavy, much too heavy. What if she couldn't help? What if she stuck her fingers in the ground and grew a field of useless poppies, or worse, nothing at all?

"Tell you what," Maer glanced at her, seeming to know Gaia's thoughts. "If you truly don't think you can help, say the word and I'll turn around right now. I'll stop the truck, and Cloudy and Godpappy will stop behind us, and we can all go back home. But if you want to find out who you really are, and what you're capable of doing, then we should do this. It's more important than any stories we can tell you. From today on you'll be writing your own story, one that the rest of us have no clue about."

Silence filled the truck as they waited for Gaia to answer. She examined the green of her hands, her fingers intertwining like vines. She heard the crunch of Cloudy's tires on the road close behind them, though she heard neither Cloudy nor Godpappy speaking. Maybe they were as flustered as she was. Then again, maybe they weren't. Like her family, or her parents at least, Lane and Cloudy had a head start on knowing who she was.

The cars passed a row of trashed, abandoned stucco bungalows freckled with bits of their former reds, blues, and greens, remnants of life that the previous hurricane had failed to fully wash away. A black shirt flapped in the wind from a sagging clothesline like a broken sail.

Jack spoke up. "Maer, you're worried about your fish growing project getting leaked. What about Gaia? Assuming she does something miraculous, how do you keep *her* a secret if everyone at the farm sees what she does?"

"That's your specialty, my dear," Maer said to Jack. "We get her to the base right afterwards if anything big happens."

The base? Why not home? This made Gaia nervous realizing her dad was right. How would other people react? What if one of them posted a videostream on the Net?

Her dad reached over the seat and grabbed Gaia's hand, kissing the back of it, holding his stubbly cheek against it for a few long moments. "I'm here for you always, no matter what. This is a lot to take in in so quickly. We'll all stick with you. But we can stop this truck right now and go home if you want."

She almost said yes, turn the truck around. But the desire to grow things was overwhelming. The *Earth Mother*? Her mom's description of it returned: The Earth Mother had appeared throughout history—even pre-history—again and again, but she had no recollection of that. How was it possible she'd been here countless times throughout the millennia and had no memory of it? Maybe different people took turns being the Earth Mother.

"It's okay, guys," she said finally. "I really want to."

Gaia turned around in her seat and stroked Selene's hair. Her big sister looked so small burrowed into their father's chest, like a balled-up jellyfish. Selene looked back at her with another expression Gaia couldn't read.

The balled-up jellyfish made Gaia think of Liesl, the one whose farm they were going to see, the feisty lady at the farmers' market who sold pickled catfish in jars. Liesl did seem batty. Her clothes went out of their way to clash, she laughed and swore a lot, and she gave off a youthful vibe that transcended her gray hair and thin, age-spotted face. The words "eccentrically obnoxious" came to mind, along with the image of Liesl as a locust flipping and snapping crazily through the air, landing only at the call of whimsy. If she really did have a community farm, Gaia couldn't imagine the woman being responsible for feeding countless families. Yet she knew her mom was close with Liesl, and Maer never got close to people unless they had what she called "unique substance."

Maer reached over to curl Gaia's hair behind a giant ear, and Gaia let her. She still felt self-conscious about her ears, and she wondered what purpose they could possibly serve the Earth Mother. But at least she wasn't a Croozer baby—or worse, a Syncro baby.

Gaia reached down and poked the power button on the receiver, but when she asked her mom to patch in some news, Maer looked at her like Gaia had grown a horn out of her forehead. "Since *when* do you listen to the news?"

"I always listen to the news," Gaia lied. She felt the urge to listen now, because the whole world was suddenly her concern, and she wanted to hear what was going on out there.

Selene slowly pushed off her dad and looked out her window, morosely wiping her eyes, watching the stark, dusty landscape of dying eucalyptus, dirt, and sad bungalows fall behind as the truck turned east and headed up into the hills. Jack let out another big sigh that flapped his lips, more proof that her tough Army Colonel dad was struggling with his thoughts.

The news came out of the old truck speakers from Maer's Telepath. There was a report about U.S. President Liz Efrain holding discussions with Chinese Premier Da Diao about how to combat the domestic terrorist group Native Americans Against America, phonetically known as 'Naaa.'" The Chinese were clearly angry about the terrorist group shooting down their water jet in sovereign Chinese airspace in Nebraska, and President Efrain said the U.S. was doing its best against the stealthy and dangerous Chief Last Coyote. Premier Diao threatened more land confiscations in all 49 states in the U.S. if progress wasn't made to stop the terrorist group.

Gaia thought of her friend Maya's farm, the one they'd driven past earlier that was now growing Chinese hemp. It was also weird hearing "49 states," since it had been only a few years since Texas had seceded. What could Gaia possibly do to help with terrorism and land grabbing? Nothing, clearly. The world was a huge, complicated mess.

The next news story was about a kid not much older than Selene, named Ouri Narcissus, who'd made his fortune inventing something called "cloud tubes" that sucked moisture from the air for small-scale water generation. Rumor had it that Ouri, an eccentric kid, had started a new city in Colorado called Vega that was rumored to be populated almost entirely of Syncros. It sounded like a scary place, and neither Gaia nor anyone she knew had ever seen a cloud tube. But it did hold out the promise of fresh water that didn't need to be treated for Copropha-G, the news anchor said. That was The Worm. Again, there was nothing obvious that Gaia could do about any of this as the Earth Mother. The Narcissus kid was already helping to solve the water problem.

Next was a replay of President Efrain's interview from earlier that morning, where she talked about the fish growing project, which made Maer seethe.

"Hell, why don't they just give the Chinese my GPS digits while they're at it, so they can torture me and steal it?" she spat.

That gave Gaia the chills, thinking again about the possibility of something happening to her mom because of the fish technology. What if Gaia were really able to do something miraculous at Liesl's farm? Wouldn't the Chinese then want *her*?

"GPS?" Jack said, chuckling. "Hey Old School, maybe because there are no more satellites up there to *enable* GPS."

Next came this:

> NEWS ANCHOR: "Meanwhile, in California news, officials confirm that the dolphin spotted swimming off the coast of San Diego last week was indeed a hoax, as Anthony Chacon reports from Chula Vista—"

"Okay, turn it off," Gaia said. "It's just making my head spin."

Between thoughts of abduction and getting closer to the place where she would try to find out what else she could do, Gaia felt queasy.

"Good choice," Maer said, and the speakers went silent, leaving the sound of popping and grinding tires on the dirt road.

The truck lurched left onto a steep, rutted road. Gaia turned to glance back at Cloudy's squad car, which was being consumed by dust. With Uncle Cloudy, a deputy sheriff, and her well-connected military father, she felt safe. At that thought the truck came to a skidding stop, and she had to brace herself against the dashboard. They'd reached a wide metal gate sporting a large triangular sign.

On it were crudely painted cartoon breasts and stick-person arms reaching for the sky. Gaia heard the hum of the electric current pulsating through the gate.

"What's this?" Gaia's heart was racing from stopping so quickly. "Military zone?"

Maer chuckled and shook her head. "It's an old hobo symbol, not military—modified a bit with the boobs. Means woman with a gun."

"Liesl?"

"Liesl." Maer punched the screen on the dashboard again. "Hey Liesl, it's us."

After a minute, the face of an older woman appeared. "Well hello there, Us," her voice crackled. "Ain't got a gate opener, so Old Ned is on his way down to open 'er up for ya. Mind the dogs."

They sat for a few moments looking past the gate for this Old Ned person to appear. Very little grew in that place, only a hillside of dirt on their left sprouting random patches of dry, yellow weeds, and a few dead oak and eucalyptus trees. On their right, the ground fell from the road into a steep bank that fed into a gentle, dropping gully sprouting no weeds at all. Just hard, cracked earth. Further down the gully Gaia saw the skeletons of two oak trees. She rolled the window down and closed her eyes. The cool, dusty air hinted at the coming evening and sunset.

Gaia took in the dead ground, resisting the urge to jump out and plunge her fingers into it. She rubbed the back of her neck where her diagnostic implant was supposed to be but was apparently no longer. Had her body somehow dissolved it? Had the hacking fried it?

The vision from the hacking flickered to life in her mind again, triggered by the apocalyptic landscape—the man with charcoal skin, the intensity of the flames engulfing him, the desperation in his reaching for her. Desperation in everything—except his eyes. They haunted her more than anything else. There was something otherworldly, almost demonic about those eyes.

His cold, milky, dead eyes. Was there any chance it was the same man who guided Godpappy and Cloudy up the mountain, then tried to take her? The one Godpappy assumed was dead? And *why* did he try to take her? It was an obvious question she'd forgotten to ask. She decided to ask Godpappy when they got out of the vehicles.

The electric humming stopped abruptly, and from nowhere two big owls suddenly swooped in and alighted on the gate, adjusted their wings, and blinked at the truck.

"Holy shit!" said Selene.

"Whoa!" Gaia heard Cloudy say in the car behind them. "Lane, look! Owls! Isn't that supposed to be good luck?"

"Yeah, I guess if you were Greek. If you were Roman, hearing an owl usually meant your army was going to get slaughtered. Beautiful birds, either way."

Gaia watched the owls and thought about good luck and bad luck sitting on either side of this gate, which to her seemed like the entrance to the world itself—the uncharted world she was about to enter as the Earth Mother. She wondered whether or not her fate were even up to her.

Then Gaia heard footsteps coming from her right. Somebody with a limp was coming, and Gaia knew she'd be the only one to hear it. A minute later the figure of a stooped, white-haired black gentleman in a worn mustard coat slowly hobbled up the side gully with a cane. When he reached the steep bank, he ascended one slow foot at a time on what must have been steps carved into the dirt, and when he finally reached the road he glanced up only long enough to take in Cloudy's squad car. Crossing in front of the squad car, he scuffled up alongside the truck, past the driver's-side window. On seeing him, the owls paced nervously, then unfurled their wide wings and pumped back into the sky.

There goes my luck, good and bad, thought Gaia. *Guess my fate really is up to me.*

The old man paid no attention to the owls. When he reached the gate, he pressed his palm onto a small pad beside it, which started the gate sliding open over the bank he'd climbed up.

Keeping his head bowed, he motioned for the cars to enter. Gaia watched him as they passed. She noticed that if he weren't stooped over he'd be quite tall.

Then, in the brief moment when Maer's side window framed the man's head, he glanced up and looked squarely at Gaia, then quickly dropped his gaze when he saw that Gaia was looking back at him.

But it was too late. In that fraction of a second, Gaia had seen Old Ned's eyes. His cold, milky, dead eyes. Just like the boy in the hacking. Just like Matthew the mountain guide.

-15-
Beasts

G aia was still in shock as Maer steered the truck through the gate and up an incline. Gaia looked in the side-view mirror, both needing to see Old Ned and not wanting to see Old Ned. Behind Cloudy's squad car she caught a glimpse of the old man's white hair and mustard coat disappear the way he'd come down the gully.

"Are you okay, Baby?" her mom asked.

Gaia realized her hands were shaking, so she interlaced her fingers and squeezed to fight the burn her body remembered from the hacking. Was it him? She wasn't sure it could be because the man in the hacked vision had been young. The eyes—those ghostly eyes—were identical. Old Ned could be the grandfather of the young man reaching through the fire in her hacked vision.

"I'm fine," she lied again, her heart pounding.

Those eyes. The hacking man's eyes. Old Ned's eyes. She couldn't shake them. Lifeless, like some demon. Gaia tensed her arms and squeezed her hands together tighter and pressed her feet into the truck floor to fight the shiver coming on.

"You cold?" her dad asked from the back seat, but Gaia just shook her head.

"What's up with that Old Ned guy?" Selene asked quietly. "You see his eyes? You think he was blind? They're just like what you guys were talking about."

She noticed it, too.

"He's not blind," Maer said. "Not completely, anyway. He might be mute. I've only seen him a few times, and he never says a word."

"Where? Where have you seen him?" Gaia asked.

"Farmers market mostly. Here at Liesl's a couple weekends ago. Why? And what's the matter with you? You've gone all frigid and quivery all of a sudden."

Selene launched a soft chortle. "Because he's hella creepy, that's why."

Gaia felt her mom's eyes on her, watching, analyzing. Her heart was racing, and she pushed her feet harder into the floorboard, feeling like a bug about to be dissected. Hacked and dissected.

"Why didn't you tell me about what happened right when you got home, Baby? If you really were hacked, it's serious. That's not the kind of thing you keep to yourself. Just so you know, I'm going to find and kill whoever did that to you. You still spooked by that?"

Gaia nodded. "That old guy's eyes reminded me of it, that's all. It's just weird that we were just talking about those kind of eyes, and now this guy has them."

"Don't worry. Old Ned's been with Liesl for as long as I've known her. It's just a coincidence."

"Godpappy doesn't believe in coincidence," Gaia said. "How long have you known Liesl?"

"Oh, I think I met her around the time you came to us."

"Gee, that's reassuring. Was Old Ned always like that?"

"Far as I remember. But I'm sure he was with her even before that." Maer looked at Gaia. "Baby, you're safe. You're with us. We'll always be by your side."

"Except when you're not," Selene criticized from the back seat, which got a "Shut it!" in unison from their parents.

The whole exchange didn't make Gaia feel any better, even though she felt Old Ned's eyes probably were a coincidence. They had to be. He was really old.

When they crested the hill, the ground dropped into a wide, flat plateau backed by rolling, dry central coast hills that softened and melted into the gray distance like a painting. At that moment, her fear thawed a little at the thought that no matter what happened, things would be okay, and her family would be there for her.

Terror one minute and hope the next, she thought. *If this is what getting your period does, I don't want it.*

The first thing Gaia noticed was white wind turbine that seemed to sit on top of an earthen shoe box of a house. The turbine looked like a massive helicopter had plunged into the ground with its tail sticking straight up and its propeller still slowly cutting through the air.

The old house had only a weathered blue door with a keyhole window in the adobe walls on each side, and two big mutts rounded the corner of the house to greet them. One was muscled, cocoa brown, and the other was black, lanky, and furry with white markings, barking and snarling. They slid between the two vehicles baring their teeth. Then a fuzzy, black, three-legged Dachshund caught up with the other two, barking at the truck, then hop-turning to bark at the squad car, then back at the truck. The screen door to the house opened a crack, and a loud whistle that hurt Gaia's ears made the dogs back up a few steps, but they kept at their violent barking.

"Just wait a sec while she calls them in," Maer said. "Duke's a mean ol' bitch that'll tear your leg off."

"Stupid dogs," Selene said. "You've got serious issues, dogs! They're gonna tear through the doors and eat us. Pop, can I borrow your gun?"

"Um, yeah. You? With a gun? That's gonna happen," Jack said.

Liesl peeked out from the blue door. Her skeletal face was drawn even tighter by a severe gray ponytail. She whistled again, then yelled, "Get in here!"

Mindlessly, as if the woman's command was meant for her, Gaia opened her door and stepped out. She'd still been deep in her own head and didn't realize her mistake until she heard her mom shout, "Gaia, wait!"

But it was too late. The truck door had already closed behind her, and the dogs were only a few steps away.

"Duke, no!" The woman yelled. Gaia stood shocked and frozen. The brown, thick dog inched closer, snarling, tight as a spring about to snap, froth building along its lips. Gaia felt a vibration in its deep growl that nobody else would have heard, which seemed to drip down through her spine. She focused on the dog's gleaming white fangs and wondered where it would sink its teeth into her first.

In her periphery, Gaia saw the woman slide quickly out the door, but she wouldn't get there in time. The dog was just about to spring, and the other looked ready to join in.

But then something odd happened. The brown dog melted into a whine and lowered its head, tucked its tail, and rolled over onto its back at Gaia's feet. The other dogs wagged their tails and started licking Gaia's pants.

"Holster that weapon, Deputy!" Liesl shouted. She'd somehow made it around the truck and come up behind Gaia, alongside Jack, who was already standing beside Gaia. From the squad car window, Cloudy was pointing his pistol at the brown dog, which still lay on its back at Gaia's feet wagging her tail like a windshield wiper, her tongue lolling out the side of her mouth.

"I didn't shoot her, Leece," Cloudy said.

"No, and you wouldn't have, either," said Liesl.

"I would have if I'd needed to, I reckon."

"Ain't got it in you to do something as manly as killin' a dog, Deputy," she said, casually spitting on the ground.

He withdrew his pistol and stepped out of the car. Gaia also doubted that Cloudy would have shot the dog. He was so mild and gentle that she couldn't imagine him hurting anything even though he had to deal with violence every day like the fight at the land grabber bus. She'd always thought it odd that Cloudy was in law enforcement. But Liesl's comment carried a venom that Gaia didn't understand.

"Leave it, both of you. Not here, not now," Jack said, kneeling down to rub the brown dog's belly. "Looks like you've got an admirer," he smiled up at Gaia.

"It wasn't me who confiscated your goats, Leece," Cloudy said.

"Cops is cops," Liesl said coldly. "But it's more about that unnatural thing you did to yourself—"

"Whoa, whoa!" Maer hollered. "Leece, enough!"

Cloudy looked down. She'd clearly stung him, and he leaned back against the squad car with his hands in his pockets and begin scraping the edge of his boot sole in the dirt.

"Leave him alone!" Gaia snapped before she had time to think. Nobody was going to talk to Uncle Cloudy that way. Gaia braced for an argument, but her command drew only a curious, almost amused glance from Liesl, who then addressed Maer.

"She doesn't know, does she."

"Leece," said Maer with obvious frustration, "a word with you. In the house."

But Liesl didn't respond. Instead, she held Gaia by the shoulders and locked eyes with her. Gaia tried to pull away, but Liesl's grip was too firm, which made Gaia angrier.

"Incredible," Liesl whispered, her breath lined with garlic. "I ain't never seen 'em up close like this before." She paused. "What is it you've done, girl? Why did your mama bring you to me?"

Gaia pulled away again, and Liesl let her go this time. Not wanting to seem intimidated, Gaia asked, "Why is your dog's name Duke?"

Liesl smiled. "I see you got some of your mama's piss." Then her scowl came back. "I like the name Duke. From an old acting hero name-a John Wayne."

"But your dog's a girl."

Liesl's eyes narrowed and she tilted her head, then glanced down at Duke who was still on her back pawing at Gaia's legs for attention, competing with the other two dogs. "Well shee-yit. Take a look at that. I'll be damned!"

Then Liesl spun away. Everything the woman did seemed abrupt. "Me an' Maer are goin' through the house," she called over her shoulder. "Meet the resta y'all out back. And take my useless mutts with ya." She stopped again and turned, tilting her gaze at Gaia, and looked down at the dogs, which were attending to Gaia as if she were slathered in food. "Unbelievable," was all she said before turning and disappearing into the house. Maer smiled and winked at Gaia before following Liesl through the blue door.

The dogs had stopped licking her and were now curled at the base of her legs like burlap around the roots of a young tree. For a few moments there was stillness, and a stroke of wind brushed her with the fragrance of dust and dry, warm eucalyptus leaves. In the distance, maybe a quarter mile away, she heard the thumps and scrapes and footsteps of people working the earth. Only one voice moved among the sounds, and it was singing a gospel-style hymn.

"*...when we've been here ten thousand years, bright shining as the sun—we've no less days to sing God's praise, than when we've first begun. Amazing grace, how sweet the sound—that saved a wretch like me. I once was lost but now am found—was blind, but now I see.*"

The voice ceased. Ten thousand years echoed in her mind. She remembered her mom talking about old mythology, saying that the goddess Gaia had kept returning to Earth for millennia. *Have I been here before? That long ago? "Was blind but now I see."* The song lyrics drifted through her mind. Was Old Ned blind? No, he'd easily navigated his way around the trucks to open the gate for them. And he'd looked at her. There was recognition.

"Come on, Blueberry," Godpappy said, yanking her out of her daydream and reaching his hand out to her. Her dad, Selene, and Cloudy were already walking around the side of the house. When she took Godpappy's hand, she felt how massive and calloused it was, and then realized she'd never really held his hand before. It struck her as weird, because he was her godfather, after all. Maybe being her teacher as well meant that he had to keep a certain distance. But even when he came over to the house for dinner he never showed her that kind of overt affection. There was always a kind of chasm between her and Godpappy that she couldn't explain. Even Cloudy gave her hugs. But Godpappy never did. Maybe it was because of who she really was. Maybe his behavior wasn't distance as much as it was some type of reverence. If so, she didn't like it. After what she'd just read in the journal, Gaia felt a closeness to Godpappy that transcended even the familial, and distance was completely wrong. She suddenly threw herself into his chest and wrapped her arms around him.

"Thank you, Godpappy," she said.

He stopped and held his arms up in the air as if he didn't know what to do.

"You need to hug me back now."

His big arms settled awkwardly around her, and after a moment he stroked her head. Gaia felt the slow thump of his heart.

"I haven't held you like this," he said, "not since you were a baby."

"Why?" she asked, not letting go of him.

"Not sure, exactly," he said after a long pause. "Maybe, somehow, I didn't want to get too attached. It always felt like you were on loan to me."

"What do you mean?" she said, letting go of him so she could see his face.

"Well, you weren't mine when I found you, and then I had to turn around and give you away to your folks, to your sister. You needed a family. I guess I didn't want to interfere with that."

"But why? You're the one who found me. You're the one who was chosen to come get me by those voices. Don't you think that means something? If you really look at it, I'm more related to you than to anyone else."

"Huh," he said, curling his lower lip. "I guess I never thought about it that way."

"Can you promise me something?"

"No," he said flatly, and she punched him in the gut.

"I'm serious, Godpappy. No matter who I am, no matter who you think I am, I need you to be normal with me, to think of me like a regular kid who needs love and help. I don't care if you're worried about losing me, and it doesn't matter who I am. All I know is I'm scared, and it's just going to make things worse if you hang back."

Lane reached down and lifted her up under her armpits and pulled her into a full bear hug. Her feet dangled, and she closed her eyes and grinned. The dogs started barking and jumping on them.

"How's that," he groaned, squeezing her harder. "Nobody calls me selfish and gets away with it. Not even little blue-headed shits like you!"

He dropped her to her feet and grabbed her hand again. Gaia was all grins.

"Thank you for saying that," he said, walking with her and shoving dogs out of the way with his boot. "When did you get so grown up?"

"I'm not going to grow up," she said. "Ever."

"Attagirl."

The mutts followed them around the side of the house giving her little space to walk. The two big ones pressed against her legs while the three-legged dachshund scampered just in front of them, darting left and right, back and forth like a metronome.

As they rounded the side of the house, the land opened into a wide, barren field freckled with patches of purple-green weeds. To their left, the field dropped off into a slope that gave Gaia a grand view of the undulating brown hills that eventually slid into the unseen ocean beyond. The dogs' ears perked up and all three suddenly bolted and disappeared over the slope's edge, growling at something, and Gaia could walk freely again. Jack and Selene had wandered over to the far end of the field and sat at the base of the giant windmill that Gaia had seen from the driveway.

Lane walked Gaia into the middle of the field where Cloudy was standing. The purple weeds, which formed a motley carpet on the hard dirt, smelled faintly of onions. Off behind a line of eucalyptus trees opposite the slope, presumably the direction of the farm, the ting of metal on metal rang out and a man cursed.

Gaia heard Liesl snap inside the house. "Maer, godsakes, why are you whispering? Speak up like you got a pair! Whadda you mean keep my voice down? She can't hear us. She's outside."

The sound of ferocious barking and snarling drifted up from somewhere down the slope.

"What the devil are those dogs barking at now. Dammit, I am in no mood for this." Liesl's gruff voice crashed ahead of her out the back door of the house. She pushed forward like an impatient breeze, a shotgun protruding from the crook of her arm that was hinged open to eat the shells she fed it from a side pocket of her overalls. "Bad timing. I'll be right back, kids."

"What is it, Leece?" Maer followed in Liesl's wake, scanning this way and that for whatever trouble Liesl might be chasing as the old wooden screen door slapped shut behind them.

"Nothin'. Just an unwelcome visitor. Prolly that Lohi kid again trying to lighten my paddy of catfish. You all stay put."

-16-
Where Hope Lies

Across the field under the big windmill, Gaia heard her dad talking to Selene, following up on her Croozer outburst.

"Godpappy," she said, "did all that really happen, all that stuff you wrote in the journal?" He and Cloudy watched her intently. Even her mom said nothing as she walked up.

Gaia couldn't read their mood; maybe sad or concerned. Or something else. The breeze tousled her blue hair across her face, and she moved it back behind her giant green ear. The sun had dropped to the top of the western hills, and she shivered. Cloudy stripped off his blue sheriff's coat and draped it over her shoulders. She was too tangled in thought to even thank him.

"Yes Blueberry," Lane answered. "It certainly did happen."

"Why did that Matthew guy try to take me from you?"

She pictured the Mt. Kenya scene, the little garden of grass and flowers and bushes—and the vine. Then it all withered and blew away, which reminded her of the grass she killed on the soccer pitch, the growing wake of brown death spreading everywhere she stepped. Was it only that morning?

"You got me there," Lane said. "I didn't stop and ask him. I was too busy trying to get him off me."

POW! A gunshot erupted, piercing Gaia's ears, and Cloudy was suddenly on his feet with his pistol drawn, jogging to where the edge of the field dropped off and disappeared.

"Stay put," Jack ordered from across the field, pointing a finger at Gaia and jogging over to join Cloudy. Selene followed him.

"Lohi!" Gaia heard Liesl shout. "Hele! Go on! Leave it!"

The dogs were barking furiously. Judging by the sound, they must have been a quarter mile down the hill. Lohi. Was it the same kid she'd met the day before? The deformed kid with the dead seagulls draped over his neck who wanted to trade for fish? "Thor thish?" He'd stared at Gaia so matter-of-factly.

Gaia ignored her father's order and walked to the edge of the slope next to Selene.

Gaia caught her breath at the unexpected sight. A giant, watery staircase sparkling in the sunlight. A terraced hillside with grassy edges spread far to the left and right, curving with the contour of the hill. Each giant step of terrace, which stuck out maybe 10 feet before dropping to the next step, looked like a mirror sprouting stubbly grass.

The dogs were gathered at the bottom, which was bordered by a grove of sycamore trees. They barked at something moving in the water. Leveling her gun, Liesl stepped in front of the dogs, and Gaia heard her say, firmly but calmly to the docs, "Hold." Then, "Don't make me fill your butt fulla salt again, kid."

A short, dark boy with half an arm cautiously pulled himself out of the water, looking like he wanted to bolt but wary of the snarling dogs. In his one hand he held the flapping gray bulk of a fish, which he let slip from his hand and splash back into the water. Lohi stayed crouching as he slowly backed away from Liesl and the dogs, then quickly turned and trotted away, looking back over his shoulder every few strides. It was the same boy, though Gaia couldn't see his melted face. But Gaia suspected Lohi wasn't the least bit afraid at that moment. It was just another scene played out in his persistent search for food. Gaia wondered if she could ever be that tough, be that matter-of-fact walking the narrow rail between living and dying. *Wha ha'n da you?* he'd asked her with that long necklace of dead seagulls. *I'm the Earth Mother*, she now said, redoing the conversation in her mind. And the Lohi in this new scene just stared back at her, uncomprehending, a string of saliva dripping from his gaping maw. He looked just as confused about it as she felt.

"Escort," Liesl commanded, and the dogs followed him. Liesl watched them all disappear further downhill over a barren knoll, then shook her head and started back up the hill.

"That's one of my frequent diners," she said when she reached the group. "Second time this week—that I've actually caught him, anyway. Makes me wonder how many he's actually gotten ahold of. Must be a handful, cuz my counts have been down. Folks are getting more brazen by the day. Gotta have my electric man check that damn fence."

"How many what?" Gaia asked.

Liesl cocked her head. "Catfish. Ain't you ever seen a paddy before?"

Gaia slowly shook her head, confused, having never heard of a catfish being called a "paddy."

"You're slackin' on your kid's education, Maer!" said Liesl.

"I've been a little busy," Maer said, shoving her hands in her pockets and looking down at the dirt.

"Oh, you know I'm just bustin' you a little." But the concern that lingered on Liesl's face said otherwise. "I know you been hot and heavy at your crazy ocean fish thing."

"It's not crazy, Leece," Maer said wearily, as if for the thousandth time. "No crazier than trying your hand at raising catfish in rice paddies."

"'Cept for I've actually *got* some fish."

Maer opened her mouth to speak, maybe to tell her about the rock fish and the pelican on the bluffs, but Liesl abruptly turned to Gaia. "We're growin' food here, Sugar. Rice and fish, among other things."

"I saw one of my mom's fish today. A rockfish." Gaia was picking up where Liesl so rudely cut her mom off. She was about to tell Liesl about the pelican, and maybe even the poppies, but Gaia noticed Maer staring hard at her, subtly shaking her head.

"That so?" Liesl raised an eyebrow and looked at Maer.

"Oh, just in the lab. I was showing Gaia some potential embryos."

"So this is your community farm?" Gaia asked quickly, not knowing how much she was supposed to reveal about her mom's fish project, not knowing how much Liesl knew.

Liesl's attention stayed pinned to Maer a few more awkward seconds, then she laughed. "No, girl, this ain't the bad part of the farm you come to see—the part your mama thinks you might be able to help with. We're in great shape on this side. The fish crap on the rice, fertilize it, and live off the dead plants. And we get a plate full o' starch and protein. It's what your mom would call 'symbiotic.'"

"Win-win," Gaia said, and looked up at Godpappy who winked at her. They'd just covered symbiosis in class the week before.

"That's right! Which you don't see too much of these days," Liesl smiled, reaching down to pick up a strange-looking green beetle and tossing it down into some rice grass. Gaia thought it odd that Liesl would chase one strange creature out of her paddy, Lohi, only to toss another one in.

"Take my little friend Lohi I just shooed off. He don't look it, but he's probably 15 or 16. He's trying to feed a bunch of brothers and sisters, all runnin' wild, ready to eat dirt and gull to stay alive."

"Is he the kid with the melted face?" Gaia asked, which made Selene snort.

The dogs returned, and at the sight of Gaia they galloped and pranced and began licking her hands and pants again. The furry Dachshund spun in a circle chasing its tail.

"Which kid with a melted face?" Liesl said. "Take your pick. They're all over, them melted Kiters." Liesl rolled her eyes and shook her head at the dogs. "Jaysus, you must be something special, kid. I ain't never seen 'em this pathetic." Then she looked at Gaia again. "I'd like to help him, but there's a thousand Lohis on the Central Coast alone, and word spreads at even a little success stealing from us. Before long—could be tomorrow for all I know—we won't be able to stop 'em all. It'll be like a human tsunami. And the folks who put what little money they have into this place and work it just so they can feed their own families will be starvin', too, and then it *all* falls apart. Feels like the thin membrane between us and an ocean of chaos will burst with a pin prick or a good sneeze."

Liesl sure could talk.

"And with an unreliable fence, the only security we can afford is keeping our eyes open and those three beasts you managed to so easily subdue. So we like to joke and laugh a lot around here to keep from weepin' and cuttin' our own wrists."

"What about getting Guard units posted to help protect the place?" Maer asked. "Didn't they promise you some?"

Jack crossed his arms and looked down as if preparing for an assault. Liesl had a way of making people look at the ground, which was something Gaia admired and hated at the same time.

"Honey, ask your husband. The only way they'll sacrifice troops is if it suddenly becomes the government's best interest to do so. You know that. No offense, Jack."

"None taken. I'm not the government," he said dully as if for the hundredth time and was tired of saying it.

"Hell you ain't! Can you spare a couple-a troops to help out around here? Didn't think so!"

Gaia felt restless, like they were all flies caught in Liesl's web, and instead of eating them she'd just talk them all to death.

"Can we go see the farm?" Gaia asked quickly before Liesl could start up again.

Liesl looked over at the sun which was about to sink into the hills. "Let's go do it," she said. "Ain't got but an hour of daylight left. By the way, what exactly *are* you gonna do?"

"We don't know yet, Leece," Maer jumped in just as Gaia was about to give Liesl an uncomfortable shrug. But Liesl kept her severe gaze locked on Gaia.

"Still need your mama's protection? Cuz it ain't always gonna be there."

"She's got a lot of help," Cloudy put in, finally holstering his pistol.

"And she always will," Godpappy said, draping a trunk-like arm around her.

"Ha!" Liesl barked. "A cop with frilly underthings, an oaf of a teacher, and a Pa who's never around?"

"Enough!" Gaia shouted, looking knives at Liesl. "I'm fine, they're fine! Pull your claws back in and stop bullying my family!"

The group sat in shocked silence, except for Selene who snorted again. But instead of fighting back, the enigmatic Liesl grinned. Her gray eyes even twinkled, and her voice came out in a growly whisper.

"There she is. I knew you were in there somewhere."

Liesl turned and led them over the purple weed-freckled hardpan in the direction that Gaia had heard the banging and cursing. It seemed to Gaia that there may have been a lot of things keeping everyone mute: Liesl's dominating, odd behavior, and the weight and uncertainty about what Gaia might do at the garden.

Something else was unsettling in the exchange with Liesl. It had awakened a cold and ominous thought: she might, one day, be completely on her own, stranded without help, like when she got hacked and was alone at the ocean's edge.

Soon they were on a path lined with gnarled juniper bushes, weeds, and dead oaks. She gazed up at the gray sky and wondered what it was like when airplanes flew freely across the heavens. She sensed that so much had changed in the world in such a very short time. She wondered why Liesl had said 'frilly underthings' about Cloudy, puzzled over why Liesl seemed to be emasculating him. There was something undeniably true about Cloudy's femininity at times, though she hadn't a clue about what that truth was. Another story for another day.

The garden wasn't far, but getting to it took longer than expected, because they talked to a handful of people on the narrow dirt road leading to it—gaunt people in dirty, worn clothes who were responsible for tending one aspect or another of the farm. None of them was Old Ned, which shot a chill up Gaia's spine. She tugged on Cloudy, Godpappy, and her dad to casually join her over by a honeysuckle bush to talk. Liesl and her mom were off arguing about whether the hope of humanity lay in the sea with fish growing or on the land with farming, and Selene had stopped to chat with the mother of one of her friends she recognized, so Gaia knew they'd have a few moments.

"I don't see him anywhere," Gaia said. "I don't see Old Ned."

"Why are you looking for Old Ned?" asked her dad. He brushed a thumb across her brow. "Gaia, you're sweating. What's wrong?"

"Jack, Old Ned has me a little spooked, too," Lane said.

"Why?" asked Jack.

"Did you see his eyes?"

"No."

"I haven't seen those moon eyes since the day we found her, on our mountain guide in Kenya. Matthew. The one who tried to take her from us."

"But I've seen eyes like that," Jack said confused. "Blind people have white eyes."

"No," Lane corrected, "these are different. They're moon eyes."

"They're seeing eyes," Gaia said.

"What?" Jack looked confused. "How do you know this, Blue?"

She felt cold. Her muscles were remembering the seizure, and the fierce burning from the fire, and the moon-eyed man.

Godpappy's term, "moon eyes," was dead-right. They were moon eyes that could somehow see.

"There's just something piercing about them," Gaia said. "Not vacant like a blind person. Like the man in the hacking, and like Old Ned."

"I see," Jack said. "No pun intended." He turned to Lane. "You said this Matthew was young, though. I know you don't believe in coincidences, but this seems like a stretch. What would this have to do with Old Ned?"

"There's something the same about them," Gaia said. "And it scares me."

The clang of metal on metal nearby made Gaia jump.

"You think it's our man?" Cloudy was addressing Lane now.

"How could it be, Cloudy? It's impossible."

"Geri-sim."

"Geris-*what*?"

Jack shook his head. "Jesus, Cloudy. You serious?"

"What the hell are you talking about?" Lane said.

"Premature aging as a disguise," Jack said. "I've heard rumors about it, but we've never actually seen it done. And we've seen a lot."

"I've actually seen it, Jack," Cloudy said. "They sometimes use it in the Croozer network."

"But Maer said Old Ned's been here for years." Godpappy Lane was struggling with it, and so was Gaia. She didn't know what to believe. She wanted more and more desperately to get to the garden. The earth felt safe to her.

"I'll bet you he's been here less than 15 years," Cloudy said calmly. "I'll bet he wasn't here before Gaia was born, which means he could have come here after she was born. Look, the guy could have followed us. He obviously wanted her pretty badly. He knew where we came from. It'd be pretty easy to find us again."

Gaia's blood was getting icy.

"But I killed him, Cloudy. I practically bashed his head in!"

"Besides Matthew," Jack said, "have you ever killed a person, Lane?"

"Of course not."

"You'd be amazed how hard it is to kill someone."

Gaia shivered as white-eyed dots connected in her mind.

"This is nuts!" Lane nearly shouted.

"Maybe. But you let me worry about that," Cloudy said. "This is why I became a lawman in the first place, to keep an eye on her, and I feel like I can finally start doing my job."

Gaia had never seen him so determined and clear.

"Take her to the garden," said Cloudy. "Stay close to her. You especially, Jack. Be sharp. I'm gonna go find our friend Ned. Or whoever the hell he is."

As Cloudy walked away, Lane started to protest.

"Let him go," Jack said. "He's right. Even if he's wrong, I'm erring on the side of paranoia. I'm not leaving my daughter."

Gaia tried to slow her breathing. All this talk was getting her worked up.

"We can go home this second, Sweet Pea," said her dad. "Just say the word. You must feel like we're blasting you with a fire hose."

When Gaia shook her head, Godpappy turned to her and held her face in his big hands. They felt warm over her ears. He looked to be on the verge of tears. "I'm so sorry, Blueberry. For everything."

Maybe it was the comfort of Godpappy's touch, but from somewhere, like the strange music that came and went, strength suddenly poured into her. And what came out of her mouth next surprised even her.

"Do you think I can kill a person if I get angry enough? Like I did with the grass?"

Lane chuckled and grinned and let go of her face. "Shit, Jack. She's okay."

"Don't cuss, Godpappy."

When they finally reached the garden it was bigger than Gaia had expected—three and a half acres, Liesl said. It made a sharp left turn at the far end, curving around the rocky slope of a small hill. She scanned for Cloudy but didn't see him.

The blight was obvious even in the fading light. The plants looked melted, scorched by an invisible fire that burned from the inside. Gaia could only guess at what some of the plants were because they were so disfigured. A dozen people hoed and dug a section near them, piling up plant remains next to an old pushcart that had "ZAZ" painted crudely on the side, and a small Latino man worked at the motor of a plow, sometimes whacking it with an old wrench. Liesl kept shaking her head, voicing mystification about the cause of the blight, and she said that a lot people would face serious hunger.

"Some will even have to risk eating Füd," she admitted.

"That's awful," Gaia said. "Kiters don't even eat that."

"Gaia Cadogan!" Maer said. "Don't use that word."

Liesl was chuckling.

"Sorry," Gaia said. "What I mean is, I've heard that the homeless Hawaiian kids won't even eat Füd."

"Only because they can't afford it," Liesl said. "They say they don't eat it for the same reasons we do: that it's unnatural and it can make you sick. But the fact is, they have no money, for anything, even Füd. Seagulls are free, and so are catfish when they get away with it. That's the only reason. Think about it. You ever watch what seagulls eat? It'll turn your belly. I saw a riot of gulls fighting over a human hand two weeks ago. You really think Kiters would play Russian roulette with skinny, putrid seagull meat, or eat rats, if they could afford 100% pure, synthetic animal guts grown in a factory?"

Gaia scanned the dead plants, watching the burn pile grow, and her mind began to whirl: dark visions of hurricane destruction, bursting splats of balloons filled with blood and piss, the piercing whine of the storm siren and the hissing, impenetrable din of a sand storm that followed, exploding pain in her face, a seagull vainly struggling against the fishing hook wedged into its guts, a raging fire that burned in pure darkness, which melted into a raging field of crimson poppies and visions of beautiful plants, memories. The terrarium. Her front-yard garden. The trees at the preserve. More poppies. Green, lush grass. Animal pictures danced in, videostreams of extinct life: whales, dolphins, sharks, coral reefs. Her dog, Prop, then rabid dogs curling at her feet. The black man looming over her in the fire. It was like her mind had suddenly cracked and everything was spilling out.

And then, from nowhere, an inner vision of warm, violet light drifted in, like her very own sun, hovering over her in the darkness, speaking to her mind, filling her with strength, courage, and peace. The music had returned, melodic, sweet. Her skin tingled, and she felt restless.

"Baby," Maer said quietly as she put a hand on Gaia's back. "You really don't have to do this if you don't want to. I—"

"No," Gaia interrupted. "I have to. I want to."

Gaia pulled away from her mom and walked slowly into the middle of the garden, which was now only turned-up dirt with skeletal plant remains. Some of the workers stopped and watched her. Her senses were alive. She smelled the sweet earth beneath her feet and heard the rush of evening breeze beginning its journey out to sea. Quail cooing, a crow cawing, chipmunks playing in a tree, the clatter of work around the rocky bend in the part of the garden she couldn't see.

She went to her knees, worked her hands through the brittle crust of the soil and into the soft, warm earth. Turning to a dead broccoli plan next to her, Gaia said, "I'm here," and a feeling of belonging cradled her soft inner places. The moment after she closed her eyes, the broccoli plant slowly turn from a sick, gray-brown color to vibrant, spring green. New leaves sprouted from its stalk.

Gaia drew a deep breath through her perfectly healed nose and slowly exhaled from her mouth, feeling herself begin a conversation with the earth without knowing what she was saying. The strange, now-familiar music rose in her mind, building and flowing, and Gaia sensed a crimson glow inside and beyond her. A single voice rose from the music—a chanting voice, neither male nor female, in a language she both knew and couldn't understand. She sensed an awakening as if thousands of eyes were opening, and the morning sun was rising up, and there were stretches and sleepy murmurs, then small shouts of joy from all the life rising into being around her.

Then without warning, nausea slammed Gaia's stomach, and torrential vomit started bursting out. A fiery, electric current ripped through her, crippling her limbs and body—an unbearable agony of the garden blight coursing through her, infecting her, burning her from within. She couldn't move, she couldn't breathe, she couldn't think. She was sizzling, sputtering, coughing, puking. She was the blight itself.

Then Gaia Cadogan, the Earth Mother, slowly fell sideways onto the dirt, took one last gasping breath, and died.

-17-
Rebirth

"**B**ack so soon?"

The voice was deep, and kind, and familiar. It was the primary voice that had risen up from the music, chanting, as Gaia had begun to commune with the earth. Both masculine and feminine, it struck Gaia as more familiar by the moment, though she still couldn't quite place it. But she knew it. She knew it intimately.

"Who are you?" she asked. Blackness had given way to the faintest amber light. Gaia felt a hum of energy surrounding her, though she couldn't see or feel her body.

"We are," the voice responded with mirth. "The fog between us has thickened."

"I feel like I know you. Why can't I see you?"

"If we let you see us, it will be a very long time before we can send you back again."

"I've been here before?" The place, with its womb-like void, was excruciatingly familiar.

The voice said nothing for a while. Gaia sensed a gentle pulse, as if she were inside a giant heart. She felt so saturated by—what was it? Goodness? There were no words for it, but she wanted to stay there forever.

"Why have you returned to us?" it asked.

She didn't understand the question. "Have I died?"

"You have asked this each time, and the answer does not change. You taught us this word, "died," from your visits. But it means nothing."

Gaia was baffled. The conversation was confusing, but it didn't matter. She felt like she belonged there, more powerfully than she'd ever felt anything.

"The thing I was trying to help harmed me."

A pause from the voice. It was more a source than a voice.

It said, "What was in your heart when you helped?"

Gaia tried to take herself back to the the place she'd come from, but her memory was murky. After a few moments, though, she had it, and she knew the source saw it, too. But she said it anyway.

"I wanted to understand, about me. I wanted to know who I was."

"And that is helping?" the source gently chided.

It was a frustrating answer. She sensed that the source, whomever or whatever it was, expected her to know more than she did. But something else was happening, some kind of separation or transition. The warmth was fading, and sensations were bursting inside of her. She had this feeling of being in a cozy room, but now it was as if somebody were opening the windows and letting a cold wind blow in. She was leaving, and she didn't want to.

"Go back now," the source commanded. "We are with you."

Gaia's mind slowly dimmed, she shivered, and then fell into a delicious sleep.

-18-

Eden Interrupted

The soft scrape of boots on a hollow wooden floor, and moments later a woman's voice.

"She's back. Oh, my sweet girl!"

Gaia opened her eyes. *This is how a chick must feel, pecking out of its shell, seeing the world for the first time.* The dim, indoor light was fuzzy, and the silhouette of her mother took shape.

Gaia was lying on something soft, and her mom sat next to her looking stricken, stroking Gaia's forehead, seeming much older than Gaia remembered.

An amber hue flashed in her mind like the feathers of a bird flitting from its perch, vanishing like mist. The dream of voices. Was it a dream? She closed her eyes and tried drifting back into it, reaching with the tendrils of thought for the impenetrable comfort of the place she'd been. But it was gone.

"Gaia, stay with me," Maer demanded.

Gaia covered her face with her arm, partly out of defiance, partly out of sadness, but mostly to muffle the throbbing in her head. "Don't boss me," she slurred. Her voice was heavy and hard to produce.

More bodies crowded around her, making Gaia feel like Dorothy in the Wizard of Oz looking up at her loved ones. There was her dad, and Godpappy, and Selene, who was looking worried and pissed at the same time. Where was Cloudy?

"Damn you," Selene said. Her eyes were wet. "Stupid gull turd of a kid!"

"What?" Gaia was confused. Why was she lying there? Why was Selene cursing her?

"Thought we'd lost you," Maer said, her face contorting, then regaining composure. "Your heart stopped."

Gaia heard the words, but they washed over her groggy shell. Had she been awake and alert, she'd have been alarmed. *What? Like dead?* she'd have shouted, then palmed her chest to make sure of her quickly beating heart. But she just lay there.

Selene lingered a moment more, then rubbed her eyes and stormed away. Gaia heard the creak of a spring hinge followed by the slap of a door closing.

"Where am I?"

Liesl's voice outside, crass and abrasive, barked orders. "No, don't touch that one, either. Dammit, I told you, just wait. We'll sort out what to do. But the big tree stays."

Then Gaia remembered. Back in the garden, her hands were dug into the earth; a whole world of life waking around her, through her. She had felt it happening, as tangibly as if she'd opened a door to a packed theater of people standing, stretching, laughing.

Then, a shadow of grief blended came, a darkness that grew until she recognized it as sickness, anguish. The blight. And when she'd tried to comfort the garden, she was flooded with agony and blinding pain. She'd allowed the blight inside of her. Subconsciously, at the time, she knew she could have kept the blight out and stopped it from entering her. It was a lesson she wouldn't have to learn twice. Next time, if there were a next time, she knew she'd have to control it better.

Gaia rolled onto her side and drew her arms in tightly.

"Do you remember now?" Maer asked.

Gaia nodded wearily.

But wait! She'd felt it as she slid into darkness. Something wonderful had happened. Along with the pain had been a sense of wild glory, of success.

Gaia sat up, which took more effort than expected, because she felt like a thousand-pound bag of Armor-Dillo concrete. Hands emerged around her, telling her to take it easy and trying to make her lie back down.

"I need to get up! I need to go see!" she pleaded. "I'm fine now!" This wasn't completely true, because her head still throbbed.

The grown-ups reluctantly backed off and gave her some room, probably having no idea what she needed or was capable of. Godpappy reached down and helped her stand, then grinned and handed her a mug, which to Gaia's delight contained tomato juice. She pulled a few hungry gulps from it, then pushed her way out the trailer door.

"Don't let what you're about to see go to your head," Lane said.

How long she'd been unconscious, Gaia couldn't tell. But it was dark outside, lit by a few barrel fires here and there and by tall floodlights along the edge of the garden.

The garden!

She froze when she saw it. The mug of tomato juice slipped from her hand and hit the ground with a soft thud.

The first thing she noticed was a young Sequoia tree, maybe 20 feet tall, smack-dab in the middle of what had been a wasteland of blighted plants. And everywhere else, the feeble, dead garden had grown wild and boisterous with life. A scatter of other juvenile trees—oak, sycamore, cypress—seemed to dance throughout the garden amid the hot red bark of Manzanita bushes. Poppies, shrubs, and wild grasses flourished, even spilled out onto the once hardpan dirt track surrounding it. So thick and wild was the growth that anyone stumbling upon this place for the first time would never know it had once been tamed and cultivated with vegetables.

At a deep level, she was completely unsurprised by the new garden. It was an ordinary confidence. Her mind went to another time when she'd been both amazed yet confident.

Last year in Godpappy's class they'd learned about internal combustion engines. Each student had to take apart, reassemble, then run a small gasoline-powered engine. Even more surprising than the story about people using these engines to mow lawns at their homes (having a lawn was illegal and completely unheard of) was the fact that Godpappy had actual gasoline and oil to use. Gaia had spent more than a week taking her engine apart piece by piece, cleaning each item with solvent, then reassembling it according to the instructions in an old videostream. She'd replaced the piston rings, snugged the piston back into the cylinder with the ring compressor, inserted the values and their springs, bolted on the oil splash, inserted the camshaft, slipped on the flywheel with it's little key to keep it from slipping, and followed the rest of the instructions until she was finally ready to pull the cord to start it up.

Her engine had fired up on the first pull. And while it startled and amazed Gaia to hear the ear-shattering roar of the little engine as she pushed the throttle, she realized that she knew every piece of that engine and how it all worked together. She knew it, and she'd done it. It was right, and thinking about it like that, there was no surprise in it. She was confident.

Now in the garden, growing all of these wild new things felt natural. In those few moments before the blight took her, Gaia realized she was much more aware of what was happening than it seemed at the time. Exactly how she was doing it, she hadn't a clue. But in those moments Gaia knew each and every plant that was coming into being. She wasn't creating them, they already existed. She was just helping them along.

"Go on," Maer said, wrapping a blanket around her shoulders. "Go say hello to your new creation."

My new creation. Pebbles poked into the soles of her bare feet as she walked to the new garden. She must not have been out long, because there was some light left. One by one, as the people moving about noticed her, they stopped what they were doing and watched. Even Liesl, who was in mid sentence bossing a short, Mexican man, stopped speaking and turned, looking uncharacteristically flustered, like she'd seen an alien spaceship land in front of her.

Except for the crackle of flames in the nearby steel drums, all was silent. The air was chill on her skin, and Gaia noticed a sliver of crescent moon hanging in the western sky above the garden, as if the heavens were giving approval.

She waded slowly into the garden brushing the new growth with outstretched hands. The soil was cool and soft and felt like home. One by one crickets began tuning up, and a bat screeched overhead.

But the peace lasted only moments.

A piercing bang suddenly shattered the air. She plunged fingers into her ears to deaden the "Pop! Pop! Pop!" that came next. Gunfire! It was close by, but Gaia could see Liesl wasn't doing the shooting, and neither was her dad. It came from somewhere behind the trailer she'd been lying in.

And then the response from a second gun.

"Down! Everyone! Get down!" Jack shouted as the confused people around Liesl hunched between standing and lying down.

"On the ground!" Jack shouted again as more gunfire popped. In a moment, everyone was down—except for Liesl, Godpappy, Maer, and Jack himself, who aimed his pistol with two hands as he moved toward the side of the of the trailer, scanning left to right as he went. Liesl was pointing her shotgun at a group of eucalyptus trees. It was the same side of the property, Gaia realized, from which Old Ned had come to open the gate for them.

Where was Cloudy?

What happened next was so sudden that it seemed oddly slow motion to Gaia. Godpappy was running to her but fell sideways and went down at the crack of a gun erupting from the row of honeysuckle lining the path to the garden. The honeysuckle was moving, inching closer, until Gaia's brain told her it was actually a row of men converging on them with rifles.

They came from every direction, closing in like a net being drawn tight. White men in dirt-colored jumpsuits wielding black rifles.

Gaia watched as her dad and Liesl were disarmed by men pouring out from behind the trailer. A man grabbed Selene's arm and forced her to the ground. Maer was screaming, "Lane, behind you!" Then suddenly, "Nooooo! My baby!" Her scream had melted into a wail.

A burlap bag went over Gaia's head, and strong hands grabbed her arms and lifted her off the ground. Gaia heard the crunch and snap of her new creation being trampled by the men's boots.

Something bit into her shoulder like a bee sting accompanied by a light click. As she fell into unconsciousness, Gaia realized that her mom had stopped wailing.

-19-

Matthew

"Stop lighting it!"

In the dream, Gaia was yelling at Stacy Williams who wielded a blowtorch, re-lighting the fuse of a spinning firework that burned red, then yellow, then green, and shrieked an ear-piercing *whiz*.

Her words barely emerged, soft like a whisper. She tried plugging her ears with her fingers but found her arms pinned to her sides.

Stacy smirked and lit the fuse again to keep it going. The noise was a metal skewer stabbing her eardrums, and when she closed her eyes and shook her head—the only thing she could do—she woke up screaming.

Something was wrong. She was on her back, and everything was different from anything she knew: a metal ceiling she could have reached up and touched if she could move her arms, the gray, padded wall next to her. The entire dim room was moving, jostling her. And the piercing whine continued, stabbed her brain relentlessly. Gaia gritted her teeth and clenched her eyes shut.

Just when she thought her brains would turn to mush, a warm touch on her temples startled her. She opened her eyes as something soft and warm entered her ear canal, mercifully killing the piercing whine.

She looked backwards as far as she could and saw who had done it.

It was Old Ned.

"It ees thee vehicle's hydrogen motah," his muffled voice said. "Thee animals also do not like it, either."

She knew that voice.

"I am sorry, my little seestah," he said.

Then things came back to her: the garden, gunfire, Godpappy falling, her mother's screams as Gaia was dragged away with a musty burlap bag forced over her head. Her heart fell into her stomach. His voice—incongruously young compared with his graying hair and old, milky, dead eyes—was the voice of the young man in her hacking.

Gaia screamed. "What did you do to them!" She struggled at her bonds. Her wrists were strapped firmly to the padded table she lay on. She tried to calm herself enough to relax the best she could, point all of her fingers together to make her hands small, and pull with all her strength to slip free. But it was no use.

"Siafu," another male African voice said. "How can she be awake? I gave her enough fo a bull!"

With a light *pop*, another sting bit her neck.

In the growing, darkening distance, Old Ned was saying, "It ees why I bound her. I think we will find her full of sah-prises."

When she woke, Gaia's head was foggy and the world was quiet. She was lying on her back unable to move.

"Hello, my little seestah," the man's voice crooned in a crisp African accent. "Good evening, jewel of thee Earth."

The words didn't completely register through the fog in her mind, through the dimness suspending her. All was blissfully quiet save for the man's voice and the light ticking of an old clock somewhere. There were no other voices, near or distant, no jarring slams or pounding of the sea, no dogs barking, none of the usual cacophony that mauled her day after day.

When her vision cleared, stars twinkled in the darkness above. But it wasn't the real sky. It was a high-domed ceiling or screen across which the bright heavens were projected, or embedded. It was peaceful. Too peaceful.

My family! The thought struck her like a hammer. She saw Godpappy Lane falling in the field. Shot? Her mom had been wailing. She tried to get up, but her neck had a strap across it. So did her wrists and ankles.

"How do you like thee stars? It ees thee sky as seen from my original home—your birthplace as well—in Africa!"

The man stepped next to her and peered down. Either he was incredibly tall or the padded table she lay on was short, because she was well below his waist.

"What did you do to my family?" she said, tears welling and running into her ears.

"Ahh," he answered softly. "Do not fret about yo family." It was a clueless thing to say, telling a young girl who'd just been kidnapped not to fret. "They are all well, mostly. They are alive. Fo thee moment."

"For the moment? What does that mean?" Gaia pulled at the hard, thin straps without taking her eyes off his. Was this Old Ned? The voice, the milky eyes were the same, but this man was younger, taller, with much less gray.

"That," he said, "ees up to you."

"Who are you?" She couldn't keep the sob out of her voice.

"Do you not know?"

"Old Ned?" she hazarded.

He considered her a few uncomfortable moments, slowly scanning her eyes, her face, her bound body. She was still in her pants and t-shirt.

"Very astute. Yes, but no. No longer. And never again shall I be Old Ned." His tone was almost resentful. "Much too painful. And thee aging template never leaves one completely. But I feel much bettah. And thees remaining gray in my hair, does eet make me look more distinguished?"

He grinned impishly, not expecting an answer, then looked over his shoulder and raised his chin briefly. Someone else was in the room, and Gaia now heard a soft set of slippered footsteps. They moved somewhere behind her head, but she couldn't see who it was.

She needed to find out what was happening. "You were Old Ned and now you're not?"

"Yes. I pree-tended. Fo far too long." He cocked his head back and forth, popping his neck, then considered Gaia like a teacher gauging the truthfulness of a student. "But don't we all pretend in one way or anothah? For example, right now you are pree-tending not to be afraid."

He was right. Her voice had come out a little shaky, and the tension in her body was making her skin feel prickly and condense with new sweat. What was the person behind her doing? She heard a light clink of metal and the shifting of things—tools?—on a soft surface. Old Ned seemed unhurried, detached from the activity behind her.

"Who are you?" she asked. But before he could answer, her mind clicked, and fresh terror gripped her. He was the man who guided Godpappy and Cloudy up Mt. Kenya. He was the one who tried to steal her, the one Godpappy left for dead. He'd aged himself. Cloudy was right. And so was Godpappy. There were no coincidences.

He drew a deep breath, then exhaled, as if the concept were burdensome.

"Yes, your mind ees trying to find some logic in your situation," he said. "But it ees my logic that ees running the show." He leaned down nearer to her face. "Do you not suspect who I am?"

She caught the faintest outline of an iris in his blank, ghostly eyes. She unlocked her gaze from his and noticed a small mole between his cheek and ear before she clamped her eyes shut, turning her head away. He whispered hoarsely, producing breath that smelled of dirty mint. "I am thee only one who undah-stands yooooooooo!" He stood up and grinned.

The final puzzle piece clicked into place.

"You hacked me. You were the one."

"Oh, not I alone," he said, puckering his lips and frowning, his face and his black button-down shirt practically disappearing into the gray light. "I am no expert in thee nuances of micro-biology hardware. But," he pointed an index finger in the air, "I did create thee vision. Apparently you did not like it as I'd hoped you would. My goal was to plant trrrust in you," he said firmly, rolling his 'r', "to make you *want* to come to me on your own free will. Howevah, when we locked eyes earlier today, when I opened thee gate fo you—"

So it was still the same day, Gaia realized. She hadn't been unconscious a long time.

"—I saw only fear, and I knew you would not come to me. So, then I knew that I had to come to you."

She remembered him opening the gate for them, and the eye contact she'd made with Old Ned.

"Old Ned," she said vacantly.

He looked up at the ceiling.

"According to thee stars, it ees technically tomorrow," he corrected, then looked down at her again. "Fifteen years. That horrid age template lived in me for fifteen years."

Gaia opened her mouth in disbelief, then asked, "You planned this for fifteen years? Capturing me?"

He ignored her question and nodded to whomever was lurking with tools behind her. Presently the sound of little wheels brought with it a short Chinese woman with drab work overalls and chin-length hair pushing a little cart up to the table on the far side of Young Ned. She looked at Gaia without expression. On top of the little cart were what looked like surgical instruments.

Gaia suddenly screamed and thrashed, pulling with all her strength at her bonds. But they only tore into her ankles, choked her, and she nearly dislocated her wrists. Her breathing came fast, heavy, and she scanned the dim, star-domed room but saw nothing else, heard nothing else.

"Nothing to frrret about," he reassured her. He and the Chinese woman had been calmly watching her thrash.

"Why am I tied up?" Gaia made no attempt to conceal her fright. She kept wiggling, hoping the straps would magically loosen or that she'd melt and slip free of them, or that some special power would suddenly emerge and she'd free herself and waste her captors. But it was useless.

She hoped for Cloudy. He'd gone off to find Old Ned at the garden, but she hadn't seen him when the shooting started. Maybe he'd slipped away, followed them, and would burst in at any moment.

"I have bound you because," he said, still ignoring the cart of instruments next to him. "I am still not sure what you are capable of."

"What do you mean, *capable of?*" Gaia lied. "I'm just a kid. What am I supposed to be able to to do? Who the *fuck* are you, anyway?!" She threw the word like a knife at him.

"Ahhh," he shook his head, tisk-tisking. "Mama—please don't cuss."

Ice water flowed through her. He was mimicking her, parroting an admonition she sometimes gave her mom—in private, with nobody else around. Had he somehow bugged her, bugged the family? How? When? And how much did he really know?

What was he going to do with her?

"I am called—"

"Matthew!" Gaia interrupted him, trying to stall whatever he was doing.

"Ah," he said thoughtfully, surprised. "So they told you."

"They should have made sure you were dead!" she spat, struggling to get free.

"Yes, yes. In retrospect, fo yoah sake, pah-haps. But it ees very hard to kill a person, even when you think you have already done the deed."

She grunted and struggled as hard as she could.

"I am called other things as well. But you, my dear, my little sistah may call me—brothah."

"Like hell!" Gaia shouted.

"But thee *real* question ees: Who are *you*? Who ees Gaia Cadogan *really*? Thees I have struggled weeth many years. Some say you created thee Earth, and thee sea. And thee sky!" he said reverently, sweeping his arm across the stars above. "My own family—seestah and brothah tried to kill me once." He grimaced and pinched a thumb and forefinger together to highlight the injustice of it.

Matthew sighed. "But, I stopped them. And my heart has grieved many years fo their loss." He set his hands on the side of the bed. "But that was long ago. Today we are here. And who ah you, then? Thees I can now finally find out, after all thees years. We will discovah it togethah, you and I."

He turned his attention to the tray.

"What are you doing!?" Gaia demanded, but Matthew ignored her and calmly lifted a scalpel.

What happened next, Gaia couldn't help. She started pissing herself. She couldn't stop it. The flow was warm down her butt, soaking her underwear and pants. She wondered if her own blood would produce the same warm sensation. She was so desperate to escape that she began aiming death thoughts at him. If she could kill grass, maybe she could kill this man. *Die!*, she thought fiery and hard. *Fall dead!* But nothing happened, and terror clipped her breath to the brink of hyperventilation.

"And as we discovah who you are, we will begin to change thee world!"

He held up a small, dull silver capsule.

"Change the world?" she panted, afraid of what he meant to do with the capsule.

"Yes!" he made a fist in front of himself for emphasis, but not elaborating. "In fact, I have already discovahed something! It appears you do not have a diagnostic chip, you naughty naughty girl!" he grinned. "Your body is magical! It seems to dissolve foreign objects, such as thee D.I. chip. I believe you were on D.I. chip numbah three when I gave you thee vision?"

How could he know that?

"It actually saved me thee trouble of removing thee chip myself, if you had one. Fo thees is how thee agencies can trrrack you. It is a bad use of thee technology. My use of thee D.I. chip, the giving of visions, is thee best use of thee chip I have yet found. But thee normal chip is not strong enough to stay inside you."

He moved the scalpel to her shoulder. Gaia felt a powerful urge to turn away, to let it happen without watching, as if under protest. But she forced herself to watch, to see exactly what this lunatic Matthew was doing.

"Many things—you, fo example—are often more useful fo things not originally intended."

Gaia's mother drifted into her mind. And Lane and Cloudy and her dad and Selene. She remembered her mother's screams, and the gunfire, Selene being forced to the ground, and Lane falling in the field, shot.

As the scalpel blade bit into her shoulder, she winced and watched it carve a deep, short trench into her avocado skin, into the muscle of her shoulder the length and depth of a fingernail. Blood rose at the cut, and with tweezers Matthew inserted the silver capsule. The insertion was more painful than the cut itself. Gaia screamed as it struck a nerve, sending a dull, sharp pain into her neck like a funny bone being struck, and her body went momentarily limp.

Seconds later it was over. The Chinese woman had quickly wiped and taped the cut and returned the scalpel and tweezers to the tray.

Matthew stretched and lengthened himself to his full height, rocking and cracking his neck back and forth.

"Thees, I hope, will not dissolve. And to prevent you from any unnecessary pain or paralysis, I must advise you not to touch me or my staff, and do not try to run. Fo if you do, I think you will find the device most unpleasant." He shrugged and held up his hands in apology. "It ees thee only way. But," he continued with enthusiasm, holding his fist in front of him, "let us focus on thee work at hand. I hope you will find that it ees bettah to help me. And who knows? You may discovah your true calling!"

While he was speaking, Gaia began to focus dissolving thoughts on her shoulder, visions of green acid. She was the Earth Mother. Surely she had more power than this. If the legends were true, she had returned many times in history and no doubt conquered countless obstacles. But she had a hard time believing this now. And even if it were true, returning as the Earth Mother meant that she'd also *left* each time. Maybe she'd died, maybe in a similar situation. But hadn't she already died, earlier in the garden? She'd gone to the warm place of voices and comfort, a place like a womb. Was that death? Was it the place she stayed between gigs?

It was all confusing and abstract, and she shook the thoughts away. She was here, and now, and she needed to get out of there, wherever "there" was.

The Chinese woman glanced up at her, and in the moment their eyes met, Gaia saw it. A flash of something, like fright or pity. But the woman turned away and left as quietly and efficiently as she'd come.

Then, to her great relief, the straps holding her wrists, ankles, and neck vanished.

Gaia quickly sat up on the table.

-20-
Zaz

Being newly unbound, Gaia's first thought was to make a run for it. But she wasn't sure what the capsule in her shoulder could do to her. She imagined a massive electric shock followed by complete limpness and unconsciousness. Matthew said was that it would be "most unpleasant" if she tried to run or touch him or his "staff," which probably meant anybody else she'd come in contact with, like the Chinese woman. She wasn't willing to risk anything at the moment. Besides, there was nowhere to go. She didn't see any doors in the big circular room, which contained nothing but the bed, the simulated stars above, the cart of surgical tools, and the man who'd used them on her.

"Fo-give," said Matthew, who was standing and holding his hands out in apology.

He *was* tall, at least 6-foot-5, maybe more. "My method, apart from thee device, was to elicit a traumatic emotional response. I have seen you kill before, my seestah, when you were in a state of great distress."

How did he know this? Had he seen her kill the grass on the soccer pitch?

"But was it from direct touch? Or was it without touch? This is thee scientific process necessary fo our discoveries."

The only discovery Gaia was interested in was discovering the way out of there and getting back to her family.

"By way of apology, allow me to show you what makes me calm in moments of high strrress! Perhaps you will find it as com-fah-ting as I find it."

He looked up and spoke, as if to invisible angels in the room: "Thee past."

Immediately, the curved walls filled with images and videostreams, pulsating with light. The sound of a wooden flute wafted in with a beautiful, haunting melody. Pictures glowed and faded, overlapping, one after another in harmonious counterpoint to the flute; pictures of rich coral reefs, colorful fishes, wide, expansive landscapes of water and jungle, brilliant sunrises or sunsets, water beasts, birds, birth, the wild, splashing violence of predator and prey. The visions curved around and filled her with wonder. Her mind couldn't keep up with all that she saw. Crocodile, hippopotamus, praying mantis, crab, whale, beetle, elephant, bees, dolphin, and other strange flora and fauna she'd never seen. It was a world that no longer existed.

"I surrround myself with home. Pic-chahs of my sky, thee sky I cannot see here. Pic-chahs of my land, of my wa-tah. Pic-chahs frrrom thee past, when life on earth was still living, be-fo man hastened her temporary death. Yes, man will die away, and thee Earth, she will sleep, then reawaken herself to what form she will take next, like a buttah-fly emerging frrrom a cocoon." He looked at her intently. "Like you."

He waved a hand between them. The videostreams faded and the stars returned. "But man will surely pass away."

"Then why bother with me?" she asked.

Matthew considered her carefully. Thoughts seemed to flit through his mind.

"My task is to provide comfort in thee last days."

The irony of this statement smacked her. "You mean as in kidnapping a helpless 14-year-old girl and killing her family?" She hoped that statement would elicit more information, which it did.

"I did not keel your family. All are alive and well, mostly. Mistah Lane Ripple has a small in-jah-ree, but he will be fine."

A gust of relief swept through her, but he could have been lying.

"And a helpless 14-year-old, you say? Almost 15—in two weeks, yes? Hardly helpless. In fact, I just took a big risk, releasing you from your bonds. I can assuah you, I am perhaps mo frightened than you are!"

She couldn't believe he just said that, and it pissed her off—especially when she'd tried with all her might to harm him just a few minutes earlier and failed miserably, helplessly. Clearly he had nothing to fear.

"You're kidding, right?" Gaia spoke with as much defiance as she dared, adding a little barb at the end. "Why are you more frightened than I am...*brother?*"

He was about to speak, but the word *brother* caught him up short. He cocked his head as if trying to read her, then grinned, completely ignoring her question. Perhaps she was somehow more dangerous than she knew, and to Matthew it was obvious. But to Gaia, knowledge of any such danger she posed was frustratingly hidden.

"But with grrrreat risk comes great reward, yes? We are both alive—we are survivors, you and I!" he said. "And our journey continues! But I see you are not convinced."

He turned and slowly paced back and forth, gathering his thoughts for a different tack. Did he think he was going to convince her that it was actually *okay* that he kidnapped her? Matthew turned to her again, alive with a fresh idea.

"You feel you are not supposed to be here," he said, clasping his hands in front of him. "Not just here with me, but in thee wahld. Who are you? Who is your true mothah and fathah? To whom do you belong? You do not know."

He was right, but she'd never admit it. *I belong to myself,* she wanted to shout.

"In many ways, I myself feel I should not be here. My birth, I am told, was a mistake. What my family—my sistah and brothah—did to me—" he motioned to his eyes, "was supposed to kill me. Thee rock that Meestah Lane Ripple hit me with was supposed to keel me. Yet here I am. Are we slaves to fate, you and I? Or are we called upon to mastah thee situation set be-fo us, as it is?" He cocked his head thoughtfully. "Fo my part, I choose the lattah, and I leave fate to play what silly games she will." He smiled, but his eyes didn't go along with it.

"If you're all about free will, then why are you determining my fate for me?"

She noticed his fists clench.

"Ah! There is thee sharp mind again!" he said, pointing a finger at her. "It is up to you to believe in fate or not, fo yo-self. My only hope is to convince you that helping me is in the best interest of thee world. If you find it is not, you are free to exercise your own free will."

"You'll let me go?"

Matthew didn't answer. "But," he held up a finger, "and thees is very important, as I mentioned earlier—while you are here, you must nevah attempt to touch me. Fo if you do, I will bind you again, or worse. I will not hesitate to take your life in place of my own. Know this." He pointed at her, his white eyes now looking gray and bloodshot. "Know this."

A chill ran through her, and she wished she'd been able to kill or at least damage this man with her thoughts when she'd tried earlier. Why didn't it work? Maybe it wasn't possible for her to consciously kill. With all he seemed to know about her, he might know she possessed some obvious power she wasn't aware of.

He'd done a lot of talking, but she still didn't know who this man was. He'd been Old Ned, and he'd played that role for a long time—and apparently in a lot of discomfort—with the sole intent of being in a position to capture her, even before she showed any signs of being the Earth Mother. Who was Matthew, and why did he want to take her from Godpappy the day she was born?

Gaia heard a swish, and the Chinese woman reemerged from a well-concealed door in the wall. The projected stars above were dimming, relenting to an unseen light on the horizon. Sunrise. Gaia wondered if the projection was an accurate depiction of the current time.

The woman brought a tray that held a white teapot and two white cups, and deftly poured the steaming brown liquid one-handed. She handed a cup to Gaia without making eye contact this time, and apparently unafraid of touching Gaia—or unaware of Matthew's demand that no physical contact occur. The situation was odd, as was this woman. Aside from a polite shyness, the woman betrayed no emotion like the brief look of fear and pity she'd shown last time she was in the room. Gaia now wondered if she'd imagined it.

"This is Mrs. Ahn," Matthew said, accepting a cup of tea from her.

She then pulled something from under her arm and laid it on the bed next to Gaia. Chinese baggy trousers, gray with a drawstring, and underpants.

Gaia's crotch was beginning to itch under her pissed-in pants, and she nearly missed another subtle moment. With what could have passed for a small change of light in the room, Mrs. Ahn again made eye contact with Gaia, and with the slightest tilt of her head indicated the trousers she'd just set down. It was a message, but Gaia had no idea what it meant. *Trousers,* she thought. *Okay.*

As Mrs. Ahn started to retreat, Gaia felt a pang that an ally was deserting her.

"Xie xie," Gaia called to her. "Thank you."

The woman stopped and turned slightly.

"That will be all, Mrs. Ahn," Matthew said. "Leave us."

But Mrs. Ahn stayed put as if trying to decide something.

"Leave us!" Matthew shouted.

When she refused to obey again, he stepped toward her. Now Mrs. Ahn moved, but Matthew stayed on her tail like a giant crow chasing a sparrow. She slipped through the open door which slid closed behind her.

"You will have to pardon Mrs. Ahn," Matthew said. "She must be a little nervous, meeting Zaz fo thee first time!"

"Zaz?" Gaia echoed, remembering all the messages and graffiti about Zaz splattered around Junipero Bay, recalling her mom's dismissal of Zaz as "cult bullshit" and Selene reciting the passage from some lost gospel about a hound and a girl rising out of the earth. Then it hit her. *She* had sprung out of the earth, according to Godpappy and Cloudy. Just like the passage Selene had read.

"Yes," Matthew confirmed. "Zaz. That is you! Do you know the story of Zaz? Thee gospel?"

Matthew was still keeping his distance. She found it difficult to look at his enthusiastically wide, dead eyes, so she looked down. "A little," she said. Her wet pants were making her itch. "But I'm not Zaz."

"And Zaz pushed back the seas," be began reciting, making a pushing motion, "and caused a garden to grow on thee poison ground. And the children spat out stones and devoured the fruit of thee garden!

"Do you know thees?" he asked.

Gaia shook her head.

"Well," he slapped his hands together, "why quote mo scripture to you when you *are* scripture! I will leave you to change out of yo wet pants."

He turned to leave but stopped.

"Please accept my apologies again fo frightening you—and I shall, in thee words of thee old television shows, 'Be back aftah these messages!'"

She wasn't sure what he meant, but she was happy to see him go. Was he really convinced she was Zaz?

When Gaia lifted the fresh pair of trousers—they smelled faintly of eucalyptus—the underpants fell to the floor, and when she picked them up something fell out of them. It was a feminine pad. She'd forgotten about getting her period. How had Mrs. Ahn known?

Gaia started to change but stopped when she heard Matthew yelling. It was faint, and she couldn't make out the words. She had barely pulled up the fresh bamboo-cloth pants when the door slid open and Matthew reappeared with Mrs. Ahn following at a distance. Against his white shirt, she noticed something strapped to his hip—what looked like the shock-baton Cloudy wore when he was on duty, though Matthew's was longer and thinner, like a short drumstick.

Cloudy. Her family. Godpappy. Gaia's heart thumped harder.

"Mo comfortable now?" Matthew asked, his eyes lingering on the soiled pants Gaia had folded and placed on the bed. She'd shoved her used feminine pad in one of the front pockets.

"Please toss thee dirty pants to me."

"Why do you want my pants?" Gaia asked, but Matthew didn't answer.

As Mrs. Ahn approached Gaia, she kept her eyes lowered. Gaia noticed that Mrs. Ahn's left cheek was bright red. Before Matthew could say anything, she retrieved the dirty pants and scurried away.

Matthew went for her with a clenched jaw but stopped. "Leave them in my study!" he called after her.

He turned to Gaia and slapped his palms together, making her jump.

"My apologies again! I forget about yo wonderful sense of hearing."

How did he know this?

His grin widened. "Yes, I know about it. I know everything!"

Then she remembered something.

"The other day when you hacked me. Were you in that old van? With somebody else?"

"Ahhh. You are curious about the logistics of how I know everything. Yo mind is sharp. But hacking? No. Thee intent was not malicious. Let's call it mo of an invitation. Yes, my assistant and I wah in thee van."

"You hacked me! You kidnapped me!" She braced herself, thinking he may try to hit her like he'd hit Mrs. Ahn, but only a muscle in his cheek twitched and he stayed calm.

"I knew you walked that way aftah school, to yo mothah's work, so I put thee van there much earlier so that you would be used to it." He seemed impressed with his own cleverness, and it confirmed that he'd been watching her. "I think I know when you discovered it. Tell me: What gave it away? What did you hear?"

"Siafu, she comes," Gaia repeated from memory. "Who is Siafu?"

Matthew nodded. "As I suspected. Good help, eet is hard to find."

"Is Siafu your African name?"

He became serious. "Yo brothah has many names. Siafu was a name given to me as a child. Siafu is a flesh-eating ant who is blind," he pointed to his eyes. "I look blind, but I am not. My eyes, a gift from my sistah, a powerful seer."

"How long have you been watching me?" Gaia asked, hoping that by holding a conversation with him he'd give away something important.

He looked surprised and hurt. "How long?" He leaned a little closer. His eyes seemed emotional, moist. "Yo whole life," he whispered, as if the experience had been long and agonizing and was finally over. "From the very first day."

Now that she saw Matthew in person, she was able to visualize a struggle between him and Godpappy fifteen years ago on the mountain. She felt hounded and harassed, and she hated him for kidnapping her, but she had begun to feel less fearful of him.

"Let's take a tour of the place, shall we?" he said brightly. "Yo new home away from home, my sistah. Come."

He turned and walked toward the wall. As he approached it, a tall, square section of it magically vanished, and light flooded the room. Her mind was still reeling, and what happened next overwhelmed her even more. As her eyes adjusted, Gaia saw a forest of dark green beyond it, and a deep, delicious, earthy aroma edged with a light bitterness floated into the room. Energy and life flowed into her. Almost against her will, she hopped off the table barefooted and followed Matthew.

Just outside the door, a short, Mexican man in a dark green jumpsuit trotted up to Matthew and handed him a pair of gloves. As Gaia cautiously approached, she examined the edge of the door frame to see if she could figure out how it worked. The wall itself was maybe two feet thick, and the edge was completely solid, white, and dimpled. Perhaps it generated some kind of solid energy field like an electric fence.

Then the humidity struck her, wonderfully heavy and damp, settling over her skin and filling her lungs with life-giving moisture. She was awestruck, and it took her a few breaths to get used to the sweet, thick sensation of it. Outside the door, the full view of the place hit her, and it was almost too much. She nearly fainted.

Straight ahead, a forest of extremely tall bushes extended in a straight line from the building, accompanied by a long catwalk of grated metal that Gaia now realized ran along the top half off the bushes. Looking through the grated floor, she saw lower catwalks at the base of the bushes, and below those, more levels of bushes and catwalks. This pattern repeated itself to the left and right. In fact, the domed building she'd been in—which from the outside now looked like half of a giant eggshell—lay at the hub of the operation, with catwalks and bushes running out in all directions like the spokes of a wheel. All along the catwalks, men and women in the same dark green jumpsuits worked the bushes, snipping clusters of whitish-yellow berries and dropping them into fat-wheeled pushcarts whose tops flared out wider in the front and back. It was hard to tell how many workers there were. All around and down into the lower levels, they swarmed like ants—like a colony of siafu ants, she thought—snipping and moving the carts up and down the lines.

The light in the complex was warm and soft, almost like dawn, and she thought it might be her imagination that the light was slowly, steadily increasing. When she looked up, another miracle stopped her breath. There was the morning sky with its deep, blue-gray in the west and brilliant shafts of sunrise streaming from the east. Wispy clouds made with divine brush strokes hung in gentle repose.

Yet they were inside. She knew it because of what she heard. There was a hollowness to the sound of everything which didn't evaporate into the air like it did outside. Sound seemed to ricochet, bounce, change location. The sky, she realized, was an unimaginably large dome, a deific parent to the dome of the room she'd been in. Gaia couldn't see the end of it in any direction.

"What is this place?" she asked.

Matthew pulled on the black gloves that had been handed to him and smiled. "Do you like eet? Eet is my garden." But suddenly his voice became severe. "No!" he demanded, which made Gaia jump. "Stand up!" But he wasn't talking to her. The man in the green jumpsuit was on his knees facing Gaia and crossing himself with religious reverence. "I said UP!" Matthew commanded again, stepping over and backhanding the man hard across the face, a blow barely audible because of the glove. He fell over sideways and reluctantly got to his feet, still crossing himself, looking down the whole time. The bipolar speed with which Matthew went from friendly to vicious shocked her. He was volatile. He'd also struck Mrs. Ahn for apparently not following orders strictly. However important she thought she was to him, she realized he might also turn on her in a flash. Yet, she wondered, maybe this act was calculated to plant that very fear in her. The man he'd struck, however, didn't act like this was a first offense. Her brain suddenly went to a chemistry lesson Godpappy gave the class a few months ago. Matthew was a pyrophoric chemical like phosphorous that would explode when simply exposed to air or moisture—in essence, anywhere, at any time.

"Eet is NOT thee time!" he scolded the man. "Go!"

The man gratefully obliged, turning and clomp-limp-jogging away around the building in his thick boots. None of the nearby workers even turned their heads to look.

"I apologize, once again," he cooed. "You were asking what is thees place."

Not wanting Matthew to think she was the least bit affected by what just happened, Gaia asked, "What are these plants?"

"Come," he said. "I will show you."

He went to a bush where a large clump of berries hung over the catwalk railing.

"Come," he repeated gently, extending a gloved hand of invitation.

She followed reluctantly, scanning the complex for sights and sounds. An industrial pump thwap-thwapped down in the bowels somewhere, and the deep lowing of some animal drifted up, thick like the air around her. The clipping of berries, the thump of berry clusters dropping into bins, and the swishing of leaves sounded like a restless breeze bumbling through an old hardware store.

Matthew moved aside so she could examine the bush.

Each branch sprouted dark, narrow, graceful green leaves in a uniform pattern, with a single leaf at the head of each branch and leaves jutting out perpendicularly in pairs down the stem. Gaia had never seen this plant before, and each branch looked to her like a multi-armed Hindu goddess. The berries, which on closer inspection seemed creamier white than yellow, hung bountifully from the branches.

Gaia cupped the berries, which were hard. The main stem of the berries was thick, reminding Gaia of her umbilical cord. She ran her hands across the leaves, circling the branch with her thumb and middle finger and letting the arms of the Indian goddess plant funnel through the hole as she drew her hand back.

In a bizarre coincidence of thought, Matthew said, "They remind me of the Indian goddess Kali, no? The multi-armed goddess of death. Do you know Kali? Do goddesses know each othah?" The question sounded like a joke, but he wasn't smiling. He seemed genuinely curious, but he suddenly brightened and laughed. "Do Zaz and Kali take tea togethah?"

Gaia didn't respond, but the question made her wonder anew about mythology. She herself, the Earth Mother, was supposed to be only mythical, yet here she was, in the flesh. Could other gods and goddesses be real, like Kali, walking the Earth in the flesh of clueless 14-year-olds? It was an intriguing notion.

A new thought shocked her awake. Why was Matthew wearing gloves? She quickly withdrew her hands.

"What kind of plant is this?" she accused.

"This," he said somberly, is my prrride and joy. "I developed thees species myself. "Thee scientific name is Toxicodendron Vernix, genetic strain 15. My pah-sonal strain! Thee common name is poison sumac."

"What?!" Gaia stepped back. She'd never seen the plant, but she'd sure heard of it, and now she knew why Matthew was wearing gloves. The plant was poisonous to the touch and could cause a bad rash. She also knew something else that was more unsettling: poison sumac was the primary ingredient in Croozer. Matthew, the thought slowly dawned on her, was a manufacturer of the most dangerous recreational drug ever known. And he was a *major* manufacturer given the titanic size of his operation.

But she didn't want to tip her hand and reveal what she knew, even though the fact was virtually common knowledge and he'd probably reveal it soon enough. However, he might not suspect a kid her age of knowing. So she took a more urgent tack to feign ignorance.

"And you let me touch it? Won't this give me a bad rash?"

Matthew shrugged. "Fo anyone else, yes. But fo you, doubtful."

"Doubtful? Why did you make me touch it?" Her hatred of him was growing. He was a mean-spirited bully who used others for his own whimsy or sick purposes. Seeing him this way made her angry, as if he were yet another playground tormentor. "Is this some kind of sick experiment?"

"Eet is something I need to know."

"One of these 'discoveries' you were talking about making with me?" She made quote marks in the air and let anger rise in her voice. This was her own dangerous experiment, but thoughts of her family kept her fuming. Her mother's screams. Gunfire. Men converging with rifles. Godpappy falling. She was getting more worked up. "Discoveries for you, with me as the guinea pig? Is that it?"

Matthew looked cross and began walking back toward the domed room. "Please do not disrespect me, sistah."

"Stop calling me that," she said, falling into step behind him. Words were apparently the only weapon she had. "I'm not your sister! You're not my brother! What have you done with my family?"

He spun so quickly she nearly ran into him. His arm was raised, poised like a snake ready to backhand her, and she winced. His milky eyes looked fierce. His next words were spat, slowly, individually, in an obvious battle of self-restraint.

"Do...not...dis...respect...me."

He lowered his hand and collected himself. Gaia's heart hammered.

"Now come. Eet is time fo thee gospel to be fulfilled. I have promised Zaz to my people, and Zaz they shall have."

-21-
Opiate of the masses

I t didn't take long for Gaia to find out what the capsule in her shoulder did.

As she followed Matthew along the catwalk around the curved edge of the room they'd been in, she misjudged one of the grated, see-through steps leading to a lower walkway and tripped, instinctively reaching out to catch herself from falling. The thing she caught herself with was Matthew's arm.

She dropped to the floor like a doll, paralyzed. As she lay there twitching on a current that felt like a million bees coursing through her, stopping her breath, her mind floated to the community garden and the feeling of the blight taking her. Gaia's thought then shifted and morphed into a beautiful view of the garden as she'd re-grown it, hovering and drifting over it like a ghost, able to reach down and nearly touch the top of the juvenile sequoia as if she were in a hot air balloon or a leaf gliding along on an invisible current. It was lovely.

The mad buzzing stopped suddenly. Her senses returned just ahead of her lungs, which she noticed were pulling hard at the air. She feared she'd never be able to gulp enough breath. Limbs still vibrating with fiery nerves, Gaia rolled onto her stomach, put one knee at a time under her, and struggled to stand with the help of the metal railing next to her.

"As I told you. Do. Not. Touch. Me. Thees is a mild setting."

So that's what the little pellet in her shoulder could do. This was the game. Matthew had also seemed confident that her body wouldn't dissolve it like her previous diagnostic implants, which meant the thing must be made out of a stronger material. But how could he know whether it would really hold up? He didn't, she realized. Maybe her body would overcome this foreign object as well. She concentrated on hydrochloric acid, or whatever it was inside of her that could dissolve things, flowing through her shoulder area. It was worth a try. Anything was worth a try.

Gaia wiped drool from her chin and spat. She squared her shoulders, and she bored her stare into Matthew's dead eyes. Counting the hacking, it was the fourth time over the past day that he'd caused her to lose consciousness or bodily control. It was ridiculous. If she ever wanted to escape, she couldn't let him have that kind of control over her, whatever it took.

"After you," she said as coldly and evenly as she could.

His hand came off the baton. *So that's how he triggered it*, she thought. Matthew's milky eyes narrowed and studied her for a moment, but he only turned and led her to a grated elevator.

They dropped past level after level. Jump-suited workers hurried from the poison sumac plants, abandoned their pushcarts, and scrambled down spiral staircases like a flow of green water pooling too quickly for a drain, then slowly twisting down, further and further toward the lower levels of the complex. The collective clomping sounded to her like steady thunder. She also picked up on a din below her, a mass of voices in congregation, mixed with the calls of animals.

As they descended, Gaia noticed some of the workers looking at her and pointing, conferring among themselves. She wondered if any of them had seen her collapse. The voices spoke other languages besides English. She heard Chinese, which she spoke pretty well, but but also some Spanish. With English or Chinese— or even when the two languages were bouncing around each other—she could pick out full phrases. Her Spanish was weaker, though she heard the words "madre" and "dios," which she knew meant "mother" and "god," but she couldn't figure out the context, whether the words were separate or combined in the common phrase, "madre de dios."

Then it hit her. Zaz. *I have promised Zaz to my people, and Zaz they shall have.*

They were coming to see her. But what did that mean? Was she supposed to speak? Would they tear her limbs off? She wished she knew more about Zaz, this mythological person from some lost gospel. She should have asked Selene to tell her more in the car on the way to her soccer game.

Selene. Gaia ached to be back in the car seat next to her meanspirited big sister, even if it meant being punched or called 'little shit.'

Now she could see the ground. They'd dropped below the catwalks of poison sumac, and a vast, unbelievable sight met her. A village, crops, people—animals. She could see the end of the complex off in the distance, or maybe it wasn't the end. In any direction the place was massive. There were rows and rows of little huts with tiny dirt yards lined with short, motley wooden fences. The only time the houses broke their straight-row formation was when they bent around occasional massive support tubes shooting up into the heights of the complex.

In the fenced yards were animals that Gaia had never seen. A few fat little birds strutted in the yards, and gangly dog-sized creatures that were white and brown and black let out funny trembling cries.

"Sheep?" The word just slipped out of her. She hadn't meant to say it aloud.

Matthew smiled, shook his head, and tisk-tisked. "Ah, how quickly thee world fah-gets her lost species. Goats, not sheep."

Run, run, run, you little goat. Last Coyote gonna slit your throat.

Last Coyote. Was it possible? Could this man, Matthew, Siafu, be Chief Last Coyote, the evil genius capable of downing satellites and airplanes with the phantom Pulse weapon and sewing fear throughout the world with his seemingly unstoppable terrorist organization? Matthew was Native African, not Native American. Then Gaia thought back to the community garden, with the men descending on her and her family with rifles. Was it possible? This beyond-impressive complex had to be the work of some kind of genius. His behavior matched his legendary reputation. Gaia shuddered.

"And do you know thee others?"

"Chickens?" she said, even though she now doubted herself and didn't want to continue her ignorant streak. More than that, she didn't want to let this bipolar sadist belittle her anymore, whether he was the infamous Chief Last Coyote or not.

"Good! And ovah there," he pointed to a large rectangular field sprouting a leafy crop. Next to the field was a barn with a big fenced yard holding larger animals that slowly moved or stood, docile, brown, black, and spotted black and white.

"Cows?" she ventured.

"Yes!" he clapped. "Moo!"

As the elevator slowed to reach ground level, Gaia wondered how Matthew got ahold of illegal livestock. It was a lot to take in: Matthew, Croozer, this gargantuan facility-slash-village, contraband animals, a hidden world. It all presented a size and context beyond anything she'd ever imagined. It felt indomitable, the sick wonder of it, and she began to lose any hope of escape.

The elevator stopped, and Matthew slid the door open. "But, you must remembah that *you* are the main attraction here. *You* are thee big deal! Come." He grinned and exited, leading her to the left around the massive center column the elevator was attached to. He seemed happier, more confident. She wondered if he thought his little shock lesson would be enough to control her from now on. If so, she thought, he guessed wrong. She was determined to fight.

At floor level, the place felt even more massive. The open ground they walked across was a smooth, level surface of dirt and stone that seemed to be carved out of the earth itself. Off to her right, the huts seemed much larger than they'd looked from higher up, and the spokes of catwalks above her rose into infinity. People of all ages hurried from the little village in the same direction Matthew and Gaia were going, some slowing when they caught a glimpse of her. One little boy pointed, but his mother grabbed him by the arm and tugged him along, glancing over at Gaia, then at Matthew who was slightly ahead of Gaia. But Matthew didn't seem to notice any of them.

The throng of people they were walking toward was huge. There were easily more than a thousand men, women, and children crowded together. Many wore the green jumpsuits, but just as many didn't.

She glanced up into the heights of the complex. A section of catwalks above her ended, and she saw the simulated gray-blue sky with wispy, bone-colored clouds slowly drifting, all lit by the sun which she guessed was hiding behind a thicker clump of clouds up and off to her left.

"Mira!" she heard a little girl say. "Mira, Mama!"

Where am I? She wished with all her might that she'd had a Telepath so that her family would know her location. But she was too young for a Telepath, and even if she'd had one she guessed her body would dissolve it like it did the diagnostic implants. Matthew would have made sure she didn't have one—would have undoubtedly cut it out of her or zapped it. The building was probably self-contained, too, with its own closed Net.

"Greetings, my fami-lee, my children," Matthew's projected voice boomed as he strode. "Please, make way so that I may introduce you to ou-wah special guest. Indeed, to yo-ah new sistah, as I have been promising you!" He held his fist in the air.

The crowd noise swelled, punctuated by random whistling and tentative applause. As Matthew approached the mass of people, they parted and formed a wide pathway, lowering themselves to their knees as he passed and becoming very quiet. He halted and turned, finally seeing that Gaia had fallen behind looking at the sky, and with a gracious smile and an outstretched hand he said, "Please, come, my sistah, honored guest. You do not have to be shy here. We are all your new family!" He wiggled his fingers.

A family that kidnaps children, shoots their real family, and brings them to a strange place to be tortured, Gaia thought.

Behind Matthew, Gaia noticed a large, circular stage, maybe two feet high, which the crowd surrounded. She took a few cautious steps forward, wary of wading into a mass of people whose heads were all bowed except for a few children whose parents quickly yanked them down.

"A bit faster please," Matthew said, grinning even wider. "They have been waiting fo you fo a very long time."

A dead plant sat in a large pot onstage, and Gaia guessed it was a poison sumac skeleton. She wondered what Matthew was playing at. Was he expecting her to do something with the plant? She was liking her situation less and less.

When Matthew saw that she was on her way, albeit slowly, he hopped up onto the stage and waited for her to ascend the steps. All around her, heads were bowed. Body odor was pungent. As she stepped up, Gaia noticed a small boy in a pure white robe gazing up at her in awe. His garment stood out from everyone else, as if he were a little white beacon of hope, and she wondered why he was dressed that way.

As she neared Matthew, keeping her distance, she could now see the full crowd which she guessed was easily 5,000 in number, maybe more. Matthew's sudden shout made her jump.

"GLORY TO MOTHAH!"

At this, the entire crowd rose and repeated the phrase in unison, which was so loud that Gaia covered her ears.

"POWER TO THE SEED OF THEE EARTH!"

The crowd shouted this, too, as well as everything else Matthew shouted.

"DESTROYER OF THE HOUND!"

"BLESSINGS TO ALL WHO FOLLOW AND ARE FAITHFUL!"

"SHE IN ALL!"

"ALL IN SHE!"

That was the last of it. He looked at her and smiled, then took a knee and bowed deeply to her with his arms outstretched.

"Zaz, mothah of all," he said softly, though it was still projected. "Your people, your faithful, have gathered in your presence." He raised his head. "Bless us."

Matthew stood.

"Thee gospel, thee law, is clear. It is written that none shall lay hands on thee mothah. None shall approach save the prophet. And who is thee prophet?"

"SIAFU!" the crowd bellowed.

"Who?"

"SIAFU!"

"Yes?"

"SIAFU!"

"As he who discovered the lost gospel, as he who dedicated his life to fulfilling the prophecy of the coming of Zaz, to usher in a new peace to thee dying world and ridding it of the Infidel, I-AM-THEE-PROPHET!"

"SIAFU!" they called.

"And at long last, thee prophecy has been fulfilled! Thee prophet has delivered to thee people..." he paused for dramatic effect, "ZAZ!"

The crowd erupted. People pumped their fists in the air, women fainted, children were held aloft to better see. A rhythmic chant of "ZAZ! ZAZ! ZAZ!" spontaneously broke out. People went berserk.

Gaia felt very small, and she started shaking. She knew she was the Earth Mother, but she still had no idea what her purpose was or what she was supposed to do in the world. But she was sure this wasn't it. She tried to calm herself, but her breath stuttered. She knew she'd already died and come back to life, but the intensity of the moment made her doubt it. Nothing was clear except her desire to flee. She wished for the power of flight, but it didn't come. Instead, Matthew raised a hand, and the crowd fell silent.

"And now, to show you that I am true, and that the goddess has finally come, a proof. Bear witness, my children."

And then Gaia heard Matthew's voice in her mind; something else the capsule in her shoulder could apparently do.

Bring it back to life. Do it now. He motioned to the dead poison sumac bush in invitation.

No, she thought back deliberately as if she were speaking, wondering if she was doing it right. *I won't.*

A shadow crossed his otherwise jubilant face.

Do it. Now. Or I'll make you.

I won't. I refuse. And you can't make me. I can only do it with my own free will, not by force. She wasn't sure about this, but he didn't need to know.

Very well. Now he smiled. *I was hoping you would refuse. Thee show goes on, and they will believe in you even more.*

Suddenly, Matthew dropped to his knees and bowed down before her, prostrate.

"My savior!" he cried, his voice booming through the hushed complex. "Fo-give your humble servant! Fo it is written, 'Zaz demands a sacrifice!'"

He jumped to his feet, crouching his giant frame as best he could in humble deference to Gaia as he crossed in front of her to the stage stairs.

The crowd rustled, and two figures in green robes ascended, bringing with them the white-robed little boy between them, delivering him to Matthew. One of the green figures turned to descend the stairs, but the other stayed, hesitating. Gaia could see it was a woman. The other, a man, came back and grabbed the woman's arm, pulling her backwards. She struggled to stay. "Mijo!" she cried "My baby!" But the man pulling her was too strong, and the woman's wails and sobs were muffled as she was pulled back into the crowd.

No! Gaia thought to Matthew. *Don't!*

But Matthew didn't respond. Instead, he spoke to the crowd, turning to face Gaia with his hand around the boy's shoulder.

"And Zaz, the mother of all, was pleased, and did bless her people!"

Gaia didn't see where the knife had come from. Matthew held it aloft, and before she could move to stop him, before she could even think another word into the Telepath, Matthew pulled the boy's hood back, grabbed him by the hair, and slit his throat.

Cries went up from the crowd. In her numb shock, Gaia heard the boy's mother shriek. Surely this was a joke, a magic trick. Surely it was just for effect. If so, it was convincing. Blood poured onto the boy's robe. Matthew still held him by the hair as the boy's body jerked and gripped at the gaping wound at his throat while Matthew calmly stared at her, unconcerned with the boy.

This is real! My God, it's real!

Gaia couldn't move. She didn't believe this was happening. The world around her pulsated like a massive heart, moving closer, further, closer, further with each beat. Blood flowed out of the boy, saturating the white robe. It pooled at his feet, and at Matthew's feet. His Telepath voice returned.

Now do it. Fo if you do not, if Zaz requires mo sacrifice, there is another waiting. A little girl.

Gaia's body moved on its own without any conscious thought from her. In a blur—she realized she was crying—Gaia found herself kneeling at the poison sumac skeleton. She plunged her hands into its dirt and pushed as hard as she could, hoping she'd break her fingers so that she'd feel something else. She clenched her teeth and growled, trying to break her voice box. An anger like she'd never known erupted, and she focused it all on the dead bush.

Then she was aware of arms pulling at her, of intense heat, and she felt herself come free, moving backwards. When she looked up, the bush was engulfed in flames.

-22-

Heart of a Goddess

G aia fought and squirmed to get free of the hands gripping her, touching her, moving her across the stage as she struggled. The hands were gloved, and above the roar of voices and shouts she heard Matthew calling instructions to take her somewhere.

She wrenched an arm free and punched and swung randomly, connecting with a head here and a nose there until she felt her body seize with the same induced epilepsy inflicted on her before. Now that she could no longer struggle, they carried her, moving more quickly. The epilepsy clouded her senses, especially her hearing, a sensation that made her feel underwater and pulled by a strong current. Gaia was vaguely aware of people surrounding her in the crowd, touching her as she was carried along.

The press of bodies lightened, the angle of her body changed, and she heard heavy rainfall before realizing in the recesses of consciousness that it was the sound of boots on metal stairs. It was the last detail she remembered before everything went black.

When her mind awoke she realized her jaw was tightly clenched and sore, and she wondered why, wondered where she was. Above her hung a gray-blue sky across which a seagull glided. It cocked its head to consider her and sailed out of view, and she realized it was a projected image like the sky itself.

Then the most incredible, rich smell of cooked food washed over her, and her stomach lurched with hunger.

When Matthew stepped into view above her, Gaia's hunger turned to nausea, which quickly turned to panic, because she remembered what had happened. Worse, she was on her back with her biceps strapped to whatever she was lying on. Then she realized that she was in the original room, strapped to the same bed, back where she started.

"I am pleased," he said. "I am very pleased, my sistah."

She tried with all her strength to break the arm straps. All she could do was kick her feet and shake her head. She saw him watching her struggle, so she closed her eyes and tried to slow her breathing. All she had was her voice as a weapon.

"*I* am *not* pleased," she said. "Zaz is not pleased."

Matthew chuckled. "Zaz," he said, then reached down and gently stroked her head, which Gaia shook back and forth to free herself from his touch.

"I have come to realize that you cannot kill me with your touch or your anger," he said. "You see? No harm can come to me. That is all I wanted to show you. Now we may sit down togethah and speak. As equals. And look!" he stepped back and indicated his hip. For a moment she wondered what he was talking about, then realized there was no baton strapped to him, or none that she could see. "No way to incapacitate you anymore. A gesture of trust!"

"Trust?!" she sputtered. "You just killed a little boy, slit his throat right in front of me! And you think you can get me to trust you? You're a beast! You're the one whose throat needs to be slit!"

"Ah," he held up a finger. "Come come. We put on a won-daful show, you and I. I nevah dreamed you had fire in you! Most exciting. We do, all of us, have a dark side, even you, my sistah. Seeing how you killed thee grass on thee football pitch—sorry, thee *soccer* pitch, as the Americans say—did reveal a darker side of your powah I find most intriguing."

He was there! He saw me! But Gaia didn't remember seeing him or anyone remotely resembling him or Old Ned. Then again, at the time, she was so taken with the grass that an elephant could have walked across the soccer field and she wouldn't have noticed.

"Trust, my sistah, is not an absolute. Trust is seem-ply a matter of context."

He touched the side of the table, and the bands popped off her arms. She was free. Gaia immediately spun off the bed away from

Matthew and landed on her feet, but her legs were still wobbly and buckled, crumpling her to the floor. Matthew was instantly next to her, but this time he reached down to help her. He was laughing. Laughing!

"My, you are a very spirited one, aren't you? Full of vee-gor and veem!"

Vigor and vim. A desperate idea came to her. Very slowly, Gaia got to her hands and knees, feigning exhaustion and panting. Matthew stepped closer, offering his hand. It was what she hoped he'd do. With all her speed and might she thrust her palm up into his crotch, connecting hard.

Matthew fell over and curled into an ball. Gaia jumped to her feet, all adrenaline now, and scurried around the bed looking for something she could use as a weapon, like the medical instruments that were there before. But the medical cart was gone. She heard Matthew cough and groan.

Gaia noticed a table a few yards away that had been set for a meal for two: plates, silverware, and food trays on stands next to it. In the place settings she found a short, thick knife with a serrated edge and a sharp point. Matthew was beginning to stand, but he was hunched over and trying to steady himself on the side of the bed. Feeling like a trapped animal, Gaia took the knife and ran to the far end of the circular room where she'd seen Matthew and Mrs. Ahn come and go through a sliding door. She searched with her eyes, and with her hands, rubbing over the surface of the wall, but she could find nothing.

"Help!" she yelled, slapping the wall. "Help me! Help me!"

Matthew hobbled toward her now, still coughing. She ran away around the edge of the room, wielding the knife while keeping him in sight and looking around for another exit. But instead of pursuing her, he stopped, then went into a coughing, hacking fit that lasted a while, but it wasn't just coughing, and Gaia now realized that mixed in with the hacking was more laughter. How could it be? Given what she'd seen him do to the boy, and given that he'd even struck one of his own people with no provocation, Gaia was sure that what she'd just done to Matthew warranted the ultimate penalty. But as he stood up to his full height, sputtering and chuckling, he made no more move to catch her. Instead, he simply shrugged with outstretched arms, shook his head, and went to sit down at the table as if nothing had happened. His bipolar nature frightened her more than ever.

It was then that Gaia knew she was trapped. Even if she were able to hurt Matthew, or even kill him, she'd never get out of that room. And even if she did, she'd have to contend with thousands of people who were perfectly willing to sacrifice one of their young in order to get Zaz. These people were delusional, insane. There's no way they'd let her just walk out of there.

She took another minute trying to think of a last-ditch solution, then gave in and approached the table. Matthew was busy lifting lids and dishing food onto the two plates, though his face was still a bit purple from pain and he coughed a few times.

Videostreams of animals and nature suddenly appeared in the domed ceiling.

"Truce," he said. "I will take that as payment for thee things I have done to you. Ah! I see you have brought your own knife to thee party. That is fortunate, because as you can see I am one knife short. Please, sit down. Let us talk."

He lifted the lid on a pan and stabbed a thick chunk of food, placing it on her plate. He stabbed one for himself. The aroma coming off it was like nothing she'd ever smelled and awoke a new level of hunger in her, trumping even her panic. *Where there's food, there's hope*, the old saying came to mind.

Despite the hopelessness of her situation, Gaia prepared herself for round 2, knowing she had no other choice at the moment. She set the knife next to her plate and pulled out her chair to sit opposite Matthew. He spooned some kind of steaming, pink-brown chili beans onto her plate next to the quinoa already there, followed by green beans and a thick slice of bread smeared with a yellow spread. He then poured her a glass of water from a clear pitcher. When he finished, he sat back and folded his hands in his lap.

"I am still pleased, and now even more that you have decided to join me fo dinnah."

Gaia tried to hold out in front of the food, but she couldn't take it anymore. She was famished, not even caring if the food was poisoned. Grabbing the fork, she dug into the things on the plate she recognized—green beans and quinoa—and chewed, forking in another mouthful before she'd swallowed. Matthew watched. Gaia reached for the glass of water but hesitated.

"It is Worm-free, I assure you," he said. "See?" He drank from his own glass. "It is not so hard, taking Thee Worm from thee water. In fact, it is my next business idea."

Gaia took a tentative sip from her glass. It was refreshing, without the usual acidic quality water had. She thought that people would go crazy for this kind of water and almost said so, but she didn't want to pay this man any compliments, and she definitely didn't want to sympathize with her captor. There was a term for that, which she knew, because it was the nickname for one of the girls on her soccer team who had an abusive father: "Stockholm Syndrome." She took another bite of green beans.

"So you think we're even?" she said with her mouth full. "We're not. You owe me. An explanation if nothing else." She ventured a bite of the chili beans, which were tender and savory. They popped in her mouth with a salty, spiced broth.

Purple-crimson blood on a white robe floated into her head and made her gag, but she fought through it and kept chewing.

...Last Coyote gonna slit your throat.

She remembered Matthew standing onstage with his long knife raised in the air. Gaia looked at the knife in her own hand and set it down.

"You're Last Coyote, aren't you."

Matthew raised his eyebrows, surprised. "Why do you think so? Most intriguing."

"Then you're not?"

Matthew didn't answer.

"Why did you kill that little boy?" She noticed he had changed into a clean set of un-bloodied clothes.

"Why did you demand that I sacrifice him?" Matthew asked.

"I DIDN'T!"

"Oh? By refusing to obey my wishes, you forced me to do it." He was uncharacteristically calm, serene even. He idly turned his plate, and Gaia wondered why he hadn't taken a bite yet.

"But you said you hoped I'd refuse!"

"Yes. I did hope that. But you disobeyed nonetheless."

"Why? Why did you do it?" She found herself holding the knife again, pointing it at him.

"Can you not guess?"

Gaia thought about this, picturing what would have happened if she'd obeyed and healed the plant like he'd first asked. She couldn't see what difference it would have made. "No," she said finally. "I can't guess."

"So that my people may continue to think that what they believe is true. According to thee gospel, Zaz demands a sacrifice. A human one."

"That's barbaric! Why would anyone believe that? It's just so that you can stay in control, then, and they'll follow you and do whatever you say!"

He smiled. "Well done, sistah, well done. This is lee-dah-ship." Matthew was speaking softly. He looked like an actor who had been flamboyant onstage, but who became himself again back in the dressing room. He seemed almost tired.

"So you don't even believe in Zaz yourself, then?"

"Oh, I believe in Zaz. But fo different reasons." He cut into his own thick chunk of dark brown food and took a bite, motioning for her to do the same. "Try thee meat before it grows cold. I will answer your questions while you eat."

"What is this?" She pointed at her portion.

"Beef. It is from a cow."

Gaia hesitated. Aside from the beef leather her mom had given her at Pelican Bluffs, the only animal she'd ever eaten was jellyfish. Even though people in different parts of the world ate meat—even in New Texas—it struck her as odd and somehow wrong to eat an animal.

"This cut of meat is called thee tri-tip. A cut made famous near where you come from."

"Kenya?"

Matthew laughed on his mouthful of tri-tip. "No, no. Santa Maria, up north."

It was a mistake, and Gaia caught it. A small mistake, but maybe one she could use. They were somewhere south of Junipero Bay. Still in California, maybe, but south could also mean Mexico, Central America, and South America, all the way down to the tip of Patagonia. And then Antarctica, which was silly, she realized, and so were Central and South America. Why would would this facility be located that far south? Gaia decided on either Mexico or California. He'd also gestured with his knife when he said "up north," seeming to imply that it was a relatively short distance. Matthew still hadn't acknowledged his mistake.

"But," he continued, "we will talk of where you truly come from, Kenya, our homeland, my sistah. Not yet, though."

If he was capable of making that kind of mistake, maybe he'd make others. For all his apparent control and invincibility, he was fallible. This gave her hope.

"Anyway, if I indeed were Last Coyote, why would I admit to it? Thee pow-ah of Last Coyote lies in thee mystery of Last Coyote, don't you think?"

Gaia only shrugged. She knew he'd only run her in circles around the truth, and whether he really was Last Coyote or not didn't matter at this point. Matthew was who he was, and Gaia just wanted him dead.

The food in her belly had triggered more hunger. She stared at the meat, then decided to go for it. When she cut into it, she saw that it was bright pink inside. And when she brought the fork into her mouth and began to chew, the intensity of flavor almost melted her face. She had to stop chewing for a moment to process what she was experiencing. Salty with pepper and garlic, rough but tender, juicy beyond belief, so juicy it left a little brown puddle on her plate. She chewed more ravenously, taste buds swelling and bursting, and cut off another chunk, watching Matthew run his bread through the juice on his plate and take a bite. She followed suit. The bread was crunchy and creamy. She could imagine only one thing tasting any better: tomato soup, the way her mom made it with sugar.

Mom. Dad. Selene. Godpappy. Cloudy. They all got together to eat every Sunday, which she realized was today. Instead of being with the people she loved most, eating the food they worked so hard to produce, delicious in its own way because it was gathered and made with honesty and love, she was sharing a gourmet meal with the very beast who had deprived her of her family and their Sunday meal. The food in her mouth soured. Yet, she forced herself to chew and swallow over and over, trying to smother her hunger as quickly as she could. If Gaia had any hope of escape, she'd need strength. She wondered if her family would ever be able to find her.

Then Gaia got an idea, thinking it might get her out of the room.

"I have to pee."

"Ah! Fo-give!" he stood and walked over to the raised bed and pulled a handle on the side of its boxed metal frame, which revealed, to Gaia's dismay, a small composting toilet. Her prison was complete. He'd thought of everything. Matthew turned the entire bed 180 degrees so that the toilet was on the other side to give her privacy, which was yet another instance of civilized behavior that she wasn't used to from him. She waited for Matthew to return before going over and trying to use it.

Then she felt something in her pants and panicked. Her period. She needed to change her pad. When she pulled her trousers down, she found the pad she was using had more than served its useful life. She wrapped it in some toilet tissue she found stacked in a compartment at the base of the seat and was about to drop the wad into the toilet, but then she remembered Mrs. Ahn. Mrs. Ahn had acted as if she didn't want Matthew to know that Gaia had her period. But why? Didn't every woman have a period? For good measure, Gaia wrapped more toilet paper around the wad to hide any color, then dropped it in the toilet.

Every woman. *But I'm not every woman*, she thought. *If I'm the Earth Mother, why do I have a period?* It was another mystery, one Matthew might have some knowledge of that she didn't. How could he know so much?

"Everything is okay, yes?" Matthew called. "You found thee tissue?"

"Oh, there it is," Gaia stalled. "I found it." She fashioned a makeshift pad out of new tissue, adjusted it a few times in her underpants, realized it was as good as it was going to get, then returned to the table and tried not to squirm in her seat.

"Good! I had begun to worry that you had fallen in, yes? I wonder if my people have ever considered the fact that even Zaz needs to piss!" He clapped his hands together, congratulating himself on his own joke. "So. Earlier you asked me if I believed in Zaz. I want to an-sah yo question. Please, continue to eat as much as you like. You must be starving like a Hawaiian child!"

Gaia ate some more chili beans, then nearly choked on them because of what Matthew said next.

"I have a confession. I invented Zaz."

"You what?"

Matthew grinned and re-filled Gaia's water glass. "Is it so difficult to imagine?"

"What do you mean, you invented Zaz?"

He leaned back in his chair. "Five years ago, and it was quite expensive. Do you have any idea how much it costs to make artifacts look thousands of years old under scientific scrutiny? Well, let us just say it is a good thing thee Croozah business is doing so well. That was thee hard part. Thee easy part was hiding thee artifacts, outside of Jerusalem. Thee fun part was planting thee rumor and watching thee archaeologists fight ovah thee discovery." Matthew took a sip from his own water and popped a green been into his mouth. "Months before thee discovery I made videostreams, prophesying about the coming of Zaz. When people realized that I had known about it before thee scientists, well, people came to me, thee prophet. One can find very cheap labor in hope, in religion."

"And you invented it knowing I was here?"

"Of course."

Gaia now realized her mom was right about Zaz. It was complete and utter hooey.

"Why do you do this?" Gaia pushed her plate away. "You're just scrambling everyone! Zaz, Croozer. Croozer is terrible! Just walk around the streets, *everywhere*, and look! People are slumped over, stumbling around. They don't want to work. They don't want to do anything. You can't even talk to them. Their brains are gone! And these poor people, they think I'm Zaz. All their hopes are stuck on me. And I was starting to think that maybe I was Zaz, that maybe there was an old prophecy, that maybe there was real hope! This is stupid. You're a fraud. You want to give people false hope and hurt them. And why are you telling me this? Aren't you afraid I'll tell the world your secret?"

Gaia wanted to stick her finger down her throat and vomit all the food back onto the table. She didn't want to accept anything from Matthew, which was easier to think now that she was no longer starving.

Matthew became deadly serious. "Thee short answer as to why I invented Zaz, as I mentioned, is simply cheap labor. True believers will work fo next to nothing. So it has always been with religion." He sighed as though impatient. "My sistah. I can sympathize with your feelings. It is a necessary stage of thinking which good-natured people must pass through, which I myself have passed through. But truly, there is no other way. What I say is true. I realized that thee world does not want to be saved. *People* do not want to be saved. They say they do, but they never do thee right thing themselves, never truly try to change. They wait for someone else." He held up his hands to fend off a fresh outburst from Gaia. "Oh, yes, some do act. People like you and me. We try to rise above, to pull everyone else along with us. But humans are crabs. Do you know crabs?"

When she didn't respond, he kept going. But she had heard of crabs.

"When I was a boy, there were crabs in thee sea. You may have seen pic-chahs. We used to catch them fo food. Very tasty and very funny. As we carried them in thee basket back to our home, some would try to escape by climbing out. But we nevah had to worry. Do you know why? Because the others would grab onto their climbing brothers and pull them back into thee basket! They would not let them escape. And so it is with humans. When one tries to climb out, he is shot. When one attempts to do something good, another takes advantage."

Gaia's mind went to the Chinese water jet being shot right out of the sky. Chief Last Coyote had taken responsibility for it, which meant that if Matthew was Last Coyote, he himself had done it— or ordered it done. It was true hypocrisy.

"I watched people fight over new crops." His brow furrowed and he pinched the air with his fingers. "I saw parents pushing away their children to fight fo food! I watched a sea of dead fishes wash up on thee shore day after day, and I saw thee tide bring in the last of the great whales. I knew we were finished as a species. My mission became to help people pass from thee Earth, to fade away, in comfort."

To Gaia, it didn't add up. Here was no philanthropist. He was a cold-blooded killer. "You mean you saw how you could make money off people instead of helping them."

"Is it not a service worth being paid fo?"

"But it's a lie," Gaia said, leaning forward and pointing at him. "It's one huge, unforgivable lie!"

"A lie, you say? If Zaz is real—if thee person, thee goddess described in thee gospel is indeed real, then it is not a lie. You are sitting right before me."

"But you don't know that's what I am! How could you? And people don't want to be on Croozer, either!"

"Oh? I could not disagree more. You are young still and do not understand people yet. It is a waste of my time to debate the truth of human nature with a child. Even a child who is a goddess, which I *do* know."

Gaia bristled. "I'm not a child."

"Indeed not," he said, swinging his fist through the air. "You are indeed more than a child! You are a goddess. In thee teachings of my own belief, if one devours thee heart of a god or a goddess who has returned to thee Earth, then that person becomes thee deity."

"What?" Her hand went involuntarily to her heart, which had picked up its pace. "You're kidding."

"But," he continued, "there is always a chance I have misinterpreted thee teachings. Thee California air can cause one to be lazy and forgetful at times."

It was another mistake! He implied that they were still in California. Hope buzzed in her briefly, and she decided on a new tack to drive some kind of wedge into this new crack and somehow weaken him, make him drop his guard.

"I can help you," she said. "I can grow things. You already know it."

But Matthew only stared back at her, then sighed.

"You told me I owed you an explanation, which I am giving to you," he said. "And you are correct. It is thee least I can do. But it ees also a way of unburdening myself of it. You see, there is no one else I can talk to about thees."

An eerie feeling rose in her. "What do mean, 'the least you can do?'"

"The teachings of my faith, my real faith, say that thee heart of thee human deity must be consumed at the blood of birth. This ees why I tried to take you from Mistahs Lane and Cloudy. I thought it ees the same for a male deity and a female deity, when thee heart must be consumed. This ees what I thought then, and it would have been a mistake."

"*When* the heart must be consumed?" Was he thinking of eating her heart?

"Aftah that, I learned the truth. For a male, a god, it is at his birth. But for a female, a goddess, it is not at her birth. Her heart must be consumed when she has arrived at the time of *giving* birth."

My period, Gaia realized. *When the goddess gets her period.* Her heart tore at her chest.

The second Gaia jumped to her feet, unsure of where to start running, Matthew held up the baton he'd assured her he no longer had.

"As to why I am confessing to you about my invention of Zaz," he said, "it ees only because you will not be able to tell anyone. Fogive." Matthew eyed the baton. "Given thee deep respect I have fo you, my sistah, I shall try my best to make it painless."

-23-
The Last Coyote

The bees had returned. Gaia clenched her teeth against their buzzing agony, coursing underneath her eyebrows in a slow parade of electric fire. How long that lasted, she hadn't a clue. But when the bees subsided and she found herself strapped to the familiar bed, Mrs. Ahn was wheeling in the cart of surgical tools. A videostream appeared on the domed ceiling: A bonfire lashed at painted, scarcely clad African men who stomped out an intricate, choreographed dance, slamming their spear butts into the ground in unison and tossing chunks of mud into the fire which responded by belching yellow-purple smoke.

"Help me!" Gaia begged Mrs. Ahn as she brought the cart next to the bed and raised the arm of a lamp over Gaia's midsection, then flicked it on. "Mrs. Ahn, please! Help me! Qing-ni bangzhu-wo! He's going to cut out my heart and eat it!"

But Mrs. Ahn didn't respond, didn't even look up.

"Mrs. Ahn already knows," came Matthew's voice from behind the bed. He stepped into view and stood next to the surgical cart drying his hands on a towel. He set the towel down, adjusted the lamp, and picked up a scalpel from the tray. Gaia screamed when he brought the shiny blade up to her throat without a word, then felt a few tugs as Matthew sliced her t-shirt open right down the middle, exposing her chest and belly but keeping her breasts covered.

"Nooooo!" she screeched at him with all her strength and began sobbing uncontrollably, unable to fathom what was about to happen.

Matthew stared down at her like a calm beast pitying its prey.

"It has been a long journey, my sistah. I have enjoyed watching you grow to become a young woman, and I have felt a kinship with you."

"Don't do this! Please don't do this! I'd rather help you than—" But Gaia stopped herself. A calm had suddenly swept into her, and she looked up into the spitting fire and dancers on the ceiling. Drums pounded, and she felt the beat of her heart in sync with them.

"Than what?" Matthew asked. "Rather help me than die?"

"No. That's not true. I'd never help you." A deep peace descended into her, illogical as it was.

"I know," he said. "I know. Now you are smiling. You have made your peace, yes?"

"I have." The voice seemed to float out of her on its own. "Have you?"

He cocked his head, curious, then smiled back. "Oh, yes. I am at peace. And now we will become one, you and I, my sistah."

Matthew looked up at the videostream of the fire, the dancers, and began speaking in his native language, an incantation perhaps.

That's when Mrs. Ahn struck. Gaia's restraints suddenly vanished, and when Matthew heard the sound of it, he looked down to see what was happening. Then he yelped and clutched the back of his leg where Mrs. Ahn had stabbed him. When she came at him again wielding a scalpel, Matthew swiped at her, but she ducked and moved so quickly that Matthew may as well have been swinging at ghosts. The next moment, like a deadly little finch, Mrs. Ahn plunged a scalpel into Matthew's neck where it joined the shoulder. He howled and fell to his knees, grasping at the foreign object sticking from his neck as blood flowed from the wound. Mrs. Ahn then stepped in wielding a metal tray and slammed it into the side of Matthew's head with a sickening thud. As he fell over, looking like a marionette whose puppet master had decided to drop him where he was, Matthew fumbled for the baton at his hip. But he was groggy, and he fell over and stopped moving. Suddenly, Mrs. Ahn went lifeless as if she'd been dropped by the same puppeteer, and she hit the ground, twitching until her body lay still. Matthew had somehow been able to do that. Gaia guessed that Mrs. Ahn had a capsule in her just like Gaia did.

Gaia looked at Matthew, then Mrs. Ahn, then back at Matthew. Surely one of them would rise and make the next move. But both lay motionless, and more blood was leaking from Matthew's neck. It was now or never; but she was so gripped by shock that it took all her will to make herself jump down from the table. What if Matthew came to and was able to push a button on his baton, sending her to the floor like Mrs. Ahn?

She carefully went over to Matthew but stayed at what felt like a safe distance, then froze when she saw his face. His white eyes were wide open. After a few moments, she realized he was unconscious or dead and staring at empty space. Poor Mrs. Ahn looked dead. Gaia stepped over to check her pulse. Nothing. She didn't dare check Matthew's pulse for fear of being grabbed, but she made a couple of quick attempts to free the baton from his belt, being as careful as she could not to press anything that looked like a control. There were two benefits to having the baton: he wouldn't be able to use it on her, and it might open the door to the room. But she couldn't get it free. Maybe it was somehow DNA secured so that only Matthew could wield it.

Realizing she was wasting valuable time, Gaia decided to abandon the baton and try something else. She stopped to think, which was difficult to do in her panicked state. What if Mrs. Ahn were still alive and awake? What would her next move have been? Mrs. Ahn had been able to enter and leave the room. Maybe she was going to take Gaia back through the same door.

Gaia lifted Mrs. Ahn under her arms from behind and dragged her toward the door. Mrs. Ahn was much heavier than she looked. But as they neared the wall, Gaia's heart leapt when she saw the door slide open. Clearly it was keyed to something in or on Mrs. Ahn. Gaia pulled Mrs. Ahn's body across the threshold and into the next room and set her down. She saw that they were in a comfortable but sparsely appointed office with a desk, a chair, an orange throw rug covered with plain black silhouettes of animals, and a head-high bookcase that was a few feet wide and crammed with a mishmash of tattered ancient spines and newer, cleaner volumes.

Off to her right, on the opposite side of the room from the desk, the space narrowed and turned into a hallway that disappeared with the curve of the building.

Then the door they'd just come through slid shut behind her. She could no longer see Matthew. If he weren't dead and came to, he'd be able to kill her like he'd killed Mrs. Ahn. Surely the chip in her shoulder was capable of killing her. *"Thees is a mild setting,"* he'd told her after he immobilized her the first time. Or maybe he'd just paralyze her and keep her alive enough to cut out her still-beating heart, which had been his plan all along.

But she couldn't help that. She needed to keep moving, get out of there. Gaia saw that her shirt was hanging wide open where Matthew had sliced it, and she was cold. She knelt down to Mrs. Ahn.

"Xie xie," Gaia whispered. "I need to ask for one more thing." She struggled to pull off Mrs. Ahn's surgical shirt. It was tricky work, but after a minute she had it. Gaia stripped off her own shirt and donned the surgical shirt, which was a bit too small, but it would do. She looked down at dead Mrs. Ahn, lying there in the helpless indignity of now being half naked in addition to being dead, and she draped her torn t-shirt over Mrs. Ahn's chest. She wondered who this woman was and why she had sacrificed herself for Gaia. The nonverbal messages she'd sent Gaia earlier that day now made sense. Maybe there were more like her in the complex.

Gaia heard footsteps, and her attention snapped to the hallway. More than one person was coming, and she heard two men speaking. Fortunately, they didn't seem to be in any hurry.

"Dude, *fuck* New Texas," one was saying. "I say we send 'em all back. You wanna start your own country? Then go live in your own country."

"Órale, puto," another said, "ain't *you* from Texas?"

"Shut your ass, Diego. Las Cruces ain't Texas."

"Oh, that's right, you're from New *Mexico*, ese." The man laughed. He talked like the Latino boys in her class.

"Man, fuck you and *fuck Mexico, too!*"

She couldn't tell if they were inside or outside of the building, but she didn't want to stay there and find out. They were getting closer, but there was nowhere for her to go except back into the room or down the hallway they might be coming from, and she'd run right into them.

Then she noticed the outline of a metal frame in the wall beside the bookcase. She ran over to it and saw that it was a square utility panel the height of her thigh. She twisted its recessed latch and swung it open. A musty, earthy, burnt smell floated out of the dark opening. She ducked into it and was able to pull the door closed the moment she heard the voices enter the office behind her.

"What the fuck?" one of them said. There was a brief pause followed by the efficient talk and movement of soldiers. Gaia knew it well because her dad was a soldier. Gaia held her breath. She didn't dare move for fear of being heard, but she couldn't stay right next to the door, either. What if they decided to open it to look for her?

"Nolan, Big Al, check the room. Beast, go back to the entrance. Nobody comes in or out."

Boots went in different directions, and she heard somebody call from inside the room where Matthew was.

"Chief, we need a medic in here. Now."

Does that mean he's still alive? Gaia wondered, tensing at the thought that he could wake and immobilize her again.

Then a muffled explosion went off somewhere in a distant part of the complex.

"Shit!" the man in charge said, then barked orders through his Telepath, requesting a medic and ordering men off to the new action. She heard another man come into the office.

"She's gone. The girl. She ain't here."

"Shit, shit," the leader said. "And I ain't sure I wanna go find her. If she did this, and she's who everybody thinks she is, I want none of that. What if that's her blowing shit up?"

Were they afraid of her? Gaia wondered if her reputation might be more powerful than she realized, which could only help her. Still, she wasn't ready to be caught, and she wasn't immune to being zapped or shot.

"Orders, chief?"

"Stay here and keep your eyes open. Ping me with anything new."

"Roger that, Chief."

She slowly inched away from the door. It was pitch black, but she was able to stand. The ground was covered with spongy pellets that smelled like burnt wood, and as she quietly moved forward and felt the walls on either side of her with her hands, she found that she was sandwiched in some narrow walkway between walls. A few moments later, she was blocked by a wall in front of her. There was nowhere to go, and the muffled voices of the soldiers inside gave her no clue as to whether Matthew was dead or alive. Another explosion went off in the complex. What was going on?

She was stuck. Gaia sat down and fought back tears while struggling to think. She tried to calm herself by slowing her breath down as best she could and digging her hands into the squishy pellets on the ground, which gave her an idea. It seemed ridiculous given where she was, but what other choice did she have? Gaia had never tried to grow anything specific before, instead deferring to what she thought the ground wanted to produce. This time, though, she had a picture of a tree in her mind: a sequoia like the one that had popped up in Liesl's garden. She saw it, tall and sturdy in the sunlight. But nothing was happening, so she dug her hand deeper down. Still nothing. Maybe she was trying too hard. Maybe it didn't work when she tried to grow something specific.

She took another deep breath and sighed. Though her parents were unapologetic atheists, Gaia herself was always on the fence about God. She'd always felt deep down there had to be something bigger, something ultimately responsible for the wonder of living things. Now especially, some power beyond human understanding was possibly the only reasonable explanation for her existence and had even possibly been the thing that had spoken to her after she'd died in the community garden. Regardless of what was real or true, if she ever needed to cast a prayer into the void, there was no better time than right now. Gaia didn't know what to say, so she tried to settle deep within herself. Her silly dog Prop wagged into her head, and she pictured her family, Cloudy, and Godpappy walking toward her across a field of poppies. Finally, she let out another big sigh and said, "Please. Help me."

She felt a tingling between her fingers.

Gaia opened her eyes and felt the slightest current running through her, a thing she didn't remember feeling the last times she'd caused growth. Then along her palm she felt movement as if the thinnest snake was slithering across it. Something tickled her cheek, like a flying bug, and she flinched. She heard a quick, merry laugh which startled her. She scanned the blackness, but it was too dark to see.

"Hello?" she said, but nothing replied. Maybe she'd imagined it. But then she saw a sliver of gray light at the base of the outer wall and the thin runner of a plant there. Her face tickled again, and when Gaia touched the thing it felt like a snake. It moved away

from her, and she saw it slip into the crack under the wall. The gap
got bigger inch by inch. Vines! More slipped through the gap and
began growing fatter.

Then a deep, startling pop broke the silence as yet another
bomb went off in the complex, followed by more pops and
crunching as the vine widened the gap even more. Then a loud
bang erupted as the dome wall cracked before her. Gaia could
have fit her arm through the space, but she waited, even though
the noise was bound to attract attention.

The thickest vine had the girth of a big tree. It was warm and
pulsated with energy. The popping and banging of the breaking
structure had given way to a steady grinding sound, and sharp
popcorn fragments of wall rained down on her. She covered her
head, trying not to breathe in any debris. Moments later the
grinding stopped, and so did the sprinkling debris. She held her
breath and squinted through the dust. Without waiting she began
sliding her body along the vine through the broken wall. As she
moved through, she heard the sound of crickets and saw that she'd
made it out onto one of the catwalks, but she wasn't sure where.
The light was dim, coming from a bright moon sliver at the far end
of the complex ceiling. She ventured a dusty breath and tried her
best to stifle a cough.

Now she could easily hear the shouts and runnings of men in
boots clanking on catwalks and pounding on the ground far below.
The sound seemed to be moving in one specific direction, and a
moment later another distant explosion erupted.

The vine had grown beyond her sight around the curve of the
broken wall. Far below, she saw the small lights of the little village.
She could tell by the position of the moon, if it truly mirrored the
movement of the real moon outside, that she had an hour or two
before dawn. What now? She couldn't just sit there, but she didn't
want to leave the warmth of the vine. It felt familiar to her core,
like the place she'd visited after she'd died in the garden. She
rubbed the vine and closed her eyes. "Thank you," she whispered.

A little bat squeaked overhead. She watched it flopping across
the starry sky against one of the simulated clouds.

"Go now," a voice said inside of her, which almost seemed to
come from the vine. It spoke with the force of command that made
Gaia spring up.

A strong hand suddenly covered her mouth. Instinctively she swung her fist down behind her and connected with the attacker's groin. The blow made him wince, but it otherwise seemed to have no effect, because the man behind her kept pulling her steadily backwards.

"I'm helping you!" he croaked. "No noise!" She was surprised that the whisper wasn't that of a man, but of a young man. "I'm gonna let go, okay? Quiet!"

Gaia nodded. He let go, and she turned to face him. In the dim light she recognized this kid. He was taller than she was and had dark, messy hair.

"Where is it?" he asked. "Did he put it in your shoulder?"

She wasn't sure what he meant at first, then realized he must be talking about the capsule. She nodded and pointed to her shoulder where Matthew had cut her and inserted it. The boy fished something out of his pocket that looked like a small, black river stone. Holding it to her shoulder with his palm, Gaia felt a warm buzz followed by a click. He put it back in his pocket.

"It's dead now," he whispered.

"How did you know?" she asked.

"He puts 'em in everybody. Now they can't track you. Let's go. Down!"

As he led her to a circular staircase, another boom erupted from somewhere else, drawing away another group of shouting men. Below in the village, lights were flicking on one by one.

"Keep up. We gotta hurry," the boy said.

As she followed him down the staircase, she realized he couldn't be much older than she was. Maybe a year or two. Then it hit her.

"You're the boy from the street!" she said. "With the pack that slammed the hood of our truck and started fighting the Chinese bus!"

He stopped and turned, putting his fingers to his lips. "You wanna get us caught? Shut it and move!"

It was him alright, the kid who was wearing the shirt with the cartoon face of Chief Last Coyote. But he wasn't wearing that shirt now. *This is weird*, she thought. *What if it's a trick?* But there was something about the boy she trusted, even if he might be a disciple of Matthew, maybe otherwise known as Chief Last Coyote. Then it hit her. Matthew was not Chief Last Coyote. She remembered the surprise on is face when she'd accused him of being the dreaded terrorist. Who was this boy, then? If he lived in the complex village, why had he been out on the street?

At the bottom of the staircase the boy slowed, paused, then suddenly pulled Gaia behind a nearby column a split second before the beam of a flashlight bathed the place they'd just been standing. The light climbed the staircase, then moved away just as another explosion went off closer to where they were.

"When I say run, stay with me and move your ass, okay? Can you run?"

Gaia nodded.

"We're headed for those huts across the way," he pointed.

The boy peered around the column, holding his hand up for her to wait. A cart of men with guns drove past.

"Run!" he whispered, and they were off across the open ground. Another boom was followed by gunfire behind them, and a moment later the boy had pulled her around the side of a dark hut and into a small walkway. A little goat stuck its head through a split-rail fence beside them. It watched them with stupid, wide eyes, then bleated. A light went on inside the hut directly across from them.

"Come on," he said, leading her down the little pathway between huts. "Wait." He darted over to a clothesline and pulled something off of it. When he came back, he tossed it to her. "Put this on. If someone comes out, just pretend like you belong here and walk calmly." It was a poncho with a hood, much too big for her, but it covered her hair and darkened her face. Now it would be difficult for anyone to immediately recognize her.

They kept to the edge of the little village, dodging behind an apple tree here, a plum tree there, trying to keep as quiet as possible. Gaia heard different sounds coming from the huts, mostly worried voices. None of the huts had glass windows, just woven curtains or nothing at all. A man's voice floated out a nearby window.

"They told us to stay put."

"But there's bombs going off!" a woman replied. "I ain't gonna just sit her and get blown up."

"Where we gonna go then? You go out there you gonna get shot or something."

Goats and chickens were getting restless in the yards, clucking and bleating nervously.

Gaia froze. Something in her periphery, which she thought was a statue, was really a human being. A small Asian girl was standing in her yard watching Gaia. Her pants were much too baggy and drawn in at her waist, and her thin, shirtless upper body made her look like a stick with an oversized root bundle. When Gaia looked at her, the girl turned and ran back into the house. When Gaia turned back to follow the boy, he was gone, and she panicked. As she scanned the pathway and huts ahead, she heard the muted coo of a dove and saw the boy backed against a tree up ahead motioning to her.

"Keep up!" he whispered when she reached him. Gaia could see him more clearly now, and she noticed there was something wrong with his face. He had a bubbly scar that ran up and down the left side of it, which looked hideous. His hair was hacked short and uneven. He had strong features, either Mexican or Native American, and when he grabbed her hand to keep moving, she noticed how big and calloused his hands were, but also surprisingly warm and gentle, as if he were holding a little bird. A tingle went through her body, and bumps rose all over her skin. She pulled her hand away but kept following as they bent with the path and hopped an occasional fence. The boy had a sure but strange gait, a bit lopsided like a big puppy that hadn't grown into its coordination.

They finally came to the entrance of one of the huts. Gaia froze when she saw the shape of a man sitting in a chair on the darkened porch, hidden under a beat-up cowboy hat. He nodded at them, then clicked the button on a small device in his hand before following them into the hut.

Gaia couldn't see anything inside. It was too dark, and she bumped into the boy, who told her to put her hands on his shoulders and follow him. As they moved through the hut, she smelled the lingering aroma of cooked food, a comforting, rich, fried oil smell that made her stomach flop with hunger. The man following them smelled of smoke. When they reached what seemed like the back of the hut, they stopped. The boy opened a door. "Bunch of stairs," he said. "Duck your head going in." As they moved forward she put her hand on the side of the wall for balance and was surprised to feel little shelves. At the base of the stairs, the light in a small room shone on a chair and a small table stacked with a few books. The boy stepped up to another set of shelves, slipped his hand into one, and pushed the bookcase open, which led them down yet another set of stairs.

As they descended, the stairs curved and the light increased. A hanging lamp at the base of the stairs let Gaia see the back of the boy clearly. He wore an old cotton t-shirt tucked into an old pair of the most incredibly wonderful pants Gaia had ever seen and had always wanted: real cotton blue jeans. His arms and neck were deep brown. He was tall and the kind of big that one day turns into huge. At the bottom they came to a thick wooden door. Gaia turned to look at the smoky man. He was older and his skin seemed like thick animal hide. His nose was flat. He wore a long red shirt buttoned at the top that was also tucked into blue jeans. He nodded at her, but his dark eyes indicated the door. The boy made a complex drum beat on the door, which then clicked. He pushed it open, and the three of them stepped into a large but cozy, well-lit room.

Inside, a handful of men stood up from the various chairs they'd been sitting in. The boy moved aside to reveal a round table, and standing up behind it was a man of a race she'd never seen before. He had strong, thick features like the rest of the men in the room, but his skin was pinkish white. His long hair was white, too, and pulled back into a pony tail. He looked at Gaia and smiled, then looked at the boy.

"What happened to *you*? Why you walkin' funny?" the man asked, amusement curling his lips.

"She clocked me in the kiwis, Pop. I thought I was gonna barf."

The men in the room chuckled. The boy looked at Gaia with a grimace, but his eyes were as gentle as his grip had been. The scar was bad, though not as hideous as she'd first thought. She found herself quickly looking down. She was starting to feel safe, but given what had happened to her, Gaia wasn't ready to trust anything.

"I'm Two Dogs, er, Marty," the boy said. "That was a good shot, by the way. You're a fighter. That's good."

"I'm Gaia," she said, realizing how stupid that was when everyone in the room chuckled again.

"Well, that's certainly a relief," the albino said. "I'd hate to think we'd brought in the wrong green-skinned, blue-haired, grass-killing, sequoia-tree-growing girl."

More chuckling.

"It's an honor to finally meet you, Miss Cadogan," he continued. "We've been waiting a long time. We were beginning to doubt ourselves, doubt Nagi Tanka, thinking that maybe he wouldn't send you. Lotta folks are worried about you, too." Then she said to Marty, "Did she have one?"

"Yeah, right here," Marty said, pointing to Gaia's shoulder. "But Pop, it didn't go as planned. There was—something big growing, a giant vine. It cracked the building and let her out."

"Oh?" He looked at Gaia. "Did you do that?" He didn't seem surprised, and she didn't know whether she should say anything. She had no idea who this man was or what he wanted. But they were helping her, and apparently it was a planned mission of sorts. *The enemy of my enemy is my friend*, she thought. *Maybe*. It was the only thing she could trust at the moment.

"I—I'm not sure. I don't know if I made it happen or not. I was stuck between the walls."

He studied her. "There would have been a woman helping him. Short, Chinese."

"Mrs. Ahn?" Gaia said.

"Yes. Mrs. Ahn. Did she help you?"

Gaia nodded. "She cut him and knocked him out, right before he was about to—"

He raised his eyebrows.

"He was going to cut out my heart and eat it." She regretted the words as soon as they came out. Was she giving these people ideas?

"I'm sorry," he lowered his head. "We didn't think he would try to do it so soon."

"You knew?"

The albino nodded. "Did he use it on you? The device in your shoulder?"

"Three times, if you mean the shock thing." The memory of the bee feeling shot through her.

"Was worried about that." His brow furrowed. "Back to Mrs. Ahn. Sounds like she wasn't able to get you out all the way."

"I think she's dead. I had to take her shirt."

The albino sighed and rubbed his face with both hands. He seemed weary. "I was hoping that wouldn't happen. Mrs. Ahn was a great lady and a good friend." He paused. "How you holding up?"

"Okay I guess. I think." Gaia studied his face, which was carved with lines that made him seem almost kind. "Who are you?"

"Ah!" He brightened. "Sorry. Manners are the first things to go in a crisis. Most people know me by the name'a Chief Last Coyote, wanted terrorist, President of Native Americans Against America, and proud card-carrying member of the Lakota tribe of the seven council fires, eight generations removed from the great warrior Crazy Horse. But you can call me Joe."

But Gaia only heard the first part of what he said as the shock of it washed through her.

He looked around. "Whadda you say, fellas? Wopes, sorry, Alice," he said, bowing to a person in a hat who'd come to stand next to Gaia. It was a woman. She smiled at him and shook her head, then looked at Gaia.

"It's okay," she said. "You ent gotta worry. We're friends." She put her arm around Gaia and squeezed, then addressed Chief Last Coyote again. "I know you probably want to, but we ent got much time."

Chief Last Coyote—Joe—frowned. "Aw, Alice, don't be that way. We gotta help send Mrs. Ahn off to the spirit world. Just a little smoke. If we can't take time for a quick smoke to send our friends off, then the terrorists have already won." More chuckles.

Alice rolled her eyes. "It's your grave. But I'm just thinkin'a this one here." She gave Gaia a little squeeze. "We at least gotta get a little food into her."

"We'll be quick" he said. "When the rest of the search party gets back, we'll do a quick smoke for Mrs. Ahn, then we'll hightail it outta here."

-24-

Vanish Like Smoke

"Food first," Alice said, moving Gaia into a chair at the circular table. The men in the room came and sat as well, except for the man they'd met at the hut entrance. He turned without a word and went back up the stairs, closing the door behind him. Gaia counted five more besides Chief Last Coyote, Alice, and Marty, and everyone except Alice crowded in together around the table. All the Lakota wore blue jeans and long, button-down cotton shirts with different designs on them. Some were simple plaids of dark blue and gray, others had patterned pictures like cacti and birds. The biggest, taller than the rest by a head, had a shirt with a single snake winding all around it. His hair was short like Marty's, but the rest of the men had longer hair either put back in a pony tail or left to hang like Gaia's. Yet unlike most people she saw every day, the Lakota had more meat on their bones. They were thin, but not gaunt. They also seemed shy, and none of them except for Marty, Alice, and the chief looked at her.

"If we should leave, I don't need to eat," Gaia said, getting more anxious by the minute. She wondered what their plan was but didn't dare ask.

"Don't worry," the chief said. "We're still waiting on a few others yet. Won't be long. Might as well eat a little."

Alice set a cup of water in front of Gaia, followed by a plate with a fat disk of golden-brown bread. The smell was sweet and savory and glorious, obviously what she'd smelled when they'd entered the hut. She stared at it.

"Ever had fry bread, darlin'?" Alice asked. "I 'spect not. Don't be shy. Just tear it apart."

"Here, lemme help you with that," the chief said, starting to reach for her plate. But quick as a snake, Alice slapped his hand.

"Knock it off, Joe," she warned. "That's the last time I'm gonna tell you."

He pulled his arm back like an injured wing. "Ah, just one little bite," he pleaded.

"You had yours. Y'all had yours. Let her be."

The chief leaned closer to Gaia and said in a low voice, just loud enough for all to hear, "Alice's fry bread will drive a man to do things he wouldn't otherwise think to do."

"Joe!" she hollered again, as Gaia noticed his hand slowly inching its way toward her plate. The next second something slammed the table in front of her, making her jump, and Gaia stared at a thick knife that was embedded deep into the table where the chief's hand used to be. The men burst into hysterics. The chief's eyes had gone wide and his mouth made a small "o" as he clutched his hands against his chest. He looked over at Alice whose stern face slowly melted into laughter.

"Sorry, darlin'," she said to Gaia. "We'll stop goofin' and let you eat. *Won't* we, Joe."

"Oh, yes Ma'am," the chief said, but a second later he pointed at Gaia's untouched plate and asked, "You gonna finish that?"

Gaia ate her fry bread as quickly as she could, but she slowed down in the middle of chewing. It warmed her soul in a way that that none of Matthew's food had.

Matthew. He might still be alive, and even if he couldn't get to her through the capsule in her shoulder, there was no way he'd easily give up his lifelong quest to eat her heart. He'd still come after her. She hoped the Lakota were enough to protect her.

Four more men entered from a hidden door at the back of the room. They looked stunned, nodding at the others, considering Gaia warily. One man leaned down and whispered into the chief's ear. He smiled, then spoke to Gaia.

"We wanted to spring you yesterday, before the Maggot killed that kid. But we weren't ready." He waved his hand at the stunned men. "These are the guys who were supposed to free you from the big room today. They don't spook easily. They're spooked now. I wondered why they weren't with you when you came. Now I know. You were already out."

"That's how I found her," Marty said. "She was just sitting there on that big vine."

"Winyan wanagi," the chief said, looking truly serious for the first time.

"Not just any spirit woman, and you know it," said Alice, who came up behind Gaia and put her hands on Gaia's shoulders. Then softly she said, "Makhá-akáŋl. But we must help her, just a little. She is so young." Then Gaia felt Alice's forehead resting on the top of her own head, then the wet drops of tears, and she stopped chewing. The room had gone completely still. Everyone's eyes were closed as if in meditation or prayer. Gaia felt overwhelmed by the attention and unworthy of such reverence.

"No time for smoke," the chief said finally. "Walks Pretty Fast says the big room collapsed on one side from a big vine, and he's pretty sure The Maggot is still alive."

The Maggot. That must be their name for Matthew, and he was still alive. That was worrisome. She was getting more anxious about leaving. Why were the Lakota taking their time? As if reading her thoughts, the chief finally got things rolling.

"We have to leave now and smoke later." He turned to Gaia. "I'm sure you have a lotta questions, like who we are and all, and why you're here with us. We'll try to answer your questions later. Just know that you're safe now, okay?"

It was a relief. Even just being away from Matthew was a relief, no matter whom she was with.

Joe turned to Marty. "Now the hard part begins. Cinks, you understand the task and are ready?"

"Yeah, Pop," Marty said. "I'm ready."

"Gaia," the chief said, "you will go with Marty. He knows the way. They will not be looking for only two. Stay as invisible as you can. Another group of us will pretend we have you, as a distraction, and we'll be setting off more bombs to keep The Maggot's men busy elsewhere. Alice will play you. Mitawin, are you ready?"

"Husband, I'm more ready than you are, you old fart," Alice said, patting Gaia's shoulders and wiping her own eyes. Gaia wondered why she was crying.

"As always. As always," the chief smiled. "Time to go. Night Jay says they've discovered she's missing and they're starting to search the villages."

Then Gaia spoke up. "They found out I was missing right before Marty found me. I overheard them when I was hiding."

Alice considered her with such compassion that Gaia felt like it was her own mother looking at her. "Well there you have it," Alice said. "She can take care of herself."

Gaia felt like this was the furthest thing from the truth.

"Okay," Alice said, snapping into business mode. "Everybody look away. Oh not you, darlin'," she said to Gaia. "We're gonna swap clothes, you an' me."

A half minute later Alice was wearing the surgical shirt, poncho, and bamboo pants, and Gaia had on a pair of blue jeans and a button-down denim shirt. Alice helped her cinch the belt tighter saying, "Can't be helped. You're so thin." Alice then removed the hair tie from her own hair and started to make a pony tail for Gaia, then stopped as Gaia flinched when her ears were in full view.

"Lordy, Lordy, but those are some beautiful flaps you got there!" she said. "Bet those come in handy. Wait, here," she said, rearranging Gaia's hair so that it formed two broad pigtails that mostly covered both ears. Then Alice said, "Any other day I'd say wear 'em out proud for everybody to see. But we've gotta keep you as incognito as possible. There. You look like a pureblood Lakota woman now! One more thing..."

Alice reached behind her and produced a pair of cloth shoes with firm soles like the Lakota wore. "Put these on. You'll love 'em. Made out of real deer hide."

Gaia slipped them on. They were a little tight, but they were soft and warm and slightly padded on the bottom. She felt a broad-brimmed hat being squished on top of her head, and Alice moved back to consider the effect. "There. Now you're one of us."

"What about my skin?" Gaia asked. "I'm still pretty obvious."

"It'll still be dark enough out," Alice said. "Just keep your head down. You'd be amazed how invisible you can be right out in the open."

The Lakota got up and assembled in front of the entrance where Gaia and Marty had come in.

"The two of you will go out the back, we'll go out the front," the chief said. "With luck, we'll meet you at the beach. We are the fire, and you are the smoke. Go, vanish like smoke." But both he and Alice held a worried gaze on Marty, who only smiled.

"Ka Dish Day, Pop. Ka Dish Day, Ma. See you soon. Stop worrying."

The chief smiled.

"Ka Dish Day, Two Dogs, Cinks," the chief said. "Guard those kiwis."

Then the fire group turned and left.

"Time to be like smoke, Makȟá-akáŋl," Marty said to Gaia. He looked determined. "Follow me."

"What does that mean?" Gaia asked, following Marty around a wooden post to the base of a dark set of spiral stairs.

"You don't get the whole smoke metaphor?"

"No, not that. I get the metaphor. That other name you're calling me. Maka-something."

"Oh, that. I'll tell you when we're out; because if we don't make it, it won't matter."

"You're a great motivational speaker."

He stopped and turned, descending the few steps he'd already walked up, and put his face uncomfortably close to hers. He wasn't angry, just intense. His scar seemed to consume the whole half of his face, yet it somehow suited Marty. There was an attractive recklessness about it.

"Listen. This is very important. We're in some serious shit right now. Don't be fooled by how calm and laid-back we all seem. That's just our way. The Maggot, Siafu, is the scariest man I've ever seen. My pop can be pretty scary, too. My ma even scarier. But nothing compared to Siafu. Ghost Shadow, the man at the front door of the hut, he's our man on the inside. He found out Siafu was going to cut you open and eat your heart, thinking that he could ingest your power and make it his own."

Gaia involuntarily put her hand on her chest.

"He's bad news. Ever heard of the kind of ants that'll kill a person and eat 'em whole? They're called siafu. And it's no coincidence."

For a split second, Marty's closeness and intensity, the hint of fry bread on his own breath, the safety he represented, made her think of kissing him.

"Anyway, we're wasting time. To summarize," he said, slapping one finger and then two fingers into his palm for emphasis, "One, deep shit, and two, really deep shit, so be ready for anything. Stay with me."

Gaia followed Marty to the top of the dark stairs until the brim of her hat bumped into him when he stopped. "We go at the next explosion," he said. "We have to go across to Kauai village. That's the hard part. Second part is easy. Stay close and try to look natural. Be like smoke."

Right after he finished speaking, a deep boom rumbled from the bowels of the complex, followed by the staccato popping of gunfire.

"Now," Marty said, and they were through a door and outside into another part of the village, on another narrow walkway. More lights blinked on in the huts, and people came outside to see what was happening. A rooster cock-a-doodled, and another boom erupted further away than the first. Marty and Gaia walked briskly away from the direction of the ruckus, weaving around huts, keeping to the center of the village, sometimes pausing to pretend to mingle with the curious residents, then edging slowly away. The light of day was slowly rising, sooner than Gaia had expected. She kept her head bowed to avoid eye contact with anyone, to avoid being recognized. Someone might notice her blue hair if they were looking carefully enough, but that couldn't be helped. She flipped the collar of her shirt up and tucked her pony tails into it. *Just keep your head down,* Alice had advised.

At the back of the village they reached a stock yard and casually walked along the fence, which took them out closer to the main complex thoroughfare.

"Cart coming," Gaia said, hearing the hum of wheels moving their direction.

"Into the yard, quick," Marty said. "Pretend you're working."

They hopped the fence and Gaia grabbed a shovel leaning against the fence, then dug while Marty knelt down to the hole she was making. A cart loaded with guards hummed past them toward the direction of more gunfire. Gaia was suddenly jolted by a loud animal whinny in the shed behind her.

"What the woody?" Gaia heard Marty say. Then she saw what he was talking about. The animals in the yard were all moving toward them in a cluster. Cows and chickens, and little goats that trotted and hopped, shaking their little horned heads at each other in mock battle. A larger, long-faced animal emerged from the barn.

"Is that a real horse?" she asked, more in shock at the presence of a horse than the fact that all the animals were coming to her. Soon Gaia and Marty were surrounded, which now made them more than conspicuous.

"They know!" he said, looking at her with awe, then snapping out of it. "We gotta git. A quarter mile across open floor. This is the really hard part. Come on. Where are you going?"

Gaia wove through the press of animals and jogged to the wall of the shed, pulling two long sticks out of an old barrel. The group of animals, slowly realizing she was no longer with them, had turned and begun to follow her. She made her way back through them as they all turned again and followed her back to the fence. Marty, who had already climbed out, climbed back in looking confused.

"Here," Gaia said, handing him a stick. "This'll work. I saw them doing this earlier. We'll drive the animals across. What was it your mom said? You'd be amazed how invisible you can be right out in the open?"

Marty grinned. "I like it."

They walked toward the main gate in the yard. Gaia flipped the looped rope off the post that kept the gate shut and pushed the gate forward.

"Wait," Marty said, "all of them?" An inextricable mixture of cows, goats, and chickens were pushing on them trying to follow Gaia.

"Just cows, if you can. Four or five," he said.

Marty stood at the gate pushing goats away and kicking at chickens to let only cows through. In the end, when Gaia closed the gate again, two goats and a chicken had gotten out, and Marty had to toss the chicken back over the fence.

"I'll lead," Gaia said. "They'll follow me. You drive them from the back. Which way?"

"That village yonder," Marty pointed.

Looking both ways for more carts, even though Gaia didn't hear any, they set off across the open floor. Gunfire blasted from at least three different areas of the complex behind them, and men yelled. The animals followed Gaia, and Marty stayed at the back pretending to prod them forward with his stick even though he didn't need to. The animals were smitten with their new shepherd and would follow her over a cliff.

Gaia heard another cart whiz behind them, but she didn't turn to look, and the cart didn't slow. Her nerves were sizzling. The thought of falling back into Matthew's clutches was terrifying despite all the help the Lakota were giving her. Having only Marty accompany her might have been a brilliant logistical idea, but it only made her more fearful. What could he possibly do if they got caught?

In a few minutes they'd reached the edge of another village and got a few strange looks from residents there who'd come out to see about the gunfire and explosions. She kept her head down and hoped nobody recognized her. The people in Kauai village were mostly Hawaiian, but their well-fed bodies distinguished them from their emaciated Raftie kin in the outside world.

Marty jogged up beside her and spoke quietly. "Best thing is to just make a break now, ditch the animals so they can't follow us."

Gaia nodded.

"Jog to the edge of that hut over there. When we get around the corner, we start running. Stay close. The hut we want is just a few back in. Okay? Go!"

They broke into a quick trot, and as they rounded the hut they were aiming for, Marty bolted. He was so fast! Gaia struggled to keep him in sight as he wove around people and huts. Gaia almost plowed into a little boy who'd suddenly run into her path, and she stumbled. When she looked up again, Marty was motioning to her from up ahead.

She caught up and followed him through the side door of a hut, which was empty of people. A lantern glowed atop a low foot table in the main room, casting light on old color photographs of waterfalls, lush forests, and large waves. One photo showed the tiny spec of a man riding a wave that filled nearly the entire picture frame. An old paddle and some netting hung on the wall.

They walked through the small kitchen into the back room of the hut, where Marty pushed the upper body of a dark wooden Tiki statue, making the Tiki man tilt slightly backwards on his surfboard. A section of thick floor popped ajar opposite the statue, and Marty heaved it open, revealing a dark hole.

"You first," he said. "Wait for me at the bottom."

Gaia saw the wooden ladder below when she came to the edge and looked down. The hole was tight, but it opened up as she descended and cleared the entrance. At the bottom of the ladder, she saw that she was in a dimly lit catacomb that formed a narrow hallway in both directions. The dank, dusty odor was a smell Gaia remembered from her early childhood, when she'd climbed into the crawl space under her house and seen an animal skeleton. The smell made her think of death, of hidden places no one would ever think to go, of forgotten souls.

When Marty joined her he said, "Now the easy part. The tunnel that way," he pointed up the tunnel, "that goes back into the complex, to another village. This other way, this leads straight up and out. Unless they know about this tunnel already, we're home free."

-25-

Hecheto Aloe. It Is Finished.

They had to crouch, Marty more so than Gaia. The small lights in the catacomb walls soon ended. Marty unsheathed the big knife at his side, turned the base of its handle, and light glowed from the hilt, making the tunnel look even more haunted. They hadn't gotten far when a thunderous boom from somewhere above them in the complex shook the earth, and dirt and rock crumbled from the ceiling.

Marty lurched forward and Gaia followed, ducking, but she suddenly slammed into him.

"Back! Back up the ladder!" he yelled, turning, pushing Gaia.

Earth and rocks fell more freely now. At the base of the ladder Gaia paused, watching transfixed as the tunnel collapsed toward them, dreamlike, from both directions. "Go!" Marty shouted, pushing at her, trying to lift her up. Marty cried out in pain, which snapped her awake. He pushed her hard, launching her up the ladder. Moments later they both rolled into the room covered with dust. Marty panted unevenly, coughing, and his blue jeans were torn at the calf and bloody. Dust poured from the hole making Gaia cough uncontrollably. Marty got up and stomped the hatch door closed. A carved wooden mask bared its teeth at them from the corner of the room.

"You're hurt," she said when her coughing stopped.

"I'm okay." He tousled dust out of his hair with both hands. His eyebrows were gray. "Shit. Plan B."

"What's Plan B?" Gaia hoped it didn't involve going back out into the riot of gunfire, bombs, and people she heard outside.

Marty rubbed his head some more. "Just lemme think."

"There's no Plan B?"

The adrenaline inside her shape shifted into terror when he didn't answer immediately. There was no Plan B. This was it. They were going to get caught, Marty was going to be killed, and Matthew would cut out her heart and become some twisted version of an earth god, if eating her heart would truly do that to him. She pictured a burning world of people wandering around listlessly in bloody white robes with their throats gaping open. It was Hell, and he was Satan, calmly watching with that fake, annoying smile from his blood-soaked throne. For all their planning and timely help, the Lakota—the Legendary Chief Last Coyote himself—had failed. He was just a nice man with a sweet family and a bad reputation. The silver lining, as Gaia saw it, was that she'd at least be dead before Matthew ate her heart. She wouldn't have to watch him do it.

She took a deep, resigned breath, then exhaled. For now, at least for the moment, they were alive, and Marty's leg was hurt. She knelt to have a look at it. The least she could do in her final moments was to be kind.

"It's not as bad as it looks," he said. A deep gash ran down his calf. "Leave it. We gotta go."

"Can you walk?"

"Course I can walk! I'm Lakota, ennit?"

When he grinned, a small, strange hope crept into her, or maybe it was just gratitude that he was still trying.

"So do you remember seeing those big vents at the walls of the complex?" he asked. "Big tubes that go up like chimneys?"

Gaia nodded.

"That's where we're headed. Time for some improv."

Gaia drew a deep breath. This was it. Marty was a sweet, resourceful kid. In these final moments of her life, Gaia let herself admit that she had a bit of a crush on him, scar and all. He was awkward and flawed, just like her.

"You okay?" he asked. "Ready?"

Gaia reached up with both hands, cradled his head, and pulled him down into a kiss, brief but warm. She would at least kiss a boy before she died. Gaia let him go and bit her lip. It was nicer than she'd imagined back in the Lakota hut.

"What was that for?" he stammered, eyes wide.

"I'm ready now," she said.

Marty cocked his head quizzically, clearly flustered. "Is that allowed?"

"I'm Mocka-whatever-that-word-is," she said. "I'll do whatever I want."

He considered her for a few moments.

"I like your style," he said finally. A smile replaced the dumb look on his face. "Let's get the hell out of this place."

When they came out of the hut, Gaia moved with the confidence of destiny, even though she believed that destiny to be her own death. And in that calm inner space, in that full resignation, her fight instinct crept back in. Everything inside of her suddenly and subtly shifted, like the pink and orange of sunrise, the color of the sea, giving way to the bright tip of a rising sun. She was determined to escape, if for no other reason than to spite Matthew. It felt good.

Kauai village had become a swarm of the curious and the confused. Guns were still going off, and parents in the village were busy pulling children back inside while they themselves tried to see what was happening. Guards with rifles moved in twos and threes in the direction of the gunfire, not noticing Marty and Gaia moving against the grain of people. At the edge of the village, though, Marty stopped and cursed, looking across the open floor to the far wall.

"They've got guards at the vents. They're just standing there looking around."

"Wait," she said. "Hush for a minute. I need to listen."

"All this noise and you want *me* to hush?"

"Shhh!" She closed her eyes, trying her best to calm her nerves as she trained her ears at the vent where the guards were standing. What she heard was slight boot scraping mingled with a hollow whoosh of air coming out of the vent. Now that she had the sound to listen for, she switched her focus away from that vent and listened off in another direction. Further off, she heard the hum of another vent, and it didn't have sounds of people in front of it.

"Follow me," she said.

"You got something?"

But Gaia was already on the move. They went deeper into the village until they came out on the other side, to the edge of wide-open ground that ran at least a hundred yards to the complex wall.

It would be a long way to move completely exposed across open ground. Gaia hopped into a yard and hid behind an an avocado tree. Marty followed.

"There," she said, pointing at a vent on the far wall. There were no guards in front of it.

"Okay, walk. Let's just walk," Marty said. "Be natural."

"Hold on," Gaia said, and went in a crouch over to a scrub of garden where there was a wheelbarrow half full of animal dung. She pushed it back to Marty. "Okay, now we can go. Doesn't get more natural than this."

Marty shook his head. "You're just full of tricks, aren't you."

They went through the little gate and walked as purposefully and normally as anyone could pushing a wheelbarrow of animal dung across a hundred yards of open floor. Gaia could tell that Marty was trying to keep from limping. She kept her head down to shadow her face, but then heard something.

"Someone's coming!" she said.

"Just keep walking. Keep your head down."

Marty pretended to fuss with something in the wheelbarrow as the sound of jogging boots got closer. Then, to Gaia's relief, the jogging men passed behind them.

But then Gaia heard the worst sound imaginable. A little girl at the edge of the village was shouting.

"Momma! Look! It's the green girl! Momma, Momma!"

Gaia's blood turned to ice water, and when she turned to look, the girl was pointing at them. One of the guards had heard the girl, too, and stopped to look. He slowly began moving toward them, then broke into a jog, pulling the rifle off his shoulder.

Marty's arm was already extended at him. A tiny blip of light pulsed out of his hand, and the guard fell. But another guard got to one knee and shouldered his rifle, taking careful aim. Marty fired a pulse at him but missed, and the guard's gun erupted. Gaia waited for Marty to fall. Instead, Marty turned and shouted. "Get in!"

Without thinking, Gaia jumped into the dung-filled wheelbarrow and Marty pushed, picking up speed. Mercifully, the dung was drier than she'd expected, and her cloth shoes didn't sink into it too much. Then her brain caught up and she wondered why she wasn't just running alongside him, until she realized how fast they were going even with his injured leg. There was no way she could have run that fast. The rifle erupted again, and again, but Marty was still gaining speed.

"Sonofabitch is a terrible shot!" he said, almost giddy.

When they reached the vent, the guard was well behind but running after them.

"In! Now!" Marty said. The base of the big tube opened on rollers, and Marty pulled it away from the wall. They ducked behind it, and Marty pulled it closed. The crack of a bullet hit the outside of the tube.

Inside, a skinny metal ladder attached to the tube wall rose up into the heights.

"Go! Climb! I'll take care of this joker," Marty said.

Gaia began climbing. The ladder rungs were uncomfortable under her feet, and her shoes slipped a little from the animal dung. She heard the vent slide open, and she looked down. The guard slid in and had his rifle already trained up the ladder. A shot went off and hit the rung above her. Gaia tucked into the ladder, her muscles frozen and her heart going off like a jackhammer as she waited for the next bullet to hit her. She wondered what it would feel like but hoped it would at least kill her. She couldn't bear the thought of Matthew strapping her down again and coming at her with a scalpel. Her guts convulsed at the thought, and stinging bile rose into her throat. Below her, she heard scuffling and grunts.

When she looked down again, tense as a petrified tree, she expected to see Marty lying dead on the floor and the guard pointing his rifle at her. But to her astonishment and relief, Marty already had the guard's rifle slung over his shoulder and he was pulling the vent closed again. The guard lay in a pile on the ground. Maybe there was more to Marty than she realized. She turned and kept climbing, but she heard boot steps and shouts approaching the tube. Gaia pushed on, amazed when Marty caught up to her so quickly. They must have been 50 feet up already.

"There's more coming," she said, looking back down.

He cursed again, not at what she'd said, but at what was above them: a locked grate blocking their ascent like a round prison door. The ladder continued maybe another hundred feet higher. Even if they made it past, they still had a long climb.

"Scoot over a step if you can." He climbed around her to examine the grate. Gaia checked the ground again. The guard's body below seemed tiny. She tightened her grip on the ladder.

"Did you kill him?" she asked.

Marty was reaching out as far as he could to feel the edges of the grate.

"Maybe," he said. "Just a little."

Something whizzed like a kamikaze bee and sparked against the ladder below them, followed immediately by the crack of a gun that sounded like thunder in the vent. Without pausing to look down, Marty pulled something out of his pocket. It looked like a big spider. He bit the edge of it, then shouted a battle whoop before dropping it.

"Sorry about the yell," he said when Gaia winced at the volume. "Makes 'em stop to see what's going on so they don't shoot."

As the spider fell, it whizzed to life, whirr-hissing like a spinning firework, hovering in the air below them. It made a pop, then another pop, and two tiny trails of smoke streaked down at the guards, two of whom fell instantly. Another shouted "Hummingbird!" and the others quickly left the vent.

"That'll give us a few minutes," Marty said as the Hummingbird spider thing kept hovering and buzzing below them. "But we ent got much time before they're waiting for us at the top."

He reached into another pocket and pulled out a blob of clay, ripping it in half and pressing each piece into one of the hinges on the grate.

"Back down a bit," he said. He followed her down and shielded her with his own body. "Hold on. Gonna be be loud."

The charges detonated with a bang that shook the ladder. It was so loud that Gaia felt her brain rattle in her skull, and her hearing went dull with ringing. Marty yelled and rubbed his neck. When he took his hand away, there was blood on his palm. "Shrapnel," he said. "Just a graze." He wiped it on his jeans. "You go on up past me."

He pushed the broken grate up and held it for her, and the two of them climbed for what seemed like an hour but was probably only minutes to the top of the ladder. Even past the ringing in her ears, Gaia was glad to hear the soft whiz of the Hummingbird below, which let out another pop. She looked down, which was a mistake because it made her a little height dizzy, but she was glad to see no guards below.

When they reached the top, they climbed onto a ledge of rough concrete that served as the floor of a hollow, gray cylinder that rose and narrowed high above them. Cool air rushed down from the top.

"We're inside a windmill," Marty said. He stepped to the door in the circular wall. Gaia had come to loathe round rooms and suddenly felt claustrophobic. Marty went back to the vent hole and looked down to see if they were being followed. Satisfied, he came back to examine the door, removing the rifle and leaning it against the wall.

Then he stopped and turned to Gaia. "What are you doing?" he asked as she pulled his knife out it's sheath.

"You're bleeding everywhere, Marty. We need to stop it."

"Too bad we don't have any duct tape," he said, watching her cut two long strips of fabric from the bottom of her shirt. "Best thing ever invented."

"Hold still," she said after he protested that they needed to keep moving. But he held still, and when she was finished, she stood back to look at her work. Between the flannel belt around his neck, the calf of his jeans all wrapped up, and all the blood on him, Marty looked like an Indian zombie. He grinned at her.

"Thanks, Makȟá-akáŋl. You know it's gonna fall off, right?"

She held up the knife. "I could always stab it with this to keep it in place. I might anyway if you don't tell me what that name means."

"Funny! A stabbing joke from a girl who almost had her heart cut out of her chest."

It was the first easy moment she'd had with him. If they were normal kids, they might have been hanging out in a secret fort, just talking, minus all the dust and blood and conversation about stabbing and being gutted. But apparently Matthew was still alive, and his men were after them, and that brought her fear back up.

"Well, about that name, some things should stay a mystery, ennit?" He winked at her and turned to a keypad beside the door. "Except for this. We need to get this open."

"Move," she said, nudging him aside. Gaia looked at the keypad, which was an old standard 12-key with four rows of three numbers, plus star and pound keys. Under each number were letters of the alphabet. Above the keypad, a small metal plate was stuck to the wall with the initials "USMC Pendleton" and a serial number. Her brain lit up. "Ha! I think I know where we are! San Diego, Camp Pendleton! The old Marine base."

"Coulda told you that if you'd asked," Marty said. "What are you doing?"

She punched in the numbers 38227 and was relieved when the light went green on the keypad and the door lock popped.

"What the—" Marty said, looking astounded.

"My dad taught me. He said a lot of old military locks like this used the same code, especially if there's no real reason for having a lock there to begin with. It's 'fubar'. It means—"

"Fucked up beyond all recognition," Marty cut in, grabbing the rifle. "You just saved our asses. Or your dad did. Let's go. Stay behind me."

As soon as they pushed the door open, Gaia and Marty were pelted by wind and sand. They crouched and shielded their faces while Marty led with the rifle, sweeping it one-handed across the landscape. It was a howler of a sandstorm, and it stung. Gaia pulled the brim of her hat over her ears and tucked her head. Then she heard Marty's rifle erupt, three, four times. When she squinted up she saw two men fall in a haze of blowing sand.

Marty grabbed her arm, and they were running into the whipping, blurry void. Gaia couldn't see anything and could barely raise her head without getting her face sandblasted. She didn't know how Marty was able to navigate, but she grabbed onto his belt and hung on. Maybe he was guessing just like she would have been, though she doubted it. He'd proven too resourceful so far. Sand bit into her neck and hands, pelted and poured into her ears, and under the thin soles of her shoes she felt the hard ground turn to sand, which slowed them down. She was spitting dirt and coughing. They stumbled along, plunging down and slogging up dune after dune. The world was nothing but sand, and Gaia's shoes were filling with it, grinding and cutting into her feet. Twice she stepped on cactus that broke needles off in her left foot, right through the thin sole of her shoe. Marty stopped suddenly, and she could see that they were at the edge of a drop-off.

"Jump!" Marty yelled.

They did, and when she landed the cactus needles pushed further into her foot, making her cry out. Where they'd landed, the wall of dune next to them blocked the wind, and she could breath easier. "Just a minute!" she said, gently pulling off her shoe and trying to pull cactus needles out of her blistered feet. She got some of the needles, but a couple were too deep and stayed lodged. Marty scrambled back up the dune and looked behind them to see if they were being followed. By the time he got back, she'd gotten her shoes back on. Her feet were in pain, but they felt better than a few minutes earlier.

"You good?" he asked.

She nodded. "You?"

He smiled and grimaced at the same time, pointing to the loose cloth around his bloody neck. "Your homemade band-aid came off. Told you. Can you walk?"

"I'm fine," she said. If Marty could keep going with bleeding gashes on his body, she could manage a few blisters and cactus needles.

They hugged the edge of the dunes and began to see sporadic patches of sky. Gaia heard the ocean, and off to their distant left, gray-pink blotches of it peeked through gaps in the swirling dirt descending from the sky, some of it coming in gusts and some drifting on its own when the gusts took a break. The storm was dying. When Gaia ventured a peek over the top edge of the dunes, little bits of sand slapped her face and eyes. Across the desert landscape Gaia could see the sun rising, red as Mars, blocked by a swath of smoke from a fire burning in the distance. But nobody came.

"There!" Marty said, pointing toward the shore at a small kite that was flailing in the sky above the ledge of a cliff. He led them closer to the shore where they had to pick their way down a rocky bluff. He kept turning to look behind them, and to check on her, because she was limping. Gaia's left foot had swollen itself tight into its shoe, but she waved him on.

At the bottom, where they reached the ocean, the foam from the rushing tide slid into the base of the dirty cliff and tumbled around rocks and patches of a stone jetty that pointed straight out to sea, a crumbling relic that had long ago outlived whatever purpose it served. Jellyfish rode the foam in and out, covering what little sand there was, floating like a giant white blanket of gelatin over the dark tangerine swells.

"Just made the end of low tide," Marty said. "We'd be out of luck in an hour."

They'd taken their shoes off for the walk up the shore, and Marty looked concerned when he saw her foot, which was twice the size as her good foot.

"Cactus?"

"Yeah," she said. "Was hurting for a while, but now I can't even feel it."

"We'll see about cutting 'em out when we get to the beach. Ma's pretty good at that."

She nodded, but she knew it wouldn't be necessary. The foot was feeling better already, and she sensed that her body had begun to dissolve the invading needles. In a half hour, maybe less, her foot would be back to normal. As she stepped around beached jellyfish, the onrushing cold salt water soothed her feet and soaked the legs of Alice's baggy jeans. She did her best to roll them up into a cuff, but they refused stay up around her knees.

The little kite danced in the air on the other side of a point just ahead. They'd have to wade into the ocean to make it around. Marty told her that the kite was where the tunnel would have spit them out. "Would have been a little easier going that way, ennit?" He stopped and looked behind them. "Weird. Somebody shoulda seen us coming by now. Not like Pop to leave a place unguarded like this."

The water around the little point came up to Gaia's waist. A bigger swell came in and surprised her, lifting her feet off the sandy bottom. She struggled to keep her mouth out of the Worm-infested brine. Gaia was now completely soaked and hoped the Lakota had an extra set of dry clothes.

As they made it around the point, Gaia saw that they had entered a large cove of beach, and back against the far recess of the curving bluff, a hard stone's throw away, there were people gathered. The Lakota. A little fire crackled, and Gaia saw the white head of Chief Last Coyote. She guessed it was Alice who knelt next to him, and a few of the other men knelt with them, as if they were at a church service. The only sounds were the sea and the little kite snapping in the wind, tied to a stick that was wedged into the sand near the people. The scene struck Gaia as odd. She would have expected a happier reception. But then again, there was much about the Lakota she didn't understand. Then she realized why it all looked so weird: everyone's arms were behind them.

Marty must have picked up on it too. He stopped and put his arm in front of Gaia.

"Something ent right," he said.

Then another sound. Sandy footsteps right behind them. Marty and Gaia spun around, then froze when they saw the rifles pointed at their chests, wielded by two white men with crewcuts. They'd come out from behind a fold in the bluff wall.

"Careful," one of the men said to Marty. "Drop it."

Marty started to raise his rifle.

"Marty, no!" the chief's yell echoed from the distance.

But Marty never got his gun up. Gaia jumped at a whack beside her, and Marty dropped to his knees, knocked in the back of the head by another gunman who'd come up behind them. She backed away in shock and watched the men tie Marty's hands behind his back. Gaia now realized why they weren't being followed. They were being ambushed.

Without thinking, she hurled herself at the man who'd hit Marty, a wiry, shorter man with a shaved head and goatee. *Eyes, throat, balls,* her dad's often-repeated words sprang to mind. *If you ever need to hurt a man, that's what you go for.* Her thought was to quickly punch the man in the throat, then kick him in the balls and take his rifle. But what her dad never told her was that fights rarely go as planned. The man was quick. He turned to face her and pushed the rifle butt forward to catch her in the face. But Gaia ducked just in time. As the rifle grazed the top of her head, she blindly slammed her knee into what she hoped was his groin. The man buckled. In the split second that Gaia saw his exposed face, she swung her elbow at it, remembering what Quinn had done to her in the fight on the soccer pitch. She connected squarely with his nose. He grabbed his face as he fell backwards, hollering in pain.

She reached down for his dropped rifle but felt herself suddenly jerked back by her hair, and before she knew what was happening her face was being pressed hard into the sand, surrounded by the sound of men laughing.

They jerked Gaia to her feet, wrenched her right arm behind her back, and started pushing her forward. When she spat sand, Gaia saw Marty being pushed along beside her. He looked dazed, and he stumbled. They kicked him and lifted him back to his feet. More men with rifles emerged from the base of the bluffs.

Then Gaia noticed the man sitting directly behind Chief Last Coyote.

Matthew.

Like a popped balloon, all the air, all the hope, was suddenly gone from her.

They'd lost after all, after all that.

The yin and yang of Matthew and Joe's opposite skin colors, the opposite expressions each wore, was striking. The chief was solemn, almost worried. Matthew was smiling, and as he watched Gaia he began chuckling. He wore a black turtleneck, which she realized hid any signs of the injuries Mrs. Ahn had inflicted on him back in the circular room.

Gaia saw the men pushing Marty forward as well. He was conscious but dazed. They searched him and found the stone-looking weapon he'd fired in the complex, along with his knife, another Hummingbird, and a few other small gizmos. They patted Gaia down as well, and when they were satisfied, they shoved both of them down to their knees. Gaia looked over and saw Marty clench his teeth. Next to Marty was a hatless man that Gaia realized was Ghost Shadow. Ghost Shadow said something to Marty in Lakota and was rewarded with his own rifle smack to the head.

"My dear," Matthew said. "Deed I not say you wah full of vee-gor and veem? And weeth so many new friends! Had I known you liked to swim een yo clothes," he motioned to her ocean-soaked clothes, "I would have given you trou-sahs that wah three sizes larger! Do you get eet? Swim een yo clothes?" He laughed aloud at his own joke. He was the only one who did.

But his face turned serious, and he shook his head. "Come, come," he said, motioning her closer with a pistol. Two of his men lifted her by the arms and dragged her closer to Matthew. Alice, who was to the right of her husband, watched Gaia as if trying to speak with her eyes.

"It ees time fo this silly game of hide and seek to end. Een a way, I feel I have cheated, fo I have known about thees tunnel fo months." He motioned behind him at a small cave in the bluffs. "But what can one do with such in-fa-mation except give thee opponent a sporting chance, yes? My one regret is that I did not know about this tunnel much soonah. I have found it a wonda-ful path to thee ocean."

Suddenly, loud female Lakota singing rose at the fire. Alice's eyes were closed, and the firelight glinted off her tears. She tilted her head back to project her voice to the heavens. Matthew took a calm step toward her and hit her on the side of the head with the butt of his pistol. The singing stopped instantly, and she tipped over onto the sand. The chief's expression didn't change, though his forward gaze seemed to harden like stone.

A Lakota man to the left of the chief let out a whoop, jumped to his feet, and stumbled at Matthew with his hands still tied behind his back.

"Wakinyan!" the chief shouted. But it was over in a flash and an ear-splitting bang. The bullet from Matthew's pistol kicked Wakinyan's head backwards, and he, too, slumped to the sand. The chief made a face and bowed his head.

It was too shocking to absorb. Gaia barely knew these people, but they felt like family, and they were starting to be slaughtered right in front of her. Seeing how Matthew had so easily slit the throat of an innocent little boy, she knew this would end quickly and brutally. Gaia looked at the dead Wakinyan, and her stomach lurched at the blood pooling under his head. She felt her body convulse and retch involuntarily, and she let the vomit struggle out of her. Bile burned the back of her eyes. More men laughed.

"No more playing," Matthew said. "Watch thees one." He motioned for his men to cover the chief as Matthew stepped around the fire to Gaia. "Do thee boy first," he said to the men behind Marty. The Lakota were now all shouts, protesting what was about to happen.

Gaia felt her hair being grabbed and twisted to force her head toward Marty.

"You must watch." Matthew's cheek was against hers. His voice was icy and his breath was rank.

And that's when it happened. A trapdoor suddenly dropped open in Gaia's soul and she felt herself falling through it, falling deep inside herself, plunging toward a fire that belched and heaved. But as she fell into it, the fire didn't consume her. Instead, she landed in its belly and stood, anger coursing through her. She stood, the master of the fire, her own defiant fury swelling the flames as it grew, as if the fire were afraid of being destroyed by Gaia's hotter, wilder wrath.

She was swelling with fury, as if she were Fury itself, desiring to kill anything that dared insult her by living. Fury now launched her from her own depths, shooting her like a rocket across sky, sea, and earth. She flew over fields, trees, torching everything in her path, setting the world ablaze. Everything would die.

She banked and flew to a place of shouts and cries, and Gaia found herself back at the bluffs, surrounded not by corporeal people, but by people-like shapes, lined in red heat, merely outlines, as if she were able to see everyone's souls, shapes that were now engaged in battle. Gaia watched, her own rage flowing and consuming her mind, and she was pleased at the destruction she wrought, at the souls that seemed to be battling on her behalf, fueled by her wrath, and she pushed fury from every pore and fissure in the earth, conducting a symphony born from Hell itself.

But a nip of cold touched her shoulder, and when she looked, a purple-lined soul, different from all the rest, reached to grip her.

"Dare you to touch me?" she said to the thing, angered by its insolence. But it grew in size and began to creep and surround her.

"Dare I?" it said, and Gaia knew it was Matthew, or a thing much greater than Matthew that powered him, some inimical power contrary to her. "Dare you to return when I have claimed the world? When I have won?" it said.

She began to feel cold and fearful, and her flames flickered and dimmed as the purple thing quickly thickened around her and became darker and colder.

"Who are you?" she asked, feeling it difficult to move.

It laughed. "Of course. You do not remember. So has it always been when you return."

Another reference to her having been in the world before, long ago. The dark coldness, the voice, was new yet somehow familiar. Perhaps it was the feeling of despair that was so familiar. Despair. Her light gave one last flicker before it went out with a pop.

"Yes," it said. "You begin to remember, as you have always known, even in your short time here. Despair is one of my names."

Gaia felt helpless and began to wonder where she was, in some underworld of consciousness; or perhaps a real place. The thought of wanting to die crossed her thought.

"Such a cruelty that my Adversary, your own parent, causes you to forget whenever you return. And now, just as your new self was beginning to feel hope—and love."

Love. Gaia thought of her mother, her father, Selene, her silly hound dog, Godpappy, Cloudy, and the loss burrowed hard into her heart. She was fading. It was so cold.

"Give my regards to the Adversary. Mine is the last word in the history of these human creatures, as it was always destined to be."

Her mind dimmed, and she felt herself becoming ice. She was becoming—nothing.

"Goodbye, child of the Adversary."

Who was this? How was this? As Gaia faded, she began to welcome the nothingness. It would all be over soon.

A flicker of light, like the tiniest spark, wove through empty space like a firefly. She saw it as herself, the last of her life force, leaving at last.

But the spark turned back and flew the other direction, and as it did, its light flared, hot green and blue.

It turned again, but this time it flew toward her and grew, getting brighter. Gaia felt the slightest thaw, the tiniest hope, and wondered what it was.

She felt an unease in the darkness, in the dark thing trying to snuff her out.

The spark kept growing, now bright green, almost blinding. It must have been very far away at the start, because as it approached, swerving as if it were fighting a mighty wind, it grew and grew until it was nearly the size and shape of a man. Immediately she knew who it was: Wakinyan, Alice's son, Chief Last Coyote's son, whom Matthew had killed. Marty's brother. He was edged with pulsating green and filled with blue shadow that defined the faintest shapes, like a hint of nose or a line of chin.

Then he let out a whoop, the most delicious, life-affirming sound Gaia had ever heard, and it fed her like a dying plant receiving water and sunshine. Her heart swelled with it. The light-man that was Wakinyan swung his arms and danced this way and that, singing and whooping.

The darkness let out a roar, and Gaia felt it vibrate and tremble. It was losing its hold on her, and she felt warmth returning. The light from Wakinyan became brighter, and her own light flickered back to life.

Gaia could move again, and she stretched her arms out to the side and wiggled her fingers. Wakinyan let out another series of whoops in acknowledgement, and joy, and battle. Then Gaia pushed hard, and flames erupted around her, swelling as she pushed harder. The darkness roared again, but from further away.

"Leave us," Gaia commanded it. She pushed harder, and her flames spread like a forest fire, and she felt the darkness leave. She saw once again the red outlines of the living souls engaged in battle around her.

Then next to her, Gaia felt a shadow of cool malice, and remembered that it was Matthew. She turned to it with a fresh rage, remembering what he was about to do to Marty, and she focused a new burst of her flame on Matthew. The fire engulfed the shadow, which slowly vanished, finally snuffed out as if it had never existed.

Marty, she thought again. *I need to help Marty.*

Gaia closed her eyes, willing herself back up into the world.

As she emerged into her human consciousness, the world was bright chaos. Men were fighting hand to hand amid shouts and an occasional gunshot. Marty and the chief fought in the center of the melee. The Lakota seemed to be getting the upper hand as one after another of Matthew's men fell and the Lakota were able to help their brothers still engaged in combat.

Matthew.

He was no longer gripping her hair. She was free. Gaia stood and looked down, still reeling from her own battle with the dark thing. But what she saw now didn't surprise her. She knew she'd done it. There was Matthew, lying dead in the sand with his eyes wide open, all his hubris dead with him. She noticed a pool of blood on his shoulder soaking part of his turtleneck, coming from the knife wound Mrs. Ahn had given him. He'd bragged about Gaia's inability to harm him, but now he said nothing.

Moments later the rest of the fight was over, and none of Matthew's men remained alive.

Then Gaia heard a woman wailing. "Wakinyan! Cinks! My son!" Alice cried, kneeling next to Wakinyan. "Le mita cola! Not my son! Not my son!"

More gunshots erupted as Ghost Shadow and another Lakota stepped to each of Matthew's men for a final insurance bullet to the head.

Marty went to Alice and held his mother, who was holding her dead son. His brother. Gaia wanted to tell them that Wakinyan had saved her life, but now wasn't the time, and they may not even believe what she told them.

The chief came to where Gaia was and knelt down beside Matthew's body. He rolled Matthew on his back, examining him. Gaia had just enough time to look away as the chief raised a knife and plunged it into Matthew's chest. She plugged her ears, but then stopped and let her arms down, turning to watch. She wanted to watch.

The chief's movements were quick and efficient. Moments later, he held Matthew's heart up in the air, examined it, then casually tossed it into the fire.

"Hecheto aloe," he said. "It is finished."

-26-
Release

C hief Last Coyote stood and went to his wife and two sons, one of whom was now dead. He wrapped his arms around them, and they rocked, and Alice sang a quavering song in Lakota.

Gaia watched them, unsure of what to do. In his mother's arms, Wakinyan's hair was a tattered frame around his vacant, bloodstained face, and his hair draped over Alice's forearm like a black waterfall that would never reach the ground.

Gaia wanted to tell them what Wakinyan had done for her, but it wasn't the time. She didn't understand how she'd been able to go to the deep place she had, or how what she experienced there affected the world above. But wherever it was she'd gone, Wakinyan had forced the despair from her, and she'd been able to kill Matthew. Why hadn't she been able to go there when Matthew had her strapped to a bed and was about to cut out her heart? Her world seemed nothing but questions. Unanswerable riddles.

She watched Wakinyan's face, feeling pulled to it. She snapped out of it when Alice stopped singing, and saw that Alice was looking at her. It was an odd expression, quizzical and sad all at once.

"Makȟá-akáŋl," Alice said barely above a whisper. "Is there anything you can do?"

"No," Joe said, but not unkindly. "Let him go."

But Alice kept her eyes on Gaia as if Joe hadn't said a word.

"If you could just try, I'd be obliged."

Joe cradled the side of her head, and kissed her hard on the forehead, fighting back his own tears, then whispered something into her ear in Lakota like a forlorn lover, but Alice didn't break eye contact with Gaia. On the other side of Joe, Marty rubbed an eye with his palm.

"Yes," Gaia nodded and stood without even thinking. The deep dream world was still in her thoughts, and she wondered if she could drop back into it and at least see Wakinyan's spirit again.

She knelt in front of Wakinyan's body, still in Alice's arms. Joe didn't say a word, didn't try to stop her, which felt like permission to Gaia. Up close like this she could see the bullet hole in Wakinyan's forehead, and the caked blood around it, and for a moment her presence there seemed ludicrous. What was she supposed to do?

"I don't expect anything, Miss Gaia," Joe said. "Let's just be here with him as he flies away."

That helped. Gaia looked at Alice, who nodded, and any pressure that Gaia felt about reviving Wakinyan melted away. She closed her eyes and put a hand on his leg. She listened to the little signal kite snap overhead. Gaia imagined that it was Wakinyan's rising soul that lifted the kite, and that he was happy and flying away.

Suddenly, Gaia felt herself drop again and enter the place of spirits. All around her was a rich violet, pure and even like the sky. In the distance, a bright light flashed, and she kicked her feet and breast stroked her arms to catch up to it. The light was moving away, and she wasn't closing the distance, until it curved a wide arc in the purple air and changed course toward her. As it grew, her heart beat faster, because she recognized it's familiar shape, getting clearer and clearer, but still blurry in its brightness. It was Wakinyan. Last time she'd seen him here, he'd let out a loud whoop that repelled the darkness and gave her the strength to defeat Matthew. But now he made no sound. There was no swishing of clothes or whisper of breeze, only a vacuous silence as he floated before her, his face too bright to read any feature or expression.

"Come back," she said, and held out her arms to him. Wakinyan's spirit said nothing, and didn't reach back to her. He just floated there watching her. "Come back with me," she said again, reaching out to pull at him back, which actually seemed to be working, because he got closer and brighter. But she felt a surge of slicing pain through her forearms that made her cry out, and when she opened her eyes she was lying on her back in the sand.

"What is it!" Alice said, her eyes wide and expectant, but Joe brought her into another embrace and told her it was time to let go. She cried freely, and the three of them gently rocked.

"I'm sorry," Gaia said as she stood and turned to give the three of them space.

It wasn't long after that Joe and Marty got up, followed by Alice who gently laid Wakinyan's head in the sand. The Lakota quickly and quietly divided into two parties: one led by Alice to take Wakinyan's body home for burial in South Dakota, and the other led by the chief to ferry Gaia home.

Alice's face had become stone, her movements efficient, but Gaia felt a brush of tenderness from her when she refused to take her own hat back. "You need it more than I do, and it'll squeeze my sore head," she said, pointing to the bump where Matthew had struck her with his pistol. She also grabbed Gaia's hand and put something into it: a smooth, round stone the size of an eyeball that was painted red. "To make the spirits happy," Alice said, "though I believe you are one of them, Makȟá-akáŋl. So to make *you* happy. I hope to see you again. Somehow I think I will. Ka Dish Day, be safe. Be good. Gunjule. Nagi Tanka guide your way."

And they were gone, lifting Wakinyan's body out on a litter.

Only five Lakota remained, including Marty, who was quiet and elsewhere. The chief introduced Gaia to Otter, Jacob, and Buck, all of whom looked both sad and bashful, reluctant to make eye contact with her. They seemed relieved when the chief spoke Lakota to them and they turned to disappear around the other side of the point.

"They've never seen a walking spirit before," the chief said, sadness also clearly pulling at him. "They don't know how to act."

Alice had wanted Marty to come home with her—said her heart couldn't take losing another son. But the chief insisted Marty stay with him. Marty moved more slowly than the others and kept his distance, gazing at the ground.

Soon Otter, Jacob, and Buck floated back around the point, each on a watercraft that looked like a wide floating motorcycle bobbing on the jellyfish-coated swells. When they were even with the beach, they drove them to the shore and surprised Gaia when they rolled right up onto the sand on wheels. She'd never seen watercraft like these before. The drivers looked like bandits with their face guards. The chief motioned Gaia over to one of the vehicles, which he called "Frogs," and pulled a set of dry clothes out of a side hatch for her. The men respectfully turned, pretending to be busy as Gaia changed into them. More denim, and a dry pair of cloth shoes. As she got dressed, she slipped the red rock into a front pants pocket and she shivered with cold. The clothes slowly warmed her, even as baggy as they were. Her once-swollen foot looked and felt better. She was healing quickly and wished she could have somehow passed that healing power to Wakinyan. The chief offered Marty dry clothes as well, but Marty waved him off. The chief didn't argue, but he did insist that Marty wear a face guard. He also handed one to Gaia. "To keep The Worm out," he said. "Especially from gettin' into your eyes." But Gaia already knew this having worn one every time she went out with her mom or Godpappy to check the fish beds. Godpappy. The last time she'd seen him there was a gunshot and he was falling in the community garden.

"Chief, uh, Joe?"

He looked at her, waiting.

"My family. Godp— Lane. Ripple. Are they okay?"

He nodded, and relief broke through her like a wave. "Everybody's okay. Lane took one in the shoulder, but he'll live. They were holdin' 'em all in a warehouse, but we got 'em out. His men ent the smartest we ever went up against. Felt a little bad for them. But only just a little."

Gaia was about to ask how he'd known about the attack and where to find her family, but he must have sensed it and said only, "I'll tell you more later." He'd just lost his son, and Gaia didn't want to press him. But she did have another question.

"What day is it?"

The chief frowned. He looked angry. "He keep you knocked out?"

"A few times."

He looked back at Matthew's body and spat. "Monday," he said as he slid Matthew's pistol into a side compartment. Gaia would have thrown it into the sea, wanting nothing to do with the former psychopath. But the Lakota seemed an infinitely practical people.

Her family was okay. It had been only two days—she'd probably missed a full day being unconscious—but it felt like weeks. No, more than that. Gaia felt like she'd aged a decade over the weekend.

She pulled the sea mask on, getting the goggles right before tightening the strap that cupped the back of her head. Masks all had that same weathered neoprene smell, like salty rubber. Like her mom's and Godpappy's boats. Like home.

Otter and Marty rode together on one Frog and led the way, driving back into the surf on wheels, then bouncing on the waves as the wheels retracted. The chief and Gaia went next. Gaia sat behind him and grabbed the handles on the Frog inside her knees, holding on as the Frog's engine gurgled and farted in the water, lifting and dropping on the swells. Gaia felt spray on her hands and forehead and looked back to see Buck and Jacob entering the water, slowly dragging Matthew's body behind them on a rope tied around his ankles.

The body carved out a smooth trough of sand. She was relieved to see him so helpless now, his face blank and muddled with sand, his arms raised and trailing as if asking for surrender.

Questions came and went in Gaia's mind, and were replaced by only more questions. How did the Lakota know about her? How did they find her? Why were they helping her? Did the chief have people living in the complex, like spies? And where did Mrs. Ahn fit into all this? She wanted to ask the chief, but a dark hole in her heart was pulling everything into itself, followed by excitement at the thought of seeing her family. Emotions churned around in her gut like a load of wash.

Moments later, Matthew was swallowed by the oncoming tide, and his body disappeared under the water. With the extra weight, Buck had to gun the Frog's engine, which shot a long tail of water behind them.

As they drove further out to sea, angling north, Gaia looked back at the cove one more time, scanning the empty bluffs, then watching the thin shadow of cave entrance that led back down into the complex. The taut rope pulling Matthew's body behind Buck and Jacob's Frog looked like a thick fishing line.

Joe and Gaia pulled up beside Otter and Marty, waiting for Buck and Jacob to put weights on Matthew's rope. Marty looked out to sea stoically. As they dropped the weights that would pull Matthew to the bottom of the continental shelf, Gaia was still a little anxious. She'd left Matthew for dead once already, and he'd come back. He'd also told her that it was hard to kill a person. But she remembered that Matthew's heart was smoldering back in the fire, and she breathed easier.

Otter adjusted something on the Frog's console as Marty continued staring out to sea. The sun pushed silver light through the hazy clouds and painted silver across the pink-tangerine sea.

Gaia thought about her mom and dad and how sick with worry they all must be. Her dad and Cloudy were probably contacting everybody they could to help search for her, and her dad would have been pulling whatever military strings he could. Thinking back to her own escape from the complex, she knew she had no real chance of escaping on her own. Somehow, there were a lot of people looking out for her.

Then there was the vine that had broken the walls of her prison after she'd prayed for help, and the happy, phantom laughter of something there with her in the dark.

The chief turned in his seat and said, "Alice will let your folks know you're okay, and that we're bringing you back to them. Won't be until tonight, though. Sorry for that. We need to make a stop on the way, then we'll let it get dark." As he turned back around he paused on Marty, watching him for a few moments. Marty never looked over.

Gaia wondered what it would be like to lose a family member. How could you even begin to process that? It was one of those things you couldn't really understand unless it happened to you. The chief had just lost his son, yet he was apologizing to *her* for not being able to bring her home right away.

Buck and Jacob caught up, having dealt with Matthew's body, and they were off, driving in a triangle formation with Buck and Jacob out front. They continued out to sea for what seemed a half hour. Finally, Buck called out something to the chief in Lakota, and the chief nodded.

Off to the right, the sun had gone behind a bank of clouds that blended into the darker gray smoke coming from a fire in the distance. Wind curled around the Frog's windshield and tugged at Gaia's baggy clothes and the broad brim of Alice's hat, which she'd cinched tight with its cord. They angled further north and cut through the sea. Gaia pictured dolphins breaking the surface alongside them, smiling at her, like she'd seen in the old footage. She thought of dark sharks patrolling below, feasting on Matthew's body—if they ever ate dead, human flesh before they went extinct. She wondered about rockfish, and about all the life that once thrived in the sea.

Maybe I can grow sea plants, she thought.

They rode for hours. Her skin got numb from the wind raking her. Whenever the sun started to peek through the clouds to warm them, it was swallowed by another cloud moments later. There was nothing to hear out in the ocean except the wind and the boiling of the Frogs. Marty remained granite sitting behind Otter, never looking over at Gaia. She began drifting off, lulled by the steady white noise all around and by the warmth of the chief's back. She must have fallen asleep, because she felt the chief patting her leg. She opened her eyes to see him pointing at some islands up ahead. "We're stopping there, at Anacapa," he said.

-27-
Malihini Kipa

Gaia knew of Anacapa Island. She'd never been there, but a couple of years ago she'd gone with her mom to the main island of Channel Islands National Farm, of which Anacapa was part, to scout possible locations for the fish reseeding project. Behind the electrified fence she'd seen hills rolling with new fonio sprouts. But her mom had ultimately passed on the location, saying that area was more prone to hurricanes than further north, and that the fish reseeding—and the fonio plants, for that matter—would be doomed. She said the place was only good for wave and wind harvesting, and that Anacapa, the tiny easternmost island in the chain, was a transient slum for Hawaiians who were routinely chased off by government patrols or deported back to their homeland. Gaia didn't want to stop. She knew she was only a hundred miles from home, just around Point Conception ahead in the distance.

They slowed as they reached the eastern tip of the island, marked by a big rock that looked like a giant anteater about to poke its nose into another rock—as if the two rocks were once joined into an arch. Without any of the drivers speaking, the Frogs moved into a line behind Buck and Jacob. Gaia watched as Jacob extended a long pole into the air with a bright yellow signal flag that snapped in the breeze. They moved slowly, staying as close to the rocky shoreline as they could, the refracted currents off the steep shore making them bob and rock. The coastline gradually curved to the left, past jagged outcroppings that formed small, dark coves.

As they approached the smaller midsection of the island, they turned in to shore, let their wheels drop, and rolled onto a thin ramp of rock. Gaia gripped the handles as they slowly crept up a steep switchback trail until they finally came out onto a large plateau that gave them a grand view of the vast California coastline to the east and the bigger neighboring islands just west of them. The plateau was barren, studded with only occasional weeds and a few yellow bits of ice plant. The wind whipped harder up there.

Then Gaia saw movement ahead of them, as if an animal had darted. Then slowly, one by one, she saw people emerge. Skeletons, more like. Some walked, some hobbled, some seemed to have missing limbs. As the Frogs got closer, some of the people raised their hands in greeting. Some had grotesque deformities on their bodies and faces, as if they had been burned or boiled: misshapen heads, clubbed hands, twisted torsos. A frightening canvas of horrific cubism brought to life, animated, walking toward them. An island full of Lohis. Many were naked.

The Frogs came to a stop, and the chief dismounted, took off his mask, and stretched. Gaia took off her mask, too. A large Hawaiian man with a deformed balloon belly overhanging tattered shorts approached, smiling.

"Don't worry," the chief smiled, seeing the look on Gaia's face. "It's not contagious."

"Aloha, aloha!" the big man said, giving the chief a firm embrace and pat on the back. "It has been a very long time, Joe!"

"Much too long, Boki, my friend," the chief said. "Much too long. I apologize."

Gaia slowly climbed off the Frog as a group of younger Hawaiians approached her cautiously, staring.

"Nonsense!" Boki said. "Look at us. We're still here, aren't we? Maybe they realized we're not worth the trouble and stopped sending patrols. So what have you brought us this time? Some pineapple trees and sugar cane?" He laughed, patting his belly.

"More of the usual," the chief said. "But this time, maybe also something unusual." He turned and looked at Gaia, curiosity mingling with the sadness. "Something unusual indeed."

"I'm sorry about your boy, Joe."

Gaia could hear bits of conversation between Boki and the chief who were sitting off in a small, battered building under a roof of patched driftwood. At first, the chief had sat there by himself in silence for a while. Once Boki joined him, the chief had told Boki about the morning, about Gaia, and about the death of Wakinyan. But other distractions kept her from hearing everything. Otter, Buck, Jacob, and Marty were opening compartments in the Frogs, thronged by children and adults, and were handing things out: bags and water purifiers to some of the older people, cassava leather and little forked trowels and tiny plastic bags to the younger ones.

A group of children had also gathered around Gaia like curious, expectant dogs. Their deformities were difficult to look at, as if a mean, careless child had pulled clay into people-like forms, snapped his fingers, and brought them to life. There were so many of them, whites and Asians and native Hawaiians. How they'd remained hidden when Gaia and the Lakota had arrived was a mystery. The kids had spilled onto the bluff like gophers coming out of their burrows. A little girl—Gaia could only tell it was a girl because she was naked—was reaching up to touch Gaia's face. Her permanently open mouth gaped around her face toward her ear. Unsure, Gaia pulled back a little, feeling foolish and vain for ever thinking of herself as freakish.

"It's all right, don't worry," a voice came from behind her. "Let 'em touch you. Human touch is important for them."

When Gaia turned, she saw a flawless Hawaiian woman dressed in khaki shorts and a faded red cotton t-shirt that read, "Christmas sucks." She had a long braid and a beautiful, hard face.

"You look like you've never seen nuclear contamination before," she smiled. "It's not contagious."

"Oh," Gaia said. "I—didn't know."

"I'm Ailana," she said, extending a hand. Gaia shook it, and Ailana held her strong grip a few moments more as she examined Gaia's face and skin.

"I'm Gaia."

"Gaia, like the goddess?"

"I guess so," she blushed.

The kids were pressing in harder now, trying to touch Gaia.

"Hele aku!" Ailana waved with the back of her hand to shoo them away. "Go play. You're missing out on the cassava. Let me talk to this weird-looking girl." Ailana winked at Gaia, and some of the kids giggled as they slowly moved away, then ran over to the other Frogs.

"So what's your story? You Lakota?" Ailana asked.

"No, I don't think I'm Lakota."

Ailana laughed. "You mean you don't know?"

Gaia didn't know how to react. She'd been called things, but she'd never been asked about her nationality. She was stumped, tongue-tied, and the familiar aloneness started to creep in. There was so much to say and so little to say at the same time.

"Sorry for asking," Ailana said, "but what happened to you? Honestly, I'm not just prying. I spend most of my time helping people who have been contaminated somehow, mostly island people."

"It's okay," Gaia said. "I'm used to it. It's just—a long story. I was adopted. I've always been like this." Then she told a white lie, not wanting to delve into it. "I don't know much more than that."

Gaia felt a tug at her shirt. A naked little boy with large, misshapen eyes and a pig nose dripping mucus was holding up a piece of cassava leather.

"Oh, Moa," Ailana said, seeming happy to change the subject. "Always my sweet boy." Then she said to Gaia, "You should take a bite off the other end of it. I think he's got a cold."

Gaia watched the snot glisten on Moa's face, blazing a slow trail into his open mouth. Gaia slowly took the cassava and tore a bite off the back end of it, then handed it back to Moa, thanking him. He took it from her and trotted away.

"It's frightening how empathetic that boy is," Ailana said. "His emotional radar is off the charts. He can spot sadness a mile away. I'd say he'd make a great possum when he grows up, but I worry that he won't be tough enough."

"Possum?"

"Yeah. Possum. Like me." But she looked fearful all of a sudden. "Wait. You're not a cop, are you? Jesus. You'd better not be a cop. Tell me you're not a cop."

Gaia stared back, a little shocked, but Ailana laughed again.

"I'm joking. Possums are sneaky but fierce. They're nocturnal and don't have permanent homes, so they move around a lot. They're immune to snake bites, and they have a pouch for carrying their babies. I'm a possum. I smuggle these kids into the mainland, one at a time. There are a lot of Hawaiian families who want to help. It's tragic what's happened back home, on the islands, and we're big-hearted people, especially for our own. And we're citizens, yeah? But our government—our very own government—has turned its back on us. So we have to do everything underground. We're on our own now, just like Texas. Except the difference between us and Texas is that the government doesn't want Hawaii anymore. We're completely third world now. But who isn't third-world anymore, yeah?"

"You mean the epidemic in Hawaii?" Gaia asked. She'd always heard there was an outbreak of some terrible disease there.

"Ha! Epidemic. That would make me laugh if it didn't make me cry. That's the story, of course. Big epidemic, big quarantine. Keep those filthy, disease-ridden Rafties out." She looked angry.

"What, then?" Gaia asked. What could be worse than an epidemic?

"I wouldn't expect you to know. It never gets talked about, which is the real crime. What happened was simple payback. Reaping what we sow. And by 'we' I mean the clueless Haoles in Washington. Payback for the dirty little nukes *our* government launched at Syria before I was even born. Boki—the guy over there talking to Joe—was just a kid, but he remembers. Some of the radioactive cloud went into Turkey. Then wham, Turkey says 'Screw this,' and before you know it most of the Middle East is now New Persia, and Turkey starts dumping their own nuclear waste off the islands."

Ailana picked up a rock and threw it at a seagull that was strutting toward the group of kids still clustered around the Frogs. It hopped over the rock and kept moving.

"Epidemic. If Turkey had been able to sneak in far enough to make their little deposit off San Francisco, I wonder what we would have called it then. Salmonella? Spineless East Coast suits. Epidemic. Shit." She punched her fist into her other open hand. "So I'm a possum. I'm a great possum. I'd be a mercenary if I had the time. But I love these kids, and I can kick a little ass when I need to. Speaking of which," she broke off and hollered at one of the older kids loitering around the Frogs. "Oy, Pahoehoe. Turn around and grab that gull. He must be retarded coming in this close."

Pahoehoe was the tallest in the group. He had a cubist face—Picasso couldn't have painted him any more strangely—a huge clubbed foot, and one good arm. The other arm was a shriveled appendage sticking out from his shoulder that looked like it was trying to be a hand, only a little more than what Lohi had. But he was surprisingly quick. He took a couple of steps backwards, moving behind the gull, then pounced, extending his body into a full dive and grabbed the bird by the legs. The gull thrashed, trying to fly away and bite Pahoehoe's arm at the same time. But it was over in seconds. Pahoehoe got to his feet and slammed the bird into the ground. It twitched a few seconds then lay still.

"Good job, buddy!" Ailana said. Pahoehoe smiled and jabbed his fist in the air. Then he looked at Gaia and his smile lost a little of its light. He picked the dead bird up by the legs and carried it over, dropping it at Gaia's feet. Gaia noticed Pahoehoe had scraped up his chest in the dive.

"Malihini kipa," Pahoehoe slurred at Gaia. He bowed a little, then smiled in full, looking at Ailana and winking. Ailana laughed again. She laughed freely, with all of her heart, it seemed, and Gaia marveled at how she could be so angry one minute and so joyful the next.

"You're a beautiful host, Po,"Ailana said. "Thank you. Mahalo."

Pahohoe dropped his head, suddenly bashful at the compliment, and slowly walked back toward the Frogs, looking back once more with a sheepish grin.

"That was pretty amazing," Ailana said, watching him go, her eyes moistening a little. "We work on keeping these kids as centered as we can. They're so hungry, but it's important that they stay respectful, that they share, that they're good hosts. Malihini kipa means guest. He gave you that gull knowing that he probably wouldn't get any of it."

"I'm going to give it back to him," Gaia said, starting to reach for the bird.

"No!" Ailana said sternly, freezing Gaia, but Ailana softened right away. "Don't you dare give that back to him. That would undo the joy of giving he just filled himself with. That's more important than food. However," she said, tilting her head to scrutinize Gaia with one eye, "being a guest also has responsibilities. Accepting this gift means you've also got to contribute afterwards." Then she looked puzzled and said, "What are you grinning at?"

"Oh, nothing," Gaia said. "I just thought of a way I could contribute."

"Yeah? Like how?"

Gaia smiled. "You'll see."

"Sneaky! I think I like you, goddess girl. Let's go see what those useless men are up to."

As they walked toward the building, Gaia looked back to the Frogs. Marty, who was smiling a little with a group of kids, looked up and watched her go, which gave her sudden goosebumps, and she felt herself blush again. It was the first time he'd looked at her since they left the cove. Had she done something wrong? Had she frightened him by killing Matthew? No, it was probably all about losing his brother.

The chief and Boki had come out of the little building, and the two men, Ailana, and Gaia talked together. They told Gaia more about what it was like trying to live in Hawaii now and why islanders were leaving in droves, some for Japan and some for the states. The nuclear contamination was obviously a central problem that affected everything, from health to food to water. Eating contaminated jellyfish was also out of the question. Purified water had to be shipped in. Even with the water shipments, there was so little to go around for drinking that none of it could be used for growing.

"We're living a nightmare," Boki said. "If it's not nuclear contamination and lack of good water, then the hurricanes come. So many hurricanes this past decade. Hawaii is like a bulls-eye for 'em. And when the crops do start to come in, the rain stops. Or we get wiped out by the next storm."

"Any progress underground?" the chief asked him.

"Not enough money," Boki said. "Underground farms are a lot more work than you'd think."

Gaia thought back to Matthew's massive complex. He couldn't have built it himself. It must have already been there when the military had it. Then she had an idea.

"Mr. Boki—"

"Just Boki!" he laughed. "I never liked that 'mister' stuff."

"Well," she said, "I just came from a place that had a massive underground growing system. Old Camp Pendleton."

Boki raised an eyebrow, and the chief nodded.

"I'll fill you in later," the chief said. "Not sure if it would work out for you, but she's right. It's huge."

"Might be worth a try," Boki said. "I mean, when you float across 2,300 miles of rough seas through a contamination zone on a little raft, anything is worth a try."

As their talking wound down, the chief pulled Gaia aside. They went into the building he and Boki had gone into, which was nothing more than an empty concrete box with door and window openings, a matted brown grass floor, and a stick roof that allowed light to bounce in at different angles. She hoped he was going to tell her about their departure plan. Despite how interesting Ailana, Boki, and the Hawaiians were, she was feeling desperate for home.

They sat on the ground across from each other, the chief with his legs folded. He didn't say anything for a few minutes. Just studied her, looked through her at times. Gaia was antsy and kept shifting her seating position. But then she remembered what the chief and his family had just gone through.

"I'm sorry about Wakinyan, Sir," she offered. "I can't help feeling like it was my fault."

"What?" he said, looking like somebody had slapped him. "No! How can you say that? The fault was mine. I was careless, and he was hot-tempered. But he went bravely, and this is good. I am proud of him. Life is so short here that it won't be long before I see him again. I am at peace with it."

"I think you will, too," she said.

He didn't say anything, but he had an odd, knowing look. She wanted to tell him about her experience with Wakinyan in the deep, spirit place, but it still didn't feel right. She wasn't sure he really would understand once she told him. So she asked the next thing on her mind.

"How did you know about me?" she asked. "Why are you helping me?"

He waited, watching her intently, pondering. "We know a lot," he said finally. "We're in the information business, mostly. For a few years now we've suspected that you are Makȟá-akáŋl, Ni' nahlin. Your name, Gaia, is no coincidence. It meant something similar to the ancient Greeks as it does to us: That you are a goddess of the Earth, an Earth spirit, the child of the great spirit Nagi Tanka. So I thought you were maybe worth the risk." He smiled.

"But how did you know? I didn't even know any of this myself until a couple of days ago. Things started to happen, and my mom told me things, and Godpappy, er, Lane and Cloudy—" she broke off, unsure how much to tell him.

"It's okay. I know all about it."

"You do? How?" He was such a mystery. So human yet so omniscient.

"Like I said, I'm in the information business. And I know your godfather, and I knew who Siafu was. I know about him being there on the day of your birth."

"You know my godfather?" That was maybe the biggest shock of all.

He smiled. "Does it surprise you?"

"Jesus! It makes me mad realizing how little they told me, about *anything*!"

He nodded sympathetically but didn't take her side. His albino face, his white hair, somehow conveyed less gravity than dark skin and hair would have. "I know your dad, too. Jack Cadogan is a good man. And then there's your mom." He grinned. "Maer Cadogan is some woman. Curses like an inmate, too. I like her. Anyway, we had people at Liesl's farm. That's when we knew for sure who you were, though we suspected when you were younger." He shook his head. "Still hard for me to take in, what you did there at the farm, who you are."

She felt faint. How did they all know each other, her family and this fearsome terrorist? She thought back to the the Chinese Fire Water Jet she'd watch cartwheel through the sky in flames only two days ago. Her parents *had* seemed awfully unsurprised.

"It's okay," he said, as if sensing her shock. "We've got a few minutes to air this out."

"But why?" she started "Please don't think I'm being disrespectful, Sir—"

"Joe, please. Call me Joe."

"Okay. Joe." It felt funny calling him that. He was definitely much more than a Joe. "But aren't you—"

"A terrorist?" he finished for her.

"Well, yes."

He sighed. "That, Miss Gaia, is a complicated question. The short answer is yes, the long answer is no." He looked at her a few moments more. "The short answer is that I work with the U.S.

government. *With*, not *for*, mind you. As a partner. The Lakota are an independent nation. The U.S. government hires us, gives us money, to destroy things."

"Seriously? But that doesn't make any sense. You're NAAA. You're Native Americans Against America. How can you be working *with* the American government?"

"It makes sense if you see what we destroy."

"Like the Fire Water Jet?"

"Ah, so you know about that!"

"I *saw* it. It freaked me out!"

The chief smiled. "Sorry about freaking you out, though I'm pleased to see it had that effect on you. Let me ask you this. Was it an *American* jet?"

"No, it was Chinese."

"Bingo," he said, pointing a finger at her like a gun and taking a pretend shot.

"But what about the other stuff, especially the farms, the buildings, the roads?"

"Chinese. Chinese. Chinese."

"So you only destroy Chinese stuff?"

"Chinese stuff in America."

Gaia rewound everything she'd ever heard about NAAA and the things they'd destroyed. What he was telling her seemed to add up.

"But—why?"

"To make them think twice, three times, four times, about taking over any more of our land. It's complicated, politically, but I'll try to explain." Joe shooed a fly away from his face. "For many decades the American government has been running low on money. So they had to borrow, mostly from China. Well, when land became more valuable than money, the Chinese called in their debts. They started confiscating American land to grow food for themselves, to build air bases, stuff like that."

Gaia furrowed her brow. *Couldn't the government just say no?* she wondered.

"I know what you're thinking," he said. "How could we just let them do that?"

She nodded.

"It's not that easy. For lots of reasons the government couldn't say no. That's where we come in."

"So the government wants to scare the Chinese."

"Yep. And what better way than with a group calling itself anti-American, a group the government seems to have no control over? The Chinese can't blame the U.S. government for that. So the Chinese slow down their land-grabbing and the Lakota make money, grow food on their own land, and live another day."

Gaia nodded and picked at some dry grass, though at the moment she wasn't tempted to plunge her fingers into it and make it live again. The confusion of world politics was writhing in her head, latching its tentacles onto the confusion and fear over what Matthew had done to her in the name of "helping the world" by slowly euthanizing everyone for profit. It was a world where people bled over scraps of food, where parents took it from their own children. Otherwise beautiful, innocent children were melted by nuclear war. Was there no hope anywhere?

Outside she heard some of the older kids and grownups trying to corral some of the younger kids. She also heard one of the Lakota teaching a younger Hawaiian how to use the small fork trowel to get the soil ready for seed.

"Something troubling you?" the chief asked.

She didn't answer immediately. She was trying to put it into words. Finally she realized that she just needed to confide, to let it all out.

"Yeah. A lot. A whole lot." The big-world angst was making her feel hopeless about her own situation. "I mean, a week ago I'm just this weird misfit kid. But since then, it's like somebody dropped a different me into my body, or I'm in the strangest dream I've ever had." She slapped herself hard across the face. "But see, that proves I'm not dreaming, right?"

The chief's eyes widened a little, but he didn't respond.

"Then I get kidnapped, and supposedly I'm this Zaz person from some old lost gospel, some savior, which it turns out is complete—" she paused, "*carpshit*, because Matthew or Siafu or whoever he was told me he made that up. And since then it seems like everyone is after me for one thing or another. I almost get my heart ripped out of my body, and I don't know what to do, because—" she broke into tears. "I'm only freakin' 14! And I'm telling this to a terrorist who's trying to destroy the world, but who's somehow on my side, who risks his own family's lives to save mine. So yeah, something's bothering me, Joe! And I feel like just running away screaming. What's so *funny*!"

Joe was chuckling. "Do you feel better?"

"No!" she yelled, but it did somehow make her feel better. The Lakota had an irresistible humor, and she allowed herself a little smile.

"Well," he said, "it's all a little weird. But so what? As to what you're able to do, your magic, that's your gift, and above all you should be grateful for it, not angry. But what I see in you has nothing to do with magic. Your spirit, your heart, is so strong. You've spoken of your family. I've come to learn that blood is not always the most important part of family."

She thought of her parents who, she'd discovered only two days ago, were really her adopted parents.

"Some people that I truly consider family do not share blood with me," Joe continued. "As for you, I see that you are a true sister of Alice and Ailana. If this world is to be helped, it will not be by your magic. The world will help itself only when people can become more like Alice, and Ailana, and Gaia. So you can drop that weight off of your shoulders that you need to save the world. You can help with your magic in many ways. But you are not responsible for the world. You are not a conceited person. So don't think conceited thoughts."

Gaia let his speech settle in. It made her feel a little less heavy.

"And you have to be able to accept yourself," he said.

"Why does everybody keep saying that? Love myself without condition, right?"

"No. Don't try to love yourself. It doesn't work. Just start by accepting yourself, letting yourself be a flawed human being who makes mistakes. I mean, look around at all of us. Boki and his family. Me, a white Indian. You know how hard it was for me to accept that? You, your wonderful skin and eyes and hair." He opened his arms wide. "We're all freaks here! How funny is that?"

But now Gaia was thinking about how she'd failed to bring Wakinyan back. There was so much she could do, yet she was so helpless at the same time—for a supposed goddess.

"Give yourself a break," the chief went on. "Appreciate yourself for who you are. What else can we do? Laugh at ourselves, with kindness and respect."

"But I'm not human, am I?"

"You're human enough. Anyway, enough psychology. I know you're anxious to see your folks. Alice will soon get word to them, and you'll see them tonight. We have to wait until it's dark to move."

"You haven't told my parents yet?" she asked. "Don't you have a Telepath?"

"No. None of us does. Too easy to track. And they rot your instincts, make you a slave to them. I don't like artificial stuff in my body, no matter how small it is. Like what Siafu put in you."

Gaia understood the point he was making. Anything inserted into her body had been troublesome, from the D.I. chip to Siafu's capsule. And Telepaths weren't always around. People used to carry bulky little computer telephones in their pockets. But Gaia couldn't even see that the Lakota carried those, or any other communication device.

"Then how do you communicate with each other?"

"Like this. It's called talking." He grinned. "Really, I'm not kidding. It's amazing how connected you can be without Telepaths. You know how blind people develop stronger senses to make up for their lack of sight? People think you're blind and ignorant if you don't have a Telepath. But to us, we do so much better without 'em. We have other tricks, too. To communicate. I'll show you sometime, if you come visit us in South Dakota."

A dragonfly buzzed into the room and startled Gaia by landing on her head, its wiry legs tickling her scalp. The chief held out his finger, and the dragonfly left Gaia and flew onto it. He turned his hand to examine its lacy wings and metallic blue body. "Good luck," he said. "It's a sign."

It was the first time Gaia could remember an animal showing preference for somebody besides her.

"Is it? Good luck?"

"Hell, I don't know. I just made that up."

The thing flew back onto Gaia's shoulder, and another dragonfly buzzed in, joined its mate in copulation, and the two flew off together, conjoined by a thin braid, back out the door into the wide world.

"I take that back," the chief said, grinning. "They're definitely gettin' lucky! Wopes, sorry. Alice woulda smacked me for saying that in front of you."

Gaia blushed and picked at the ground, because Marty had appeared in her thoughts and she feared if she looked at the chief he'd know it. Thinking of Marty at that very moment—inspired either by the dragonflies or what the chief said about them (or even randomly happening at a very bad time)—was exciting. More than anything it was confusing, and she pushed him out of her mind with something obnoxious and distracting: Selene. She'd get to see her sister soon, and her mom, and dad, and Cloudy, and even Godpappy.

"Joe?" Gaia said. It was time to tell him.

"Yes Miss Gaia?"

"I saw your son. I saw Wakinyan."

"You did?" Joe froze, his pink eyes like strange, hopeful planets. "When you held him on the beach?"

"Yes, but before that. When Matthew told them to kill Marty."

His face hardened when she said that. Gaia realized it was the first time she had ever really looked at him, noticed the details of his features. His white hair was out of its pony tail, and it hung about the length of hers, to his shoulders. It was as white as Wakinyan's was black as hers was deep blue. His eyebrows were only slightly darker, hovering over his pink planet eyes like clouds, as if his face were a different universe where space was white and the celestial orbs in it stood out like playful, colored marbles. His eyes were softening again.

"When did you see him before that?" he asked.

Gaia realized she didn't know where to start or how to describe the deep place she'd gone.

"I was furious, and I dropped down deep into somewhere. Maybe it was the spirit world. I don't know. But there was a darkness there, and it spoke to me. It called itself Despair, and it said it had claimed the world, and that I was interfering. It spoke as if it had seen me before, like I'd fought it before. But I don't remember anything like that."

She paused, watching for some response from Joe. What he asked her next surprised her.

"The voice," he said. "Was it male or female?"

Not only was he believing her story, but he was asking a very specific question about it, as if it were something not unfamiliar to him. The validation put her more at ease.

"It was male," she said. "Deep voice."

Joe nodded. "Silly question, sorry. Of course it was male."

"Why? Why of course?"

"Because in my experience, women are seldom the forces of despair." He shook his head. "Sorry. Didn't mean to interrupt. Keep going."

Gaia smiled. It was such an otherworldly conversation, yet it felt as normal as if they were talking about their plans for the upcoming weekend. If she'd been sharing this with anyone else, Gaia thought, they'd excuse themselves, leave the hut, and have her committed.

"I tried to fight it, the dark thing, but it was winning. It was snuffing me out." She scrunched her brow trying to remember exactly how Wakinyan had come to her. She wanted to get it right, because Joe seemed keen to know specific details. "Then I saw a firefly. I've seen fireflies before, when I went to Washington, D.C. with my family a few summers ago. This was just like that. It was dark, but there was only one firefly, way in the distance. It was green, and blue, and it kept getting closer."

Joe was all eyes now, and his lips were parted. A gust of breeze swirled into the little hut, and the smell of dust and dry grass filled her lungs.

"When it got closer, it got whiter, and bigger, and it was the shape of a man. And somehow I knew it was Wakinyan. Like he had some signature that fit perfectly into a spot in my brain."

She looked up as his eyes, which were suddenly damp.

"He let out a cry, like how I imagine a war whoop sounding, and he danced. It felt like he and I were one thing, growing with strength and light, and it drove the darkness away."

A tear dripped down Joe's cheek. Then another on the other side. He didn't wipe them away.

"And the Maggot with it."

Gaia nodded, knowing he meant Matthew.

"You were brave."

"It was your son. He saved me." Gaia knew that if it hadn't been for Wakinyan, she'd have—well, she wasn't sure what would have happened. But she knew she wouldn't be sitting here talking to Joe, or getting ready to see her family again, if it weren't for Wakinyan.

"Oh!" Joe gasped, his face suddenly lit with clarity. His eyes moved back and forth, their gaze reversed as if watching the idea move about inside his skull. Seeing him this way made her more hopeful.

"He did it on purpose," Joe said.

"Did what on purpose?" she wasn't following. Coming to help her? Or—

"He got himself killed on purpose."

"What?"

"Wow," he said, slowly letting out his breath, then looking her in the eye. He was smiling now. "Clever little bastard."

"What? What do you mean?" Gaia was antsy to find out. Yet more magic was at play.

"Wakinyan is not normally impulsive. He wouldn't have jumped up and run at the Maggot like that unless he had a good reason. He knew he was going to get shot. In fact, he was counting on it. Anything less and he'd only have gotten the butt of a gun across the head and knocked out."

Gaia wasn't following, and it looked like Joe could see that, so he kept going.

"Wakinyan knew things were going to get very, very bad. There was nothing he could do to help in this world, so he got a head start. He knew he'd be more of a help in the spirit world, and damned if he wasn't right."

"You mean," Gaia said, beginning to understand but still unable to comprehend, "he sacrificed himself to help me in the spirit world?"

"I ent sure he knew *who* he was gonna help. Maybe he thought his mother would show up in the spirit world, or me, or Marty. He just wanted to be ready, maybe get used to the place ahead of time."

"You're serious," Gaia said. She still couldn't comprehend. It would take a lot of trust to know you actually *were* going into the spirit world. What if there wasn't a spirit world? What if when you died, that was it? Nothing? But given her recent experiences with "death" and the deep place, she knew it existed. But how could Wakinyan know?

Joe nodded. "I'm serious. We train for the spirit world."

"Train? How? Why?"

"Cuz we're all going there someday, and if we happen to get there unexpectedly, it makes sense to be a little prepared. We think the spirit world is more like the dream world, when you're asleep. So we practice lucid dreaming, where you control what happens in your dreams."

"You can do that?" Gaia had heard of it, and even tried a couple of times, but it never worked.

"Sure. It takes practice, a lot of practice, but it gets easier. I hope it helped Wakinyan. By what you say, he did well."

"But I couldn't bring him back. I tried."

"Maybe he didn't wanna come back," Joe said.

Gaia thought back to it. She'd reached out to him, but—

"It seemed like he was thinking about it," she said. "But then I felt a sharp pain in my arms, and he left. And I came back to the world."

Joe smiled and stretched. He looked satisfied, and he finally wiped his wet eyes and cheeks. He stood, looking down at her with an expression of pride.

"You did your best. Alice asked for your help, and you tried. We will always be grateful for that, Makȟá-akáŋl."

Warm air and the warm sounds of the Hawaiians and Lakota outside wrapped around her. It was the first time she'd felt truly content in a very long time. Thinking of seeing her family soon, sitting there in the protective fatherly presence of the chief, wanted terrorist, President of Native Americans Against America, and proud card-carrying member of the Lakota tribe of the seven council fires, eight generations removed from the great warrior Crazy Horse, also known as Joe, filled her with lightness and hope.

She thought of Ailana, and the generous spirit of the Hawaiians, which made her want to help. Then, the urge to dig her fingers into the ground overcame her.

-28-

Tomato. Sort of.

When Gaia opened her eyes, she realized she'd gone into something of a trance. She'd gone to the deep place of music, where the one-but-many, male-but-female voice or voices flowed like an underground river of life.

The first thing she saw was the chief, wide-eyed, staring at the juniper bush that now existed in the space between them. The rest of the hut floor was blanketed with wild onion grass, and outside the door grew new little bushes with red berries, bushes of wild nuts, the prickly yellow heads of squaw root. And more poppies.

The chief looked outside and slowly rose and walked out of the hut. He just stood there, looking left, looking right, then stared back at Gaia, who was sitting cross-legged and smiling.

"Wh—" he started. "It's—it's *everywhere!*"

She walked out and joined him. It *was* everywhere, covering the little island. Wild, mismatched bushes, grasses, and flowers. Happy shrieking came out of the boy Moa, but everyone else was stone quiet, gazing around in wonder.

"I wish Alice could see this," the chief said. "I'd heard from my people about Liesl's garden. But actually *seeing* this for myself..." He looked even paler than usual, and his pink eyes were wet.

Ailana was the first to approach them and speak. She kept her distance and looked wary.

"You did this?"

Gaia opened her mouth to speak, but nothing came out at first, then, "Yes. But I don't know how I do it."

"Gaia. So that's really no bullshit. Are you really—her? Are you some kind of goddess or alien or something?" Ailana looked almost as pale as the chief, and Gaia could sense a wall going up between them.

"I don't know who I am, exactly."

"For real?"

"Yeah, for real."

"Ailana," the chief cut in. "Meet Makhá-akáŋl. The Earth goddess."

So that's what that word means, Gaia thought. Hearing the chief pronounce it so matter-of-factly gave her chills, as if she were just learning about it for the first time.

"But she just said she doesn't know who she is."

"It's because she is new to it. She's still very young."

"So how do *you* know this?" Ailana asked the chief. "How do you know she's not some alien from space?"

Gaia felt extremely alien with Ailana talking about her in the third person, all her previous warmth gone. Despite what Gaia had just done, old feelings of isolation crept in, a sadness of not belonging, which opened the floodgates and pushed everything bad into her mind: being kidnapped, missing her family, the little boy with the slit throat, Mrs. Ahn, Matthew shooting Wakinyan, and the heaviness of being this all-important Earth Mother who hadn't the first hint what she was supposed to do. Despite what the chief had just told her about self-acceptance, the opposites—self-pity and self-loathing—were rising in her. And what she'd just grown on the island, this new miracle rooted in joy, had suddenly turned to grief. Gaia ran back into the hut to get away from everyone and hide her tears. But her isolation didn't last long.

"Hey." It was Ailana at the doorway. "Can I come in?"

Gaia shrugged and dried her face as best she could. Ailana came in and took Gaia by the hands to sit her down. Ailana put her palm on the little juniper and shook her head.

"'E Maui! I'm a little freaked out here, okay? I'm sorry for what I said."

"I really don't—" Gaia stammered, "know what I'm supposed to do. I just found out about this two days ago."

"Seriously?"

Gaia nodded.

"You don't know where you came from or anything?"

Gaia somehow trusted Ailana. The woman was too honest not to trust, and she wanted to talk to someone. "All I know is that I was born on Mt. Kenya, and two men found me there. I grew up in Junipero Bay. And things just started happening on Saturday. Well, Friday really, when I got hacked."

"Got what?"

"Nevermind," Gaia shook her head. "But I just found out I can grow things. And kill things when I get mad enough."

Ailana let out a low, falling whistle. "That's heavy. I hope I'm not making you mad." She slapped Gaia playfully on the shoulder. "Seriously, though. How did you do this? Grow these things?"

"I just put my fingers into the ground and sort of meditate."

Ailana shook her head. "Aiwaiwa! So can you grow whatever you want?"

"I don't know. I tried once, but it didn't really work. Things just randomly grow, I guess. Things that want to grow."

Ailana rubbed her hands together with excitement. "You should try! Do you want to try?"

Gaia did want to try. "I don't know if it'll work, though."

"Only one way to find out! Go on, pick something. Do I need to move out of the way? Let me move out of the way." She scooted back.

Gaia decided on a tomato plant but didn't want to tell Ailana in case it didn't work.

"Well? What are you gonna grow?" Ailana was now a giddy little girl in a "Christmas sucks" t-shirt.

"Tomato," she caved in.

"Blech. I hate tomatoes. Sorry! Go, go. Try it!"

Gaia gently set her fingers between patches of onion grass and lightly dug them into the ground as if she were playing a dirt piano. She closed her eyes and filled her thoughts with a big heirloom tomato plant that had thick, dark green leaves and fat, crimson fruit. In her mind, the fruit suddenly grew little mouths and started singing to her in squeaky chipmunk voices.

"Holy shit!" she heard Ailana screech, and Gaia opened her eyes to see what had happened.

A cactus. A small prickly pear cactus whose paddle-shaped leaves sprouted swollen fingers of purple fruit.

Ailana shrieked and lost it, rolling on the ground laughing. "That's the craziest thing I've ever seen!" She sat up and palmed the sides of her face with both hands. "Fuck! I mean, it just came out of the ground and got bigger and bigger!"

Gaia herself was amazed but a little disappointed.

"Wow!" Ailana said. "Wait, are you sad? Why do you look sad?"

Gaia shrugged and sighed. "It's not a tomato plant."

Ailana laughed and clapped her hands together. "Are you kidding me? So what! Hell, at least it's edible. Just need a knife and some thick gloves!"

Gaia wondered if the singing tomatoes in her head had anything to do with it. Was somebody messing with her, this Source of hers, this power that had helped her escape from Matthew's room with that big vine, that spoke to her when she died in the community garden, that she'd heard when she went into the trance a few minutes earlier? Was she not supposed to—or unable to—grow specific things?

"I don't know what happened," Gaia confessed. "I guess it kind of looks like a tomato plant. In a way."

She looked up and noticed the chief leaning against the doorway with his arms crossed, smiling.

"You just need a little practice, that's all!" Ailana said.

But Gaia wasn't sure she shared Ailana's optimism or agenda, based on what Ailana said next.

"You're coming back to Hawaii with me."

-29-
Mahalo, Aloha

Back outside, Hawaiian kids were picking, pulling, and yanking at plants like deformed, wingless, dirty bees finding pollen for the very first time. They hauled in nuts, berries, little onions, and anything else that looked edible. Seagulls started to appear in droves, flying by in cautious groups and landing at a distance from the humans. The once-barren little island had become an Eden-like carnival.

To Gaia's relief, when Ailana told Boki and Chief Last Coyote about wanting to take Gaia back to the islands, the chief forbade it.

"She needs to get back to her family," he said with a finality that nobody questioned. She felt almost giddy. But her heart sank at what Boki said next.

"We'll have to leave right behind you, Joe." He gazed around at the wild new growth covering the island. "We'll get too much attention with all this." But Boki didn't seem sad, just matter-of-fact. He even winked at Gaia and smiled.

Gaia never would have thought that what she'd just done would hurt anyone, especially her new friends. What good was her gift if it was only going to cause trouble? When she confessed her regret to Ailana, whom she thought might be angry about having to leave, and also about not being able to take Gaia to Hawaii, Ailana surprised her with a parting pep talk.

"For one, get a spine. Don't let anybody walk on you, jerk you around. Not even me. We Hawaiians will get along just fine. Always have."

"I think I have a pretty good spine," Gaia said, feeling defensive that Ailana thought she might be soft.

"Okay, well get a stronger one. I don't know what the 'other plans' are for you," Ailana said, quoting the air with her fingers. "One, you're gonna have to be a hundred times as tough as you've ever been. And two, you need somebody to help you focus your power, to use it in a disciplined way, instead of randomly growing things wherever you go. Don't call attention to yourself."

Gaia saw the benefit of that. If she hadn't performed the miracle in Liesl's garden, she might not have gotten kidnapped by Matthew. And while Ailana was being bossy—which no doubt helped her succeed as a possum—it was the first practical advice anyone had given her so far, which was refreshing. But how could Ailana, or anyone else, really know what she should do or how she should do it? It was all uncharted territory.

"Then what am I supposed to do?" she asked, really hoping for a usable answer.

"That's why you need help, and I've got a name for you. What you just did won't always be a good thing to do."

Gaia felt guilty again, and Ailana must have picked up on it.

"Don't get me wrong," she quickly added. "This is amazing. I still can't believe it. But let me tell you what's gonna happen now. Boki chose Anacapa *because* it's so desolate, because it was easy to hide here, and close for me to transport kids to the mainland. It's been perfect for a while. Nobody's bothered with this place because it's a dead zone. Or was a dead zone. Now look at it." Ailana stretched out her arms. "If you'd have grown a little patch of ground with some berries, that would have been great, something we could handle. But all this?" She laughed and shook her head. "'E Maui, girl! It's like a miniature jungle everywhere. It's beautiful! So you need to learn how to focus and practice somewhere safe."

"I'm sorry," Gaia said, feeling more deflated. "I didn't— I'm just a kid."

"Spine!" Ailana barked. "You need to be the toughest person on Earth right now. Don't give me this kid shit, either. Give yourself more credit than that. You're already more together than most grownups I know. You just need help, that's all."

"But how? Who?"

"Remember this name: Chester Green, at U.C. Davis, up north. I took some graduate courses with him. He's brilliant, he's well-connected, and he can make sure you're protected. You ever hear of humigenesis?"

"Yeah, on the news. Where you can get soil to grow itself, right?"

"Yep. That's one of the things. But there's a lot more."

Ailana pulled a piece of cassava leather out of her back pocket, tore off a bite, and handed the rest to Gaia. Gaia nibbled on its dry sweetness, which roused a great hunger in her. The last thing she'd eaten was a piece of Alice's fry bread before escaping from Matthew's complex. Ailana continued.

"And Chester's the man. He'd definitely know what to do with you. Go find him."

Ailana looked at her hard, as if trying to bore the command into Gaia's brain. A wisp of excitement flicked inside of her. Humigenesis was often talked about, but nobody had ever figured out how to re-grow soil. Her mom had had more luck growing fish in a contaminated, extinct ocean. Had this Chester Green person figured it out? Would he teach her?

Then another thought hit her. Was *she* capable of it herself, the same way she was able to grow plants out of nothing? Maybe there *was* a way to help her focus her new abilities.

"Meantime," Ailana finished, "we'll figure out where to take these kids next. You didn't mean to cause trouble. They probably would have found out about us in a week or two, anyway, even if you hadn't shown up."

Little Moa trotted up to Gaia and grabbed her hand, pulling her to a big circle of people forming around a growing pile of bounty. He'd also grabbed the chief, who was sitting cross-legged and looking serious, almost sad as he came out of his daydream. But Boki was all smiles and even gave Gaia a full hug, his big belly forcing her to bend over a little.

"I don't know what to tell you," Boki said. "Mahalo, I think. No, just mahalo! I mean, look at them. I have never seen them this happy, this hopeful. I myself have never felt so hopeful. I can say without any fear of contradiction that this place, where we are now, is the most beautiful, the most bountiful place on all the Earth. It has been an honor to see this, to receive this gift from you. Thank you, Miss Gaia." He bowed. "How lucky for the world that you are real, that you are with us!"

Gaia wasn't sure what to make of this. Was Boki trying to put a good face on a bad situation, or did he really mean what he said?

But she was quickly distracted by more seagulls, who continued to flood the island from all directions, landing even closer now that the humans seemed to be otherwise occupied. Boki called out to the bounty-gathering kids.

"Children, not too much! Only what we can carry out! Bring what you have now."

The Hawaiians brought their armfuls of berries and nuts, spilling little bits as they approached, then dumping their loot into the growing pile.

Pahoehoe, the boy who'd caught the seagull for Gaia, brought the dead bird to Boki, and the two exchanged heated words in Hawaiian, with Boki pointing at the pile of food. Eventually Boki relented and led Pahoehoe over to a makeshift cooking grate. Pahoehoe looked over at Gaia, a grin spreading across his cubist face, and gave her a thumbs up with his good hand. She wondered why, with all this new bounty, Pahoehoe would still want to eat seagull—and even give some to her. Maybe he was following through on his generosity, some spirit of Aloha that made him proud. Maybe it was habit, or maybe they'd still need to know how to do it again in the next day or two when all the bounty was gone. After all, she couldn't stay with them and keep growing things for them to eat. Maybe it was all those things.

Gaia sat down and hugged her legs. She lowered her face toward her knees and closed her eyes, listening to the happiness all around that she knew would soon come to an end. She couldn't imagine the hardships they'd run into next. Through the press of bodies all around, she felt a calm presence sidle down next to her.

"Are you sad?" Marty asked.

When she looked up she could tell he'd been crying. She didn't say anything, just turned to look at the pile of food in the middle of the circle.

"They would have had to leave soon anyway," he said.

She looked at him again. "Are you okay?"

"I'll manage."

It was the first time they'd spoken since before they were re-captured by Matthew's men at the cove. Since Matthew had killed Wakinyan.

"I'm sorry about your brother, Marty."

"Yeah, me too." Marty twisted a piece of onion grass between his fingers. "He was a good brother, a good son. A good Lakota. I hope I see him again. But not too soon. I'm not ready for the spirit world yet. I worry most about how Mom's taking it."

"Your mom's tough."

"She is. Tougher than I am." He took a deep breath. "Can I tell you something? For some reason I feel like you're the only person I can tell right now. Pop understands, I think, without needing to talk. But I need to get it out. I think if I keep it in it'll eat my insides."

"Okay," she hesitated, watching him, his young face caught somewhere in that odd place between boyhood and manhood.

Marty lowered his voice. "I've never killed a person before today."

The memories flew into her. The man he fought down at the tube entrance, the little Hummingbird killing men to protect their escape up the ladder, the gunshots when they emerged out of the windmill tube.

"Stopping a life," he said, "a life just like your own, feeling it happening right there. Taking somebody from their parents, from their children, from all they were and all they could become. Part of my soul is gone now. Part of my own life. I feel it. I can't ever get it back."

Gaia knew that she herself should be feeling the same way, having killed Matthew. But for now she had zero regrets about it.

"But they would have killed *you*, Marty."

"I know. I've been thinking about that. But it doesn't help. And in some ways I think it would have been better if they'd killed me instead."

"No!" she almost shouted, but lowered her voice again. "You can't say that."

He looked at her, then looked down and nodded.

"Those were bad men, Marty, working for the devil."

"Were they?" he looked back up into her eyes. "How do we know that? Maybe that's the only way they could survive, help their families eat."

"But isn't that a choice they make? They don't have to make that choice. It's like the people who choose to break into a community pantry and steal other people's food. Or that woman who killed a nurse while trying to steal breast milk from the baby bank in Santa Maria. So they're doing it to feed their families. Does that make it okay?"

"Doesn't make them evil," Marty said.

"Doesn't it?"

"No. It just makes them human."

Gaia disagreed, but she kept it to herself. People always had choices, she figured. The ability to choose, to think logically, whether those choices were good or bad, was what really made people human.

"Siafu," Marty continued, "now he was a bad man. Seeing him die didn't bother me." He pulled out another shaft of onion grass from the ground, which made Gaia wince. It was an odd feeling, like he'd uprooted one of her children. "Wanting to take the greatest gift the world has ever seen and rip her heart out?" He shook his head again. "You did that, didn't you. Killed him."

Gaia felt a tingle at Marty's idea of her. Was she the greatest gift the world had ever seen? Whether she was or not, the fact that he thought so made her blush again. But she didn't answer his question about killing Matthew, and he didn't press.

"How old are you?" she asked him.

"Just turned 16. What about you?"

"Almost 15."

"You're 14?" He looked shocked, but now he smiled back at her, almost grinned. "You're a lot older than that, Makhá-akáŋl."

They were interrupted by Boki calling everyone to the circle. Ailana led the group in singing a Hawaiian gratitude song. The sound of the language was beautiful, dancing like a playful breeze or a tide that gets caught among rocks, meanders, and twirls its way back out.

After the singing, Ailana told the legend of Maui, and how he had captured the sun to make it move slower through the sky, which seemed fitting given that the real sun was now frosting a bank of clouds on the western horizon with the last of its pink light. Ailana kept adding details, bullshitting here and there.

After the story, Boki said something in Hawaiian that sent a current of excitement through the circle. Apparently it was time to eat. But instead of a mad dive into the food, a strange order commenced that surprised Gaia. Two of the younger children walked around the circle passing out old bamboo bowls, after which the very youngest leaned into the pile, taking little bits of everything instead of big piles. Then some older children went, and the order proceeded up in age until it was the adults' turn to go. The process commenced so quietly that Gaia could hear the gulls shuffling around them. Any other time she'd witnessed hunger, it was accompanied by some level of greed or violence. But not here. Here were the poorest of the poor, the most unfortunate of all, and they were being considerate. That, Gaia realized, was the real miracle.

Then Pahoehoe appeared with a block of wood that served as a plate, and when he set it reverently on the ground in front of Gaia, she saw the cooked carcass of the gull he'd caught, beautifully browned, wingless but still with it's head and feet and only a few blackened feathers remaining.

"Malihini Kipa!" he slurred.

Everyone fell silent and watched. Then, child by child, a chant rose up, gaining volume with each word. "Kaukau! Kaukau! Kaukau! Kaukau!"

"They want you to eat it," Ailana said in her ear, amused.

Gaia whispered back. "Why eat seagull with all this other food?"

The look Ailana gave her was almost piteous before whispering back. "He was so proud of that catch, and what he feels in his heart by being able to share it with you—" she broke off. "How do *you* feel about giving us all this? Pretty good, right?"

Gaia nodded, then nodded again, finally understanding.

"And you're not gonna be with us every day to do this again, right?" Ailana said.

"I get it," Gaia said, nodding some more.

"Just take a little bite and offer it back to him," Ailana said. "Unless you want to eat the whole damn thing! Then go for it."

Gaia chose option one, picking it up and nibbling a tiny piece off the breast while Pahoehoe watched, hanging on her every movement. All in all it tasted decent. Charred and a little tough. Nothing like the beef she'd eaten with Matthew, but in this context it tasted more satisfying. More real. She ventured another bite, then thanked Pahoehoe out loud and asked if he'd like to share the rest with her. He jumped to his feet, came over and took the plate from Gaia, set it with the rest of the food, and took a seat in the circle as another group of younger children filled their bowls.

Soon the chief got up, and the Lakota began to assemble away from the group. Boki and Ailana joined them and motioned for Gaia to come over.

"We leave soon," the chief told Gaia. "Your journey is about to end, then begin again." Then he said to Boki, "Can we help? Want us to tow you?"

"No, thank you, Joe," Boki said. "Ailana's got a Frog. After she gets back from her drop tonight we'll get the rafts loaded and she can tow us. She found a home for little Moa!"

Ailana pulled Gaia aside.

"Who are you going to find?"

Gaia thought for a moment. "Chester. Chester Green. Up in Davis."

"That's right. Don't forget. Remember what I told you."

Gaia nodded. Ailana was holding her firmly by both shoulders and looking her square in the face. She pulled Gaia into a tight hug, running her strong fingers up and down the middle of Gaia's back.

"There's that spine," Ailana said. "Feels strong. Keep it that way."

Then Ailana abruptly let go, shot Gaia one last smile, and walked back to the circle of children, cheering them on as they played hot potato with the skeleton of Pahoehoe's seagull.

-30-
Things Fall Apart

A t the docks of Junipero Bay, Friday evening had begun to fill and dribble with cars, hopeful stray dogs, people queuing up at the big green shipping container that served as the farm vault for their weekly share of whatever vegetables had made it out of the ground. Next to the vault, cops with nimble necks scanned for trouble.

Broo-swilling regulars made a beeline for the Gulper Tavern, and up the street, a few nicer, washed cars pulled up in front of McLintocks, a legendary establishment whose owner had managed to stockpile enough dried beef to feed its wealthy customers for another few years. Or so he bragged. Nobody seemed to know whether he kept the beef on premises or brought it in as needed from a more secure location. A year ago, a group of men made a bold run at the place to try to relieve it of its stash, but the armed guard in front repelled them so quickly and violently that nobody had dared try it since.

Catty-corner to McLintocks, the usual line had begun to form on the sidewalk in front of Salty's, with people trying to decide whether they were in the mood for ice cream or hashish, or both.

"Why they call it 'ice cream' when there ain't no ice *or* cream in it?" a woman in line asked her friend, who only shrugged in response.

By all outward appearances, it was a standard Friday in Junipero Bay except for Maer Cadogan, who looked antsy. She'd made three trips from her boat to her office, each time carrying nothing back. Cloudy leaned on his crutches and watched her, gently rocking his leg cast forward and back.

"Maer, take it easy," he said. "It's going to be okay. We know she's safe now, and it's a simple pick-up. We just need to hop on the boat and go get her."

"Simple pick-up, Cloudy? Simple pick-up?" She stopped and put her hands on her hips and looked right at him. It was the first time she'd actually stopped moving all evening. "When you're going to meet the most wanted man on the planet, who just happens to have your daughter, nothing is simple."

Cloudy held up his hands in defense. "Fair enough. I'm just saying everything's going to be all right."

"Once we actually have her back, it'll be all right. Oh, where *is* that man?" said said, then cursed, seeming to remember something, and started speed walking toward her office again, skirting around ancient Bum the Jim as he tottered toward Cloudy.

"Evenin', Jimmy," Cloudy said as the old man got closer. Bum still had his hair, long and straw gray, which at some indistinguishable point became his carpet of beard. He wore a long overcoat that was cleverly patched together with bits of rubber tubing and plastic bags scavenged from an old landfill.

"My good officer," Bum croaked at Cloudy. "Have you by any chance happened to see my manatee?" His eyes were clear, but elsewhere. "I seemed to have lost him, you see. I told him not to set one fin in that poisoned ocean, but does he ever listen to a word I say? No, no he does not." Bum held up a crooked finger, not waiting for Cloudy to answer. "Ah, and word to the wise, word to the wise, since you are an officer of the law. Sir, I have it on excellent authority, from my manatee, no less, that you should watch out for the Chinese tonight! The CHINESE, those damn yellow bastards!" Bum turned and hobbled away, mumbling, tracked by the stares of a dozen Chinese people.

Maer brushed past Cloudy with an old SONAR machine. "Why do you keep humoring that poor old man? You could help me carry things instead," she huffed, then turned and stepped onto the boat and started rooting through a gear box.

"What he said actually has me spooked a little," Maer.

"What did he say?"

"He says to watch out for the Chinese tonight."

"So? Shouldn't that be a daily standing order? I'm certainly doing that already."

"He was a scientist for the old CIA, you know."

"What, 90 years ago? He's a doddering fossil who wets himself."

"True, he *is* almost 130 years old. But I've honestly found that one out of every 58 things he says is actually true."

"So what do you want me to do about that? Are you saying that I shouldn't go pick up my daughter?" She cursed. "Do you have an extra beam?"

Cloudy flicked his on and waved its light onto the boat deck.

Maer stopped and looked at him. "You know I don't blame you for any of this, Cloudy."

Cloudy nodded slowly, looking down at his shoes.

A voice came around the corner of the Gulper Tavern. "Did you hear Bum? I just passed him, and he was mumbling something about Chinese tonight?" It was Jack, walking with two men in camouflage.

"Jack. Tony. Scott." Cloudy greeted them. "You see, Maer? Somebody else takes Bum as seriously as I do. Too bad it's your husband. You don't believe a word he says, either."

"Lane not coming?" Tony asked.

"Nope," Cloudy said. "Still in the hospital. Be out soon, though."

"There you are, Jack! Jesus!" Maer said. "Why was your Telepath dark?" She turned back to rummage some more. " I've been trying and trying to reach you for an hour. Gaia? Gaia Cadogan? Your daughter? Remember her? Gotta go pick her up from the most wanted man alive?"

"Mind lowering that voice a little?" Jack said. "Sorry, but we got word about something, which is why I was curious about what Bum said. About the Chinese."

"That we should watch out for them tonight," Cloudy said. "Those damn yellow bastards."

"Hm," Jack mused. "It makes me nervous. He may be a nut, but sometimes he gets ahold of some shockingly accurate classified information."

"It *was* about the 58th thing he said to me," Cloudy agreed.

"Sweetie," Jack addressed his wife, "you're gonna hate hearing this."

Maer spun around and slammed the lid of the gear box. "Don't call me 'Sweetie.' That's what I *really* hate. And where are the goddamned flares? They're always right here in this box."

"Maer. Stop."

"What is it?" she snapped, continuing to rummage.

"Maer, STOP!" Jack commanded. "I don't think you should go out there with us tonight."

"Not a great time for jokes, Jack." She turned and hollered up to her office. "Selene! Now!"

"And *definitely* not Selene! Maer, we agreed on this!"

"Tell it to the Injuns," Maer waved him off. "Ah! There are the flares. Who fucking goddamn put 'em in here?"

Jack boarded the boat and grabbed his wife by the shoulders. "Maer. Listen. We're getting a credible threat. About you. It's the Chinese. The Secret Service is coming to fetch you. You need to stay here. We'll go out, and we'll bring our daughter right back."

She took a deep breath and sighed a stream of air that would have been fire had she been a dragon. "They can all go to hell. You, the Secret Service, the Chinese, and all this goddamn fish growing tech they seem to want so badly. I'm going to get my baby."

* * *

As Gaia and the Lakota carefully maneuvered their way down the switchback trail on the Frogs, she heard the ocean washing harder into the rocks. A big swell had come in, which meant the ride would be rough. But that didn't matter, because she'd be home soon.

They set off from Anacapa, and the chief led the group further north and further out to sea for well over an hour until the glow of the Santa Barbara hills disappeared behind them. The wind had reversed itself when the sun went down and cut back in to rush onshore. Gaia thought about little Moa, about Pahoehoe and the others, hoping they'd be warm enough during their exodus off the island—all because of her.

A few gulls had followed them from the island, and Gaia caught flashes of body and wing in the darkness beside them. In the red glow of lights emanating from their Frog, Gaia saw gray jellyfish floating dumbly in the swells.

The Frogs stayed in a wide triangle formation, and Gaia could see only the lower half of the other riders in their own red glows.

The sea was dark except for the occasional tanker in the distance or the light buoys marking a power-generating wave farm.

After a couple more hours of bucking and cold wind, the Frog engines stopped and they slowed to bob on the swells. In the distance, Gaia saw the twinkle of her hometown, Junipero Bay, and she noticed a the faint lights and hum of a boat moving toward them. When she focused her hearing, Gaia's heart did a backflip at the faint sound of her mom giving orders. For all the bossing her mom gave her in the past, for all the times it annoyed Gaia, the sound of it now was musical.

She'd be home soon.

But Gaia heard something else. It was an odd, high-pitched purr coming from the direction of her mom's boat. She wondered if they'd parked over a wave farm.

"Do you hear that?" she asked the chief.

He stopped and listened, scanning the water around them. "What are you hearing?"

"I don't know. Maybe nothing. But it's kind of a purr, or the sound of tiny popping bubbles."

The chief didn't respond, but pulled something out of a pocket and sent a series of red light flashes toward Buck and Jacob, who gunned their Frog and they sped off toward the oncoming boat.

In response, a green light swung away from Maer's boat, and Gaia realized it was a small watercraft coming to meet Buck and Jacob. When the two craft met in the middle, Gaia watched their dim lights bobbing on the swells as they spoke. Gaia could hear their voices but couldn't quite pick out what they said. The breeze was too gusty and carrying the sound away toward the shore. But she knew one of them was her dad, and she let herself feel the wave of excitement and relief washing through her. She was almost home. Gaia pictured the big bowl of tomato soup her mom would make for her, and she imagined Prop hopping and whining and licking her mercilessly the second she walked into her house. He'd snuggle with her, in her own bed, and she'd fall asleep for a week.

After a minute or two, a red light from the watercraft flashed a series of long and short bursts.

"You ready?" the chief asked her.

"I am," Gaia said. "Are you sure you don't hear that? Seems like it's getting louder."

The chief turned in his seat to look at her. "Probably the wave farm. Jacob didn't pick anything else up on his scan." Now he smiled at her, his white face and hair looking gray and ghostly in the glow of the Frog's red running lights. "We part ways now, as friends. Your path is your own. Walk it wisely. Walk it with a clear heart."

"Will I see you again?"

"I'm counting on it. Your path is your own, but Coyote, my spirit guide, did tell me to keep an eye on you. If you ever need us, we'll help you."

"How do I find you?"

"We'll find *you*. We'll know. Come visit us in South Dakota if you get a chance. Just get yourself to the chin of Crazy Horse." He tapped his chin. "That's all you have to do."

"The chin of Crazy Horse? What's that?"

"You'll figure it out." He smiled.

The chief turned to start driving, but Gaia put a hand on his shoulder. He turned back around.

"Thank you, Joe. For everything. And I'm sorry. I'm so sorry. But what I said about Wakinyan is true. It *was* him, I know it. He saved my life at the cove, when I was fighting that dark thing."

"I know." The chief's smile widened. He almost seemed proud. "We're all in this together. Our job is to help each other. Nobody can go it alone. Even you. *Especially* you. Always remember that."

Gaia nodded and let out a weighted breath.

"And I forgot to tell you," Joe said. "I talked to Wakinyan earlier, after dinner."

"You what?"

"He says the spirit world is nice. Kind of like back home, but he misses everyone."

"Really?" Was he able to do what she had done, to go deep into the spirit world?

"Yeah. Really. He also said he felt you pullin' on him to come back when you were holding his body at the beach, just like you told me. He said he almost turned around and came back. But he knew it was time for him to move on, so he had to cut loose from you. Hoped his knife didn't hurt you where he made the cut. Said you'll be a powerful healer someday."

Gaia remembered the inexplicable stabbing pain in her forearms when she tried, and failed, to bring Wakinyan back to life. She smiled at the thought of him cutting her loose and willingly moving on.

"Time to go home," the chief said.

He hit the jets on the Frog and they sped off. Gaia watched the lights of her mom's boat getting closer, anticipating the reunion with her family. Even in the dark she could almost make out the forms of her sister and her mom out on the deck.

But something odd was happening. The purring sound she'd been hearing suddenly got louder, and a bright green ring slowly formed in the water around her mom's boat, accompanied by an intense electric hum like the sound of cicadas. She'd never seen or heard anything like it before.

Joe suddenly slowed, and the men on the small crafts stopped talking. Something was wrong.

Inside the green circle of light, which was getting brighter by the moment, a handful of tiny red lights rose and surfaced as small crafts, maybe five or six of them. Was this supposed to be part of the rescue, Gaia wondered?

But what happened next answered that question. Buck, Jacob, and her dad suddenly gunned their crafts and split off in different directions. Then gunfire erupted, and Gaia saw white blips of light come from the Lakota, exactly like those that came out of Marty's little stone-shaped weapon.

"Hang on!" the chief shouted, launching the Frog hard right to swing around the melee, then burning open-throttled toward shore as Gaia was finally able to wrap her arms around his stomach. She held on tightly as the Frog bucked suddenly and picked up a new burst of speed in the calm waters of the bay. Gaia heard shouts, and Selene screaming, and more gunfire and chaos. She looked back at her mom's boat getting smaller as they sped away, watched the little blips of light fading, and her body seized with panic.

"What's happening?" she screamed, but Joe didn't answer. He kept their Frog at full tilt and started angling for the docks and the Friday night lights. Gaia launched a scream of anguish into the cold wind whipping at her, but her voice was lost. It came out in a helpless croak that burned her throat.

When they reached the docks, Gaia thought Joe was going to slam them into the sea wall. But at the last second he banked hard left and reversed the jets, setting them right next to a ladder. Swift and effortless as wind, Joe lifted her over his shoulder, carried her up a ladder onto the docks, then started running. He was incredibly strong. Suddenly, he stopped.

"Get in," Gaia heard a man's voice say. The chief set her down, and Gaia had just enough time to see that she was being pushed into the back seat of a black car. Joe got in with her, slammed the door, and the car sped away.

"What happened, what happened?" Gaia cried.

"I don't now," the chief said. "Change of plans."

"We have to go back! What's happening to them?"

But the chief didn't answer. Instead, he put his arm around Gaia and began quietly chanting a song in Lakota with his eyes closed.

After a series of jolting turns, the car slowed and came to a stop, and the door on the chief's side opened.

"Move," a suited man ordered.

The chief helped Gaia out of the car as more suited men guided them toward another black car, thick and bulky with blackened windows. From a couple of dim streetlights nearby, Gaia could see that they were in a vacant lot. A man opened the back door of the car, and a moment later Gaia found herself sitting next to the chief on a wide seat. Somebody was sitting across from them in a facing seat. A woman. Gaia recognized her, though she looked a little different, smaller, than she looked on the videostreams.

"Madam President," the chief said.

"Hello, Joe," said the President of the United States, Liz Efrain. "Little trouble tonight?"

"What? What trouble?" Gaia cried. "What's happening?"

The President paused to stared at her, tilting her head. "What an interesting person," she said.

"Did you know about this?" Joe asked the President.

She kept her eyes on Gaia. "Rumors," she said. "We warned Jack Cadogan, but apparently Maer Cadogan is as stubborn as ever."

"So it *was* the Chinese," Joe said.

"What? What about the Chinese?" Gaia pleaded.

"Yes, it appears so," the President said. "The reason I'm here is to pick up Maer Cadogan. A few moments too late, apparently. I was planning to bring you along with your mother as well," she said to Gaia. "If what I've heard is true, you could be very useful to us. To your country, I mean. But now we only have one Cadogan, and not the one we set out to retrieve." She scratched her neck and thought. "But this may have worked out better than expected, especially if half of what I've heard about you is true."

"What do you mean, 'better than expected?'" Gaia said. "What does that even mean?" Her guts were in knots.

She ignored Gaia and addressed the chief. "I imagine you'd like to go back? Join the fight?"

"Fight's over. I want to stay right here, with her."

"And miss all the fun everyone's having? No, you go play."

"No."

"Oh, I insist."

The door next to the chief opened. Gaia's panic rose. She didn't want him to leave her, and she looped her arm through his to keep him there.

"I'll take good care of her, Joe."

"I ent leaving her." Joe stared at the President.

"Let me get her out of here to where it's safe," the President said coolly. She seemed to be measuring him. "You can come visit her soon."

"Promises have been made to Indians before, Liz."

"Joe, come now. This is me."

"I know. That's what I'm worried about."

"We're done here."

Joe paused and thought, but Gaia only pulled on his arm tighter.

"It's okay," he finally said to her and squeezed her hand. "You'll be safe."

"I don't want you to go," Gaia said.

"I know. But I have to."

"But what's going on? What happened to my mom?"

"The President will explain it to you. For now, don't worry. The Chinese don't want to hurt your mom."

With great reluctance, she let him pull his arm away, deciding to trust him one more time.

He turned back when he stepped out of the car. "Remember what I told you." He tapped his chin, which Gaia took to mean the chin of Crazy Horse. The door closed.

"Yes, yes, chin up and all that," the President said. "Well, I certainly have heard a lot about *you* these past couple of days. And he's right. The Chinese don't want to hurt the legendary Maer Cadogan. They need her alive."

"What do they want her for?" Gaia was crying and grinding her frustration and anger between her teeth. She felt completely helpless.

"Same thing I want her for. Fish."

Gaia thought back to a few days ago. Was it only that short a time? Gaia was with her family at their kitchen table, and the President—the very woman now before her—was talking on the news about the secret fish reseeding project her mom was working on. And her mom was upset, and made a dark joke about being kidnapped by the Chinese. Only now, Gaia realized, it was no joke. Her mom had just been kidnapped by the Chinese. Gaia felt so naive and blind and foolish for not paying more attention to her mom's urgency. But what could she have done? The world was so hard and complicated. And heartless. She wondered if the rest of her life, however long it lasted, would be nothing but one kidnapping after another.

The President, she realized, might have even known her mom was going to be taken.

"Why is Joe leaving?" she said.

"Because I asked him to."

The President reached forward, and Gaia flinched as the President gently lifted up her chin to make eye contact with her. "We are strong women, and now is not the time for tears. Now is the time for patience."

"Patience?!" Gaia yelled. "What do you mean, patience?!" Her mind went back to Ailana and her lecture about Gaia's spine, but it didn't seem to be helping. Gaia was melting down.

"Here," the President said, handing Gaia a bottle of water. "Drink this. The important thing at the moment, at this very moment, is that you're safe. You're in good hands."

As the big car pulled away, Gaia saw only dim light outside and could hear nothing through the thick, black window glass. She felt like sobbing as the memory of deformed Hawaiian kids singing songs of gratitude filled her mind, and the echo of gunfire and her sister's desperate screams from the boat moments ago rang out as if it were just happening.

"Stop the car," Gaia demanded, not knowing what she'd do even if the car did stop.

"Drink your water," the President said. "We stop when I say. Don't let my temporary soft spot for your situation give you the wrong idea about me."

At that, anger began to replace Gaia's grief. She was angry about being taken from her family again, she was angry at how the President had dismissed Joe and made him leave. She felt as if she were being kidnapped again. Gaia closed her eyes and focused on the road ahead of the car, trying to go to a deep place again.

Seconds later, the car did stop, suddenly, as if it had crashed into something, and Gaia found herself lying on top of President Efrain in the opposite seat. The President quickly pushed Gaia off her, cursing. Gaia flopped back in her own seat.

She heard the sound of opening doors and quick footsteps as the Secret Service detail exited and surrounded the vehicle.

"TJ!" a man yelled. "Watch my six! I'm going under!"

More shuffling.

"Anything?"

"Nothing at twelve."

"Nine clear."

"Three clear."

"Six is clear. Whadda you got, Dan?"

Gaia heard mumbling. Minutes passed. Finally, their door opened and an agent poked his head in.

"What the hell happened, Dan?" the President snapped.

"Uh," the agent hesitated, dirt smeared on the knees of his black pants. "Looks like we got caught on something."

"Caught?" President Efrain said. "What do you mean, caught? Caught on what? What could *possibly* stop a goddamned armored car this heavy?"

"Not sure yet, Madam President. We're cutting it off now. Whatever it is, it's wrapped around the axle."

He held something out to her. His hands were greasy like a mechanic's. The President took it and turned it over in her hands. It was dark green. She sniffed it.

"Smells like broccoli," she said. "What the hell is it?"

"Plant of some kind," the agent said. "We think. We'll be on our way in a minute."

Excitement poured into Gaia. It sounded like she'd grown something she actually meant to grow, and in a place she wasn't standing on at the time.

As President Efrain eyed her, Gaia realized the woman wanted to blame her but was doubting her own sanity, which pleased Gaia immensely. As Gaia moved for the open door to get out, the door slammed in her face. There was no handle that Gaia could see that would open the door, so she sat back in her seat.

The President watched her but said nothing. Her look was something along the lines of confusion mixed with fear, but she quickly got control of it.

"No," the President said finally. "You stay, and we keep moving."

"Are you sure about that?" Gaia said. If she could get the car to stop, maybe she could free herself and get back to her family.

The President watched her, then spoke louder.

"Dan."

The car door opened again and Agent Dan stuck his head in again.

"Please secure our guest."

"Ma'am?"

"I want her secured and attached to this vehicle."

"Yes ma'am."

As Agent Dan climbed in next to Gaia, she realized it would be futile to struggle, and while her mind churned for answers, nothing landed. She could only watch as she allowed the agent to bind her wrists together with a soft, strong band, then attached a kind of cord to the band and secured it to a loop in the floor. It was such a convenient setup that Gaia wondered how often the President did this to people. When Agent Dan left and closed the door again, the President reconsidered Gaia.

"Yes," she said. "I'm sure about that."

When the car started moving again, the President looked out the tinted window, smugly.

Patience, Gaia thought as she closed her eyes, wanting to use the President's own advice against her. *Now is the time for patience.*

Epilogue

Dawn crept into the dirty dew of Pelican Bluffs, and Sergeant Carl Renneck was finishing his dawn walk before reporting for duty in the guard booth.

It was a good day, because he was getting his new gate installed. The woman who'd blatantly destroyed it—that arrogant Cadogan woman—wasn't going to be back anytime soon. Rumor had it she'd been kidnapped by the Chinese. Why the Chinese would want her, he hadn't a clue. But she was their pain in the ass now, and that pleased him.

He removed his military cap and wiped his sweaty brow with the sleeve of the same forearm, still surprised by the field of poppies that had sprung up seemingly overnight. Maybe the Cadogan woman was experimenting with plants.

He frowned.

Sergeant Renneck had intentionally walked the perimeter of the field—away from the poppies—not because he didn't want to trample them, but because he wouldn't be able to see his boots. The poppies were too tall and thick. Sergeant Renneck always wanted to be able to see his boots, which were worn but well polished. In the early days of the war with New Persia, he'd seen men lose legs walking through sketchy places where they couldn't see the ground. Today he knew he was being overly paranoid, but that caution was the reason he was still walking around on two good legs. That caution was what allowed him to control situations before they controlled him, like that pre-dawn morning months ago when he dispatched those raft niggers from Hawaii who were sneaking up the cliffs. The Cadogan woman might have had a soft spot for them, but he didn't. They were probably armed. If they were, he'd saved his own life, quickly and efficiently, and he'd only used one bullet apiece. Hell, even if they hadn't been armed, he was still doing the country a service by reducing the social burden of more hungry mouths to feed.

It was that exact sensibility that could get a man like him promoted again.

He scanned the field. Apparently a park cleanup had begun. He was a little sad to see that the gull carcasses at the base of the windmill had been removed. They helped make the place less attractive, a deterrent for numb-skulled civilian visitors.

But when he saw the giant mower emerge from the trees, rolling through the poppies like a ravenous beast, his heart warmed, and he smiled. Sergeant Renneck suspected the driver was a man worthy of respect; a clean, orderly man who understood the value of precision, starting his work at the top of the field and guiding his mower back and forth across perfect row after perfect row, no less carefully than if the man had been shaving himself with a straight razor.

As he watched the driver convert verdant poppies into a tangled, flat mulch of burnt-orange and green, he wondered if the driver also planned to rake away the debris. A man like Sergeant Renneck would. On the other side of the coin, a person like that Cadogan woman, who had blatantly driven through his guard gate, had no respect for his authority or property—and certainly neither did her poisoned offspring, that strange one with the blue hair and that odd island skin. Neither could hold a candle to him with regard to proper respect.

He was still miffed about the gate, about how that Cadogan woman had carelessly destroyed what he'd been charged to protect. It was a mistake he wouldn't make again. Given the right chance, he'd do her, and even her daughter, just like he did those Hawaiian niggers.

But Sergeant Renneck was, if nothing else, a man of proper self-control. Everything in its time and place.

He watched the mower neatly cut down more poppies, row after row, and that soothed him a bit. He allowed himself another smile, then looked down at his worn but well-polished boots.

It was a good day.

Thanks

A book tells a story. What it doesn't tell is the story within the story about the struggle, learning, joy, and reward of doing the work—a process that makes the writer grow as a human being, better able (one hopes) to walk the earth side by side with his fellows.

I have many to thank for their encouragement, generosity, and beautiful insights. Without these folks in particular, this book either would not have happened or been some grosser shadow of itself.

My wife, Lila, and our amazing kids, Sascha, Tatiana, and Hailey, have been a perpetual fountain of inspiration to me. Carving time out of a busy life to write a novel is beyond tricky and requires the patience and sacrifice of loved ones at every turn. I'm a lucky man.

And humble thanks go to my writer's group and colleagues at Wooden Stake Press, past and present: Jeff Chacon, Jack Maness, Kim Baack, Sean Maslow, and Jonna Gjevre; especially Jonna, for her razor instincts about the craft of storytelling and her wicked editing skills. Thanks also to Laurie O'Neil for development edits, and to a handful of friends and family who were kind enough to read cruder drafts of my drivel and urge me along.

About the author

Floyd Jones has worked as a paperboy, golf course monkey, dishwasher, busboy, soup cook, journalist, editor, presidential campaign ghostwriter, waiter (yes, this is chronological), White House staffer, camp counselor, technical writer, and software documentation coach. He lives in Colorado with his wife, dog, and ginormous children. They sometimes laugh at his jokes (knowing they're in his will, after all).

Send Floyd at note at gaiacadogan@gmail.com.